In the safety and anonymity of the confessional, Hope St. Germaine spilled her deepest secret—and her greatest fear.

"The women of my family are evil and wanton, Father. They're sinners, they sell themselves, their bodies. We are cursed women."

Hope twisted her fingers together, heart thundering. "I escaped, but now I fear that my baby daughter will grow up evil and wanton. I see the Darkness in her, Father, and I'm so afraid."

The priest began to speak with a strength that filled Hope with calm. "We are all in the possession of the darkness, child. Eve offered Adam the apple, he took the forbidden fruit and original sin was born."

He shifted; Hope heard the rustle of robes and the click of his rosary beads. "You must teach your daughter to fight the darkness."

"But how, Father?" Hope leaned toward the partition. "How can I help her?"

"You have the power to mold her into a woman of high moral character. This child has been sent as a test of your strength and your faith. This child can be your glory or your defeat."

Hop̲e _____ n't lose to the
Dar_____  _____ter. She would stamp
the _____ worked to stamp it
out _

This _____

Also available from MIRA Books and
ERICA SPINDLER

RED

Watch for her newest blockbuster

FORTUNE

in April 1997

FORBIDDEN FRUIT

ERICA SPINDLER

MIRA BOOKS

ISBN 1-55166-071-7

FORBIDDEN FRUIT

Printed in U.S.A.

To Melissa Senate
For all the years and all the books.

My heartfelt thanks to the following people for their part in bringing *Forbidden Fruit* to life:

Linda Kay West
Lieutenant John Jackson
Sergeant Michael Pfeiffer
Metsy Hingle
Jan Hamilton Powell
Karen Stone
Gary Weissert
Dianne Moggy
Melissa Senate
Nathan Hoffman
Evan Marshall
and
MIRA Books

Prologue

Vacherie, Louisiana
1959

Hope Pierron sat in the window seat of her third floor bedroom and gazed out at the Mississippi River. She smiled to herself, anxiousness and excitement coiling in the pit of her gut. She controlled both with icy determination. She had waited all her life for this day; now that it had come, she would not reveal herself by appearing too eager.

She pressed a hand to the sun-warmed glass, wishing she could break it, leap out and fly to freedom. How many times during her fourteen years, years spent trapped within the red walls of this house, had she wished the same thing? To be a bird, to leap from the window and fly to freedom?

After today, she wouldn't need to wish for wings. After today, she would be free of this house. Of the stigma of sin. Free of her mother and all who she had known.

Today she would be reborn.

Hope closed her eyes, thinking of her future, yet picturing her past and this hated house, instead. The Pierron House had been a fixture on River Road, a part of the culture of southern Louisiana since the summer of 1917. That had been just before the demise of Storyville, when her grandmother Camellia, the first Pierron madam, had moved her daughter and her girls here.

Surprisingly, neither hue nor cry had erupted then, nor when the gentlemen began calling. All these years later, this house, the activities within, were still accepted, just as the heat and mosquitos of August were accepted—with resigned dismay and sugar-sweet disdain.

Hope supposed one could expect no less; after all, this was Louisiana, a place where food, drink and other sensory intoxicants were as much a part of day-to-day living as mass and confession. Louisianians accepted their penance with as much *joie de vivre* as they did their pleasure; they understood that in a strange way, The Pierron House represented both.

The building itself, a Greek Revival structure with twenty-eight imposing Doric columns and sweeping wraparound galleries, was an architectural wonder. Ironically, when the afternoon sun struck it just so, the house glowed a virginal, almost holy white. When the sun set, however, the illusion of holiness ended. The house came alive with the music of men the likes of Jelly Roll Morton and Tony Jackson, the walls rang with the laughter of those who had come to taste the forbidden fruit and of those who sold it.

Every evening of her life she had been forced to hear that laughter, had been forced to witness the regularity with which her mother's girls led their gentlemen up the serpentine staircase. Cloaked in a sinfully plush, bloodred carpet, those stairs led to the six large bedrooms cn the second floor, bedrooms outfitted opulently with silks and brocades and large, soft beds.

Beds designed to make a man feel like a king or, on a particularly good night, a god.

For as long as she could remember, Hope had known what went on in those bedrooms. Just as she had known who and what she was—the whore's daughter, a trick baby, tainted by sin.

From secret places and small, unnoticed peepholes, Hope had watched with a mixture of fascination and horror the things that men and women did with each other. And sometimes, while the couple writhed on the bed, she would rock back and forth, her thighs pressed tightly together, her breath coming in small, uneven gasps.

Those were the times The Darkness held her in its grip, clamoring for unholy release.

Afterward, guilty and ashamed, Hope would punish herself. The way she touched herself, the things she watched, were wrong. Sinful. She had learned of her sin at mass and in catechism, as she sat alone because none of the other children would come near her. Yet, outside the church walls and inside these, such behavior was lauded—especially by the men who laughed by night and averted their eyes by day.

At the creak of the stairs that led to her bedroom, Hope turned away from her window and faced the door. A moment later, her mother appeared in the doorway.

Lily Pierron was an incredible beauty, same as all the Pierron women had been. Her face and figure seemed not to have aged with the years; her hair was the same velvety blue-black it had been in Hope's childhood. The other whores commented on it behind her mother's back; Hope had heard them whispering. They speculated that Lily had made a pact with the devil. They speculated that all the Pierron women had.

All except Hope. Hope was not nearly as beautiful as her mother—her own hair was a deep brown instead of black, her eyes a watery rather than brilliant blue, her features sharp instead of soft.

She was not as beautiful because The Darkness was not as strong in her.

"Hello, Mama," Hope murmured, fixing a sweet, sad smile on her mouth.

The older woman returned her melancholy smile and took a step into the room. "You look so grown-up standing there like that. For a moment, I hardly recognized you."

Hope's heart began to thud against the wall of her chest. "It's just me, Mama."

Her mother laughed softly and shook her head. "I know. But it seems only yesterday you were a baby."

And only an eternity of yesterdays that she was a prisoner of this place. "To me, too, Mama."

Lily crossed to the bed and the suitcase that lay open on top of it. Hope saw the effort it took her mother to keep from falling apart, and wondered if her mother noticed that her daughter's eyes were dry, her hands and voice steady. She wondered what her mother would say if she knew the truth, if she knew that her only daughter planned to never see her again.

"Is this the last one?" her mother asked. "The car will be here any moment."

"Yes. I've already taken the others down."

Lily carefully tucked the final few items into the case, then closed the bag and fastened the clasps. "There." She lifted her swimming gaze to Hope's. "All ready to . . . go." Her throat closed over the last, and the word came out choked.

Hope forced herself to cross to her mother. She caught Lily's hands with her own and brought them to her cheek. "It's going to be all right, Mama. Memphis isn't that far."

"I know. It's just that—" Her mother drew in a ragged breath. "How am I going to manage without you? You're the best thing . . . the only good thing in my life. I'm going to miss you desperately."

Hope curved her arms around her mother, fighting a smile. She hid her face against her mother's shoulder. "I'm going to miss you, too. So much. Maybe I shouldn't go. Maybe I should stay and help—"

"No! Never!" Lily cupped Hope's face. "You will not end up like me. I won't allow it, do you hear? This is your chance to escape. It's what I've always wanted for you. It's why I named you Hope." She tightened her fingers. "You were always my hope for the future. You mustn't stay."

This time Hope couldn't contain her smile. "I'll make you proud, Mama. You wait and see."

"I know you will." Lily dropped her hands. "Everything's set. St. Mary's Academy is expecting you. You're from Meridian, Mississippi, the only child of wealthy parents.''

"Who travel abroad," Hope filled in. She laced her fingers together, nervous suddenly. "What if someone discovers the truth? What if one of my classmates is from Meridian? What if—"

"No one will discover the truth. My friend has seen to everything. Not one other girl from Mississippi attends the academy. Even the headmistress believes you're Hope Penelope Perkins. No one will question your story. Feel better now?"

Hope searched her mother's expression, then nodded. She knew her mother's "friend" to be none other than the Governor of Tennessee. He and her mother went way back; Lily knew many—if not all—of his darkest secrets. Secrets she would go to her grave with. Of course, such loyalty sometimes demanded return—in the form of favors.

The sound of a horn sliced through the humid afternoon. Hope's heart flew to her throat, and she raced to the window. Three stories below, the airport shuttle idled in the driveway while Tom, the houseman, helped the driver load the bags.

Lily followed her to the window. "Dear Lord, it's time already." She laid her hands on Hope's shoulders, her cheek against her hair. "I don't know how I'm going to bear this."

Hope sucked in a deep breath, joy a living thing inside her. Almost free. *Just a few more minutes and she would never see her mother or this hated house again.* She struggled to keep from laughing out loud.

Her mother sighed, dropped her hands and took a step away. "We'd better go."

"Yes, Mama." Hope collected the suitcase, then she and her mother started for the stairs. Her mother's girls were waiting for them in the foyer. They each hugged and kissed Hope, they each wished her well and made her promise to write.

The youngest of the group—a girl not much older than Hope—handed her an apple, lush and red and ripe. "In case you get hungry," she said softly, her eyes bright with tears.

Hope took the girl's offering though the fruit burned like acid against her palm. She longed to fling it away and run, but forced herself to meet the whore's eyes and smile. "Thank you, Georgie. It was sweet of you to think of me."

Hope stepped outside, her mother beside her. The breeze off the River was hot and slow, but sweet still; it washed over her, cleansing her of the stench of the house and its history. Her history.

Her mother drew her into her arms and clung to her. "My darling, darling baby, I will miss you so much."

Hope fought the urge to tear herself from her mother's arms and race to the waiting vehicle. She allowed her mother to kiss her one last time, promising herself that she would never again have to endure her vile touch.

The touch of sin.

The driver cleared his throat. Hope said a silent thank-you and eased from her mother's grasp. "I have to go, Mama."

"I know." Lily curved her arms around her middle, battling tears. "Call me when you arrive."

"I will," Hope lied. "I promise."

She started for the car, counting the steps. With each she felt as if another piece of her past was falling away from her, like layers of smothering clothing, ones made of wet, rotting wool.

The driver opened the door. She moved to get in, then stopped and looked over her shoulder at The House, at her mother standing in its shadow, at the whores, clustered in the doorway. Her lips curved into a small, satisfied smile.

Today she was reborn as Hope Penelope Perkins. Today she left The Darkness behind.

Letting the apple slip from her fingers, she turned and stepped into the car.

Part 1

Hope

1

The perfume of flowers hung in the air, almost overpowering in its sweetness. The scent mixed strangely with those of the maternity ward, creating another that was both appealing and repugnant. Even so, fresh arrangements arrived hourly, enthusiastic offerings sent to herald the birth of Philip St. Germaine III's first child.

The excitement was understandable. After all, this child would be heir to the family's wealth and social position, this child would be heir to the venerable St. Charles, the small luxury hotel built in 1908 by the first Philip St. Germaine.

For this child, nothing was too much.

Hope gazed down at the newborn, nestled in the bassinet beside her bed. Despair and disappointment, so bitter they burned her tongue, roiled inside her. She had prayed for a boy. She had done the rosary, she had done penance. She had been so certain her prayers would be answered that she had refused to consider names for a girl.

Her prayers had not been answered; she had been cursed instead.

She had given birth to a daughter, not a son. Just as her mother and grandmother had, just as every Pierron woman had for as many generations back as she could recall.

Hope drew a deep breath, bile rising like a poison inside her. She hadn't escaped the Pierron legacy, after all. She had managed to believe, to convince herself for a while, that she had. In the eight years that had passed since she'd walked away from the house on River Road, she had brought each of her plans to fruition: she had left behind her mother and the stigma of being the whore's daughter; she had married Philip St. Germaine III, a wealthy man, a man from an impeccable and prominent family; she was now one of New Orleans's premier matrons.

But today she saw that although she had left her past behind, she hadn't escaped it. The Pierron curse had followed her.

The baby girl was already a beauty, with light skin, vivid blue eyes and velvety dark hair. As with all the Pierron women, this one would possess the ability to bewitch and enslave men; she, too, would have the great, ugly darkness inside her. The ugliness that would chain her to a life of sin and an afterlife of eternal damnation.

Hope shuddered. For didn't she, too, have The Darkness inside her? Didn't it sometimes burst free, despite how hard she fought to keep it locked way?

Philip entered the room, his face wreathed in a beatific smile, his arms laden with a huge bouquet of pink roses. "My darling. She's beautiful. Perfect." The florist's paper crackled as he laid the bouquet on the bed. He bent and pressed a kiss to Hope's forehead, careful not to disturb his sleeping child. "I'm so proud of you."

Hope turned her face away, afraid he would see her true feelings, afraid he would see the depth of her despair and revulsion.

He sat on the edge of the bed. "What is it? Hope, darling..." He turned her face to his. He searched her expression, his own concerned. "I know you wanted a son for me. But it doesn't matter. Our little one is the most perfect child ever born."

Tears stung her eyes, and she blinked against them. Still, one slipped past her guard and rolled down her cheek.

"Oh, love, don't cry." He drew her against his chest. "It really doesn't matter. Don't you see? Besides, we'll have other children. Many more."

The pain inside her grew almost unbearable. Hope knew what her husband did not: there would be no more children for them. She, like her ancestors, would be unable to carry another child to term. That was a part of the curse, the Pierron women were allowed only one child, always a daughter. To that daughter they would pass The House and the legacy of sin.

Hope curled her fingers into the soft, fine fabric of his jacket. She longed to share her thoughts with him, but knew he would be shocked, horrified, to learn the truth about his *perfect* wife. And now, his perfect daughter, too.

He could never know. She swallowed hard and pressed her face to his shoulder, breathing in the scent of the rain that lingered on his jacket, preferring it to the cloying atmosphere of the room. *No one could ever know.*

"I just wish," she whispered, working to achieve just the right mixture of grief and wistfulness in her tone, "that my parents could have lived to see her. It's so unfair. Sometimes it hurts so much, I . . . I almost can't bear it."

"I know, my darling." For several moments, he cradled her against his chest, then eased her away, his lips lifting into a small smile. "I have something for you." From his jacket pocket he drew out a jeweler's box. Stamped on the lid of the midnight-blue leather case was the name of New Orleans's finest jeweler.

With trembling fingers, Hope opened the box. Inside, nestled on the white velvet, lay a strand of perfectly matched pearls. "Oh, Philip." She took out the necklace and brought it to her cheek. The pearls were cool and smooth against her skin. "They're exquisite."

His lips lifted, and he shifted his gaze to the baby, who had begun to stir. "They'll be hers one day. I thought it appropriate."

Hope's pleasure in the gift vanished, and she replaced the necklace in its box. He adored his daughter already, Hope thought, following his gaze. He had been bewitched, snared by The Darkness. And the fool didn't even know it.

"She's caused a sensation in the nursery," he continued, not tearing his gaze from the bassinet. "Nurses from all the floors have heard about her, about her beauty, and have come to see her. She's caused a traffic jam at the viewing window." He turned back to his wife, covering her hand with his, curving his fingers reassuringly around hers. "I'm the luckiest man in the world."

The baby stirred and whimpered, then began to cry. Hope shrank back against the pillows, knowing what was expected of her but unable to bear the thought of holding the child to her breast.

The baby's cries, at first small, pitiable mewls, became shrill, angry demands.

Philip frowned, obviously confused. "Hope, darling ... she's hungry. You have to feed her."

Hope shook her head, cringing deeper into the pillows. To her horror, her breasts, engorged and aching, began leaking milk. The baby's face grew red as the fury of her wails increased. Her features contorted into something ugly and terrifying. Something Hope recognized from her nightmares.

The Darkness. Dear God, it was strong in this child.

Philip tightened his fingers over Hope's. "Darling ... she needs you. You must feed her."

When Hope didn't move, Philip scooped up his daughter. He rocked her awkwardly, but her cries didn't diminish. He held the child out to Hope. "You must."

Hope looked wildly about the room, desperate for a way to escape. Everywhere she looked, she saw The Darkness, everything reminded her what a fool she had been.

She hadn't escaped the Pierron legacy. She never would.

Trapped, she thought, a frantic hopelessness beating inside her. She was trapped. Just as she had been all those years ago.

"I can't," she said, hearing the hysteria in her own voice. "I won't."

"Darling—"

"Mrs. St. Germaine?" The nurse rushed in. "What's wrong?"

"She won't feed her," Philip said, turning to the nurse. "She won't take her from me. I don't know what to do."

"Mrs. St. Germaine," the nurse said crisply, her voice brooking no disobedience. "Your daughter is hungry. You must feed her. She will stop crying the minute—"

"No!" Hope drew the blanket to her chin, her fingers curled so tightly into the fabric that they went numb, panic pumping through her until she shook with it. "I can't." She turned to her husband, tears slipping down her cheeks. "Please, Philip, don't make me do this. I can't do it. I won't."

He stared at her as if she had sprouted horns. "Hope? What's wrong? Sweetheart, this is our child, our baby. She needs you."

"You don't understand . . . you don—" The last caught on a sob and she turned her face to the pillows. "Go . . . away. Please, just leave me alone."

2

Philip August St. Germaine III had an idyllic life, one of those existences so untroubled that others commented enviously on it. He had the right family, all the right and best things; he was healthy, athletic and handsome enough. He had sailed through school, in part because of native intelligence, but more because of the charm he had acquired through breeding.

In truth, Philip had never had to work for anything, not for grades or girls or a living. Everything had been handed to him not only on a sterling platter—the St. Charles being the crown jewel on that platter of glittering gems—but with an adoring smile. For Philip, the years flowed effortlessly one into the other.

Far from being bothered by his lack of effort in shaping his own life, he accepted it all graciously, as his due and his wonderful lot in life. He did feel for those poor souls who struggled and suffered, and he never forgot to give—and give plentifully—to the Church, both in thanks for his bounty and as a sort of insurance policy against guilt.

Frankly, until thirty-six hours ago, Philip August St. Germaine III had thought, with justifiable arrogance, that nothing ugly or unhappy could ever touch him.

Now, as he stood at the maternity ward's nursery window and watched a stranger feed his baby, his beautiful, perfect daughter, that same arrogance mocked him. Now, he felt as if his idyllic life was crumbling around him.

The last day and a half had been like a nightmare from which he couldn't awaken. The wife he adored, usually sweet-tempered and genteel, had become a person he didn't recognize. A person who frightened him.

He brought a hand to his head, heavy and aching from stress and lack of sleep. It wasn't only that she had cursed at him, spitting out words he would have sworn she didn't, and couldn't, know. It was more than the fact that she had told him she hated him when he had tried insisting they pick out a name for their child.

No. It was the way she had looked at him, an almost maniacal light burning in her eyes, that frightened him. Because when she'd looked at him that way, he had felt, deep down in his gut, that the life he had known was gone forever.

Philip jammed his hands deep into his trouser pockets and gazed at his daughter, sucking greedily on a bottle of formula. She was the image of her mother already. He couldn't understand how Hope could look at her with such horror, how she could recoil from touching her. He pressed the heels of his hands to his burning eyes. When she looked at their precious daughter, what did she see that he didn't?

If only he could understand, if only he could crawl inside his wife's head, maybe he would be able to help her. And then, maybe, his world would stop rocking around him.

Her behavior had come out of nowhere. She had looked forward to the birth of their first child. Her pregnancy had been an easy one; she had suffered from neither morning sickness nor mood swings. They had talked about all the things this child would do and be. Other than her absolute conviction that she carried a boy, her attitude about motherhood had seemed completely normal.

Now this. A shudder of fear moved over him. What would he do if he had lost her? If the woman he had known and loved so desperately had ceased to exist forever? How would he go on? He loved her beyond reason; he had from the first.

Inside the nursery, the attendant finished feeding and burping Philip's daughter and laid her in her crib. Philip watched, seeing instead Hope as she had looked the night they first met. He had been in Memphis on business; they'd been introduced by friends. She had been laughing, her head tipped to the side, her long, silky hair falling softly against her cheek. He'd had the urge to touch it, to bring the dark strands to his lips to test their texture and taste. He could recall the exact rose shade of her mouth, could recall the way she'd pursed her lips in amusement, could remember that he had become aroused just watching her speak.

She had turned and met his eyes. He'd sensed that she knew exactly what he was thinking, that she was glad he was thinking it. In that moment, he had fallen madly in love with her. It had been as simple, and as complicated, as that.

That night and for the remainder of his business trip, they had been inseparable. He had told her everything about himself, and she had shared her life with him. The tragic story of her parents' accidental death while traveling in Italy, of how she had been left alone in the world at seventeen, had touched him deeply.

Something about her had made him feel like the most powerful, the most important man in the world. He had wanted to shield her from the harsh world, had wanted to protect her from all of life's unpleasantness. He had wanted to bring her into his charmed circle.

If he had been a less cautious man, he would have proposed on the spot. Instead, he had waited six long, agonizing weeks.

Family and friends had thought him insane until they met her. Then they, too, had fallen under her sweet spell. Even his demanding, ever-critical parents had thought her the perfect choice.

Not that it had mattered what they thought. He had been prepared to defy them, he had been prepared to give up everything for her.

Their wedding night had been an experience beyond his fantasies. She had done unimaginable, incredible things to his body, yet with such sweet, almost tentative innocence, that he had felt as if he were deflowering a virgin. Even now, standing in plain view of the world, his life in turmoil, thinking of that night brought swift, stunning arousal.

Sometimes he felt as if his life revolved from night to night, from one opportunity to make love with her to the next. Those times when she couldn't—or wouldn't—were a kind of torture beyond his previous experience. No woman before Hope had had such a hold on him; it was as if without her his heart couldn't beat.

"There you are." Hope's doctor came up to stand beside him. Harland LeBlanc had delivered a host of St. Germaine babies, and although nearly sixty, he looked a decade younger. Since the man was considered the top obstetrician in New Orleans, Philip took some comfort in knowing Hope had the best care available.

The older man motioned to the nursery. "You have a beautiful daughter, Philip. In fact, I don't think I've ever seen a more beautiful infant."

Philip looked at the other man, then returned his gaze to the nursery window. "Yet, Hope can't bear to look at her. She's yet to hold her. She won't even consider a name."

"I know it's been difficult, but—"

"Difficult?" Philip said, his tone caustic. "I don't think you do know, Harland. I don't see how you can. You weren't there this morning when Hope swore at me. When she told me she hated me. All because I wanted to pick out a name for our daughter." He drew a painful breath. "The way she looked at me was...chilling. I never thought my wife would look at me that way."

The physician laid a hand reassuringly on Philip's shoulder. "Believe it or not, I do understand what you're going through. I've seen this type of behavior before, and it will pass. Everything is going to be all right, Philip."

"Are you so certain of that?" Philip drew a hand across his forehead. "What if it doesn't pass? I couldn't bear to lose her. She's everything to me, she's—" He cleared the lump from his throat, feeling exposed and foolish. He shifted his gaze to the nursery and his sleeping daughter. "I love my wife, Harland. Too much, I sometimes think."

The doctor gave Philip's shoulder a comforting squeeze, then dropped his hand. "What Hope's going through isn't as uncommon as you might imagine. A surprising number of women experience depression after childbirth. On occasion, the depression is so severe, so all-encompassing, the woman abandons her family. Or worse."

Philip met the other man's gaze once again. He lifted his eyebrows at the physician's solemn expression. "Worse, Harland?"

"Women in the grip of this blackness have killed their newborns, Philip. As horrifying and foreign as that may seem."

Philip made a sound of shocked disbelief. "Surely you're not suggesting that Hope might...that she could...kill our child?"

"Of course not," Harland said quickly, his tone confident. "But I do think we should keep her here a few more days. We need to monitor her. Just to be sure."

Dear Lord. Just to be sure? Of what?

Fear thundered through Philip, taking his breath, stealing the remnants of his peace of mind. Harland LeBlanc, Philip realized, considered top in his field, a doctor who had seen everything, was worried. More worried than he wanted to let on.

Philip breathed deeply through his nose, working to steady himself. But Harland didn't know Hope the way he, her husband, did. All she needed was a return to normalcy. She needed to be surrounded by her things and the people who cared about her.

"Do you really think that's necessary, Harland? Hope needs to be home. Our baby needs to be home. Once there, Hope will adjust. I know she will."

"What if she doesn't? Postpartum depression is caused by the tremendous imbalance of hormones in a woman's body. Hope has no control over these feelings she's having, she's awash in them. She's not trying to be difficult or unreasonable.''

The doctor shook his head. "What if I send her home too early and she doesn't adjust? What if I send her home and the unspeakable happens? I don't want to take that chance." He met Philip's gaze evenly. "Do you, Philip?"

The unspeakable. Or worse. Philip swallowed hard. "No. Of course not."

"Good. Your wife needs you now. You say you love her, well, now's the time to prove it."

Philip willed away his frustration and selfish fears. Hope needed him. His daughter needed him. He had to be strong. "What can I do?" he asked. "Just tell me what I can do."

"Be supportive. Understanding and loving. I know it's hard, but you must remember that Hope is not in control of her emotions. She's as frightened as you are right now. Probably more. She needs time. She needs your patience and love."

Philip turned his gaze to his sleeping daughter, so tiny and helpless his heart broke for her. She needed her mother. She needed to go home. "And if my love and support aren't enough? What then, Harland?"

For a moment, the physician said nothing. Then he sighed. "They'll have to be, Philip. Right now, you don't have any other options."

3

Hope awakened with a start. Breathing hard, clammy with sweat, she moved her gaze over the dimly lit room, expecting to see the outfittings of the third-story bedroom she had grown up in. Instead, she saw the simple, functional furnishings of her hospital room.

Hope drew in a deep, shuddering breath, relief spiraling through her. *She was in New Orleans. She was Hope St. Germaine; the River Road house was far away. Part of a previous lifetime, someone else's lifetime.*

Hope drew in another deep breath, the effects of the nightmare still clawing at her. In it, she had been back at The House, crouched low and spying on a couple having sex. Only, in the dream, it had been her daughter on the bed, her daughter performing the lewd sex acts.

Yet, when her whore-child had looked over her shoulder, as if sensing Hope's spying gaze, it was her own face Hope had seen staring back at her.

Making a helpless sound of fright, Hope pulled herself into a sitting position. She clutched the bedding, willing away the image from the dream. She knew what was happening to her; she knew why, night after night, she was being tormented with nightmares of the past she had left behind.

The Darkness was upon her, taunting and challenging. It thought it had won already.

No! Hope brought her trembling hands to her face. She wouldn't let The Darkness win. She couldn't. She had worked too hard for all she had achieved to succumb now.

Hope hugged her knees to her chest. She rocked, her head pressed to her knees, her mind whirling. Who could she turn to for help? Who could she trust? Philip was losing patience with her. Their family and friends were acting strangely, distant and suspicious. She saw the questions in their eyes. She saw the disapproval in their expressions. How long until someone uncovered the truth about her past? How long until the life she had built for herself crumbled to bits beneath her feet?

She had to accept her child; she had to behave like a doting, besotted mother. She had to behave as if she didn't see her daughter's vile core, pretend she didn't see that the beautiful fruit was spoiled by worms.

Tears, hot and bitter, welled up in her eyes and slipped down her cheeks. But when she held her daughter, how would she keep her revulsion from showing? How would she be able to hide her despair and feign affection? She couldn't; she knew she couldn't.

Hope threw aside the covers and climbed out of bed. She crossed to her half-open door, the linoleum floor cool against her bare feet. She peeked out at the deserted hallway and nurses' station. She heard a woman's weeping from down the hall, heard another's comforting murmur.

The Vincent woman had lost her baby. Philip had shared that information with her earlier today, she supposed in the hope of making her thankful for their own baby's good health. Instead, she had wished it was her own child who had been taken. If the Lord had chosen her baby, her problems would have been solved.

But the Pierron daughters were strong with The Darkness that beat inside them; the Pierron daughters never died.

She had to escape, she thought, frantic suddenly. She had to get out of this place and breathe fresh air; she needed to be away from the constant prying, the insufferable compassion, of the hospital staff. She had to find someone who would understand and help her.

The church. She could turn to the church. The priest would help her. He would understand.

And in the anonymity of the confessional, she would be safe. Her secret would be safe.

Whimpering with relief, Hope turned away from the door and moved blindly to her closet. She rifled through it, pulling out her street clothes, tugging them on as quickly as she could, fumbling in her haste. Throughout her life the Church had been her solace, her rock during times of turmoil and confusion. Surely this time would be no different. Surely the priest would know what she should do.

But what if, this time, the priest couldn't help her? What would she do then?

Fear pumped through her, taking her breath, her ability to think, to act. She struggled to get control of her emotions; she couldn't afford to fall apart now. If she did, The Darkness would have her.

Never. Taking a deep, steadying breath, Hope crossed to the phone and as quietly as she could, called a cab. That done, she collected her purse and tiptoed to the door. Luck was on her side—the nurses' station was still empty. Smiling to herself, she ducked out of the room and went quickly to the elevator. She didn't want Philip alerted to the fact she was leaving the hospital. He would try to stop her; the hospital staff would try to stop her. None of them understood.

As she had hoped, the elevator was unoccupied. It whisked her to the lobby; she stepped out and started for the double glass doors directly ahead. A security guard stood at the front desk, flirting with the receptionist. Neither spared her more than a glance.

Hope pushed through the doors and stepped out into the humid New Orleans night. Air, thick with moisture, enveloped her like a womb. She breathed deeply, grateful, so grateful, to be free.

She moved away from the building, out of its circle of light, and the dark swallowed her. Moonlight glistened on the wet pavement; tree branches, their leaves heavy with a recent rain, hung low, their loaded leaves splattering her as she walked beneath them.

A streetcar rumbled past; a youth darted across the avenue, shouting a greeting to another passing in a car. From the canopy of oak leaves above her came the sound of some small animal scurrying for deeper cover.

The cab drew to the curb. Hope slid inside. "St. Louis Cathedral," she instructed, then settled against the worn seat. In hopes of catching the faithful either in anticipation of their sin or in repentance of it, the Jackson Square cathedral heard confessions into the night. She had always thought it ironic that New Orleans's oldest, and to her mind, most awe-inspiring cathedral stood sentinel at the very heart of debauchery.

Hope clenched her hands in her lap. The cab smelled stale, like old cigarettes and mildew. The driver said little; his silence saved her having to rebuff him. She turned her face to the window and watched as the grand residences of uptown gave way to the high rises of downtown, then to the old-world architecture of the Vieux Carré, or French Quarter.

Within minutes, the driver drew the cab to a stop beside the cathedral. Hope asked him to wait, then stepped out into the night. She lifted her gaze to the church's mighty spire, feeling a measure of relief already. St. Louis Cathedral stood watch over Jackson Square, just as a chaperon would over a pair of anxious teenagers, just as the Catholic church had always stood watch over the eternal souls of the faithful. Rebuilt twice from ashes and once from the rubble wrought by a hurricane, its rigid lines provided a stark contrast to the whimsical ironwork of the buildings adjacent to it. Hope had always thought of this church as a type of anchor, its rigidity balancing and securing the lives of the *laissez bon temps roullé* Creoles who had once inhabited the Vieux Carré.

Taking a deep breath, she hurried toward the church's welcoming portal, her heels clicking on the cobblestone walkway. From the Mississippi River, located just beyond the square to the east, came the lonely call of a barge; from nearby Bourbon Street, she caught the strains of Dixieland jazz and raucous laughter.

As she entered the church, those sounds faded, leaving a silence that echoed, that reassured. A sense of calm, a feeling of serenity flowed over Hope. Her agitation, the desperation that had held her in its grip for days now, melted away. Here, The Darkness couldn't touch her. Here, nestled in the arms of the church, she would find her answers.

A marble cistern stood inside the entrance. Hope dipped her fingers into the holy water. She crossed herself, and started for the confessionals that flanked each side of the sanctuary at the front.

She slipped into the first she came to and drew the curtain closed behind her. She knelt, facing the interior wall, and bowed her head. A moment later, the panel slid open. Obscured by a screen, she could make out the priest's form, but not his features. Just as he could not make out hers.

"Bless me, Father, for I have sinned. It's been two weeks since my last confession."

"What sins do you have to confess, my child?"

Hope twisted her fingers together, her heart thundering so hard it hurt to breathe. "Father, I ... I've come to you under false pretenses. I've come not to confess my sins, but to seek your counsel. You see, I—" Her throat closed over the words, and she fought to clear it, fear and despair rising in her again, threatening to swallow her.

"I have nowhere else to turn, Father. No one to turn to. If you can't help me, I don't know what I'll do. I'll be lost." Hope brought her hands to her face and wept into them. "Please, Father. Please help me."

"Calm yourself, child. Of course I'll help you. Tell me what's troubling you."

Hope shuddered. "The women of my family are evil and wanton, Father. They're sinners, they sell themselves, their bodies. It's always been so in my family, we are cursed women."

She swiped at the tears on her cheeks. "I escaped, but now I fear for my baby daughter's eternal soul. I fear she, too, will grow up evil and wanton. I see The Darkness in her, Father, and I'm so afraid."

For a moment, the priest said nothing. Then he began to speak, softly but with a strength and surety that filled Hope with calm.

"We are all in possession of the darkness, child. Eve offered Adam the apple, he took the Forbidden Fruit and Original Sin was born. Each of us come into the world tainted by that act of Original Sin. We are all unclean. But God sent His only son to die for us, for our sin. Christ is our promise of salvation."

The priest shifted, Hope heard the rustle of his robes and the click of his rosary beads. "You must help your daughter. You must show her the right path. You must teach her to fight the Serpent."

"But how, Father?" Hope leaned toward the partition. "How can I help her?"

"You're her mother. You have the power to mold this child into a woman of high moral character. Only you. You show her the way, teach her right from wrong, holy from unclean. God has sent you this child as a test. Of your strength and of your faith. This child can be your glory or your defeat."

Hope's heart began to thunder, and suddenly her path— her purpose—was clear. It wasn't the Lord who was testing her, it was The Darkness.

She curved her hands into fists, so tightly her nails dug into her palms. Let The Darkness test her, let it taunt and mock her. She wouldn't lose to it; she wouldn't let it have her daughter. She would stamp the Bad Seed out of her child, just as she had worked to stamp it out of herself.

This child could be her glory or her defeat.

Glory, she thought, determination rising like a tidal wave inside her. This child would be her Glory.

Part 2

Santos

4

Living in New Orleans's French Quarter suited fifteen-year-old Victor Santos just fine. No place else he had lived was quite like it. Day and night, the Quarter vibrated with energy and excitement; he never lacked for something to do or someone to hang out with. He liked the sounds and the smells, he liked the old buildings whose cracked plaster walls were always damp, he liked the lush, hidden court-yards and the fanciful iron balconies.

But most of all, Santos—called that by everyone but his mother—liked the people. The Quarter was home to all ages, persuasions and colors, home to the good, the bad and the ugly. Even the crush who flocked to Bourbon Street at night—most of them dedicated party animals, the rest curiosity seekers come to ogle the outrageous—fascinated him.

His school counselors were always telling his mom that the Quarter was no place to raise a kid because of the *bad element*. Of course, they would lump her into that cate-gory, too, if they knew she was an exotic dancer and not the waitress she had told them she was.

As far as Santos was concerned, those counselors were a bunch of full-of-crap know-it-alls. As far as he was con-cerned, hookers, junkies and runaways had a lot more heart than no-good sons-of-bitches like his daddy. No, from what he had seen of life, the folks who'd had nothing but hard times and hurts didn't have room inside them for hate.

Santos crossed Bourbon Street and shouted a greeting to Bubba, the guy who worked the door of Club 69, the place his mother danced nights.

"Hey, Santos," the burly bouncer called back. "You got any smokes? I'm out."

Santos laughed and lifted his hands, empty palms up. "Gave it up, man. Haven't you heard? Those things'll kill you."

The man flipped Santos a friendly bird, then turned his attention to a couple of tourists who had stopped outside the club and were craning their necks to get a peek at the show.

Victor continued down Bourbon, then cut across to St. Peter, hoping to shave a few minutes off his walk. He had promised his mother he would pick up a couple shrimp po'boys on his way home.

His mouth started to water at the thought of the big, sloppy sandwiches, and he stepped up his pace, though not too much. August in New Orleans didn't lend itself to hurrying. Although the sun had begun its descent more than an hour ago, the sidewalk was still hot enough to fry an egg. Heat emanated from the concrete in sweltering waves, and the air, heavy with the ninety-plus–percent humidity, could suffocate the overzealous. Just last week, a tourist-buggy horse had fallen over dead in the street, a victim of August in New Orleans.

"Hey, Santos, baby," a woman said from behind him. "Where you goin' in such a hurry?"

He stopped, looked over his shoulder and smiled. "Hey, Sugar. Going to the Central Grocery, then home. Mom's waiting." Until about six months ago, Sugar had danced at the club with his mother. She'd been forced to start working the streets full-time when her man had taken off, leaving her and their three kids.

"Your mama always did like them sandwiches. Bet you do, too, a big boy like yourself." She laughed and patted his cheek. "You tell your mama I said hello. You tell her Brown Sugar's doin' okay."

"I will. She'll be glad to hear it."

Santos watched her walk away, then shook his head and started off again. Sugar was an example of the kind of folks those do-gooder school counselors called a bad influence. The way he saw it, she was doing the best she could to take care of her family. The way he saw it, sometimes life didn't offer anything better than a shit sandwich. When that happened, you had to eat it or starve.

Not that there weren't some bad people in the Quarter. There were plenty; just like everyplace else. He figured folks came in three varieties: the haves, the have-nots and the want-to-haves. The way he saw it, the lines between these three groups were very clearly drawn. It was economics, pure and simple.

The haves were easy. They liked their lives, and as long as members of the other two groups stayed out of their way, they weren't any bother at all. But the want-to-haves were trouble. They came from all walks of life, they grappled for money and power, they would do anything to anyone to get it; the want-to-haves burned in their gut to lord it over somebody else.

Santos considered himself a pretty tough kid, but he steered clear of that kind. Experience had taught him well. His daddy had been like that, always hungry for what he didn't have, always yearning to lord it over somebody else, ready to raise his fist to somebody smaller or weaker. Like that would make him a big man.

His daddy. Santos curled his lips in distaste. He had nothing but bad memories of Samuel "Willy" Smith. The man had been pure oil-field trash, but too good to marry the "spic-squaw" girlfriend he had knocked up, too good to give their baby his name. He used to call Victor and his mama half-breed wetbacks and tell them *they* were no good.

Santos remembered feeling little but relief the morning the sheriff had come by their trailer to tell them Willy Smith had been killed—his throat slit from ear to ear—in a bar-room fight. Every now and then, however, Santos did wonder about his old man—he wondered how he was enjoying hell.

Santos reached the grocery and went inside, grateful for the blast of cold air that hit him as he opened the door. He ordered the sandwiches, shot the breeze with the counter girl while he waited, and ten minutes later was back on the street, the po'boys and a couple bottles of Barq's in a brown take-out sack.

He and his mother lived on Ursuline, in a small, second-floor apartment. The place was clean, cheap and unair-conditioned. They endured the summer months with two small window-units, one for each bedroom. Sometimes it was so hot in the kitchen and living room, they ate on their beds.

Santos reached their building, jogged up the one flight of stairs, then let himself into their apartment. "Mom," he called. "I'm home."

His mother stepped out of her bedroom, a brush in her hand, her features masked by the thick layer of makeup she wore to work. She had told him once that she liked wearing the makeup when she danced, because it made her feel as if it was somebody else up on the stage, as if it wasn't really her the men were staring at. She had told him, too, that those guys, the ones that came to the club, liked her to look cheap. Like a whore, or something. It was part of their thrill. Santos thought it was really fucked-up. He wished his mother didn't have to put up with it.

She shut the bedroom door behind her, careful not to let the cool air escape. "Hi, darlin'. How was your day?"

"Okay." He fastened the safety chain. "I have the sandwiches."

"Great. I'm starving." She motioned toward her bedroom. "Let's eat in here. It's hot as hellfire today."

He followed her and they sat down on the floor, then dug into the sandwiches. While they ate, Victor studied his mother. Lucia Santos was a beautiful woman. Half American Indian—Cherokee, she thought—and half Mexican, she had dark hair and eyes, and an exotic-looking, high-cheekboned face. He had seen men look at her, when they'd been out together, just the two of them, her in her blue jeans, her hair pulled back into a girlish ponytail, her face free of the makeup that exaggerated and hardened her features.

He took after her; everybody said so. And every time he looked in a mirror, he said a silent thank-you for it. He didn't think he could have faced getting up every day, looking in the mirror and being reminded of Willy Smith.

"Mrs. Rosewood called today."

One of those know-it-all do-gooder counselors. "Great," Santos uttered. "Just what we need."

She put down her po'boy and wiped her mouth with a paper napkin. "You start school next week. You need some things."

His gut tightened. He knew what that meant. Tonight, tomorrow night or the next, she would come home with a "friend." Suddenly, there would be plenty of money for clothes and doctor's visits and book bags. He hated it. "I don't need anything."

"No?" She took another bite of her po'boy, chewed slowly, then washed it down with a long swallow of the root beer. "What about the two inches you've grown over the summer? Don't you think your pants are going to be a little short?"

"Don't worry about it." He crushed the paper his po'boy had come wrapped in and shoved it into the empty take-out bag. "I've got some money saved from my job, I'll get new clothes myself."

"You also need to visit the dentist. And Mrs. Rosewood said your records show that you're due for—"

"What does she know?" he interrupted, angry suddenly. He jumped to his feet and glared at his mother. "Why can't she just leave us alone? She's just an old busy-body."

Lucia frowned and followed him to his feet. She met his gaze evenly. "What's the problem, Victor?"

"School's a waste of time. I don't see why I can't just quit."

"Because you can't. And you won't, not while I'm alive." She narrowed her gaze, her expression fierce. "You need an education if you're ever going to get out of this dump. You quit school and you'll end up just like your daddy. You want that?"

Victor clenched his hands into fists. "That really sucks, Mom. I'm nothing like him, and you know it."

"Then prove it," she countered. "Stay in school."

He flexed his fingers, frustrated. "I'm big enough to pass for sixteen. I could quit school and get a full-time job. We need the money."

"We don't need the money. We're doing fine."

"Right."

At his sarcasm, she flushed, obviously angry. "What's that supposed to mean? Huh?" She poked her index finger into his shoulder. "What do you want that you don't have?"

He said nothing, just stared at his feet and the remnants of their meal, an ugly mess on the pieces of white butcher paper. Like this whole, fucking situation. Anger and helpless frustration balled in his chest until he thought he might explode with it.

"What?" she asked, poking him again, this time harder. "You want some high-priced stereo system? Or maybe you *need* some of those fancy, name-brand jeans or a color TV in your room?"

He lifted his head and met her eyes, the blood pumping furiously in his head, "Maybe what I want, maybe what I *need,* is a mother who doesn't have to turn tricks every time she has to buy her son a new pair of shoes or take him to the doctor."

She took an involuntary step back, as if he had slapped her, her face going white under her foundation and blush.

He held a hand out to her, contrite. "I shouldn't have said that, Mom. I'm sorry."

"Don't." She took another step back from him, working to get control of herself. "How did you know about the... tricks?"

Santos dragged his hands through his hair, frustrated, wishing he had never started this. "Give me a break, Mom. I mean, I'm not blind. Or dumb. I'm not a kid anymore. I've known for a long time."

"I see." She gazed at him another moment, then turned and crossed slowly to the one window in the small room. She stared out at the street below, her view partially obstructed by the small air conditioner. The seconds ticked past, seeming more like minutes. Still, she said nothing.

He took a step toward her, then stopped, cursing himself. Why hadn't he held his tongue? Why hadn't he just let her believe he didn't know her little secret? He couldn't take his words back now, and her silence hurt him more than one of his daddy's blows.

"What did you expect?" he said, softly now. "Every time I needed something, you came home with a *friend*. He would stay an hour or two, then leave. Of course, we'd never see him again."

She bowed her head. "I'm sorry."

A catch in his chest, he crossed to her and wrapped his arms around her. He pressed his face to her sweet-smelling hair. Tonight when she returned from work, it would reek of cigarettes and the dirty old men who had pawed at her. "Sorry for what?" he asked, choked.

"For being a... whore. You must think—"

"You're not! I think you're the greatest. I'm not..." His voice thickened, and he struggled for a moment to clear it. "I'm not ashamed of you. It's just that I know how much you hate it. You're always so quiet after. You always look so sad."

He breathed deeply through his nose. "And I hate that you do it for me. I hate that I'm the reason why you let those guys..." His words trailed off.

"I'm sorry," she said again, her voice small and broken. "I didn't want you to know about the tricks. I thought…" She shook her head. "This isn't the kind of life I wanted you to have. I'm not the kind of mother you deserve."

"Don't say that." He tightened his arms around her, wishing he could protect her, wishing he could take care of her. "You have nothing to be sorry for. I just wish you…if I quit school, you wouldn't have to do it anymore."

She turned and faced him, her eyes and cheeks wet with tears. "I would do anything for you, Victor. Don't you see? You're the best thing I've ever done. The best thing in my life."

She cupped his face in her palms. "Promise me you'll stay in school." She tightened her grip, her gaze on his intense. "Promise me, Victor. It's important."

He hesitated, then nodded. "I'll stay in school. I promise."

"Thank you." She smiled, but he saw that her mouth trembled. "You always keep your promises. You always have, ever since you were old enough to make them to me." She shook her head. "Sometimes I wonder how you can be so honorable, coming like you did from Willy and me."

She made a move to lower her hands; he caught them. "I'll take care of you someday," he said fiercely. "You won't have to put all that crap on your face, you won't have to work the way you do now. I'll take care of you," he said again. "I give you my word on that."

5

"Victor, darlin', I'm off."

Santos tore his gaze from the small black-and-white TV on his dresser to glance at his mother. "See you."

She hooked her purse strap over her shoulder. "You going to get up and come give your mama a kiss?" He made a face, and she laughed. "I know, you're too grown-up for that now."

She crossed to him, bent and planted a light kiss on the top of his head, then threaded her fingers through his hair. "You know the rules, right?"

He tipped his face up to hers and arched his eyebrows in exaggerated exasperation. "How could I not? You repeat them every night."

"Don't be a smart ass. Let's hear 'em."

"Put the chain on," he said in the sassiest voice he could manage. "And don't answer the door for anybody. Not even God."

She rapped her knuckles against the top of his head. "And don't leave the apartment. Except if it's on fire."

"Right."

"Don't you look at me that way." She narrowed her eyes, all traces of amusement gone. "You think my rules are a big joke. But take it from me, there are some real creeps on the streets. And if the creeps don't get you, the state will. Merry, from down at the club, lost her kid that way. Social Services found out she left him alone at night and took him away."

"Yeah, but Merry's a doper and her kid's only six." He swung his legs over the side of the bed and stood. "It's not going to happen, Mom. You worry too much."

"Is that so, Mr. I'm-fifteen-and-know-everything?" Hands on hips, she leaned toward him. "When I was your age, I was damn cocky, too. I sure as hell never imagined I'd have to make a living by shaking my tits and ass for a roomful of strangers. I didn't even know women like me existed."

She shook her head, her expression sad suddenly, resigned. "That's one of the things life teaches you, darlin', one bad choice can screw up your entire life. Remember that the next time you think you know everything."

Santos knew the mistake she was talking about—hooking up with Willy Smith, getting pregnant by him. Her family had disowned her, and Willy had taken to using her for a punching bag. Bad choice, all right. A real doozy.

He swallowed hard. "I'll be careful, Mom."

"You do that." She touched his cheek with her fingertips, lightly, lovingly stroking. "I couldn't bear to lose you, Victor."

He opened his mouth to say the same to her, then feeling silly, he swallowed the words. "You won't," he said instead, covering her fingers with his own, squeezing them. "You're stuck with me."

She smiled and motioned with her head toward the front door. "I've got to go. You know how Milton is if I'm late."

Santos nodded and followed her to the front door, watching as she walked down the hall. When she reached the top of the stairs, she looked back at him, smiled and waved. A lump in his throat, he returned her smile, then closed the door. He reached for the safety chain, then stopped, taken by the urge to run after her and give her the hug and kiss she had asked for earlier, taken by the sudden and overwhelming need to hold on to her, the way he hadn't allowed himself to in a long time, to hold on to her and tell her he loved her.

What would he do if he lost her?

He opened the door and started into the hall, but caught himself short, feeling more than a little bit silly. He was too old to cling to his mother the way a baby would, too old to need her coddling and reassurance. He laughed to himself. All her talk of losing him, all her worries and warnings, had momentarily unnerved him. He laughed again. Next, she would have him believing in the bogeyman and the kid-eating monster in the closet.

With a snort of amusement at his own imagination, Santos fastened the chain, and made a beeline for his room. He dug his shoes out from under the bed, put them on, then sat to wait.

He checked his watch. He would give his mother a ten-minute head start before he left to meet his buddies. He met them every night at the abandoned elementary school on Esplanade and Burgundy, at the northern edge of the Quarter.

His mother's words filtered through his head, the ones about Social Services, about her fear of losing him, and he pushed them away. His mother worried too much; she treated him like a baby. He had been meeting his friends this way for the entire summer and weekend nights during the previous school year. He always made sure he beat his mother home; he, like all the kids, steered cleared of both the cops and trouble. And as he had promised his mother, he was always careful. He had never even come close to getting caught.

Exactly ten minutes later, Santos unlocked the door again and headed out into the hallway. Moments later, the hot New Orleans night enveloped him. He muttered an oath. Nine-thirty at night and it was still hot.

Santos brought a hand to the back of his already damp neck. That was the thing people didn't get about New Orleans summers, the thing that made those long months nearly unbearable—it never cooled down. Sure, other places got hot during the summer, some got hotter. But those places got some relief when the sun set.

New Orleans remained at the boiling point, May through September. In August, they were all nothing more than human crawdaddies. The tourists he talked to acted so surprised by the heat. Invariably, they asked how he stood it. New Orleanians didn't "stand" the heat, they just got used to it. To his mind, there was a difference.

Santos lifted his face to the black sky, and breathed deeply through his nose. The air may not have cooled, but in the last few hours it had changed, the Quarter with it. He found the difference both subtle and glaring—like the difference between natural light and neon, between the scent of flowers and perfume. Like the difference between saints and sinners.

Indeed, the shoppers and businesspeople had disappeared with the day, making way for the night people. Night people came in two varieties, those who lived on the fringe, and those who lived on the edge. Fringe people were people like his mother, ones who didn't quite fit into the standard, all-American, Norman Rockwell mold, though they wished they did. Those who lived on the edge did so by choice, because they liked the life.

Music, bluesy and sad, trickled from an open balcony somewhere above him, from another the sounds of sex. Santos jogged past them, ducking down an alley, choosing the less-traveled streets, careful to avoid the paths his mother might choose, careful to avoid being seen by anyone who might report back to her.

From a corner restaurant came the clatter and clank of pots and pans, the enticing smell of boiling seafood. Santos passed behind the restaurant, then wrinkled his nose as he dodged a particularly ripe garbage bin. Nothing like a day or two in the heat to transform crabs and shrimp from enticing to sickening.

The school in sight now, he slowed his pace. It wouldn't do to be seen running in this neighborhood—with the amount of poverty and crime here, the cops were always cruising the area, always on the lookout for a young male fleeing the scene.

Santos circled around to the back of the school. After making sure nobody was watching, he ducked behind a row of wildly overgrown oleander and sweet olive bushes. There, as he knew he would, he found a window propped open with a brick. He hoisted himself up to the ledge and swung inside. From deep within the building he heard the sound of laughter; his buddies had already arrived. He dropped to his feet.

A match flared. Startled, Santos swung around. A kid called Scout—so named because he was always on the lookout for cops, pushers, winos or anyone else who might intrude on the group—stood in the corner, his amused expression illuminated by the match's flame.

"What gives?" Santos asked, frowning. "You scared the shit out of me."

Scout lit a cigarette, then tossed the match. "Sorry, man. You're late tonight."

"I got hung up with my mother."

"Drag." Scout pulled on his cigarette, then blew out a stream of the acrid smoke. He indicated the length of iron pipe propped against the wall beside him. "Glad it was you. For a minute, I thought I was going to war. Got to protect our turf."

And he would have, Santos knew. Most of the kids Santos hung with, including Scout, lived on the street full-time. They were runaways, either from their families or the foster-care system. A few, like Santos, were neighborhood kids who didn't have adult supervision at night. They ranged in age from eleven to sixteen, and the group shrank and swelled in size on an almost daily basis. New runaways joined the group, others moved on or were caught and returned to wherever—or whomever—they had tried to escape. Santos and a handful of the others had been part of the group since its beginning.

"Where is everybody?" Santos asked.

"Homeroom. Lenny and Tish lifted a bag of crawfish from the back of a truck. They're still hot. They were thirty minutes ago, anyway."

Santos nodded. "You coming?"

"Nah. I'm going to stand watch for a while."

Santos nodded again and started for the area they called homeroom. Because the school was so large, they had selected four rooms to be their regular meeting places and had given each a name—drama club, arts and crafts, sex ed. and homeroom.

Homeroom was located on the second floor at the end of the main hall. Santos made his way there, picking around rubble and weak spots in the flooring. As he expected, he found the group gathered around the bag of crawfish, laughing and talking as they shucked, sucked and generally made pigs of themselves on the stolen mud-bugs.

Razor, the oldest of the group, saw Santos first and motioned him in. Nicknamed Razor for obvious reasons, he had been on the street the longest of anyone in the group. He was a good guy, but he didn't take any crap from anybody. Living on the street did that to a kid. Toughened him. Santos figured Razor wouldn't be hanging out with them much longer. At sixteen, he was ready to move on.

"Nice score, Tish, Lenny." Santos exchanged high-fives with the two teenagers, then took a seat on the floor.

Conversation flowed around him. Social Services had picked up Ben again and sent him back to his foster family; a pimp had cornered Claire and had tried to scare her into tricking for him; Doreen had caught Sam and Leah making out; and Tiger and Rick had left New Orleans, planning to hitch their way to the good life in southern California.

After a time, Santos noticed that there was a new girl with them tonight. She sat just outside their circle, joining in neither the talk nor the crawfish, her arms wrapped tightly around her middle. Santos nudged Scout, who had joined the group and taken the place on the floor next to him. He motioned the new girl. "Who's that?"

The other boy followed his gaze. "Tina," he said. "Claire brought her. She hasn't said more than two words since she got here."

"She new to the street? A runaway?"

"Yeah, I think so."

No "think" about it, Santos decided, cocking his head slightly as he studied her. She had *lost, alone,* and *scared to death* written all over her. She kept her eyes downcast and repeatedly bit down on her lower lip, as if to keep it from trembling. Whatever she was running from, he would bet his meager summer earnings that it was pretty bad.

He felt for her, the way he did for all his friends. Over the years, they had told him stories that made his daddy's beatings seem tame. Santos peeled a crawfish and popped the tail into his mouth. He tossed the head and shell onto a pile of others, and reached for another. Every time he heard a new kid's story, he appreciated his life—and his mother—more.

He thought of the discussion he'd had with his mother earlier that day, remembered her shame at his knowing that she sometimes hooked. She just didn't get it. She might not be Mrs. C from "Happy Days," but she loved him. They might not have much, but they had each other. And his friends made him realize that in this mostly rotten world, having someone, having love, was something special, something worth holding on to.

The crawfish gone, the group began to shift, some splitting into smaller groups, some of the kids heading out to the streets, some crashing. Tina didn't move; she sat as if frozen to the spot. Frozen by fear, no doubt. By uncertainty.

Santos stood and made his way across the room to her. "Hi," he murmured, shooting her an easy smile. "I'm Santos."

She lifted her gaze to his, then dropped it once more. "Hi."

Her voice was soft and sweet and scared. Too soft, too sweet for a girl on the streets. It would harden up fast, just as she would. *If she was going to survive.* He sat down next to her, though careful to leave plenty of distance between them. "Your name's Tina. Right?"

She nodded but offered nothing more.

"Scout says Claire brought you in." She nodded again. "First thing you'll learn about us," he said, smiling, "is Scout knows everything. The second thing is, we're a good group. We watch out for each other."

When she still didn't look up, he figured she would rather be alone. He started to his feet. "If you get in a jam, let me know. I'll do what I can to help you."

She lifted her face, and he saw that her eyes and cheeks were wet. He saw, too, that she was pretty, with light brown hair and big blue eyes. He guessed her to be his age, maybe a little older.

"Th . . . thank you," she whispered.

"No problem." He smiled again. "I'll see you around."

"Wait!"

Santos stopped and met her gaze.

"I—" Her throat closed over the words, and he saw her struggle to clear it. "I don't know where to . . . go. I don't know . . . what I should do now. Can you . . . help me?"

"I'll try," Santos said, though he doubted he could give her what she really wanted—a safe place to sleep, freedom from fear. He sat back down. "Where do you want to go, Tina?"

"Home," she whispered, her eyes filling. She clasped her hands tightly in her lap, fighting the tears. "But I can't."

He understood. He pursed his lips in thought. "Where are you from?"

"Algiers. My mother and—"

The scream of a police siren ripped through the night, stealing her words, punctuating the quiet like an obscenity.

"Oh, my God!" Tina leaped to her feet. She looked wildly around her, the way a trapped animal would, as if seeing her surroundings for the first time.

Santos followed her to her feet. "Hey, Tina . . . chill. It's okay. It's just—"

A second siren followed the first, then another after that. The squad cars passed close to the building, flashes of red-

and-white light penetrated the darkness, squeezing through cracks and crannies, creating a weird, frightening kaleidoscope. It was as if a dozen cop cars had descended directly on top of them.

"No!" Tina screamed, covering her ears. "No!"

"It's okay... Tina—" Santos put his hand on her arm, and she whirled to face him, her face a mask of horror. In the next instant, she tore free of his grasp and ran for the door. Santos ran after her, catching her a moment before she reached it. He put his arms around her and held her tightly.

Hysterical, she fought him, kicking and crying, pummeling him with her fists. "Don't! You have to let me go! You have to!"

"You'll hurt yourself." Santos dodged her blows as best he could, wincing as her fist caught him in the side of the neck. "Dammit, Tina, the stairs are—"

"They're coming... he sent them! He—"

"He who?" Santos got a hold of her upper arms and shook her. "Tina, nobody's coming. Nobody's going to hurt you. Listen, they're gone, the sirens are gone."

She crumpled against him, sobbing, shaking so badly he thought she was having convulsions. "You don't understand. You don't understand." She curled her fingers into his T-shirt. "He'll send them... he said he would."

After a while she quieted, then totally spent, went limp in Santos's arms. He led her to a corner, to a mattress shoved against the wall. She sank onto it, curling into a ball of despair.

Santos sat next to her, his knees drawn to his chest. "You want to talk about it?"

Although she remained silent for a long time, something about her breathing, about the way she caught her breath every so often, as if preparing to speak, made him think she wanted to. Finally, she did.

"I thought... they were coming for me," she said dully, her voice drained of everything but despair. "I thought he had sent them."

"The cops? You thought the cops were coming for you?"

She nodded and curled herself into a tighter ball.

"But why?" Santos murmured, almost to himself. "You thought *he* sent them. Who?"

"My stepfather. He's a cop." Her teeth began to chatter, and she hugged herself tighter. "He told me if I ever...tried to get away from him, he would find me. He said he would find me and..."

She let the last trail off and Santos could only imagine what the man had promised he would do to her. Judging by her fear, it had been bad.

Even worse than what he had probably already been doing to her. The bastard.

Santos laced his fingers together. "I live with my mom. She's pretty cool, but my dad was a real prick. He used to beat me. He's dead now." Tina didn't say she was sorry; because she knew he wasn't. Kids who had lived through hell understood each other without having to be told. "I guess your stepdad's a real prick, too."

"I hate him," she said fiercely, her voice choked with tears. "He...hurts me. He...touches me."

Santos's gut tightened. "So, you ran away."

"It was either that or kill myself." She pulled herself into a sitting position and looked at Santos. He saw by the expression in her eyes that she meant it, that she had considered death an avenue of escape. "I didn't have the guts."

"Did you tell anyone about him?"

"My mother." Tina tipped up her chin. "She didn't believe me. She called me a liar and a...a slut."

Santos swore. He wasn't surprised by her story; he had heard it before. "How about a teacher, a neighbor, or someone?"

"He's a cop, remember? A real top cop, too." She bit down hard on her bottom lip. "Who would believe me? My own mother didn't't."

Santos squeezed her fingers. "I'm sorry."

"Yeah, me, too." She looked away. "I'm sorry I didn't have the guts to take those pills. I had them in my hand, but I couldn't do it."

"Don't say that. I'm glad you didn't." She met his eyes, and he forced a smile. "It's going to be okay, Tina."

"Yeah, right. It's going to be okay. I have no money, no place to go." She started to cry again and brought her hands to her face. "I'm so scared. I don't know what to do." She lifted her tear-streaked face to his. "What am I going to do?"

Santos didn't know, so he comforted the only way he knew how. He put his arms around her and held her for a long time, until she had cried all she could, until the room grew quiet as, one by one, others of the group left for the places they called home. Still, he held her, though he was aware of time passing. His mother would be home soon. When she found him gone, he would be dead meat.

Santos made a sound of regret and drew away from her. "Tina, I have to go. I—"

"Don't leave me!" She clutched at him. "I'm so scared, stay a little longer. Please, Santos." She buried her face against his chest. "Don't go yet."

Santos sighed. He couldn't leave her. She had no one, no place to go. His mother would have to understand. And she would—after she killed him.

They talked. Santos told her about his life, about his mother and father, about school and living in the Quarter. She told him about her real father, about how much she had loved him and how he had died.

Santos heard the pain in her voice when she spoke of her father, he heard the longing. For the first time, he thought of what it must be like to lose someone you love, how much it must hurt. He had been so relieved that his father was gone, he had never considered what it would have been like if it had been his mother taken from him.

It would have been hell. He doubted he could have gone on.

They talked longer, sharing their dreams, their hopes for the future. Finally, as exhaustion tugged at them both, he drew completely away from her. He searched her expression. "I have to go, Tina. My mother's going to kill me."

Tina whitened with fear, but nodded bravely. "I know. You have to go."

"I'll tell her about you," he said, catching Tina's hands. "I'll ask her if you can bunk in with us for a while. I promise I will."

A cry escaped her lips, and he cupped her face with his hands. "Wait here. I'll be back tomorrow." He tightened his fingers. "I promise. I'll come back for you tomorrow."

He bent and kissed her. She made a sound of surprise. It mirrored his own. He pulled away, gazed into her blue eyes, then kissed her again, this time deeply, eagerly. His chest grew tight, his breath short. Arousal kicked him in the gut.

She slipped her arms around his neck; she pressed against him. "Stay with me. Please. Don't leave me."

Santos thought for a moment of doing just that. He was already late, already in the biggest trouble of his life.

"I couldn't bear to lose you," he'd heard his mother say just that night. She would think she had. She might have already called the cops, might have gone out to look for him herself.

"I can't," he whispered. "I want to, but I can't."

He pressed his mouth to hers, then freed himself from her arms and stood. "I'll be back tomorrow," he said. "I promise, Tina. I'll be back."

6

Santos passed a shop that had a neon clock hung in the front window. Chartreuse light spilled through the glass, staining the sidewalk and his skin an eerie yellow-green. The clock registered just after 4:00 A.M.

He was a dead man.

Unlike earlier that night, Santos didn't bother with stealth. He took the fastest, most direct route home, alternating between a jog and a flat-out run. Even the streets that were normally well-populated were deserted.

As he ran, he thought of his mother's fury and of how he was going to convince her to let Tina bunk in with them, especially in light of his behavior. And he thought of Tina's mouth against his, of her fear and the way she had begged him to stay with her. He flexed his fingers, frustrated, torn between what he had done and what he could have done.

He should have brought her home with him. He could have insisted his mother let Tina stay. If that hadn't worked, he could have pleaded with his mother. If Lucia Santos was anything, she was a soft touch. One look into Tina's desperate, frightened eyes, and his mother would have caved.

His steps faltered and he thought of going back, then decided against it. It was nearly dawn already; Tina would be safe at the school. He would smooth things over with his mother, then go back for her in the morning.

He darted down an alley off of Dauphine Street. The cutthrough dumped him out onto Ursuline, two blocks from his home. Up ahead, police lights shattered the darkness.

Three squad cars and an ambulance, their lights flashing, were stationed in front of a building down the block. One near his.

His steps faltered; he narrowed his eyes. Not just *near* his apartment building, Santos realized. *His* building; *his* home.

He started to run.

The police had cordoned off the area. Despite the ungodly hour, a small crowd had gathered. He saw an old lady from the first floor. "What's going on?" he asked, out of breath, his heart thundering.

"Don't know." She looked at him suspiciously. "Somebody's dead. Murdered, I think."

"Who?" He sucked in a deep breath, willing his heart to slow, frightened by the panic tugging at him.

She shrugged and lit a cigarette, squinting against the smoke. "Don't now. Maybe nobody."

Santos turned away from the woman. He searched the assembled crowd for his mother, the panic inside him growing. *She wasn't here.*

That didn't mean anything, he told himself, struggling to stay calm, struggling against the black fear that threatened to overwhelm him. Other of his neighbors were missing, probably asleep in their apartments. She could have brought a "friend" home with her; she could be out searching for him.

"Merry lost her kid. Social Services found out she left him alone nights."

This could be about him. His mother could have called the cops and reported him missing.

Then why the ambulance?

Santos shook his head, feeling light-headed suddenly, feeling like he might puke. He had to see her; he had to make sure she was all right. Even as he told himself she was, he pushed through the crowd, ducked under the police line and started for the building's front entrance.

"Hey, kid."

Santos turned. One of the police officers strode toward him. Santos could tell by the cop's expression—and by the way his right hand hovered over his revolver—that he meant business. *"Somebody's dead,"* the old woman had said. *"Murdered, I think."*

"Yeah, you." The cop pointed. "Where do you think you're going?"

"Inside." Santos swallowed, his mouth so dry it felt as if he had been eating dirt. "I live here."

"That so?" The cop looked him over.

"Yeah." He rubbed his damp palms on his thighs. "My mom's waiting. I'm late, and she's...she's probably pretty worried."

Another officer came up to stand beside the first. He looked too young to be wearing a badge, let alone carry a gun. He had a face that had never lost all its baby fat; his blue eyes were kind.

"You got a name?" the first one asked.

Santos moved his gaze from one to the other. "Victor Santos."

The cops exchanged glances. "Santos?"

He nodded, his stomach turning.

"Where've you been tonight, Victor?"

"Hanging out with friends. I...I snuck out while my mom was at work. I promised I wouldn't, but—" Santos took another deep breath, feeling as if his world was crashing in on him. "Have a heart. I mean, she's probably worried sick."

"You got ID, Victor?"

He shook his head. "No...but my mother can—"

"How old are you, Victor?"

"Fifteen." He swallowed hard, thinking again of his mother's warning about Social Services. He started to shake. "Look, don't blame her. She's very careful, a really good mother. It's my fault." He looked pleadingly at the officer with the kind eyes. "I snuck out. She's going to kick my butt when I get in there. Please don't call Social Services."

The cops looked at each other again. "Calm down, Victor," the baby-faced officer said, looking uncomfortable. "Everything's going to be okay."

"What do you mean?" Santos looked from one to the other again, panic rising like a tidal wave inside him. "What's wrong? What's happened?" He grabbed the officer's sleeve. "Why are you guys here?"

The young officer pried Santos's fingers loose, then put an arm around his shoulders. He steered him toward one of the squad cars, speaking in a calm voice, one meant to soothe. "Have a seat over here, Victor, and I'll call someone to come speak with you."

"But my mother—"

"Don't worry about that right now." They reached the car and the cop opened the rear door. "You need to sit here for a few minutes and I'll call a friend of mine—"

"No!" Santos broke away from the man and started to walk away. "I'm going home. I'm going to see my mother."

"I'm afraid I can't let you do that." The officer clamped a hand over Santos's shoulder, his voice now devoid of sympathy and discomfort. Suddenly, he seemed plenty old enough for both the badge and the gun. "You stay here until I tell you otherwise. You got that, Victor?"

Santos stared at the officer in horror. *His mother. Where was his mother?*

The crowd made a noise then, a collective gasp, a murmur of appreciation that their wait was finally over, that finally their curiosity would be appeased. The sound spilled over Santos's nerve endings like acid.

He swung toward the building's entrance, toward the cops and paramedics emerging from the entrance. He stared at the stretcher, at the body obscured by a white sheet.

Somebody was dead.

Murdered.

Santos tore away from the police officer's grasp and ran toward the building, toward the stretcher and the lifeless form it carried.

Santos made it past the barricade before the officer caught him and held him back. Santos fought him; freed himself. He reached the stretcher; he ripped away the sheet.

The cops grabbed him from behind and dragged him back. But not before he saw the blood, not before he saw the victim's face, frozen into a twisted mask of death.

His mother's face. His mother's blood.

A cry of pain sawed through the night, shattering it. His cry, Santos realized, clutching his middle. His mother. Dead. Murdered.

His stomach heaved. He doubled over and puked on the baby-faced officer's shiny black shoes.

7

Santos sat in the N.O.P.D. Homicide Division's waiting area, staring at the scarred linoleum floor beneath his feet. Shock and grief warred inside him, creating a kind of aching numbness, a pain so great he could no longer feel.

His mother was dead. Brutally murdered seven days ago. Stabbed sixteen times—in her chest and throat, her abdomen and back, in places too vile to be printed in the newspaper.

He bit down on the sound of grief that rushed to his lips, bit down so hard his teeth and jaw ached. The linoleum swam before his eyes. He fought off the tears, although in the last week he had learned that fighting the visible signs of his grief neither conquered nor lessened the pain.

Around him a sort of controlled chaos reigned. Officers came and went, a variety of perps in tow; family members of both victims and criminals milled about the waiting area; and lawyers, like sharks smelling blood, seemed to be everywhere at once. The noise level stayed at a dull, busy roar, punctuated by the occasional wail of anger or grief. Above it all, the desk sergeant's booming voice drilled directions, be it to civilians or fellow officers. Any moment, Santos expected to hear him shout, "Okay kid, Detective Patterson will see you now."

Santos had been through this before. He and Patterson were becoming big friends. *Right.* Santos flexed his fingers, the urge to hit someone or something—preferably Patterson's arrogant mug—barreling through him.

From both the *Times Picayune* and the *State's Item*, he had learned the details of the murder. They had described where and how Lucia Santos had been stabbed. They had detailed the events of the last night of her life—she had gone to work at Club 69, where she danced nights; she had picked up a john, who had come home with her; she had been killed after intercourse. They had found a half-eaten apple beside the bed.

They had called her a prostitute. They had speculated that she had been killed by the john.

After Santos had read the story, he'd thrown up. Then he had gotten angry. Something about the tiny articles—less than three paragraphs each—had had an *"Oh, well,"* quality to them. *"Just another dead hooker. Who gives a shit?"*

He had called the papers, called the reporters who had written *that*. His mother was not a prostitute, he had told the man. She was an exotic dancer. She'd been his mother. He had loved her.

"Sorry for your loss, kid," they had both said. "But I write 'em as I see 'em."

The police hadn't been any better. He had called. At first they had been kind, if condescending. They had patiently explained how the system worked. They had nothing new; they were doing their best. They had even questioned him; they had checked out his alibi. Then they had blown him off, same as they would a pesky insect.

Don't call us, they had all but said. *We'll call you.*

Santos would be damned if he would let them do that to him; he sure as hell wouldn't allow them to do that to his mother. Just because they thought she was nothing but another dead hooker.

He had called them every day—at least once. He had stopped by the station. Now, after a week of taking his calls and visits, they were less kind, less patient. No leads, no lucky breaks. On to a new victim.

Her body was barely in the ground, and they had closed the case. They hadn't told him that, but Santos knew it to be true. Some things didn't have to be spoken to be real.

Who cared about a nobody hooker?

Who gave a shit?

Santos dropped his head into his hands, his mother's image filling his head. He pictured her the way she had looked that last time he'd seen her. With his mind's eye could see her looking over her shoulder at him, smiling, waving goodbye.

He hadn't kissed her goodbye. He hadn't told her he loved her. He had thought himself too grown-up for that.

His eyes burned, and he pressed his lips tightly together. He kept his tears at bay, but the image in his head changed, shifted, becoming the nightmare images he awoke from every night, awoke from bathed in sweat, tears on his cheeks. Slasher-flick images of his mother and her attacker; his mother calling out for her son, begging Santos to come help her. And then he saw his mother as she had been when he'd ripped away the white sheet.

She had cried out for him; he hadn't been there for her. He had laughed at her fears. He had done what he wanted to, without concern for her feelings. Without concern for her safety.

And now she was dead.

Guilt clawed at him. He brought the heels of his hands to his eyes. She had been with that john because of him—because he needed school clothes and expensive doctor visits. She was dead because he hadn't been there to save her.

Had her last thoughts been of him? he wondered for what seemed like the millionth time. Had she been angry with him? Disappointed? Tears lodged in his throat, choking him. Why had he disobeyed her? Why had he stayed so late with Tina?

He hadn't remembered Tina until two days later and only then because the police had made him recount every detail of the night his mother had been murdered. They hadn't found her, but several of the other kids had verified his alibi.

Too caught up in his own pain, he had wondered only fleetingly what had happened to the girl, wondered if she

Forbidden Fruit   63

had gone home and what she had thought when he hadn't returned for her. Those wonderings always dissolved into his own guilt and shame. His own pain.

If he had been home, his mother would be alive.

He knew it, deep down in his gut. It was his fault his mother was dead.

"You okay, Victor?"

Santos looked up into the kind eyes of the baby-faced officer from the other night. Jacobs, his badge said. The man had been more than decent to him, he had gone beyond his duty as an officer to try to comfort him. Santos's vision blurred; he tried to speak but couldn't.

The cop put his hand on his shoulder. "I'm really sorry, Victor. Is there anything I can do for you?"

Santos fisted his fingers, fighting for control. "Find her killer."

The man's face registered regret. "I'm sorry. We're trying."

"Right. Tell me another one."

Officer Jacobs ignored his sarcasm. "I know how tough this must be for you."

"Do you?" Santos asked, helpless anger rising in him. "Was your mother brutally murdered? Was her murder all but ignored? Treated like nothing but a . . . a two-bit, page-six news item?" Santos's voice thickened with grief. "And did you know in your heart that you could have prevented her death, if only. . . if only you had been home. If only you hadn't been—"

"Whoa, Victor. Hold it." Jacobs sat beside him. "What do you mean, you could have prevented it?"

"What do you think I mean?" Santos clenched his hands harder, his eyes and throat burning with unshed tears. "If I'd been home . . . maybe the guy wouldn't have done it. Maybe my being there would have scared him away. Or, I could have fought him. I could have helped her, I know I—"

"You could have gotten killed, too. You probably would have." The cop looked him straight in the eyes. "Listen to me, Victor. This man, whoever he is, is a vicious killer. The kind not likely to be scared off by a boy. This was not a random act of violence. He came home with your mother, planning to kill her. He's smart. We know that because he didn't leave any evidence. Because he made sure he wasn't seen. Our guess is, he's done this before. If you had been there, he would have adjusted his plan to include killing you. Those are the facts, Victor. Ugly as they are."

"But, I could have—"

"No. You couldn't. If you had been in that apartment, you'd be dead. Period."

"At least I would have been there, at least I could have tried to help her. At least she would have known that I...that I—" His voice broke, and embarrassed, he looked away.

"She knew you loved her, Victor. And she wouldn't have wanted you dead." He patted Santos's clenched hands. "Let's go talk to Detective Patterson. Maybe there's something new."

"I doubt it. All I've gotten from him is the runaround."

Today was no different. More runaround. More bullshit. Santos stared at the detective, fury rampaging through him. He longed to lunge at the man. It would feel good, even though the burly officer would probably have him on his knees and cuffed before he landed the first blow.

But if he did manage to get in just one blow, it would be worth it, Santos thought, itching to try. It would be worth any amount of pain or punishment, if he could erase the man's arrogant, disinterested expression for just one moment.

"Look," Patterson was saying, "I know she was important to you, but I have other, more pressing cases. If we find anything, we'll act on it."

Santos jumped to his feet, sending his chair crashing to the floor. "You son of a bitch, you're not even trying. The only way you're going to get something, is if the killer waltzes in here and confesses."

The detective folded his arms across his chest and cocked an eyebrow. "It happens."

Jacobs put his hand on Santos's arm, as if sensing how close to violence he was, then shot his fellow officer a narrow-eyed glance. "Victor, we are trying. I promise you. But there's nothing for us to go on. I told you, this guy was smart."

"So you're just going to let him go free? He's out there. Don't you care, doesn't that mean anything to you?"

"Yeah, it does. I hate it. And so does Patterson. But all we can do is follow the leads we have and wait."

Santos shook his head. "Wait? What do you—"

"He'll do it again," Patterson interrupted dismissively, returning to the seat behind his desk. "He'll do it again, and maybe he'll make a mistake. And then we'll get him."

Santos stared at the detective, disgust and hatred roiling inside him. "Why bust your asses on this, the guy's only killing hookers. Right?" He fisted his fingers. "You think she was nothing. You think she was just a nobody hooker, so her murder doesn't matter. Well, it does matter." Santos took a step toward Patterson's desk. "She was my mother, you bastard. I care. I give a shit."

"Victor—" Jacobs caught his arm "—come on. I'll buy you a Coke."

Santos jerked his arm free of the cop's grasp, not taking his gaze from Patterson's. He narrowed his eyes. "I'm going to find out who did this. Do you understand? I'm going to find out who killed my mother, and I'm going to make him pay."

The detective made a sound of annoyed exasperation. "What can you do, Victor? You're a kid." He shook his head. "You'll end up getting yourself killed. Leave the police work to us."

Santos bristled at both the man's words and tone. "I would leave it to you, if you were doing anything."

The detective's jaw tightened, all traces of understanding gone from his expression. "Look, I've had it with you. We're doing all we can, now beat it. I've got work to."

"No problem, *Detective*." Santos took a step closer to the officer's desk, feeling like his equal, no longer intimidated by the man's size, his position. The feeling was heady, empowering. Suddenly, he understood what it was to be a man instead of a boy. "But remember this, I don't know how or when, but I'm going to find the bastard who killed her, and I'm going to make him pay." He placed his hands on the desk, his gaze still unflinching on the other man's. "And that's a promise, Detective Patterson."

Part 3

Glory

8

New Orleans, Louisiana
1974

To seven-year-old Glory Alexandra St. Germaine, the world was both a magical and frightening place. A place filled with everything a girl could want: beautiful dresses with lace, ribbons and bows; fine dolls with silky hair that she could brush; riding lessons and her own pony; real china tea sets for the parties she gave in the gazebo, and anything else she might point to and say she desired.

Her daddy was a part of that world, the most magical and wonderful thing of all. When she was with him, she was certain nothing ugly or unhappy could touch her. With her daddy, she felt safe and so special—like she was the most special girl ever. He called her his precious poppet, and although she thought the name too babyish for a soon-to-be third-grader and complained whenever he called her that in front of other people, secretly she liked it.

Her mother never called her by anything but her given names.

Glory shifted on the hard wooden chair, her bottom numb from sitting so long in the corner. Her corner. The bad-girl corner.

Glory sighed and stubbed the toe of her mary jane against the gleaming wooden floor, careful not to make a scuff. Her mother would inspect the area after releasing Glory from her punishment, just to make sure she hadn't been up to mischief during her penance. After all, her time

in the corner was to be spent on prayer and self-reflection.
Her mother had told her that at least a million times.
"Glory Alexandra St. Germaine," her mother would say,
*"you sit in that corner and think about what you've done.
You sit there and think about what the Lord expects from
His good little girls."*

Glory sighed again. Other mothers called their daughters sweetheart or darling or love. She had heard them.
Glory drew her eyebrows together, searching her memory,
trying to recall even one time her mother had called her by
one of those sweet names.

As always, she drew a blank.

Because her mother didn't love her.

Glory brought her knees to her chest and laid her head
against them. She squeezed her eyes shut, wishing she could
close out her thoughts as easily, wishing she could shut out
the truth. But she couldn't, and her thoughts made her feel
afraid. And sad. They changed her world from a wonderful, magical place, to one that was dark and confusing. The
one that frightened.

Many times she had tried to reassure herself that, of
course, her mother loved her. Hope St. Germaine was simply a different kind of mama, one who didn't like to hold
or be held, one who believed discipline was more important than affection.

But Glory didn't believe her own assurances, deep in her
heart she knew what was true, no matter how much it hurt.

Tears stung her eyes, and she blinked against them. Why
didn't her mother love her? What had she done to dis-
please her? She tried to be a good girl, she tried to be everything her mother wanted her to be. But, somehow, no
matter how hard she tried, she always fell short. She either
laughed too loudly or too much. She ran when her mother
wanted her to walk, sang when her mother wanted prayer.
Even when pleasing other people, she disappointed her
mother.

Glory sighed again. Her mother thought wanting others
to like her, letting them do things for her, was wicked. But

Glory didn't try to do that. With others, she got her way with nothing more than a smile; with others, she won affection without even trying.

Glory dropped her feet to the floor, longing to get off her chair and run and play. She loved to laugh. She loved to sing and dance and skip, her hair flying behind her. Mama said showing off that way was wicked, too. She said that wanting to be the center of attention was not what the Lord expected of His children.

Glory tried so hard to remember that, but sometimes she forgot. Like today. She squeezed her fingers into fists. Why couldn't she remember, the way her mama wanted her to?

A tear slipped down her cheek, and she brushed it away. At least her mother would be up to collect her soon. She could see by the gathering shadows that it was getting near dinnertime, and her mama's punishments always ended in time for Glory to take part in the evening meal.

Her stomach growled at the thought of food, and she rubbed it, her mouth watering for the toasted cheese sandwiches Cook had prepared for lunch. The sandwiches she had missed because of her bad, wicked behavior.

"Mama," Glory called. "Please, may I come out? I'll be good, I promise."

Silence answered her. She bit down on her lip, so hungry her tummy hurt. She longed to suck on a finger, but her mother had caught her at that once and punished her again. Glory wrapped her arms around herself, struggling to deny the urge. Unclean, she reminded herself. Sucking on flesh was wicked, unclean behavior.

She heard the key in the lock and turned expectantly. "Mama?"

"No, precious. It's Daddy."

"Daddy!" She flew out of the chair and raced toward him. With her father, she didn't have to ask permission to leave her corner. With her father she didn't have to apologize or explain what she had learned during her penance. Her daddy always loved her, no matter what.

He swung her into his arms and hugged her tightly. She hugged him just as tightly, feeling as if the day had just begun, sunny and full of promise.

When he set her away from him, she knew by his expression that tonight she would hear her parents' raised voices. Her father would call her mother too harsh, she would call him lenient. Her mother said that if left to him, Glory would grow up evil and wanton.

Her parents' fights always ended the same way—with absolute silence. Once, Glory had crept down the hall and listened at their bedroom door. She had heard her father groaning, as if he were in great pain. She had heard her mother's breathless laugh. The sound had been triumphant and had seemed full of power.

Something inside the bedroom had fallen, hitting the floor with a crash. Terrified, Glory had scurried back to her own room, climbed onto her bed and under the covers, drawing them tightly over her head.

Breathing hard, heart thundering, she had waited—for her mother to come and punish her; for the morning when she would learn that her daddy was hurt or dead. What would she do if she lost her daddy? she had wondered. How could she live without him?

She couldn't, Glory had realized. She would die herself.

She hadn't slept for the rest of that night, the fears roiling inside her, colliding, stealing everything but her ability to cry.

"Precious?" Her father tipped her face up to his, his expression concerned. "Are you all right?"

"Yes." Tears flooded her eyes, and she hung her head. "But I . . . I was bad, Daddy. I'm sorry."

He didn't respond, but when she peeked up at him, she saw that his throat was working, as if he wanted to say something. She lowered her eyes once more. "I picked some flowers from the garden and gave them to Mr. Riley. He's so nice to me, and I wanted to make him smile. He looks so sad sometimes. I'm sorry. I won't do it again."

Her father squatted in front of her and tipped her chin up. "It's all right, precious. We have plenty of flowers in the garden. And it's good to want people to be happy. I told your mommy that you can pick as many as you like and give them to whomever you like. She just didn't know." His mouth tightened. "Do you understand, Glory?"

"Yes, Daddy. I understand."

And she did, because they had been through this many times before. But it was her father who didn't understand. If she did as he said she could, whether it was picking the flowers, or running down the church steps after mass, or playing hide-and-seek without permission, her mother wouldn't punish her, but she would still look at her in *that way*. The way that made Glory feel ugly and bad. The way that made her want to curl up and die for shame.

Glory shuddered. She couldn't bear that look from her mother, it was worse, much worse, than any amount of time in her corner, any amount of physical reproach.

So, despite her father's assurances, she wouldn't pick flowers for Mr. Riley or anybody else—until she forgot again and acted without thinking first.

"I have an idea," her father said suddenly. "How about going to dinner at the hotel tonight? We'll go to the Renaissance Room."

Glory could hardly believe her ears. Every Sunday after mass, for as long as she could remember, her father took her down to the French Market for *beignets* and café au lait. Just the two of them. Afterward, they went to the St. Charles, and he walked her through, explaining every aspect of the workings of the hotel to her, letting her spot-check the café dining room, pretending not to notice when she sneaked nuts from behind the bar or chocolate mints from the cleaning carts.

But he had never taken her to the Renaissance Room, the hotel's five-star restaurant. Her mother said she wasn't old enough, that she was too ill-mannered for the elegant restaurant.

"The Renaissance Room?" Glory repeated. "Could we really?"

He tapped the end of her nose. "We really could."

Glory remembered her mother, and her spirits sank a bit. Visiting the hotel wasn't nearly so fun with her mother. When her mother accompanied them, Glory had to be quiet, as good girls are seen and not heard. She had to concentrate on her table manners, remembering to sip and nibble and use her napkin often. When her mother accompanied them, the usually friendly hotel staff was stiff and solemn; they never winked at her or gave her treats.

Glory bowed her head. "Mama says I'm too young for the Renaissance Room."

"We won't invite her," he said, tilting her face back up to his. "It'll be just you and me." He grinned. "But remember, you'll have to wear a dress. And your good shoes, the ones that pinch."

Glory didn't care if she had to wear mousetraps on her feet, she still wanted to go. She threw her arms around her father, unable to suppress her excitement. "Thank you, Daddy. Thank you!"

Glory did, indeed, wear the shoes that pinched. She and her father had only just arrived at the hotel, and already her toes hurt. Ignoring the discomfort, she gazed up at the St. Charles's balconied facade, her chest tight with a combination of pride and awe. Glory loved the St. Charles, everything about it, from the old, paneled elevators that creaked as they took passengers up to the thirteen guest floors, to the constant flow of people moving through the lobby, to the way it always smelled, of furniture polish and flowers.

Everyone here liked her. Here she could laugh and skip and have as many yummy minty chocolates as she wanted; here she could roam about at will, without worry of a scolding.

And, too, she loved the hotel because it was completely her father's. Everything here had been touched by him, and in a strange way, to her, bore his resemblance. She felt safe in the hotel, as if her father's arms were wrapped protectively around her.

Sometimes Glory thought that as much as she and her father loved the St. Charles, her mother hated it. Because she had no influence here, no say in how Philip ran the hotel. On a couple of occasions, Glory had heard her mother make a suggestion concerning the hotel, and Philip had responded sharply, in a way Glory never heard him speak to his wife.

The valet rushed over and opened her car door. He smiled. "Hello, Miss Glory. How are you tonight?"

She returned his smile, feeling very much like a grown-up lady. "Very good, thank you."

Her father came around the car and handed the valet his keys. "We'll be a couple hours, Eric." Her father took her hand. "Ready, poppet?"

She nodded and they crossed the sidewalk to the hotel's grand, leaded-glass doors. The doorman greeted Glory with a wide grin. "Evening, Miss St. Germaine. It's nice to see you again."

She returned his greeting, acting as adult as she knew how. "Thank you, Edward. It's nice to see you again, too. We've come for dinner." She lowered her voice reverently. "We're going to the Renaissance Room."

"Very good." He opened the door for them. "I hear the strawberry sundae is excellent tonight." He winked at her, and she giggled.

Her father laced their fingers and together they stepped into the St. Charles's sweeping front lobby. As always, her first moment in the hotel took her breath away. It was so beautiful, so grand. Above their heads, a huge chandelier sparkled like a thousand diamonds; under their feet, thick oriental carpets cushioned each step. The brass fixtures gleamed, the solid cypress woodwork had been waxed to a high shine.

Her mother called the hotel's decor tasteful opulence; Glory thought it, simply, the most beautiful place in the world.

"You did very well out there, Glory," her father murmured, squeezing her hand lightly. "I'm proud of you. You'll be a wonderful general manager one day."

Glory beamed up at him, feeling about to burst with pride. Her father had been bringing her here since she had been old enough to walk beside him; he had talked her through almost every aspect of the day-to-day running of the hotel. Many of those she didn't understand, but she always listened raptly, enthralled as much by what her father was saying as by the fact that he was saying it to her.

Now, from all those years of careful listening, she knew a great deal about the hotel, from its history, to its worth, to how her father kept it running smoothly, day in and day out.

The St. Charles had one hundred and twenty-five rooms or suites and a penthouse that encompassed the entire top floor. Three presidents had slept under its roof: Roosevelt, Eisenhower and Kennedy, as had every Louisiana governor, at least once during his tenure, since the hotel first opened its doors. Countless movie stars had chosen accommodations at the St. Charles during their visits to New Orleans. The list included Clark Gable, Marilyn Monroe and Robert Redford. Just this year the rock star Elton John had stayed here, although her daddy hadn't been too happy about the hordes of squealing teenagers who had descended on the hotel, all determined to get a glimpse of the star.

Glory and her father crossed the foyer into the main lobby. The registration desk was located up ahead and to the right; to the left was an open lobby bar. High tea was served there in the afternoon—Glory liked the scones and jam best—cocktails in the evenings. Situated beyond both, its entrance set back in an alcove, was the Renaissance Room.

As she knew he would, her father stopped at the front desk. The woman behind the counter smiled. "Good evening, Mr. St. Germaine. Miss St. Germaine."

"Hello, Madeline. How are things tonight?"

"Very good. Quiet, considering occupancy is seventy-five percent."

"And the dining room?"

"Brisk tonight, I understand."

"Where's Marcus?" he asked, referring to the night manager.

She hesitated a moment. "I think he's in the bar."

Philip inclined his head. "We'll be in the dining room. If he happens by, send him in."

They walked away from the desk, and Glory peeked up at her father. "You're mad at Marcus, aren't you?"

"Not mad, Glory. Disappointed. He's not doing his job."

Glory pursed her lips. "He drinks too much, doesn't he?"

Her father looked down at her in surprise. "Why do you say that?"

"He was in the bar the last time we were in." She shrugged. "I do know about things, Dad. After all, I'm not a little kid anymore."

He laughed. "That's right. Almost eight, already. Almost grown-up." She frowned at his amusement, and he ruffled her hair. "Here we are. After you, poppet."

They crossed through the alcove to the maître d's stand. Philip spoke to the man, waving aside his offer to escort them to their table. As they made their way through the dining room, Glory watched her father. He swept his gaze over the room, and she knew that his dark gaze missed nothing, no matter how small or insignificant. He nodded at the patrons who caught his eye, stopping and greeting many—some of whom he knew, some of whom he introduced himself to. Of each he inquired as to their satisfaction, each he wished well and expressed the hope that they would return soon.

When they reached their table, he pulled out Glory's chair for her, waiting for her to be seated before he took his own place at the table. That done, he leaned toward her. "Everything must be perfect," he said softly. "That's what people expect from the St. Charles. You must never forget that."

"I won't," she promised breathlessly. "You can count on me."

He smiled at her response. "Remember, too, the importance of the personal touch. We are not a chain hotel, Glory. We must treat each patron as if they are personal friends, guests in our home."

She nodded, hanging on his every word. "Yes, Daddy."

"You see the table before you? Always check for flaws. Even the tiniest is unacceptable." He lifted his utensils in turn, inspecting each carefully, a ritual they had been through dozens of times before. "There should be no fingerprints, no water spots. God forbid it should be soiled."

He did the same with the crystal. She followed his lead, studying, inspecting, pursing her lips ever so slightly as she did, in a perfect mimicry of him. She saw her reflection in the soup spoon and smiled, liking how grown-up she looked.

"The linen should be spotless and crisp," he continued. "And the flowers must always be fresh. If one droops, it must be removed."

"The china can't be cracked or chipped," she piped in. "Even the tiniest chip is..." She stopped, searching for the perfect word, the one he always used.

He helped her out. "Unacceptable."

"Right. Unacceptable."

He leaned toward her once again. "At the St. Charles people pay for the best, and the best is perfection. We must give it to them. If we don't, they'll take their business elsewhere."

After that, they ordered, then enjoyed their meals. While they ate, her father talked more about the hotel, sharing stories about his father and grandfather, telling her about the early days of the hotel. Even though Glory had heard most of what he said many times before, she never grew tired of hearing him tell her again, and urged him to share even more details with her.

It wasn't until their dinners had been cleared away and her dessert and his coffee served, that Glory thought again about her mother. She realized she hadn't seen her since her punishment.

"Where's Mama tonight?" she asked, licking a drop of strawberry sauce from her thumb.

Philip took a sip of his coffee. "She went to mass."

"We went this morning, too." Glory looked glumly down at her ice-cream sundae. "She must still be angry with me. About the flowers and Mr. Riley."

His mouth tightened. "That's all over now, poppet. She just made a mistake about those flowers. Remember?"

Glory looked up at him, then away, her heart hurting. "Yes, Daddy."

"Your mama loves you very much. She just wants you to grow up to be a good person. That's all."

"Yes, Daddy," she murmured, though she didn't believe it was true. She peeked up at him and knew he didn't believe it, either. She knew, in her heart, that he, too, wondered what was wrong with Glory that her Mama didn't love her.

That hurt so much, she wanted to die.

"Poppet? What's wrong?"

"Nothing, Daddy," she said, the words small and sad.

For a moment, he said nothing, and she silently begged for him to ask her the question again, silently wished for him to insist she tell him the truth. Instead, in a voice that sounded false, he said, "Have you thought about what you want for your birthday?"

She didn't look up; the tablecloth swam before her eyes. "It's still two months away."

"Two months isn't long." His coffee cup clicked against the saucer as he set it down. "You must have given it some thought."

She had, Glory thought bitterly. She wanted the same thing she had wished for last year, the same thing she wished for every year.

That her mother would love her.

"No," Glory whispered without looking up. "I haven't."

"Well, don't you worry." He reached across the table and covered her clenched hands with one of his own. "Your daddy has something special in mind. Something fitting his precious poppet's eighth birthday."

When she didn't respond, he squeezed her hands, then drew his back. "Let's do a quick tour of the hotel before we head home."

She shrugged, still battling tears. "Okay."

At first, as they strolled down the halls, Glory's hurt and feeling of betrayal prevented her from enjoying this ritual, one she usually found such pleasure in. But as each minute passed, those feelings dimmed and the magic of the St. Charles, the magic of being with her father, swelled inside her. Her father loved her, she knew. They shared this, their love of the hotel. Here, her mother couldn't come between them.

When they had checked each floor and made sure everything was in perfect order, Philip summoned an elevator, their tour over. "Occupancy is the key," her father said as they stepped into the empty elevator. He punched the lobby button. "You must keep the hotel booked. Empty rooms are not only lost revenue, but lost capital, as well. The staff and the premises must be maintained to the same standard, whether the hotel's occupancy is twenty percent or one hundred percent. Do you understand?"

She nodded, and he continued, "You must never abuse your ownership. Guests' needs must always come before the owner's needs. Never give away a room or service you can sell.

"It will be tempting, I know. It's fun to give away dinners, to throw lavish parties for your friends, to do favors for people you like. But over the years I've seen hoteliers get into trouble that way. They've lost either all or part ownership of their hotels. That must never happen to the St. Charles. We have kept her strong and in the family by being good businessmen, and by being determined to hold on to her. The needs of the hotel come first. Always."

"I couldn't bear for us to lose the St. Charles," she said softly, lifting her face to his. "I love her."

"That's good. Because someday she'll be yours." The elevator doors slid open, but her father didn't make a move to get out. Instead, he caught her hand and held it tightly. "The St. Charles is in your blood, Glory. It's as much a part of you as your mother and I. It's your heritage."

"I know, Daddy."

He tightened his fingers more, meeting her eyes, the expression in his fierce. "You must never forget, family and heritage are everything. Who you are and who you will be. Never forget," he said again. "Family and heritage, no one can take them away from you."

9

Glory awakened suddenly but without a start. She didn't open her eyes but even so, she knew her mother stood beside the bed, staring down at her. Glory felt her presence, felt her gaze burning into her, marking her like a brand.

Seconds ticked past, becoming minutes. Glory kept her eyes shut tight. She didn't want to alert her mother to the fact that she had awakened, she didn't want to see her mother's expression. She knew, from countless times before, just what that expression would be. And how it would make her feel.

Glory began to sweat under her light blanket; her heart thundered so heavily against the wall of her chest, she was certain her mother must be able to see its beat. Time seemed to stop and hold its breath; her every sense, every nerve ending strained, focusing on her mother, waiting and wishing for her to go away.

But her mother didn't go away. Instead, she moved closer to the bed. Glory heard the soft scrape of her slippers on the floor, felt the mattress move as her mother's knees connected with it. Her mother bent over her, the rhythm of her breathing changing, deepening to a sort of pant.

Fear turned Glory's mouth to ash. What if it wasn't her mother beside the bed? What if it was a stranger gazing down at her, or a monster?

What if it was the devil himself?

A cry raced to her lips; she held it back—barely. The fear squeezed at her. She pictured The Great Red Beast there beside her, waiting for her to open her eyes so he could steal her soul.

Glory curled her fingers tightly into the damp bed-sheets, the darkness closing in on her, her imagination creating vivid, frightening movies in her head. Finally, she couldn't bear the unknown another moment; finally the *what ifs* overwhelmed her. Terrified, she cracked open her eyes.

And wished with all her heart that she had not.

Her mother stood beside the bed, gazing down at her, her face twisted into an ugly mask, her eyes burning with an emotion, a light, that made Glory's skin crawl.

Glory shuddered, even as tears built behind her eyes. Her mother looked at her as if she, Glory, was the monster she had feared only moments before. As if she, Glory, was the devil.

Why, Mama? Glory wanted to scream. *What about me is so ugly? What have I done to cause you to look at me this way?*

She swallowed the words, though not without great effort. A moment later, without so much as blinking, her mother turned and left the room. She snapped the door shut behind her, leaving Glory in total darkness once again.

Glory's tears came then, hot and bitter. She curled into a tight ball, her face pressed into her pillow to muffle the sound of her shame, her despair. She cried for a long time, until her tears were spent, until all she could manage was a dry, broken sound of grief.

She rolled onto her back, bringing one of her soft, plush animals with her. She clutched it to her chest, remembering the first time she had awakened to find her mother above her, looking at her in *that way*, her face almost unrecognizable with hate. Glory had been young, so young she couldn't recall any other details of the experience.

She could recall, however, the way she had felt—ugly and afraid. And alone, so very alone.

The way she felt right now.

Glory hugged the toy tighter to her chest. Why did her mother look at her that way? What had she done to cause her mother's face to change into one she barely recognized? One that was ugly and frightening?

Why didn't her mother love her?

It always came back to that, Glory thought, tears welling again, slipping down her cheeks.

At least her father loved her.

Glory clasped that truth to her, much as she did her plush toy, denying the little voice that taunted, the one that insisted he loved her mother more. That didn't matter, she told herself, thinking of their evening at the hotel, of their dinner at the Renaissance Room and the things he had said about family and heritage.

Glory ran his words through her head, holding on to them, letting them soothe and comfort her. They made her feel less alone, less frightened. She was a part of her mother, a part of her father. She was a part of the St. Germaine family and of the St. Charles.

No one could take that away from her. Not her mother's burning gaze, not the darkness of her own fear.

She wasn't alone. With family, she never would be.

10

Glory stopped at the library door, looked over her shoulder to make sure her mother wasn't anywhere about, then ducked inside, partially shutting the door behind her. She tiptoed across the floor, heading toward the shelves containing the *forbidden* books, the ones her mother had made strictly off limits.

And now she knew why.

She reached the wall of books, glanced behind her one last time, then tipped her head back, scanning the titles on the fourth shelf. *Art Through The Ages; The Postimpressionists; Pierre Auguste Renoir: The Last Years; Michelangelo.*

Glory stopped on the last. Her grand-mère had called Michelangelo the greatest sculptor of the human form ever. She would bet that book contained what she was looking for. Now, all she had to do was figure out how she was going to get it off the shelf.

She looked around her, eyebrows drawn together in thought. The library ladder was on the opposite wall; the two chairs, big, old leather things, were too heavy for her to move by herself, the sofa too big to even contemplate.

"Darn," she muttered. "What to do?"

Her gaze lighted on the brass wastepaper basket in the corner. She crossed to it and plucked out the wadded papers, then carried it across the room. She set it upside down in front of the shelf, then climbed onto it. She stretched; the wastebasket wobbled; the book remained out of her reach. Bracing herself with one hand, she stood on tiptoe and reached her other hand as high as she could. She still didn't come close.

"Darn," she said again, this time loudly, forgetting stealth.

From behind her came a yawn and the creak of leather. Glory gasped and swiveled, nearly toppling the basket and herself. Danny Cooper, the housekeeper's six-year-old grandson stared sleepily at her over the top of one of the leather wingbacks.

She glared at him, her heart still racing. "You about scared me to death. What are you doing in here?"

"Staying out of the way." He yawned again. "Mom had to go to the doctor and Grandma said to be good. She's always telling me that when I'm here. I wanted to play, but I couldn't find you."

"Mama has a headache this morning. Grand-mère took me out for *beignets*."

He rested his chin on top of the chair back. "You want to go play?"

Glory tipped her head, studying the six-year-old. She and Danny had played together since he was a toddler, and although he was too young to call her best friend, secretly she thought of him that way.

She hopped off the wastebasket. "I've got a better idea. Can you keep a secret?"

"You bet." He nodded, punctuating his answer.

"I need you to help me get one of those books." She pointed toward the books on the fourth shelf.

He lowered his voice to a whisper. "How come?"

She looked to her left, then to her right. "Grand-mère," she said in an exaggerated whisper, "took me to the art museum yesterday. And I saw something that—" Her cheeks heated, and she shook her head. "Anyway, when I asked Grand-mère about it, she turned red and said we had to go home. And we had just gotten there, too."

He lifted his gaze to the shelf of art books. "What you saw is in those books?"

"Uh-huh." She followed his gaze. "And I want to see it again."

"I can get Granny to help."

"No!" Glory held out her hands to stop him. "You can't." She brought a finger to her lips and tiptoed over to him. "I'm not supposed to see *those* books. They're *forbidden.*"

"Oh." His eyes twinkled. "Can I see, too?"

"I'll let you see, if you'll help me. But you have to keep it a secret. Can you?"

He nodded solemnly. "Cross my heart and hope to die."

"If we're caught, we'll get in trouble. Big trouble." At the thought of her mother discovering her disobedience, a quiver of fear moved through her. Glory caught her bottom lip between her teeth, and glanced at the partially closed library door. Her mother had not gotten up that morning; she never did when she had one of her headaches. Most times, when she had one of her headaches, Glory didn't see her until dinner. Sometimes not even then.

Reassured, she returned her gaze to Danny's. She tipped up her chin in challenge. "Can you handle that?"

He straightened and puffed out his narrow chest. "If you can, I can."

"Good." Glory rubbed her hands together. "The first thing we need to do is to move this chair over to the shelves. If we both push, I'll bet we can do it."

He climbed off the chair and together, giggling, they alternately pushed and pulled it across the room. They parked the chair directly underneath the Michelangelo book; Glory climbed up and a moment later, she closed her fingers over it.

The volume was large and heavy; Glory very nearly couldn't get it off the shelf. She wiggled it to the edge, then lost her grip and it crashed to the floor, making a huge racket. Glory's heart skipped a beat. She looked at Danny, he looked at her. They both turned toward the library door, half-frozen with the certainty that they were about to be found out.

One moment became many, and finally Glory was able to draw an even breath. She held a finger to her lips, then scrambled off the chair to retrieve the book. She opened it, flipped through, and found what she had been seeking. The sculpture was called *David*; he had curly hair and a pretty face.

And he was naked.

Cheeks burning, she lowered her eyes, almost afraid of what she might—or might not—see. But there it was, at the top of the man's thighs, like pieces of rolled-up fruit or a cannoli.

Glory narrowed her eyes, studying. It looked so weird, so strange and out of place. She touched the photograph lightly, both intrigued and repelled. Did all men look like this? Did all men have a cannoli between their legs?

"No fair!" Danny craned his neck. "Let me see...let me see."

Glory tore her gaze from the strange and beautiful image, though it took great effort. "Are you sure you're old enough?"

He lifted his chin. "If you are, I am."

"I'm two years older than you."

"But I'm a boy."

She glared up at him. "Big whip. I'm still older than you are."

He stuck out his lower lip. "You promised."

"Oh, all right. But don't blame me." Glory handed him the book. He looked at the page, his expression blank. "What?"

"That," she said, reaching up and pointing.

He tipped his head, studying the image. "What?" he said again.

Cheeks on fire, Glory stood on tiptoe and pointed to the exact place in question, the rolled kernels of flesh at the apex of the man's thighs. "That!"

"You mean, his penis?"

Glory stared at him aghast. A penis? It was called a penis?

"I have one, too. All boys do."

All boys had a…penis. Dumbfounded, she climbed back onto the chair and took the book from Danny's hands. Admittedly, she'd had little contact with boys. She attended an all-girls school, and other than Danny and a couple of distant cousins, she had never been allowed to spend time alone with boys.

Her mother had told her that was because nice girls didn't associate with boys. But Glory knew that other boys and girls went to school together, that they played together. She had seen them over the estate wall, she had seen them get on the streetcar together, had seen them riding their bicycles, side by side, down the avenue. And she had listened to the other girls at school talk, girls who she had always thought were nice.

Glory frowned. But still, it smarted that little Danny, just out of kindergarten, was privy to this *important* information. It smarted, too, that he acted so casual about it, as if *everyone* knew about penises. Everyone but her, that was.

Danny was a boy, Glory remembered suddenly. *That's* why he knew. He probably had no idea what girls had. She drew herself up to her full forty-eight inches and told him so.

"Girls have vaginas," he said, nodding his head for emphasis.

She made a choked sound. "How do you know that?"

"My mom told me. Boys have penises, girls have vaginas. That's the way God made us, special and unique."

She drew her eyebrows together, confused and annoyed. "Then, it's not a secret?"

"Heck, no." He shook his head. "Everybody knows about 'em. Well, almost everybody," he amended. "And my friend Nathan, he calls his penis a hooter."

"Hooter," she repeated, trying to adjust to all this new information. Why, she wondered, had her mother kept this from her? And why, when she had pointed to the man's penis at the museum and asked about it, had her *grand-mère* acted so weird, then dragged her off? It made no sense.

Glory looked at Danny, an idea coming to her. "Can I see yours?" she asked, surprising herself. "I mean, I've never seen a…a penis before." The word felt strange on her tongue, and she blushed. "If you show me your penis, I'll show you my vagina."

"I don't know," he said, pursing his lips. "You might make fun of me. An' what if we get caught?"

She shook her head. "I wouldn't make fun, I promise. You're my friend, and that wouldn't be nice. And we're not going to get caught. I just want to see."

He thought a moment, then nodded. "Okay."

He pulled down his shorts and underpants. Glory made a sound of surprise and crouched in front of him to get a better look. He *did* have one. But it looked different than the one in the art book, and not like fruit or a cannoli at all. She narrowed her eyes and leaned closer, studying it. It was much smaller. And bumpier. Like a bumpy little cocktail frank.

A horrified gasp broke the quiet. Glory jerked her head up. Her mother stood in the doorway, her face pinched and white, her eyes wide and wild-looking. Even from across the room, Glory could see that she was shaking.

Glory swallowed hard, fear rising in her like a tidal wave. The book slid from her hands and hit the floor, falling open to the naked *David*. "Mama, I didn't—"

"Whore," her mother interrupted, advancing on her. "Dirty, little slut."

Glory shook her head. She had only ever seen her mother look at her this way deep in the night, while she stood beside the bed staring down at her. She had never heard her speak those words before. They sounded ugly and they frightened her.

"Mama," she whispered, tears slipping down her cheeks, "I wasn't doing anything. I didn't mean—"

Hope grabbed Glory's arm and yanked her off the chair. Glory landed on her knees, and her mother jerked her upright. Pain shot through her shoulder, and she cried out.

At her cry, Hope's rage seemed to escalate instead of diminish. She closed her hands around Glory's upper arms and shook her so hard her teeth rattled. "I will not allow such pernicious behavior in my house! Do you hear me? It's evil and dirty. I will not allow it!"

"Mama...I didn't mean to. I didn't...it was Danny's idea... He made me do it...he made me... Please, Mama...please..."

Danny, his shorts down around his thighs, began to cry, too, loud wails of despair.

Mrs. Cooper rushed into the library. "Madam, what's—" She stopped, taking in the scene, her expression dismayed. "Oh, dear," she said, hurrying forward. "Danny, love, what have you yourself gotten into?"

Danny's tears became howls. "Didn't do it, Granny! Wasn't me! Wasn't!"

Hope spun around, her hand raised as if to slap him. Mrs. Cooper darted between them. She pulled up Danny's pants and gathered him into her arms. "Calm down, Mrs. St. Germaine. Children will be children. They were merely curious and no harm's been done."

"Get out!" Hope raged. "And take that...vile little beast with you. I never want to see either of you again. Is that clear?"

Mrs. Cooper reeled back, her expression stunned. "But, madam, certainly you don't mean—"

"But I do." She took a step toward the older woman, eyes narrowed. "Get out, now. Get out, for *'God's servant is an agent of wrath to bring punishment on the wrongdoer. With eyes like blazing fire, he will strike down her children.'"*

Mrs. Cooper paled. She took another step back, then turned and ran, Danny howling in her arms. Glory watched them go, a sense of horror stealing over her. This time, she had done something really bad. This time, her mother wouldn't forgive her. Not ever. She began to shake.

Her mother turned to her, her expression suddenly, terrifyingly calm. "Now then, Glory, come with me."

Glory shook her head, frozen to the spot with fear, trembling so violently she could hardly stand.

Bright spots of color burned her mother's cheeks. "Very well." She curled her fingers around Glory's arm and half led, half dragged her out of the library and up the stairs. Hope took her to her bedroom, but not to the corner, as Glory expected, but to her private bathroom. She shut and locked the door behind them.

Glory scurried to the corner and huddled in it, her arms wrapped tightly around herself. Her mother went to the tub and shoved aside the frilly pink shower curtain, bent and twisted the faucets on. A moment later, steam billowed from the tub into the air.

"Mama," Glory whispered, "I'll be good. I promise, I will. I'll be good."

"You've sinned against the Lord. You must be punished. You must be cleansed." Hope turned to her then, the expression in her eyes straight out of Glory's nightmares. "Get in the tub."

Glory shook her head, her teeth chattering. She tightened her arms around herself. "It wasn't me, Mama. It was Danny. It was his idea. He made me do it. We were just playing."

Her mother advanced on her. "Like Eve, you can't be trusted. She took the apple, she tasted. You have The Darkness, Glory."

Glory pressed herself farther back into the corner. "Please, Mama," she said again, tears running down her face. "It wasn't my fault, it was Danny's. Please, Mama. You're scaring me."

"I will cleanse you of The Darkness," Hope said, her voice devoid of emotion, more terrifying for its absence. She yanked Glory to her feet, stripped her roughly, then dragged her to the tub and forced her into the steaming water.

Glory screamed. Her mother held her down. "This is nothing compared to the burn of hell's fire. Remember that, daughter."

Hope bent and rummaged in the basket beside the large, marble tub. She drew out a nailbrush. "I will cleanse you," she said again. "If I have to, I will scrub the flesh from your bones. You will be clean, daughter."

The next minutes were a nightmare. Her mother raked the brush over her skin, scrubbing every inch and part of her, alternating between whispered prayer and shouted rage. Glory recognized biblical passages interspersed with words she had never heard before, creating disjointed, frightening thoughts she didn't understand. Her mother spoke repeatedly of a bad seed and of sin, of darkness and light. She spoke of Glory's birth, of The Beast and of a mission.

Glory's skin burned; her most tender places bled. She felt hot, then trembled with the cold. Numbness stole over her; with it her physical pain lessened. Her sobs became whimpers; her whimpers, silent shudders of despair.

Finally, when Glory no longer had the strength to sit upright, her mother drew her from the tub. She dried Glory roughly, slipped a plain cotton gown over her head, then led her to the corner of her bedroom. She forced her onto her knees.

"You must see the evil of your ways." She curved her fingers around Glory's shoulder, gripping tightly. "You must see the evil and understand the folly of heeding its call."

Shuddering, Glory lifted her gaze to her mother's face. It swam before her eyes.

"The Darkness will not have you, Glory Alexandra St. Germaine. Do you understand me? I will not allow it to have you."

Without another word, her mother left the bedroom, locking the door behind her.

11

Glory had no idea how long she remained on her knees in the corner, frozen with shock and grief, frozen with fear that if she moved, her mother would come upon her and fly into another rage.

Her skin burned as if on fire, every place and part of her body. The wooden floor bruised her knees. Her back ached; her head pounded.

But her heart hurt more. Much more.

Her father, not her mother, came for her. He didn't speak, just scooped her into his arms and carried her to her bed. He sat on its edge and cradled her in his arms, murmuring sounds of love and comfort.

Glory sank into him, too weak to do more. She longed to tell him she was sorry, that she hadn't meant to be such a bad, wicked girl, but she couldn't make her mouth form the words. Just as she couldn't cry, though she felt like weeping. She had cried herself dry hours ago.

The room grew dark. Still her father rocked her. She squeezed her eyes shut, wishing she could block out the image of her mother's face, twisted with rage, her eyes hot with something that had frightened Glory clear to her core.

And later, much later, as she lay alone in her bedroom, dark save for the closet light her father had left burning for her, she wished she could block out the sound of angry voices. Her mother's. Her father's.

Glory dragged the blankets over her head. She had never heard them shout at each other this way. And although she couldn't make out much that they were saying, she heard her name, many times. She heard her daddy say divorce; she heard her mother laugh in response.

Glory hid her face in her pillow, guilt overwhelming her physical pain. She was to blame for her parents' fight. If her parents divorced, that, too, would be her fault. She was to blame for kind Mrs. Cooper being fired. It was her fault Danny had cried.

Her fault, it was all her fault.

Guilt and fear mixed inside her, leaving a bitter taste in her mouth. She had lied to her mother about Danny. She had told her mother that it had been Danny's idea to look at the books, Danny's idea to pull down his pants.

Glory drew in a strangled breath. She had promised Danny that everything would be all right. That they wouldn't get caught.

But they had. And then she had lied.

She was bad and wicked, just as her mother said. She wouldn't blame Danny if he never wanted to be her friend again.

Just as the rest of the household staff no longer wanted to be her friend, she learned the next morning as she sat alone at the breakfast table. They came and went, silently, their eyes averted or downcast. When they did happen to meet her eyes, they looked quickly away.

Glory wrapped her arms around her middle, eyes burning. Usually, the staff joked with her. Usually, they laughed and winked. No more, she thought, tears choking her. They knew that she had lied. They knew she was to blame for Mrs. Cooper's being fired. They didn't like her anymore. Now they thought she was bad, too.

Glory gazed at her plate, at her fried eggs, their gooey yellow yolks spilled across the china plate, and her stomach hurt. She hugged herself tighter and thought of Danny, of the way he had looked at her the day before. He had been her friend. He never would have lied about her to save himself.

She had betrayed him.

She hung her head, remembering all the times they had played together, remembering all the times he had made her smile when she was sad. She remembered, too, how Mrs. Cooper would bring her a snack when she had missed lunch because of one of her mother's punishments, recalled the times the woman had allowed her a bit of something her mother had forbidden.

Despair pinched at her chest, hurting, making it difficult to breathe. She missed Mrs. Cooper. She wanted Danny to be her friend again. A tear spilled over and rolled down her cheek, another followed. What she had done was wrong. Lying had been wrong. She wanted her mother to ask them back.

Glory heard her mother in the foyer, returning from morning mass. Glory brushed the tears from her cheeks. If her mother knew the truth, surely she would reconsider. Once she understood that none of it had been Danny's fault, she wouldn't blame poor Mrs. Cooper anymore.

Glory straightened. Danny had done nothing wrong, neither had his grandmother. If she told her mother the truth, her mother would ask them to come back. Surely she would. Surely she couldn't punish them for her daughter's sins.

All Glory had to do was face her mother. And tell her the truth.

Glory began to shake as the image of her mother from the day before filled her head. She recalled the punishing scrape of the nail brush against her skin, recalled the accusatory rasp of her mother's voice as she had preached about evil and darkness.

Her mother might punish her again.

Glory whimpered, afraid. She shrank back in her chair, making herself small, as small as she could. Maybe she could tell her daddy instead. He could talk to her mama, or rehire Mrs. Cooper himself.

She thought of her parents' fight. Divorce, her daddy had said. Glory squeezed her eyes tight shut. What would she do if her parents divorced? She knew how these things worked; she would have to live with her mama. How would she be able to stand it?

Glory straightened, fear souring the inside of her mouth. She couldn't ask her daddy to do this. She had to talk to her mother herself.

And if she chickened out, she would never see Mrs. Cooper or Danny again.

She had to tell. *She had to.*

Glory swallowed hard, the taste in her mouth turning her stomach. She scooted off her chair and, heart pounding, tiptoed across the floor. She paused at the doorway to the foyer and peaked around the doorjamb. The foyer was empty, but she had a good idea where her mother was. Every morning after mass, her mother had a cup of tea and read the paper in the garden room.

She found her there. Glory hesitated in the doorway, her heart thundering. Her mother looked so pretty now, with the sunlight spilling over her, softening her, making her lacy white blouse glow like angel-garb.

She looked like an angel, Glory thought, struggling to control her fear. A dark-haired angel.

"Mama?" she said softly, her voice shaking.

Her mother looked up, and the celestial image evaporated. Her mother's eyes had not lost their fevered light; her mouth was set in a tight, unforgiving line. Glory caught her breath and took an involuntary step back.

Hope made a sound of impatience. "What is it, Glory?"

Glory clasped her hands in front of her, so tightly her knuckles popped out white in relief. "May I...may I speak with you, please?"

Her mother hesitated a moment, then nodded and folded her paper. That done, she met her daughter's eyes once more. "You may."

"Mama," she began, her voice quivering, "I wanted...I needed—" She cleared her throat. "Mama, I lied to you."

Her mother arched her eyebrows but said nothing. Glory continued anyway. "I lied about Danny. It wasn't...his idea to look at the books. It wasn't his idea to look at . . . It was mine."

Still her mother remained silent. One moment became several, and Glory swallowed hard, more afraid than she had ever been. Tears flooded Glory's eyes. "I wanted you to know that it was my fault. All of it."

"I see."

Those two words held a world of disapproval and disappointment, and Glory hung her head. "I'm sorry, Mama. And I'm ashamed."

Her mother brought her teacup to her lips and sipped. She then returned it to its delicate china saucer and patted her mouth with a napkin. "Is that all?"

"No." Glory took a step into the room, a measure of her fear easing. Her mother was not flying into a rage. Her face was not contorting with fury, not transforming into that of a person she didn't know but feared beyond measure. "I thought...I hoped that you might ask Mrs. Cooper back."

Save for the way Hope tapped one fingernail against the teacup handle, she didn't move. She seemed to not even breathe. Finally, she lifted her gaze to look thoughtfully at her daughter. "Why should I?"

"Because...because *I* lied." Glory pressed a hand to her chest. "It wasn't Danny's fault. It wasn't his grandmother's. They shouldn't be punished for my behavior. Please, Mama. I'm sorry and very ashamed. Please ask them back."

Her mother stood and crossed to the window. For long moments she gazed out at the bright, hot day, then turned back to her daughter, a small smile playing at the edges of her mouth. "It's good that you're ashamed of your behavior, you should be. It's good that you're sorry. But how do I know you really are?"

"I am, really!" Glory took several steps toward her mother, hope surging through her. "I promise I am. Please ask Mrs. Cooper back."

"I may," she said softly. "I just may."

Glory brought her clasped hands to her heart. Her mother would ask Mrs. Cooper back. Danny would be her friend again. The rest of the staff would like her again. "Oh, Mama, thank you! Thank you so mu—"

"I'll ask her back," her mother interrupted. "*If* you can prove to me that you can be a good girl. *If* you can show me that you can be the kind of girl the Lord expects you to be."

Glory burst into a smile. "I can, Mama! I'll show you! Just you wait, I'll be the best girl ever!"

12

Hope knew of places in the French Quarter where she could get anything she needed, where she could fill any dark, uncontrollable desire that raged inside her. Many of these places were public and appeared to be nothing more than bars or shops or strip clubs. Most were frequented by wide-eyed tourists who never suspected what went on behind the public show.

Tonight, The Darkness had brought her to one of them.

Hope slipped through a rear door and headed down a narrow, dimly lit hallway. The walls were damp; the air fecund. From between the hundred-year-old plaster walls she could hear the scurry of cockroaches. A place as old as the French Quarter harbored many creatures. Some of them human.

She had disguised herself, not that anyone from her circle would see her here. But she knew not to take chances. She had visited this place, and others like it, many times before.

With each step, The Darkness grew stronger inside her, beating...beating...building to a fever pitch. Building until all that was left of Hope St. Germaine was a throbbing shell. Inside her burned an inferno that needed to be quenched before it consumed her live.

She would hate herself tomorrow. As always, she would curse her mother, her past, all the Pierron women. She would punish herself; she would do penance.

But at least The Darkness would be sated. At least, for a while, it would slumber inside her. And maybe, this time it would slumber forever.

And she would finally be free.

She stopped before the door marked by the number three. She drew in a shuddering breath, the blood thrumming in her head, the call so loud it reverberated through her like tribal drums. She reached for the knob and the metal felt cold against her fevered skin. She twisted and pushed; the door eased open.

On the bed, naked, the man waited for her.

13

Glory did as she promised her mother. Her every waking moment she devoted to being the good girl her mother wanted her to be. She walked instead of ran, prayed instead of sang; she neither laughed too much nor too loudly; she never complained, talked back or expressed a wish that ran counter to her mother's.

The days became weeks. Still, her mother did not ask Mrs. Cooper or Danny back. Still, Glory sometimes awakened in the night to find her mother looking at her in *that way*.

At first Glory didn't understand. Then she realized what her mother was up to: she planned Mrs. Cooper's return to be a birthday surprise. So Glory waited eagerly for her eighth birthday to arrive. She counted the days, then the hours. She continued to be the best girl she could be.

Her birthday finally arrived. That morning, she raced down to breakfast, eager to welcome Mrs. Cooper back, eager to see her soft smile and kind blue eyes. Eager to ask about Danny.

Instead, she was greeted by grim Mrs. Greta Hillcrest, the new housekeeper.

Disappointment, so bitter she tasted it, welled up inside her. Turning, Glory ran to her bedroom and locked herself inside.

She threw herself on the bed and cried, cried until she had no more tears. She had been so certain her mother planned to surprise her; she had worked so hard to earn that surprise.

Now she knew the truth.

Her mother would never rehire Mrs. Cooper. Because no matter how hard Glory tried, no matter how much she wanted it, she would never be a good enough girl for her mother. She would never be able to make her happy or proud, she would never be the daughter her mother longed for.

Glory hugged herself hard. She didn't understand what she had done, she didn't know why she always fell short. But she did fall short. And she always would.

Her mother had known that. All along, Glory realized, suddenly angry. Even as she had been making the deal, she had known Glory wouldn't please her. She'd never had any intention of rehiring Mrs. Cooper.

Anger took Glory's breath. Her mother had lied. She had tried to trick Glory. All along, she had known that her daughter would never be a good enough girl to please her.

The anger built inside Glory; it stole her tears, her hurt and disappointment. And it brought her, oddly, a measure of peace.

Much later, Glory gazed at her birthday cake, at the eight flickering candles. Around her, the last chorus of "Happy Birthday" ended and the assembled group burst into applause. For as long as she could remember, every birthday she had wished for the same thing—that her mother would love her.

Not this year, Glory decided defiantly, chest aching with her unshed tears. She would never again waste one of her wishes on her mother.

Taking a deep breath, Glory blew out her candles.

Part 4

Family

Part 4

Family

14

He'd had it. Santos dug his duffel bag off the top shelf of the bedroom closet. He had taken all the paid-for caring, all the phony concern he was going to. He was out of here.

And this time the state wouldn't find him. This time they wouldn't be able to drag him back; they wouldn't be able to force him into another foster home.

In the year and a quarter since his mother's murder, the state had provided him with four foster families. Each family had been a learning experience. The first had taught him not to think—even for a minute—of them as a real family, as his family. He was nothing more than a job for them, a crusade, an income-earning cause.

The second family had taught him not to cry—no matter what was said or done to him, no matter how much he hurt. They taught him that his pain was a private thing, something that mattered only to him. He learned quickly that when he exposed his true feelings, he opened himself to ridicule.

The third family had taught him to expect nothing from other people, not even basic human decency. He had learned nothing from this, his fourth family, because he had no spot left that was vulnerable to such a lesson. He had no hopes, no illusions, no small, secret wishes of love from them. He had closed himself off from his foster family and everyone else, as well.

Consequently, he had been labeled difficult and uncommunicative by the families who had taken him in and by the social workers, his teachers and the school administrators.

Santos fisted his fingers. In a little over a year, he had suffered through the aftermath of his mother's murder, he had lived with four different families in four different areas of the city and had attended four different schools. He had lost all his old friends and made no new ones. His whole life had changed. And yet, he was branded as difficult and sullen. It was just as his buddies had always said, the system sucked.

This time they wouldn't find him.

Santos emptied his drawers and stuffed his meager belongings into his duffel. They wouldn't find him because now he understood where he had gone wrong, the mistake he had made each time he'd run away.

He hadn't run far enough.

He had to leave New Orleans. If he stayed, they would find him, they would drag him back, put him in another home. He couldn't bear another "new" family. He couldn't bear another school, new surroundings, new faces. Not ones that were forced on him. He was sixteen now, practically a man. He could make it on his own.

He had planned his escape carefully. He had saved—a dollar here, a dollar there—fifty-two dollars. He had studied a Louisiana map and decided on Baton Rouge as his destination. It was big enough to disappear in, it was a university town with a lot of kids and was close to New Orleans. A mere ninety or so miles.

Santos hadn't forgotten his vow to find his mother's killer. As soon as he was old enough to be beyond the state's grasp, he would return to New Orleans and make good on that vow.

His mother.

A catch in his chest, he fished a small jewelry box out of the back of his desk drawer, leaving behind the school supplies he would have no need for now. He opened the box and drew out the earrings, made of colored glass beads.

Carefully, almost reverently, Santos trailed the earrings across his palm. Inexpensive, more than a little gaudy, his mother had loved these earrings. "Austrian crystal," he could hear her telling him the day she had bought them. He remembered her laughing as she clipped them on. They had almost brushed her shoulders, they were so long. She'd called them shoulder dusters. With his mind's eye, he could see her wearing them, see how they caught the light when she moved, sparkling like colored diamonds.

The memory was at once sweet and painful, and he laid the earrings back onto their bed of cotton, then tucked the box with the rest of his things into his duffel. He began to zip the bag, then thinking better of it, retrieved the box and slipped it into one of the front pockets of his jeans. The earrings would be safer there.

His mother had had nothing of monetary value, but these earrings meant more to him than a thousand real diamonds. He couldn't bear to lose them.

He finished zipping his bag, then took one last glance around the room that had never felt like his. He had no regrets, he thought. Not about leaving this family without a goodbye, not about sneaking out in the middle of the night or about the twenty dollars he had borrowed from the coffee can in the pantry. This family would not be sorry he had gone, and as for the money, he would return it when he could.

Santos crossed to the window and carefully slid it open. After checking below, he tossed out his bag, then headed out into the night.

Thirty minutes later, Santos climbed into the front passenger seat of an almost-new Chevy van. "Thanks, man," he said to the driver who had picked him up. He rubbed his hands together in front of the heater vent. "I was afraid I was going to freeze before I got a lift."

"Glad to help." The guy smiled and held out a hand. "I'm Rick."

Santos shook his hand, though it made him feel strange. "I'm Victor."

"Good to know you." Rick slipped the van into gear and eased back into traffic. "Where are you heading, Victor?"

"Baton Rouge. My grandmother's in the hospital." Santos leaned toward the vent and rush of warm air again. "She's in pretty bad shape."

"Sorry to hear that. But you're in luck—" he flashed Santos a smile "—I'm heading back to L.S.U. I can take you all the way in."

He was on his way. Santos smiled. "Great. I really didn't want to go back out in that cold."

"I've got a thermos of coffee in back, if you want some."

"No, thanks. I can't stand the stuff." Santos glanced around the interior of the car. It looked even newer from the inside than it had from the outside. There wasn't even a parking or inspection sticker on the windshield. "How long have you been at L.S.U.?"

Rick glanced at him, then back at the road. "I'm graduating this year. In psychology. I'm going to have a 'doctor' in front of my name."

Santos thought of what his mother had said about staying in school, and experienced a pang of regret. And guilt. He hadn't kept that promise to her. Or any of the others, either.

He pushed the regret away, though not without effort. "What does a doctor of psychology do?"

"Works on people's heads for a living. You know, help nut cases work out their problems. We studied all sorts of abnormal shit. You wouldn't believe some of it, Victor. Unfucking-believable."

He doubted that. Santos pictured his mother's face, twisted in death. He swallowed hard. He had a feeling he would believe it all.

"I'm kind of tired," Santos said. "You mind if we don't talk for a while?"

"No problem." Rick flashed him a smile. "You look wasted. If you need to crash, have at it. I promise I won't fall asleep at the wheel."

Santos glanced at the guy, finding something about him disturbing. Something about the man affected him like fingernails on a chalkboard. "Thanks, but I'm okay."

Rick shrugged. "Suit yourself. We've got a couple-hour trip ahead of us." He flipped on the radio, playing with the dial until he found a station he liked. Suddenly, the Rolling Stones' classic "Satisfaction" filled the quiet.

Santos leaned back in his seat and gazed out the window, watching the traffic, scarce though it was this time of night, gazing at the eerily dark buildings they passed.

Seconds became minutes as the van ate up the interstate. Relaxation crept up on him; his limbs and head grew heavy, his head lolled back against the seat. It felt as if his muscles were loosening for the first time in a year. It felt good.

Santos drew in a deep, even breath, lulled by the rhythm of the van and the highway. This time they wouldn't find him, he thought sleepily. This time they wouldn't be able to drag him back. And when he was older, he promised silently, when he was safe from their reach, he would come back and find his mother's killer.

Santos awakened with a start. As he often did, he had been dreaming of his mother. And of Tina. He rubbed a hand across his forehead, and found that he was sweating. In the dream, both women had been crying out for his help. He had tried to reach them in time, but he had been too late. Both had slipped through his fingers, falling into a great, dark chasm he had known was death.

The van hit a rut or pothole and lurched sideways, and Santos came fully awake. He blinked and looked around, disoriented and confused.

"Welcome back, man."

Santos smiled, embarrassed. "Sorry about that. I had no intention of dozing off." He caught a yawn. "How long was I out?"

"Not long. Thirty minutes."

It felt longer, Santos thought, rolling his cramped shoulders and neck. A lot longer. He ached as if he had been sleeping hard for a long time.

He glanced out the window. They appeared to be on a deserted country road. He frowned, a prickle of unease moving up his spine. *Something about this ride felt wrong.*

He shook his head, hoping to clear the sleep from his brain. "Where are we?"

"On River Road. Near Vacherie."

"River Road," Santos repeated. He had studied the map, had planned his route. Baton Rouge was a straight shot from New Orleans—Interstate 10 west all the way.

Why were they on River Road?

As if reading his thoughts, Rick said, "A chemical truck overturned on the spillway. They've got the whole damn bridge closed down. I figured we could take River Road clear to Baton Rouge."

Santos struggled to recall if River Road went to Baton Rouge. He couldn't even picture it on the map.

"Ever visited any of the old plantation homes, Victor?" Santos shook his head, and Rick continued, "They're located all along River Road, and they're really something. Back then, they needed the river for everything, their supplies, to ship out their crops, for travel. You should go see one someday."

Santos rubbed his forehead. How could he have fallen asleep? he berated himself. How could he have been so stupid? So trusting and naive? "Won't River Road take us a lot longer?"

"Not longer than sitting in traffic, waiting for a chemical spill to be cleared away. I don't know about you, but I don't want to chance breathing in any of that shit."

"Good thinking," Santos murmured, willing away his unease. Rick was an okay guy, he told himself. Taking River Road sounded like a sensible idea.

Then why couldn't he shake the feeling that something was wrong?

"You okay, Victor?" Rick looked at him in concern. "You look a little pale."

"I'm fine." Santos inched a fraction closer to his door. "Just tired."

Rick began to talk, telling Santos more about L.S.U. and psychology. Every so often, Rick questioned Santos about his life and his family, and each time Santos steered the conversation away from himself and back to Rick.

And as the other man talked, Santos kept repeating to himself that Rick was okay, that the ride was cool.

But he didn't believe his own assurances. Something *felt* wrong. Santos couldn't put his finger on it, but whatever it was lay heavily in the pit of his gut, warning him to get the hell away.

"You can be straight with me," Rick was saying. "Your grandmother's not really sick, is she? There's no one waiting for you. No one in the world."

Santos looked at the man, the hairs on the back of his neck standing straight up. Rick took his gaze from the road and smiled at him, an open, friendly, you-can-trust-me smile.

People weren't always what they appeared to be.

The last year had taught him that lesson. Big time. Santos worked to look totally surprised—even a little indignant—at Rick's comment. "Of course, my grandmother's sick. She's very sick. And she's waiting for me." He shook his head. "Why did you say that?"

"Look," Rick said, handling the van effortlessly, hardly looking at the winding road, "I've been around. A kid like you, your age, out alone this time of night. It doesn't add up. You're on your own, aren't you?"

Without waiting for Victor to reply, he added, "I could help you. Give you a place to stay for a while, whatever."

"But why would you? I'm nobody to you."

"Because I've been where you are now, Victor. I know how tough it is. Believe me, it's a lot tougher than you can even imagine."

A part of Santos wanted to capitulate, to come clean and accept Rick's help. The guy's offer sounded so sincere, so inviting. But another part, the cautious part, the part that had learned more about people and their real motives than he had ever wanted to, didn't believe the man's offer was anything but a lie. Or a trick. People didn't help other people for no reason.

"I bet it is tough." Santos met Rick's eyes evenly. "But I wouldn't know about that. I'm not on my own. And my grandmother is waiting for me in Baton Rouge. She's expecting me."

"Suit yourself." Rick shrugged and grinned.

Something about the curving of the man's lips was cold. Cold and cunning. Santos hid his shudder of distaste. "I will. But thanks, anyway."

Rick slowed the van, then pulled to the side of the road. "I have to take a leak."

Santos nodded and turned toward his window and the dark hump of the levee beyond. He heard Rick unfasten his seat belt, then from the corners of his eyes saw him reach under the seat.

Get the hell out now.

The warning shot through Santos head, and he reacted without hesitation. He grabbed the door handle and yanked; at the same moment, Rick lunged, knocking him sideways. Santos's shoulder slammed into the door, and it cracked open. Light flooded the interior.

Something clattered to the floor. Santos swung around with his fist, catching Rick in the side of the face. With a grunt of surprise, the man fell backward. It was then that Santos saw the length of yellow nylon rope on the floor between the seats, saw the knife, its blade glinting coldly.

His mother's image, battered and bloodied, filled his head. For one unholy second, panic stole his ability to think, to act. In that second, Rick recovered from the blow and reached for the rope. With a cry of fear, Santos lunged for the door. It flew the rest of the way open and the cold night air stung his cheeks and the smell of the River rushed over his senses.

He was almost out.

Rick caught his foot, his fingers closing over his ankle like a vise, dragging him back. Santos felt the bite of a rope as Rick tightened it around his ankle.

Santos looked back at his attacker, nearly hysterical with fear. He couldn't think. His heart was pounding so wildly, beating so heavily, he could hardly breathe. His thoughts, lightning fast, raced from one thing to another, one image to another. His mother, her murder, her beautiful face frozen into a terrible death mask.

As if understanding—and enjoying—Santos's fear, the man smiled. "We can do this easy, Victor. Or we can do it hard. And easy is always a lot nicer." He grabbed Santos's other ankle. "Now why don't you be a good boy for your uncle Rick and cooperate."

He would not die this way. He would not allow his mother's death to go unavenged.

With a cry of rage and fear, a cry primordial in its intensity, Santos wrenched his foot away, drew back and struck out at the other man. His foot connected with Rick's jaw, and the man's head snapped backward at the blow.

Rick released his grip, and Santos dived out of the van. He tumbled onto the muddy shoulder, then scrambled to his feet, slipping in the mud, falling to his knees. He tried again, half crawling, finally making it to his feet.

Heart thundering, he looked around frantically. His labored breathing sent puffs of condensation into the air. The car was flanked on one side by the levee and the Mississippi River beyond, on the other side by fenced property, heavily wooded.

The driver's-side door flew open; Rick leaped out. Without pausing for thought, Santos ran, darting into the road.

Headlights sliced through the night. A car whipped around the curve, moving too fast to stop, too fast for him to dodge. As if from a great distance, Santos heard the blare of a horn, the screech of tires.

Pain shot through him, exquisitely sharp, piercing in its intensity. Brilliant white light filled his head, followed by the the sensation of weightlessness, of flying, soaring like an eagle.

A moment later, his world went black.

15

Dear Lord, she had killed him.

Heart in her throat, Lily Pierron crouched beside the young man's still form. She reached out and touched his forehead, somewhat reassured to find his skin warm and damp. She brushed his dark hair away from his eyes, and he moaned and stirred slightly.

He was alive, Lily thought, dizzy with relief. Thank God. She lifted her gaze to the dark stretch of road before her, uncertain what she should do next. She doubted that at this time of night another driver would happen along anytime soon, and other than her home, there wasn't another residence for nearly a half a mile. She brought a trembling hand to her forehead. Should she try to move him or leave him to go for help?

Neither option appealed. Depending on his injuries, she could seriously hurt him by trying to move him. She was neither young nor strong, and in all probability, without his assistance she could do no better than drag him to her car.

That left leaving him alone while she went for help.

Lily thought of the driver of the van. As she had called out to him to stop and help, he had flown back into his vehicle and peeled out, so fast he had sprayed gravel clear across the road. Whatever had been going down when she happened along, this boy had been trying to escape. Why else would he have been running across the road that way?

Another thought occurred to her, one that sent a shiver of apprehension up her spine. What if that driver was up the road a bit, watching and waiting to see what she did? Waiting to see if she left the boy alone and helpless?

A long shot, she told herself, rubbing her arms, noticing the cold for the first time. Most criminals didn't hang around the scene, "just to see what happened." No, criminals usually put as much time and distance between themselves and the crime as possible. But still, the idea of leaving the boy alone, hurt and vulnerable, frightened her.

The boy moaned again, and she returned her gaze to his face. His eyelids fluttered, then opened. He stared blankly at her.

"Are you all right?" she asked, her words tumbling out in a jumbled rush. "I didn't see you. I came around the curve, and there you were. I tried to stop, I really did. I'm so, so sorry."

His eyes drifted shut again, a grimace of pain twisting his features.

"Dear God." Lily brought a hand to her chest. "Where do you hurt? How bad is it?" She made a choked sound of exasperation. "As if I could do anything about it if you did tell me. Dammit, where's a doctor when you need one? Overpaid quacks." She drew in a deep, calming breath. "Don't you worry. I'll go get help."

As she made a move to stand, he caught her hand, his grip surprisingly strong. Startled, she looked at him. His eyes were open, but this time the expression in them was so fierce she caught her breath. He moved his gaze, looking toward the other side of the road.

Lily followed his glance, then understood. "Gone," she said. "Just took off when I stopped the car." She frowned. "If he was a friend of yours, you need to choose a little more carefully."

"He . . . wasn't . . ."

The boy slurred his words, and as he spoke his eyes fluttered as if he was experiencing a wave of dizziness. Lily swore. "Look, you need help. I hate to leave you, but I live just across the street." She pointed. "I'll call 911 and be right ba—"

N . . . no. I'm . . . fine."

Lily watched in horror as he struggled into a sitting position, his face twisting into that awful grimace of pain as he did. "But, you're not fine," she said holding out a hand to stop him. "Son, you could be really hur—"

"I'm not your son."

Though little more than a hoarse whisper, she heard the defiance and bitterness in his voice. His tone and words told her much about him, things he would not want her to know.

Even as her heart went out to him, she understood that with a boy like him, the last thing she could afford to be was a pushover. "You're hurt," she said firmly, brooking no argument. "I don't know how badly. If you can help me get you to my car, I'll take you to the hospital. If you can't, I have to call 911."

Fear shot into his eyes. He grabbed her hand. "Don't call anyone," he managed to say weakly. "I'm fine. I am." As if to prove his words, he started to stand.

And ended up on his knees, doubled over.

Lily's worry became panic, but she quickly got a grip on it. "You can be as pigheaded as you like, I can't leave you here. And I won't. When I hit you, you became my responsibility."

He looked into her eyes. The desperation in them told her everything. "No... Forget about it. Please," he said again, when he had caught his breath. "I'm fine. Just promise... you won't call... anyone."

Lily clasped her hands together, torn. The boy was in some sort of trouble, that was obvious. Running from someone or something. Maybe the law, though she doubted it. He had the look of the hunted, of the outcast. Not of the criminal.

And he was hurt. He could have internal injuries or a concussion. He was slurring his words slightly; he couldn't even stand, he was so hurt or dizzy.

So, how could she do as he asked?

She couldn't.

Lily came to a decision. She knew someone she could call, an old friend who wouldn't ask any questions. But she wouldn't share that bit of information just yet.

"You have nothing to fear from me," she said softly. "And I won't call anyone... if you come with me." When he started to protest, she cut him off. "I can't just leave you. I won't. So those are your choices. Come with me, or I call the cops. I don't think you have the strength to crawl far enough or fast enough to elude them. If you think I'm wrong, go ahead and give it a try."

She took his silence for acquiescence. "I'm glad we're in agreement about this. Now, I'm going to try to get you to your feet, then to my car. You're going to have to help me, because I'm too old and too weak to carry you."

She did as she said, and in moments he was on his feet, though unsteadily. "Like I said before, I live right across the street. I'm going to make sure you're okay. You'll be safe with me until you feel strong enough to continue on your way."

He hesitated, as if considering fighting her, then nodded. They started for her car. With each step, he leaned more heavily on her for support, though she sensed he hated it.

It took several minutes, but finally they reached the vehicle. She helped him into the front passenger seat, then went around to the driver's side, climbed in and started the car. She drove the two hundred or so feet to her long driveway, and turned in. Only then did she dare peek at her young, unwilling companion.

He kept his gaze trained straight ahead; he held himself tautly, as if on guard, ready to spring from the vehicle at a second's notice. He had drawn his mouth into a tight line, and Lily sensed that it took every ounce of his strength to keep from slumping over in his seat.

Poor boy, she thought, understanding him more than he would ever have believed if she told him. She understood him because she knew what it was to be an outcast, to not belong. To be alone.

Alone, always alone.

Lily drew in a shallow, aching breath. The Lord had exacted a harsh and appropriate payment for her sins. For how much worse this earthly hell than the fires that waited could ever be.

She tightened her fingers on the steering wheel, the pain inside her a living thing, twisting and turning, squeezing at her until taking even the smallest breath hurt. *Her darling Hope. Her beautiful Glory.* She longed to be with them, longed to share their lives.

So much so, she had spent the entire day waiting, hoping to get just one glimpse of them. She had sat in her car, across the street from the St. Charles, alternately too warm and too cold, her gaze trained on the hotel's grand front entrance.

It hadn't been the first time; it wouldn't be the last.

And this time, her wait had been rewarded. Hope and Glory had emerged from the hotel, and for one perfect moment, as the sun spilled over their faces, Lily had drowned herself in the joy of just looking at them.

Lily sucked in a sharp breath, the pain of wanting so great, she thought it would consume her. It ate at her day and night, until she felt stripped of everything but hopelessness.

She flexed her fingers. All she had ever wanted was for her daughter to have a good life, a clean life untainted by her mother's sin. Hope had that now. And Lily understood why her daughter wanted nothing to do with her, why she had become so upset the one time Lily had approached her to beg for another chance; she understood why Hope feared association with her. After all, she had lived her life as outcast and leper.

Lily understood, too, why Hope didn't want Glory to know her grandmother, why she was ashamed for Glory to know who—and what—her ancestors were.

Lily was ashamed, too. She despised herself for her past actions.

But understanding didn't lessen the ache inside her. Until the day she died, she would yearn for what she could never have, she would grieve for what she had lost. And just as she would spend her last years living alone, she would die alone.

Lily drew the car to a stop at the end of her driveway. "We're here," she said unnecessarily. "I'll come around for you."

"I can make it on my own."

"Fine." She went around the car, anyway. He glared at her but said nothing.

Stubborn, she thought as she watched him grimace with each step. Prideful and pigheaded. But even as those descriptions moved through her head, she acknowledged admiration for the strength of will it took him to stand on his own, to refuse her help though he was hurt and no doubt frightened.

She had known others like him, had helped others like him. Kids who had no one to depend on but themselves. Kids who had been hurt and let down again and again. This boy hadn't had anyone in his corner for a long time. She didn't blame him his defiance; he had probably earned it.

They entered the house through the side entrance—the servants' entrance that led into the kitchen. She flipped on the overhead light. And saw that he was bleeding. His pant leg was wet with it, the blood creating a dark, ugly stain on the thigh of his jeans.

She made a soft sound of dismay. "Sit here," she instructed, easing him onto one of the chairs set up around the old, oak table. "I'll get some bandages."

He caught her hand. "You promised you wouldn't call anyone."

She met his eyes, a modicum of guilt easing through her. Misplaced guilt, she told herself. Her first consideration had to be his physical well-being. "I know what I promised. I'll be right back."

Minutes later she returned with antiseptic, bandages and a bath towel. She filled a bowl with warm, soapy water and got a washcloth. "You'll have to take off your pants. I don't think I'll be able to get to the cut if you don't."

He flushed. "Lady, I am not taking off my pants."

She bit back a smile at his embarrassment. It didn't fit his tough-guy image. "I've seen the male of the species without their pants many times. You have nothing to fear from an old woman like me." She held out a towel. "If it will make you feel more comfortable."

He snatched it from her hand, and fighting a smile, she turned her back to give him a little privacy.

"Okay."

She turned back to him. He had returned to the chair, the towel wrapped snugly around his middle. He scowled at her, and she scooped up his jeans. "I'll just throw these in the washer. Don't go anywhere."

Minutes later, his jeans safely in the washer, she returned to the kitchen. He scowled at her again. "You don't have to look so fierce, I promise I'll give you your pants back," she said.

Lily knelt in front of him and gently probed his wound, relieved to see that, although long, it wasn't too deep. She dipped the washcloth in the soapy water. "This might sting. Sorry."

"I'll just bet you are." He stiffened and gritted his teeth as she moved the cloth over the gash.

"A friend of mine is a retired doctor—"

"No."

"He lives close by," she continued, unperturbed. "If I were to tell him you're my nephew, he would accept that. He and I share many secrets. In fact, I would trust him with my life."

"It's not your life you would be trusting him with."

"You could have internal injuries. You could have a concussion, or need stitches."

"I don't need stitches." He winced. "Besides, you promised you wouldn't call anyone."

"I know. And I'm sorry about that. But, I would rather break a promise than have you die." She lifted her gaze to his. "You're much too young to die."

Panic raced into his eyes. "What are you saying?"

"My name's Lily Pierron. You may call me Miss Lily. Or, for the next few minutes, Aunt Lily."

"I won't be around long enough to call you anything." He started to stand, making a sound of pain as he put his weight on his right leg. He swore and sat back down. The front bell pealed, announcing the doctor's arrival.

"Don't answer that." He caught her hand. "Please... Lily."

She squeezed his fingers, then stood. "I'm really sorry. But, you'll thank me for this, I promise you."

He swore again. "And we both know how much your promises are worth, don't we?"

She ignored both his sarcasm and the way it made her feel. "I need to know your name."

He folded his arms across his chest and glared at her. "Go to hell."

The bell pealed again. "You must have a name. And if we're to pull this off, I have to call you something. I don't think go to hell is going to cut it."

"Todd," he said gruffly, not meeting her eyes. "Todd Smith."

She nodded. "I'll be back, Todd Smith. I hope you're smart enough to still be here."

16

As soon as Lily left the kitchen, Santos stood. He looked down at himself. "Dammit." The old lady had thoroughly outsmarted him. How far could he get not only injured, but without his pants?

"Dammit," he said again, picturing himself limping down River Road wrapped in a bath towel. He had to trust her. *Right.* He'd trusted plenty in the last year and a quarter, starting with those bumbling, good-for-nothing homicide detectives. *So much for trust.*

Heart pounding, Santos sat back down and waited, a feeling of doom settling over him like a dark cloud. He closed his eyes, certain that in one minute a police officer would walk through the door and haul his butt back to New Orleans.

She wasn't going to do that to him, Santos thought suddenly and with certainty. This Lily talked tough, but she had kind eyes. Something about her made him trust her instinctively.

He called himself a fool. Whether he could trust her or not, he was trapped.

She hadn't lied. A moment later his *Aunt Lily* escorted an elderly man into the kitchen. Instead of a badge and a gun, he was carrying a black medical bag.

And true to her promise, the doctor played along with their story about Todd being her nephew; he asked few questions about how he'd received his injuries or about anything else.

Twenty minutes later, the doctor pronounced that Santos would live. "You'll have some nasty bruises in the morning. A lot of soreness.'' He snapped his bag shut. ''But, you'll be all right.''

He advised Lily to watch her ''nephew'' closely for six hours, to wake him every two hours if he slept and to call if anything about his condition changed.

She had said that she and the old doctor shared many secrets. What secrets? Santos wondered, watching as Lily Pierron walked the doctor to the door. She slipped her arm through the old doctor's and their shoulders brushed as they walked, suggesting a familiarity beyond that of neighbors or old friends.

A moment later, she returned to the kitchen, her expression all business. ''Would you prefer the couch in the parlor or one of the bedrooms upstairs?''

He studied her a moment. ''The couch.''

''Fine. Do you need assistance walking, or—''

''I can make it on my own.''

''Of course, you can.''

Without another word, she went on ahead. He scowled at her back as he limped behind her. When he reached the parlor, she was waiting for him, hands folded primly in front of her.

He frowned at her. ''If you're waiting for me to apologize, you're going to have a long wait.''

''Did I ask for an apology? After all, I'm the one who hit you.'' She motioned toward the couch, already made up for him. ''I hope this will be all right.''

He shot her an annoyed glance. ''If you had already planned for me to sleep on the couch, why did you ask which I would prefer?''

''I didn't plan for you to sleep here, I simply knew it was where you would choose to sleep. I gave you a choice, anyway.''

''Really?'' he said, drawing out the word with obvious disbelief. Like everyone else he had come into contact with in the last year and a half, Lily Pierron was full of shit. ''And how did you *know* I would choose the couch?''

''Because it's closer to the front door. Of course.''

Irritated that she was right, he glared at her. "So what's the story with you and the old geezer? He your boyfriend?"

"Smith," she countered, softly but evenly. "That's a rather common name, isn't it?"

He cocked up his chin. "You don't believe me?"

"I didn't say that, now, did I?"

"You didn't have to." He moved his gaze over the large, opulently furnished room. "It's kind of gaudy, isn't it?"

"It served its purpose." She started for the door. "I've left an extra blanket, in case you get cold. I'll be checking on you every two hours, so don't be frightened if you awaken to find me in the room."

Santos muttered an oath. He couldn't ruffle her. If there was one thing he had learned to do well during his tenure in the foster-care system, it was how to ruffle feathers and upset applecarts. At times he had felt it was the only way he had of fighting back, of exerting his independence and need to be left alone.

And now, more than anything, he wanted to fluster this woman. He looked the room over again, this time with deliberate slowness. He brought his gaze back to hers, then smiled thinly. "Do you live alone, Lily?"

She looked him straight in the eye. "Yes, Todd, I do."

He had expected her to lie. He had expected to see fear or distrust race into her eyes. He had seen neither. She had been honest. He looked away, denying the grudging respect he felt for her.

"Why do you want to know, Todd? Are you going to murder me in my sleep? Or just rob me?"

"That's for me to know and you to find out."

She laughed then, the sound a haunting combination of amusement and despair. "Things are nothing, Todd. They mean nothing. And if you murder me, well, I really have nothing to live for, anyway."

Without waiting for him to comment, she went to the parlor's double doors, stopping and turning back to him when she reached them. "Let's strike a bargain, Todd

Smith. I don't expect anything from you, you don't expect anything from me. You don't ask me any questions, I won't ask you any. And if Todd Smith isn't your real name, I don't really care.''

Santos awakened to the succulent smell of bacon cooking. He opened his eyes and the events of the night before came rushing back—hitching a ride; being attacked; running, only to be pinned in the headlights of an oncoming car; being struck, then the sensation of flying.

Fear clutched at him as, for one awful moment, he allowed himself to consider what could have happened. If Lily Pierron hadn't come along, or if she had been going faster and had struck him harder. If she had called the cops. Santos shuddered. If he hadn't escaped the van and its driver's rope and knife.

He shook his head to clear it, fighting off the fear, willing his heart to slow. Today, tomorrow and every day after that he would have to take care of himself, he would have to fight to survive. He couldn't afford to dwell on the past and on what could have happened. He had to focus on his future. And for now, he was safe; he was free.

Santos drew himself into a sitting position and groaned. As the doctor had predicted, he was sore as hell. Each time he moved, another muscle group screamed in protest. His head and thigh throbbed. He felt as if he had been hit by a Mack truck instead of a twenty-five-year-old Mercedes sedan.

Santos swung his legs over the side of the couch. She had laundered his blue jeans. They were laid neatly over the back of the couch, along with a worn chambray work shirt. On top of them both sat a small, white box and a couple of rumpled bills.

His duffel. He'd left it in the van.

Santos moaned and dropped his head into his hands. He hadn't even thought of his bag until now. Most of his money and all of his clothes had been in it. Now he had nothing.

Except for six dollars, a five and a one.

And his mother's earrings. Thank God, he hadn't lost the earrings.

Santos stood and dressed as quickly as his aching muscles would allow. He limped into the kitchen, the smell of bacon causing his stomach to rumble. As his mouth began to water, he realized how long it had been since he'd eaten.

Miss Lily stood in front of a great, old-fashioned stove, turning bacon in a black iron skillet. She looked over her shoulder at him and smiled. "I see you're still here."

Last night, he hadn't thought much about the way she looked. He had noticed her eyes and her approximate age, but little else. This morning, in the sunlight, he wondered how he couldn't have. She was a striking-looking woman. Once upon a time, she must have been an incredible beauty.

Santos folded his arms across his chest. "And you're still alive. The family silver's still in place."

She laughed and shook her head. "I knew you weren't going to kill me."

"Yeah?" He moved farther into the kitchen. "And how did you know that?"

She shrugged. "Experience, I guess. It's given me a sense about people. Grab a plate, everything's ready."

He shifted his gaze to the pile of bacon draining on paper towels, and his stomach growled once more.

She followed his gaze. "I had a feeling you would be hungry. We're having biscuits and gravy, too. And I warn you, my gravy is pretty special."

Santos glared at her, pride warring with hunger. "You don't have to feed me."

"No?" She took a pan of biscuits, big and golden brown, from the oven and set them on the stove top. "I rather think I do owe you something. After all, I did hit you with my car."

Santos thought of the state. One of the social workers had told him the state owed him a family, since he had no one else. His second foster mother had told him he owed her and her husband because they'd taken him in. He didn't want to be owed anything. And he didn't want to owe anyone else. He told her so.

Lily stirred the pot of gravy. "Well, then," she said thoughtfully, "you can pay me for the meal."

"Pay you?" he repeated, thinking of the few dollars he had to his name. "For the meal?"

"Of course, I don't expect you to." She wiped her hands on her apron. "But, if you really don't want to owe me for the meal . . . pay me for it."

Santos set his jaw, frustrated. "How much?"

She lifted a shoulder. "I don't know, a few dollars. What does a home-cooked breakfast go for these days?"

He said nothing, and she turned back to the stove. "Or, you could work it off. There are some things I need done around here. Repairs to the garage. Ripped screens. Stuff like that. My regular man up and died on me. He'd been working for me for forty years."

She split a biscuit, covered it with the white gravy, then added a heap of bacon to the plate. She turned and held it out. "You decide what the meal's worth. And if you want to stay a few days, get your strength back, I'll pay you a little something on top of room and board."

Santos gazed at the loaded plate, his mouth watering. He hated to stay. He hated the idea of feeling beholden—to this woman or anyone else. But the truth was, he had no money, no clothes and nowhere he was expected to be. Lily Pierron's offer was a godsend. And he hated that, too.

He stiffened his spine and reached for the plate. "A couple days. Then I'm out of here."

17

Santos stayed. Days stretched into weeks, weeks into months. Now, three months to the day since Lily had taken him in, he sat on the steps that led to her first-floor gallery and stared out at the levee, wondering how it had happened. He hadn't planned to remain so long. As he had announced that first morning, he had intended to stay only a few days or a week, just long enough to save some money and get his strength back.

Santos picked up a piece of a shell that had, no doubt, been carried from the driveway on the bottom of someone's shoe. He turned over the broken bit in his hand. What was her deal, anyway? What was she getting out of this situation? He didn't buy that she couldn't find another handyman to fix up her place. And he certainly didn't buy that she cared about him.

No, she had another reason for keeping him around. Experience had taught him that everybody had an angle, everybody wanted something from everybody else. He just hadn't figured out Lily's angle yet.

He frowned. Judging by her home and car, she was rich. And rich people had no use for poor ones—except as servants or to hold up as their *cause*.

Santos narrowed his eyes. But Lily treated him in neither of those ways. She treated him as an equal and with respect. She didn't expect him to work out of a sense of obligation, but instead paid him a fair wage for any jobs she asked him to do. She gave him space, neither pressuring him with questions about himself and his past, nor suffocating him with sympathy and understanding that rang false.

What was she after?

Santos tipped his face to the purpling sky. He sensed in Lily a deep need for love and companionship, a loneliness so sharp he could almost feel it. And despite the great diversities between them, he sensed that she understood him. Understood him in a way no one had in a long time. And as much as he hated to admit it, he liked her.

Understood him? Liked her? He scowled at his own thoughts. He was being ridiculous. Softheaded and too trusting. The fact was, Lily Pierron was just as he had first thought her to be—no different from anybody else, just working her angle, whatever it was. He would be a fool to forget that.

Santos looked down at the piece of shell in his hand, then flung it as far from him as he could. He didn't like or trust her. He hated that he needed her handout and despised himself for having accepted it for so long.

The time had come for him to go.

Lily stepped out onto the gallery behind him. She moved quietly, as was her way. He'd become accustomed to her stillness, her way of appearing as if out of nowhere. She was the most self-contained person he had ever known. She seemed to know who and what she was, and although he wouldn't say that she was at peace with herself, he sensed that neither was she at war with herself. She was resigned to her life.

A lump formed in his throat, and he swallowed past it. Her life was her own damn business. Let her be resigned to it; he had nothing to do with it.

Lily crossed to him. "It's a pretty evening," she murmured, gazing toward the levee and river beyond. "I've always loved this time of day. The color and smells. The hushed quality."

Santos fisted his fingers, wishing she would go away and leave him alone. Wishing that, deep in his gut, he didn't long for her to sit beside him.

He didn't need her or her company. He didn't need any-one.

Lily sighed, obviously undaunted by his silence. "I remember being a girl and doing just what you are now."

"And what was that?" he asked sharply, irrational anger surging through him. Anger at her intrusion, anger that he was here, on this porch, that he hated the idea of leaving. Anger that, despite his own self-assurances to the contrary, Lily reminded him how much he missed what he'd had with his mother. What he'd had—and lost.

She lowered herself to the step beside him. "Gazing out at the river, thinking of all the places I would rather be." She laughed lightly. "Funny, how some things change so much and others change not at all."

How did she know him so well? he wondered, as furious with himself as with her. How, in three short months, had she acquired the ability to crawl into his head and read his mind?

He swung to face her, ready to fight it out with the whole, fucking universe, starting with her. "Why are you being so nice to me?"

She met his gaze. "Shouldn't I be?"

"No!" Santos jumped to his feet. He strode to the other side of the gallery, then swung to face her once more. "No," he said again. "You have no reason to be nice to me. Unless you want something. Just tell me, Lily. Just tell me what you want."

She shook her head. "I don't want anything from you, Todd."

"That's bullshit!" He took several steps toward her, then stopped. He clenched his hands into fists, frustrated. "You're using me. I just don't know what for."

She stood slowly, using the stair rail for support. She crossed to stand before him and looked him straight in the eye. "Then, why don't you leave?"

He should leave. Go now and not look back.

He wheeled away from her, his every instinct fighting the thought. He crossed to the railing. Curving his hands around it, he gazed out at nothing for long moments. *He didn't want to go, dammit. He felt safe here. Safe and cared for.*

Right. And at any moment he would feel a knife at his back.

Santos sucked in a sharp breath and swung to face her once more. "Why don't you have any friends, Lily?" She said nothing, and he crossed to stand directly before her. He looked her square in the eye. "You never have visitors, no one calls. Except for mass and errands, you never go out. Why is that?"

She folded her hands in front of her. He noticed they trembled, though she kept her gaze unflinchingly on his. "You have a point here, Todd?"

"Why are you treated like a leper, Lily Pierron? Why do children whisper behind their hands when they see you? Why do their mothers pull them to the opposite side of the sidewalk when you're near? Why do you always sit alone at mass?"

Pain tightened her features, but she didn't move or look away. She didn't strike out defensively at him. "Why don't you tell me."

"Okay, I will." He made a sweeping gesture with his right hand. "This place was a whorehouse. And my guess is, you were the head whore."

To her credit, she flinched only slightly. He fought the way that made him feel, and kept on, though even as he spoke the words, he regretted them, even as he flung them at her, he wished he could take them back. "Judging from the memorabilia I've seen around the place, you ran one hot little business here. No wonder you're so popular with your neighbors. And no wonder you want me around, no one else will have you."

For long seconds she said nothing, just gazed at him, her eyes reflecting not just the wounds he'd inflicted, but a lifetime of wounds inflicted by others. "Is that all, Todd?"

He wanted her to fight back, to strike out at him. Maybe then he wouldn't have a knot in the pit of his gut. Maybe then he wouldn't feel like crap. He took a step closer to her. "No, it's not." He hiked up his chin, "Where's your kid, Lily? I know you had one, I saw pictures. What, did she think you were a leper, too?"

Her pain, he saw, knew no bounds. "You're a good student of human nature," she said finally, her voice thick with tears. "I'm just what you called me. A whore. Completely alone. And yes, even my daughter abandoned me." She drew in a short, ragged breath. "I believe I'll go in, now."

Without another word, she turned and walked into the house, her head held high.

Santos stared after her, his heart in his throat. He had deliberately hurt her. Because he liked her, because he was afraid of needing her, then being hurt himself.

He had done the only thing he could think of to push her away.

Santos swallowed hard, his eyes burning. All she had ever been was kind to him. She had allowed him into her home, she had given him a job, a place to stay and food to eat. She had expected nothing from him but that he do an honest day's work.

He hadn't even trusted her enough to tell her his real name.

He felt like the mangiest, low-life dog on the face of the earth. He felt as ugly and mean-spirited as anyone who had ever hurt him and put him down.

He had become as bad as those he had fought to escape.

Without pausing for second thought, Santos followed Lily inside. The large foyer was empty. He called her name. She didn't answer, so he went in search of her.

He found her in the front parlor, standing stiffly in the middle of the room, staring, it seemed, at nothing. For long moments he gazed at her back, hurting for her.

"Miss Lily?"

She didn't turn. "Please go away, Todd. I prefer to be alone now."

He cleared his throat. "Miss Lily, please . . . I'm sorry."

She bowed her head. "For what? Telling the truth?"

"It isn't the truth. I was just being—"

"It is the truth. You're right to despise me." Her voice lowered; he had to struggle to hear her. "Even my own daughter despised me."

He took a step toward her, then stopped. "But I don't. I—" His throat closed over the words as panic settled over him. He fought the emotion, though the thought of being honest with her, of exposing his real feelings terrified him. "I was just being mean," he said finally, softly. "I'm sorry."

"Go away, Todd," she said again. "It's all right. I'll be fine."

"It's not all right." He shoved his hands into the front pockets of his jeans. "You didn't deserve that. And you haven't deserved my lies."

She turned then and met his gaze. He saw that she had been crying. He looked away, then back, ashamed. "My name's not Todd Smith," he said softly. "It's Victor Santos. Everyone has always called me Santos. Except my mother. And she's dead."

He drew a deep breath, his next words the most difficult, the most terrifying to admit. "I wanted to...hurt you. To push you away. Because I like being here. Because I like...you. And that—" Emotion choked him, and he looked away.

Lily crossed to him, but he couldn't bring himself to meet her eyes. She gently touched his cheek. "It's all right, Victor. I understand."

He lifted his gaze. In hers he saw understanding and real compassion, he saw the wisdom that comes with a lifetime of hard knocks. In them he saw himself.

How could her daughter have deserted her?

As if reading his thoughts, her eyes flooded with fresh tears. "My daughter wanted a new life. A clean life. One that had no part of the Pierron past. It didn't include me." Lily drew a deep, shuddering breath. "She left me behind."

"I think that sucks!" Santos exclaimed, angry for Lily. She had loved her daughter. The way his mother had loved him. He never would have done that to her. Never.

Lily shook her head. "I understand. I know what I am."

Santos swallowed hard, stunned. Lily acted as if she thought she deserved to be hurt, as if she deserved to be abandoned. He drew his eyebrows together, recalling the things he had said to her, hating himself for them.

"You don't have to worry," she continued quietly. "I don't want anything from you. And I'm not going to let you down." She cleared her throat. "But I do like having you around. Maybe that's selfish of me, but...I've been so lonely."

Santos covered her hand, feeling for the first time since his mother's death that he wasn't alone. Feeling as if there was someone who cared about him, someone he could turn to. A part of him doubted his feelings, a part of him warned him to be careful, disbelieving. He ignored those parts. He denied them.

He told her everything then. About his mother and father. About his mother's murder and his vow to avenge her; he told Lily about the foster homes he had been in and how he had run away from each. He shared with her his fears and his frustrations, the promises he had made to his mother and the ones he had made to himself.

He laid his heart bare; she listened and comforted him.

Santos talked long into the night, until he felt completely drained, but better for it—as if sharing himself with Lily had released him from some measure of his past, from a modicum of his pain.

And later, as they said good-night to each other, his eyes burning with fatigue, his throat raw, both knew by mutual yet unspoken acknowledgment that Santos was staying for good.

Part 5

Lovers

18
_____

New Orleans, Louisiana
1984

By age sixteen, Glory had accepted the fact that her mother would never love her. She didn't know what unpardonable sin she had committed, but she no longer cared. That her mother's love and approval would remain forever beyond her reach no longer had the power to hurt her.

For as Glory's acceptance had grown, so had her anger. And her defiance.

The years between eight and sixteen had changed Glory in more than the customary ways. Glory had honed her keen intelligence into a sharp and sometimes sarcastic edge. Her energy and enthusiasm had become indefatigable defiance.

Of course, with defiance came punishment. Glory understood that very well. She understood that she always had a choice. But, she would rather suffer her mother's most severe punishment than bend to her will.

To Glory, breaking her mother's intolerable rules had become a game. A dangerous, dizzying battle of wills and wit. She had learned what her mother's hot buttons were—anything to do with boys, her body or sex—she had learned how far she could push her. Glory delighted in outmaneuvering her mother; nothing in Glory's life came close to being so satisfying, especially when she managed to do it right under her mother's nose.

When her mother did catch her, the punishment was always severe, though the severity depended on the crime. Once her mother confined her to her room until Glory had memorized the entire Book of Judges; another time, she made Glory scrub every floor in the house with a toothbrush; still another—when she caught Glory necking with a boy in the parking lot behind the church—she had whipped her with a switch from the willow tree, wielding the supple branch as though she had been doing it all her life, manipulating her blows to punish and shame, but not to scar. Even so, she had left a crisscross of red welts across Glory's back that had taken a month to heal.

But Glory hadn't bent to her mother's will even then, she hadn't begged her to stop or for forgiveness of her transgression. Nor had Glory run to her father afterward. She had accepted her punishment and vowed to herself that the next time she would not get caught.

In a strange way, Glory looked forward to the times her mother caught her, not because she enjoyed doing her mother's penance, but because her mother seemed to derive a twisted pleasure from punishing her only child; she seemed to find satisfaction in the fact that her daughter was living up to her lowly expectations.

It seemed to Glory that the only time she actually pleased her mother was when her mother was punishing her.

Perhaps the most startling change in Glory was in her relationship with her father. Her anger had spilled over onto him and a rift had developed between them. Where she had once lived for their times together, for their visits to the St. Charles, now she avoided them. She feigned indifference for the workings of the hotel. She proclaimed loudly and vehemently to all that she was not about to spend her life playing nursemaid to a dusty pile of bricks and mortar.

Those were the times she broke her father's heart.

And when she did, her own broke, too.

Secretly, she loved her father and the St. Charles as much as she always had. Secretly, she longed for the times she and her father had spent together, their outings and the way those moments had made her feel—special and loved.

But they couldn't go back to those times, no matter how she longed to. Everything had changed; she didn't really know why, but it had.

The truth of that hurt. Sometimes more than anything else, even more than the way her mother looked at her when she thought no one could see.

Glory attended the Academy of the Immaculate Conception, an all-girl's high school located uptown on St. Charles Avenue. Girls from the best New Orleans families attended the academy and had since 1888. Families registered their daughters at birth; a degree from Immaculate Concept, as Glory called it, was the local equivalent of one from William and Mary or Radcliff. When it came to schools and their snob appeal, the academy boasted the biggest in the city. And in a city as old, as wealthy, and as hierarchical as New Orleans, that was saying a lot.

Glory leaned closer to the bathroom mirror, inspecting the bright shade of lip gloss she had just applied. Smiling in approval, she capped the lip gloss and dropped it into her purse. From the hall outside came a burst of girlish laughter; in a moment, she knew, the fifteen-minute warning bell would sound and the bathroom would be instantly overrun with girls, all wanting to take a last look into the mirror before class started.

Sure enough, just as the bell rang, a large group of girls burst into the john. They caught sight of her and rushed over. "Glory," one of them said, "we heard about you and Sister Marguerite! Is it true? Did she really ban you from participating in the sophomore formal?"

"Yeah, it's true." Glory shrugged with indifference. "Some people just can't take a joke."

A girl named Missy giggled. "I wish I could have seen Sister's face when she found you in the chapel, reading a romance novel and munching on communion wafers."

"It was something, all right." Glory flipped her long hair over her right shoulder. "Worse part of it was, she confiscated my book. And I'd just gotten to the good part."

Missy shook her head. "One of these days you're going to go too far, Glory. I mean, communion wafers? Isn't that a sin, or something?"

Glory rolled her eyes. "You sound like Sister. They hadn't been blessed yet or anything. And until they're blessed, they're just crackers."

Another, smaller, group of girls entered the bathroom, whispering and giggling. When they saw Glory and Missy, they sauntered over.

"Have you seen what *the charity case* is wearing today?" one of them asked. "That blouse looks like it's ten years old." The girl wrinkled her nose. "And even when it was new, it was ugly. It's polyester."

Glory turned away from the group, disgusted. Although the majority of girls who attended the academy were from New Orleans's wealthiest families, the school occasionally awarded a scholarship to a deserving and exceptionally gifted girl. Like the one being lampooned at this very moment. Glory had heard this girl was brilliant.

"It's pathetic," Bebe Charbonnet said, sashaying to the bank of mirrors to gaze admiringly at herself. "I can't believe they let girls like her into the academy. I mean, my parents have to pay. Everyone's should."

"After all, we have to keep our standards up," Glory said sarcastically. "Just because she's brilliant, doesn't mean she belongs at the Academy of the Immaculate Conception."

Bebe missed the sarcasm completely. "Exactly," she said. "She doesn't belong. And I, for one, will not make her welcome."

The bathroom door swung open and the girl under discussion walked in. Conversation ceased; and gazes settled on everything but the new girl. Glory's heart went out to her. She looked completely miserable, but to her credit, she held her head high.

She started for the stalls, only to have Bebe and her group close ranks, blocking her way. She stopped at their barricade, then made a move to go around. But when she moved, so did the group. "Excuse me," she said finally, flushing.

Bebe looked at her with exaggerated innocence. "Oh, we're sorry. Did you need to get through?"

"Yes." They didn't move, and the girl's flush deepened. "Please."

Bebe stepped aside; the new girl passed. They closed ranks again, and Glory suspected what they planned to do next.

Sure enough, when the girl emerged from the stall, she found her way to the sinks blocked. "Excuse me," she said again.

And again Bebe turned to her, her expression one of feigned surprise. "Oh, we're sorry. Did you need to get through?"

Glory had had enough. To stand by and watch cruelty was weak and cowardly, and Glory despised both. She had never forgiven herself for her own cowardice all those years ago when she had tried to blame little Danny for the incident in the library. She had vowed to never again allow someone to take the blame for her actions; she had promised herself she would never be weak and cowardly again.

"Yeah, Bebe," Glory murmured. "I think she does. Unlike you, she washes her hands after she pees."

Bebe's color rose, but she stepped aside. Glory smiled at the new girl. "It's a matter of breeding," she said. "Bebe here thinks that just having money makes her classy. She's mistaken, of course."

Several girls exchanged uneasy glances. Glory, they knew, had hit Bebe's sore spot. Bebe's family, unlike Glory's and many of the other Immaculate Conception girls, were new—new to New Orleans, new money, no invitation to The Mystic Krewe of Comus. But, even so, Bebe was the most popular and powerful girl in the sophomore class; the rest of the girls always deferred to her.

As far as Glory was concerned, Bebe Charbonnet had only ascended to her position of power by also being the meanest and most arrogant girl in the class. Glory didn't give a flip if the girl blackballed her.

"You're going to regret this, Glory," Bebe said, sending Glory a furious glance. She flounced to the door, stopping and looking back when she reached it. "I promise you, you will."

Glory mock-shuddered. "I'm so scared."

A moment later, the bathroom was empty save for Glory and the new girl. Glory dug in her purse for a cigarette, aware of the other girl's gaze upon her. "You didn't have to do that," the girl said quietly.

Glory shrugged and lit the cigarette. She inhaled, then blew out a long stream of smoke. "Yeah, well, I did it anyway."

"Thanks."

Glory shrugged again. "Nothing to thank me for. Those girls aren't my friends."

"But, I—" The girl bit the words back. "Thanks anyway."

Glory cocked her head and met the other girl's eyes. "What were you going to say?"

"It's none of my business."

"I'm making it your business."

"All right." She folded her arms across her chest. "I always see you with them. Why do you hang out with them if they're not your friends?"

It was a fair question. One Glory wasn't sure she had a good answer to. "I guess because there isn't anyone else. Immaculate Concept pretty much caters to Bebe's type."

"I'd rather be alone," the girl said with more than a trace of bitterness.

"I know what you mean." Glory studied the tip of her cigarette for a moment before meeting the new girl's eyes once again. "Don't let them get you down. They're just a bunch of spoiled little bitches."

"But you're not?"

Glory laughed, liking this girl's direct manner. "No. I mean, I don't think so. I'm just bad."

The girl laughed, too, then self-consciously folded her arms across her chest. "I'm Liz Sweeney."

"Good to meet you, Liz." Cigarette in hand, she saluted. "I'm Glory St. Germaine."

"I know who you are." She blushed and tucked her hair behind her right ear. "Everybody knows who you are."

"That's the thing about being bad." Glory smiled and scooted onto the counter by the sink. She took another drag on her cigarette. "Personally, I think people need a little scandal to liven things up. Without it, things would be pretty boring. Don't you think?"

"I've never really thought about it. But I suppose you're right."

"Of course, I am." Glory leaned against the mirror, and studied the other girl. She wasn't unattractive, but she wasn't pretty, either. She had a sort of plain, but nice, face. She looked wholesome and honest. She looked like the kind of person you could trust with your life.

"You're here on scholarship, right?"

Liz looked at her feet. "Yes."

"Why are you embarrassed by that?"

"I know what they call me. *The charity case.*"

She drawled the words and again Glory heard the bitterness. Glory drew her eyebrows together. "Is that why you're here? Because you're poor? Or because you're smart and poor?"

Liz lifted her gaze to Glory's. "Smart and poor."

"You know, Liz, it seems to me that's nothing to be embarrassed about." Glory took a last drag on her smoke, then slid off the counter and crossed to one of the stalls. She flipped the cigarette butt into one of the commodes and turned back to Liz. "I'm here because my family has money. Unlike Bebe, I'm not particularly proud of that fact, because the way I see it, it doesn't have a thing to do with me."

The final bell sounded, and Liz jumped. "Oh, no! I'm going to be late." She snatched up her book bag and headed for the door, then stopped and looked back at Glory. "Aren't you coming?"

"No rush." She grinned. "I wouldn't want to go and spoil a perfect record."

Liz returned her smile. "No, I suppose you wouldn't. See you." She started through the door, then stopped once more. "Glory?"

"Yeah?"

"Thanks again for helping me out. I'll return the favor someday."

Glory mock-saluted. "Forget about it. After all, what are friends for?"

19

Liz didn't forget about it. Not about that act of bravery on Glory's part, nor about any of the others that followed over the next couple of weeks. It seemed to Liz that every time she looked around, Glory was there, sticking up for her by facing down girls the likes of Bebe and Missy, challenging their snobbery by tossing it back at them.

After the third or fourth time, Liz realized that Glory had decided to take her under her wing, though Liz hadn't a clue why. Liz was both a newcomer to the academy and a nobody. Glory was beautiful, rich and considered the coolest girl in their class. She was thought to be absolutely fearless, cool under even Sister Marguerite's stare, and a complete daredevil. Many of the girls whispered disparagingly about her wildness, but the truth was, they were all in awe of her. Liz certainly was.

Liz also admitted awe of Glory's looks. She was more than the most beautiful girl in the academy, she was the most beautiful girl Liz had ever seen. And not in the cute or pretty way of most high school girls, but in a full-blown, knock-your-socks-off, womanly way.

Sometimes, when Liz looked at Glory, she wondered what it would be like to have not only brains, but beauty, bravery and a rich, classy family, too. And sometimes, she would feel a great, gnawing longing to have all that Glory had.

Liz leaned against the school's front-office counter. She propped her chin on her fist, oblivious to the noise around her. A condition of her scholarship required her to work five hours a week in the school office, and every day she spent her third-hour free period doing just that. Usually, the secretary kept her busy making copies, filing and playing gofer, but, today the secretary was out sick.

Liz sighed, thinking of her own family, comparing it to Glory's. The best her family could be called was modest. The worst was trashy. Her father was a hardworking laborer who drank too much. Unfortunately, drink turned the usually affable Mike Sweeney mean. Her mother was a devout Catholic who believed the use of birth control was a mortal sin, and who happened to be uncommonly good at getting pregnant. To help make ends meet, Katherine Sweeney cleaned houses in the afternoons.

Liz was the oldest of the Sweeney brood—there were seven of them—and from the time she had been old enough to follow directions, much of her brothers and sisters' care had fallen on her shoulders. The first time Liz had gotten a glimpse of how the other half lived, she had decided that she wasn't going to spend the rest of her life in an overcrowded apartment in the By-Water section of town. As soon as she got the chance, she had promised herself, she was getting out.

She had seen from the beginning that her only way out would be by way of her IQ, and when she had been offered a scholarship to Immaculate Conception, she had grabbed it with both hands.

The scholarship, the academy, was her chance, her route to the way the other half lived.

Her father had been against it. He didn't think much of the richies, as he called them. According to him, the richies were selfish, greedy and dishonest. And those, he had told her, were their good qualities.

Liz had chalked up his warning to his uneducated, working class mentality and to sour grapes. Even so, to placate him, she had promised to watch her back.

After a month at the academy, however, Liz had begun to believe he was right. Then she had met Glory.

And, now, she had a friend, Liz thought. At least she thought of the other girl as that. She smiled to herself. She had even thought about asking Glory—

"Liz?"

Liz blinked. Mrs. Reece, one of Immaculate Conception's few lay teachers, stood on the other side of the office counter. Liz hadn't even heard her come in.

She flushed and straightened. It wouldn't do to be caught daydreaming on the job. "Hi, Mrs. Reece. What can I do for you?"

The woman smiled. "You looked like you were a million miles way."

"I'm sorry," Liz said, her cheeks burning. "It won't happen again."

"Don't worry, I'll never tell." The woman smiled once more and held out a file folder. "Could you make some copies of this for me? I need the contents by sixth period, collated and stapled."

"I'll do them right away."

Liz took the folder, noted the job on her work sheet and carried it to the copier. She began the job and had almost finished it when the copier ran out of paper. She squatted, took a pack of paper out of the cabinet and started to stand up, stopping when she heard Bebe's voice, coming from the hallway outside the office.

"I warned her," Bebe was saying. "I promised I would pay her back, and now's my chance."

Glory. Liz's heart began to thunder. *Bebe had to be talking about Glory.*

"I don't know, Bebe," another girl said, one whose voice Liz recognized after a minute as Missy's. "What if she finds out you're the one who snitched?"

"Who cares?" Bebe made a sound of disdain. "What's she going to do? Unlike her, I have nothing to hide." Bebe laughed. "Besides, at least a dozen of us saw her skip out of gym class. How would she ever know it was me who turned her in?"

The girls entered the office. Liz held her breath and
crouched lower behind the machine, not wanting them to
see her. They went to Sister Marguerite's office and tapped
politely on her half-open door. The principal called them
in. They closed the door behind them.

Liz stood. *Bebe planned to turn Glory in for skipping out
of class. She had to warn Glory.*

Without pausing to think about the unfinished copy-job
or to consider the trouble she would be in if she was caught,
Liz darted out of the office and headed for the rest room
located across from the art lab. It was the least frequented
rest room and, she had learned, Glory's favorite. She took
a chance that Glory would be there.

She was.

Liz found her in the last stall, calmly smoking a cigarette. Liz skidded to a stop in front of her, and sucked in an
agitated breath. "Glory! You've got to get out of here.
You've got to get back to class now!"

Glory smiled, but made no move to get up. "Hey, girl.
What's up?"

"I overheard Bebe and Missy talking." Liz sucked in
another deep breath. "Bebe's turning you in for cutting
class. She's in Sister Marguerite's office right now!"

"So?" Glory exhaled a long stream of smoke.

"So?" Liz repeated, stunned. "She could be here any
moment. You could be expelled! And please, put that thing
out. If Sister smells smoke—"

"I'm not going to be expelled," Glory said, but stood
and tossed the cigarette in the commode, anyway. She
flushed it, then waved her hands in the air to disperse the
smoke. "I won't even be suspended. My family's too important, sits on too many boards and donates way too much
money to this dump. Come on, I'm going to wash my
hands."

Liz followed her, dumbfounded by her attitude, so different from her own. "But, what about your parents? I
mean, aren't you worried about getting in trouble with
them?"

Glory rinsed her hands. "You have to know my family."

"What does that mean?" Liz frowned. "They don't care what you do?"

"Quite the contrary." Glory laughed, the sound tight and, to Liz's ears, unhappy. "My mother cares about everything I do. And everything I do is wrong. It always has been. In fact, my mother all but thinks I'm the devil himself. So, you see, it doesn't really matter what I do."

Liz shook her head, shocked. "I can't . . . believe that."

"Believe it. But, it's no big thing." Glory dug in her purse, pulled out her lip gloss and applied a layer of the shiny pink to her mouth.

But, it was a big thing, Liz thought, watching the other girl. Glory pretended to be completely tough, but, something about the way she was avoiding Liz's gaze suggested otherwise. Something about her tough-girl routine suddenly rang false.

Liz let out her breath in a huff. "Well, that makes me really mad. I mean, I think you're the nicest, bravest person I've ever known!"

"Me?" Glory laughed. "Nice and brave? Wouldn't my mother get a hoot out of that one."

"It's true. You've stood up for me, and I'm just a nobody. You didn't have to do that. Heck, you didn't even know me. And you're the first girl in this school who's treated me like I wasn't some sort of disease, though it certainly hasn't earned you any popularity points."

Glory lifted her shoulders. "But who needs them?"

"See what I mean?" Liz shook her head. "It takes courage not to care what other people think."

"Not really." Glory fluffed her hair. "I don't like their behavior and they're not my friends."

"Who are your friends?" The question spilled past her lips before she could stop it. She flushed. "I mean, do you have an . . ." She brought a hand to her mouth, embarrassed. "I'm sorry, that came out wrong. What I meant was—"

"Forget about it." Glory met her eyes, her gaze defiant. "But, no, I don't. Not real friends, anyway. It's always been that way. And it suits me just fine."

"It does?"

"Yes." Glory jutted out her chin. "Do you have a problem with that?"

The other girl's vehemence surprised her, and Liz took a quick step backward. "No, of course not. I just—" Liz bit back the words, feeling like a total fool. "Never mind. I have to get back to the office."

"Wait." Glory touched her sleeve. "Sorry I was so, I don't know, such a bitch. What were you going to say?"

Liz flushed and took a deep breath. "I wasn't being critical, it's just that I wish... I mean, that I'd like to be your friend. I really like you, Glory."

Glory gazed silently at Liz a moment, then cleared her throat and looked away. She fiddled with her purse strap, fastening and unfastening the metal clasp.

Probably to keep from laughing out loud.

Liz fought tears. *How could she have said that? "I want to be your friend. I like you."* She sounded pathetic and desperate.

Liz lowered her gaze to her feet, horrified to realize how near tears she was. She would not further humiliate herself by letting those tears fall. No doubt Glory St. Germaine felt sorry enough for her already.

Liz swallowed past the lump in her throat and took a step backward, toward the door. "Look, forget I said that. It was really... dumb." She took another step, anxious to get away before she cried. "I'll see you around."

She turned and raced for the door.

"Wait!" Liz stopped but didn't turn to face Glory. "You want to know the truth?" Glory asked. "What you said earlier, it wasn't right. You're the brave one. Not me. I've never had to bear the snubs of the other girls. I've always had my family name and money to protect me. I can't even imagine having the kind of guts you have."

Liz turned around slowly. When she did, she got a glimpse of a girl very different from the one who boldly broke rules and proclaimed indifference to everyone's opinion of her. Glory stood, gaze lowered, arms wrapped around her middle, the picture of vulnerability and uncertainty. Of loneliness.

"You were right," Glory continued, trying to laugh but failing miserably. "I don't have any real friends. Because I don't let them close enough."

"But why?" Liz asked, searching Glory's expression. "Why don't you want people close to you?"

"Because everyone thinks I'm so brave. 'Glory St. Germaine's not afraid of anything,' they say. I like it that way. It's who I am." She lifted a shoulder. "If I let people close, they'd know the truth."

"You're a lot braver than you think."

"Yeah?" Glory smiled. "Well, so are you."

From outside the bathroom, they heard the sound of someone approaching. Not just someone—Sister Marguerite and her assistant, Sister Josephine. Glory winked at Liz, then held a finger to her lips. Liz nodded, and Glory ducked into the end stall, climbed up on the commode and held the door almost shut. A second later, the sisters entered the bathroom.

Liz smiled at the nuns. "Hello, Sisters."

"Hello, Liz, dear," the principal said. "We're looking for Glory St. Germaine. Have you seen her?"

Liz felt her cheeks heat and prayed the women wouldn't notice. "Yes, Sister. She just left."

"She did?" Both nuns looked suspiciously toward the stalls, then back at her. "We didn't pass her in the hall."

"That's odd, it was just a couple minutes ago. And she felt just awful. She was sitting on the floor with her arms around her middle when I came in." Liz lowered her voice to a whisper. "She had terrible cramps."

"Cramps," Sister Josephine repeated. "Poor thing."

"I told her she should have the office call her mother, but she said she had a quiz this afternoon, and she couldn't miss it. I think she went back to class."

"I see," Sister Marguerite said. "Thank you. We'll check on her there." The nuns started for the door, but Sister

Marguerite stopped when she reached it and looked back at Liz. "Aren't you supposed to be in the office this hour?"

"Yes, Sister," she murmured, almost light-headed with fear. "I was just going back. But I . . . I have to wash my hands."

"I'll see you in a moment, then."

"Thank you, Sister."

The moment they cleared the door, Glory popped out of the stall. She raced over to Liz. "You were great," she whispered. "They believed every word you said."

Liz held out her hands. They were trembling. "Poor, but, smart scholarship students have a lot to lose. I was so scared. I was sure they'd know that I was lying."

Glory hugged her. "But, you were so great. The best."

"Then why do I feel like I'm going to pass out?"

Glory laughed. "Hang with me, I'll teach you to thumb your nose at danger. Before long, you'll even like it."

"Not me. I never want to—" Liz brought her hands to her cheeks, suddenly remembering the office, her job and Mrs. Reece's copies. "Oh, no! What time is it?" When Glory told her, Liz groaned and started for the door. "I've got to go."

Glory followed, catching her arm. "Liz, wait. I wanted to . . . to thank you for helping me out just now. Nobody's ever . . . done that for me before. It . . . meant a lot to me."

Liz smiled. "Forget it, Glory. The way I see it, I still owe you." She started through the door.

"Hey, Liz?"

Liz stopped and looked over her shoulder. "Yeah?"

"I like you, too. And I think . . . I think it would be pretty cool to be friends."

Beaming, Liz darted into the hall.

20

From that moment on, Glory and Liz were inseparable. They met between classes and ate lunch together, at night they talked on the phone, and in the morning they rendez-voused at the streetcar stop five blocks from school so they could walk the rest of the way together.

Glory shared with Liz her most intimate secrets, her hopes and her fears; as Liz shared hers. Their approaches to life, their families and backgrounds, differed in the extreme. Yet they understood each other so completely that one would only have to look at the other to know what she was thinking or feeling.

Having a real friend was a new and heady experience for Glory, and she reveled in it. She had never imagined having a friend would make her feel so good about herself; she had never imagined it would be so much fun. And she hadn't realized that until Liz, she'd been lonely.

But Glory also lived in fear that her mother would disapprove of Liz and find a way to end their friendship. Or find a way to turn Liz against her. Glory didn't know what she would do if she lost Liz's friendship. She couldn't go back to living the way she had before.

Glory need not have worried. Hope was well aware of her daughter's friendship with the scholarship student. Little happened at the academy that Hope didn't know about. She had done some checking and learned all she needed to about Liz Sweeney—she was soft-spoken, polite and a conscientious student; she was also painfully shy and rather plain, not the type to be chasing boys or to have boys chasing her.

But, the thing Hope liked best about Liz was her tenuous position at the academy—her scholarship could be revoked at any time and for any reason the administration saw fit. As one of the academy's largest benefactors, Hope knew that, if need be, she could control her daughter's friend by threatening her scholarship.

She hoped, of course, that resorting to such measures would never become necessary.

For the time being, Hope decided, Liz Sweeney was a good influence on her daughter. Indeed, since the two had become friends, Glory's behavior, grades and attitude had improved. Hope gave the friendship her blessing. She made her feelings known by inviting Glory to have her friend over to the house anytime.

Anytime at all.

21

Philip St. Germaine sat at his massive desk. Over eighty years old and made of Louisiana cypress, the desk had belonged to four generations of St. Germaines. Back when his grandfather had had this desk fashioned, all fine furniture had been crafted out of imported mahogany, walnut and cherry. Cypress had been considered junk wood.

But, his grandfather had insisted on using the native cypress. When you have the choice, his grandfather had always preached, never stray far from home for what you need. For home is where your heart is, and there you will find your strength.

Home. Heart. Philip ran his hand over the desk's smooth, polished top. No paperwork littered its surface, no file folders, catalogs or reports. They rarely did. Home was for family. That, too, he had learned from his father who, in turn, had learned it from his.

Several framed family photos graced the desktop, and he scanned them, his gaze stopping on one of Hope from the early years of their marriage. Bitterness rose like bile inside him. What had happened to that soft and sweet-tempered young woman? What had happened to the girl who had made his heart sing, the girl who had made him believe in flesh-and-blood angels?

He had lost all his starry-eyed illusions about his beautiful wife. He supposed they had begun to slip away the day she had rejected their newborn daughter. He had managed to convince himself, for a time, that everything would be all right, had managed to convince himself that his perfect life and wife had not begun to disintegrate before his very eyes.

Those times were long gone.

Looking at the photo hurt, and Philip swiveled his chair so he faced the window directly behind his desk instead. The window and the dying garden beyond.

He didn't love his wife anymore. He hadn't in a long time.

Even so, she still had a powerful hold on him. A hold he had been unable to break free of.

Philip pressed the heels of his hands to his eyes, then dropped his hands to his lap. He leaned his head against the chair back, self-disgust replacing bitterness. Her hold on him had nothing to do with trust or love of family or even respect. No, it was more base than that. It was sexual. It was a gut-wrenching, adolescent lust that he couldn't shake loose of or outgrow.

He had tried. He had slept with other women, had even had an affair. Not because he was bored with his wife and their sex life; on the contrary, because he had hoped having another woman would free him from the sexual stranglehold Hope had on him.

But other women hadn't satiated his hunger for his wife. If anything, they had made him more ravenous for her, more desperate for the pleasures she offered.

Philip fisted his fingers. Dear Jesus, even Hope's stomach-turning abuse of their daughter hadn't killed his desire for her—though it had killed all else.

Including his self-respect.

When it came to his wife, he was less than a man, weak and impotent. Because of her, because of his inability to break free of her sexual grip, he had lost not only his self-respect but his daughter's love and respect, as well.

Glory. Philip brought the heels of his hands to his eyes once more, wishing he could block out the truth. He loved his daughter beyond measure. He longed for their relationship to be as it had once been, longed to have her look at him as if he were more than a hero.

But those times were also long gone. Now, she only tolerated his company. Now, she hardly looked at him. And when she did, he saw anger in her eyes. And, he thought, pity.

She, too, knew that he was less than a man.

Philip stood and crossed the room, for no other purpose than a need to move. He stopped at the open study door, then turned and crossed back to the desk. Again, he gazed down at its clutter-free top. At least through it all, the horror and heartbreaks, he'd had the St. Charles. It had been his, a place in which to lose himself and forget his failures, a success to pride himself in.

And now he faced losing the hotel, too.

He dragged his hands through his hair. He realized they were shaking, like a woman's might, or a baby's. He swore and straightened his spine, furious with himself. He had perpetrated the mess he was in. He couldn't point a finger at Hope or anyone else. He had ignored the things his father had taught him, important things, about not overextending or relying on credit, about investing cautiously and never depleting personal funds.

But when he had started renovating the St. Charles, New Orleans had been experiencing a renaissance of sorts, a financial boom the likes of which the city had never seen before. The oil and gas industries had been thriving—the price per barrel had reached a new high and exploration was up. The World's Fair had been right around the corner, promising a flood of tourists from all over the world.

Everyone had been making money. Lots of money. The all-afternoon–Dom Perignon lunch had become the norm. Philip, like many others in the city, had taken to being driven about town in a limousine. Anything worth doing had been done to excess.

At the time, sinking half a million dollars into a complete renovation and updating of the hotel had seemed a simple and risk-free venture.

And a necessity. The pressure had been on. With the fair in the offing, new hotels had sprung up almost overnight—the Sugar House, Le Meridian and Hotel Intercontinental, to name only a few. All were elegant, luxury hotels, all could offer guests what the St. Charles could not—the best of what "new" had to offer, a location in the midst of both the action of the fair and the French Quarter. He'd felt he had to compete or die.

Some had cautioned him, but those, his failing father included, had been in the minority. More than a dozen lenders had been eager to make the loan.

He'd had it all figured out—he would simply repay the loan with the hotel's increased revenues, both from higher occupancy and increased room rate.

He'd had it all figured out, all right.

Philip sank back onto his chair. Only he had no increased revenues with which to repay the loan. Who would have guessed that the bottom would drop out so quickly or so completely? OPEC had all but disintegrated, and the market had been flooded with oil. The price per barrel had fallen straight into the dumper, and oil and gas exploration had come to a screaming halt.

To top that off, the much-ballyhooed New Orleans World's Fair had been a financial disaster of epic proportions.

Philip shifted his gaze to his hands, laid flat on the bare desktop. Businesses were closing daily, layoffs were slicing deep, paring to the bone. High-paid oil executives and their families were fleeing Louisiana at the speed of light and tourists were staying away in droves. Instead of increased revenue at his newly updated St. Charles, occupancy had fallen to thirty percent and less.

Philip dropped his head into his hands. The loan had come due twice before. Both times the lender had agreed to roll over the loan. This time they had refused. They wanted their money. He didn't have it.

"Philip?"

He lifted his head. Hope stood in the doorway to the study. She was wearing a silky wrap robe in a deep purple, her matching slippers peeking out from beneath the gown's hem. She'd freed her hair from her customary chignon and brushed it to a high shine; it floated about her shoulders like a black halo.

The sheer fabric of her garment combined with the bright light of the hallway behind her illuminated the sinuous outline of her body. He stared at her, his mouth dry, his body stirring.

With a muttered oath, he tore his gaze away.

"You've been holed up here for hours."

"Have I?"

"You know you have." She entered the room, crossing to its center. "What's wrong?"

He looked at her, then away. "We're in trouble," he said emotionlessly. "Financial trouble."

She paled. "What do mean, we're in financial trouble? How can that be?"

"The loan on the hotel's renovation is due. The lender won't extend. We don't have the money."

She brought a hand to her throat. He saw that it trembled. "How much?" she asked.

"Five hundred thousand."

"But that's not so much. Surely we have that. Somewhere, we must have . . . that."

Philip stood and crossed to the window. He gazed out at the darkness a moment, then swung to face her once more. "We don't."

"We don't?" she repeated, as if she couldn't quite comprehend—or believe—what he was saying. She took another step toward him. "But surely there's something we can liquidate. Bonds or notes or whatever those things are called. Surely one of the bank accoun—"

"There's our home," he said, cutting her off. "Your jewelry. The art. Various pieces of property around the city." He tipped his face toward the ceiling, thinking of the bad deals he had made over the last several years. "I invested heavily in real estate. In commercial property, mostly. Commercial space was leasing for as much as eighteen dollars a square foot. Eighteen dollars *a square foot,* Hope! Even so, the buildings were at ninety percent, or more, occupancy.

"Of course, I paid top dollar for the properties, I leveraged us to the hilt. Now, most of those buildings have a lower occupancy than the hotel."

He dared a glance at his wife. She looked shaken, devastated. He realized he had never seen her look that way before.

"Sell them, Philip," she said softly. "Sell them, now."

"Do you really think I'm so stupid that I wouldn't have thought of that?"

"In the light of this conversation, do you really want to ask me that?"

He gazed at her a moment, heart thundering. "They're not worth what I paid for them." He turned back to the window. One moment became many. "A venture capitalist has offered to pay the renovation debt in exchange for half ownership of the hotel."

"Oh, my God." Hope grasped the back of a chair. "The things people will say about us. We'll be the laughing-stocks of the entire city—"

"I told him, no."

"You told him . . . no?" She shook her head, as if confused. "Then what are we to do about the loan?"

He faced her fully once more. "The hotel is everything, Hope. We can't lose it. Not any part of it. It would be the ultimate shame." He came around the desk and crossed to her. Stopping before her, he looked her straight in the eye. "There are your jewels. The art collection and the Rolls. Our home. The summer house. Those things we own out-right."

She began to shake. "What are you saying?"

"We have to liquidate what we can."

"Dear, God." She drew in a sharp breath. "How will I face our friends? What will I tell them?"

"I don't give a damn what you tell our *friends!*"

"Don't you yell at me, Philip. I was not the one who got us into this mess."

"Of course, you didn't," he snapped. "Not Mrs. Holier-than-thou St. Germaine."

"You said you'd take care of me, Philip. How can you stand here and talk of selling our home and my jewelry? Where will we live? And what of Glory? What of her future?"

Her words cut him to the quick. He swore and swung away from her. He strode to the desk and stared down at it for long moments before turning back to her. "I have taken care of you. I've taken care of Glory. And I will continue to do so."

"How?" She lifted her chin. "By selling our home?"

"We wouldn't sell it outright, simply mortgage it. We're not going to be thrown out in the streets."

"Until you can't make the payments on that loan, anyway. And how long will that be, Philip?" She closed the distance between them, and fisted her fingers on his chest. "Two weeks? Two years? Ten?"

He stiffened. "That's enough, Hope."

"How could you have let this happen?" she demanded, curling her fingers into his cashmere sweater so tightly her knuckles went white. "You stupid, ineffectual man. How could you have been so...careless? So shortsighted?"

Philip felt her words like a blow. He caught her hands and covered them with his own. He narrowed his eyes. "Have you forgotten your wedding vows, my darling?" He tightened his fingers over hers. "Wasn't there something in them about love and honor, in good times and in bad? Better run right off to confession. Your eternal soul's going to go up in flames any moment."

"Go ahead," she said softly, "blaspheme. I'll pray for you, anyway, Philip."

He made a sound of disgust. "We will mortgage the house and sell the summer place. The Rolls has to go, and if necessary, we'll take a look at the art collection and your jewelry. We don't have another choice."

He released her hands and turned away from her.

"What about the venture capitalist? Couldn't we—"

"No, Hope." He dragged a hand through his hair, feeling older than his fifty-one years. Much older. Burned-out. Used-up. "Good night."

"Philip?" she murmured, her voice low, breathy. "Look at me."

He recognized that tone from many times before. It called sharply, and hotly, to his memory. She only called his name that way when she wanted something. He looked at her, anyway. He couldn't stop himself.

She eased her robe slowly from her shoulders; it floated to the floor. Her translucent gown left nothing of her body to his imagination—her full breasts and dark nipples, the pinch of her tiny waist, the tempting curve of her hips, the black triangle of her sex.

His mouth turned to ash, his heart to a drum.

"Come here."

He did and she leaned fully against him. She ran her hands up to his shoulders and lightly stroked. Through her gown he felt the pillows of her breasts, the vee of her sex. He felt her heat, her promise.

As with a will of their own, his arms went around her, his hands to her buttocks. Instantly aroused, he curled his fingers into her firm flesh, pulling her to him, pressing her against his erection.

She made the small, throaty sound that drove him crazy, the sound he heard in both his dreams and nightmares. He wanted her to make the sound again, deeper and louder. For him. Because of him.

She stood on tiptoe and ground her pelvis against his. "But we do have another choice," she whispered against his ear. She slid her tongue around its curve, then dipped it inside. He shuddered.

"Take this venture capitalist up on his offer."

Her words penetrated his fog of desire, but didn't dim it. "No" sprang to his lips but not past them. If he uttered the word, she would turn cold and unforgiving; she would retreat. He swallowed the word even though he despised himself for it.

"You would still own half." She eased her hand between them and found his erection. She curved her hand around it, squeezing and stroking in the way that had always stolen both his senses and free will.

"It wouldn't be so bad." She found his mouth and kissed him, deeply, wetly, rhythmically making promises with her tongue. She closed her teeth over his bottom lip, then pulled slowly away. "What can I do to convince you?"

He caught his breath. Even though he knew she was manipulating him, he wanted her now, on the cypress desk. He wanted to give in to her so he could sink into her.

She lowered his zipper and slipped her hand inside his trousers. He shuddered as she circled him. If he did as she wished, she would let him have everything, in any way he wanted. And not just once, or tonight. But again and again, days would become weeks, maybe even months.

He arched his back and let his head fall backward, his face to the ceiling. He closed his eyes. It would just end, when she decided she was no longer indebted to him. The ending would be agony; but until then, he would know complete bliss.

He hated her almost as much as he wanted her.

He hated himself more.

Still, like some sort of a junkie, he couldn't deny himself her. She worked her fingers over his flesh. "We could say you were tired of the day-to-day grind," she continued softly, sinking to her knees. "That you had no son to one day take over, so you decided to ease your burden of responsibility."

He felt her breath against him. He groaned and dropped his hands to her black halo of hair. "It's so perfect, don't you see? We could be together like this . . . all the time."

"Yes," he muttered, arching his back, desperate for the feel of her mouth. Again her breath stirred against him, closer, hotter; he tightened his fingers in her hair, trembling with need.

"Say it again, my darling," she said. "Tell me what I want to hear, so we can be happy."

He heard a quiver of satisfaction in her voice, the self-satisfied edge of triumph. He opened his eyes and looked down at her. As she swallowed him, she lifted her gaze to his.

And he saw clear to her soul. And what he saw terrified him. Something great and dark and without decency.

The breath left his body. He sprang away from her, chilled to his core.

"Philip...my darling. What's wrong?"

He turned his back to her, cursing his weakness, sickened at what he had become. Sickened to realize he had almost given in to her.

"Philip?" she whispered. "What did I do?"

He stiffened at the sweet plea in her voice, the quiver of hurt. It called to his memory, bringing back times between them that had been warm and wonderful, reminding him of the girl she had once been and of how much he had loved her.

Once upon a time, he would have slain dragons for her.

"Philip," she whispered again. "Please, look at me."

He didn't; he couldn't. If he did, his resolve would be lost. He yanked up his zipper and started for the study door. When he reached it, he stopped but didn't look back. "The St. Charles has been in the St. Germaine family for almost a hundred years. I don't care what it takes or what I have to do, I won't give up ownership of even one brick. Don't ask me to again."

22

Hope paced her bedroom, her heart fast, her palms damp. The Darkness had come for her again, the challenge issued, the gauntlet thrown down. How it laughed at her. How it taunted her arrogance. She had thought herself impervious to its tricks.

So, it had gotten to Philip instead. And through Philip, it had another chance at her.

Hope wrung her hands as she paced, twisting her fingers together, growing more agitated by the moment. How could she not have seen it happening? How could she not have anticipated such an attack? Weak, malleable Philip. He was the perfect target.

In the week since Philip's revelation in the library, she had made some discreet calls: their banker and corporate accountant, a friend in commercial real estate. Everything Philip had told her was true: he had dug them a deep financial hole, one they now couldn't climb out of.

Stupid. She had been so stupid. And trusting. In this one area of their lives, she had never interfered, had never asked questions. That night in the library, she had tried to show him the way, had tried to lead him down the right path. But she had been too late.

Philip had turned away from her; he had left her on her knees, The Beast's laughter ringing in her ears.

Hope stopped pacing, a shudder of apprehension moving over her. She brought her shaking hands to her face. She couldn't lose control now; she couldn't weaken. She had to find a way to fix this situation. She had worked too hard and too long to have it all wrested from her now. And, it would be. One hint of their financial woes, one hint of how badly Philip had screwed up, and she would find herself suddenly on the outside of New Orleans's most powerful inner circle.

She could hear the speculation now, the whispered jeers. The A-list invitations would stop coming. Board positions would suddenly be filled by others whose coffers had not been depleted by ineptitude; doors would close, backs would turn.

She would be on the outside looking in, shunned, just as she had been all those years ago.

A cry escaped her lips. *She had been on the outside once; she would never be again.*

No matter what she had to do.

Beyond the French doors, the wind howled. Hope crossed to them. They led to a small balcony that overlooked the back garden and swimming pool. She threw open the doors and stepped out into the black October night.

The cold hit her first, then the wind. She lifted her face to the sky. A storm was brewing. The tops of the oak trees bent under the force of the wind; the clouds rushed across the black sky, alternately obliterating and revealing the moon's light.

Hope crossed to the edge of the balcony. She gripped the railing and leaned out. The wind caught her hair and tore it free of its pins; it whipped at her silk gown and robe causing it to alternately billow out around her and plaster to her form.

She leaned farther out, not stopping until she grew lightheaded and weak-kneed. The swimming pool jumped up and reached for her; The Darkness inside her took flight. It soared, dragging her in tow, rushing through the treetops and past the moon. Branches tore at her skin and gown; a bird screamed in her ear, its huge, beating wings narrowly missing her eyes.

And then she saw her mother. She took shape out of the clouds, swirling up like oily, black smoke, black surrounded by gold. The clouds parted, momentarily revealing the moon. The gold gleamed in that moment of light, winking at her.

Hope gazed at the beckoning image in both fascination and horror. If she reached for it, the gold would be hers. But so would The Darkness.

Hope crashed back to her balcony, to her bedroom and reality with a gasp. Fear choked her. She hung halfway over her balcony railing, so cold she could no longer feel her extremities. What if she had let go? What if she had reached out, as she had been beckoned to do?

She would have been killed.

Heart thundering, she ever so slowly righted herself. One by one, she coaxed her fingers free of the railing, then backed away.

Once inside her bedroom, she slammed the doors shut behind her, locked them, then sank to the floor, too weak to do more. She drew her knees to her chest and wrapped her arms tightly around them. She pressed her face to her knees, shaking uncontrollably.

As the minutes passed, her trembling eased, her flesh warmed. She squeezed her eyes shut, her head filling with the image of swirling black surrounded by gold. Hope breathed deeply through her nose, her fear and agitation evaporating, replaced by absolute calm. And clarity. She saw what she needed to do; the answer had been before her all along.

Her mother would give her the money she needed. Though tainted by sin, the money belonged to Hope; it was her legacy, her heritage. As was The Darkness. She would swallow her hatred and pride and go to her mother.

She would never be on the outside again. No matter what she had to do.

Hope stood and crossed to the phone. She had made it her business to keep track of Lily Pierron. She knew that she and a young male companion had moved to the city five months ago; she knew they had taken an apartment in the French Quarter.

Hope found the number; she made the call. Her mother answered. Hope managed to achieve the right note of desperation and childish deference, playing off her mother's breathless surprise. Hope made Lily vague promises: about agreeing to see her once this mess was settled, about repaying the loan, the proof of that being the promissory notes she would give her mother in exchange for the money.

As Hope had known she would, her mother agreed to give her everything she needed, although she had warned that it would take some time for her to get all five hundred thousand. She would have to liquidate almost all her assets; she would be left with little more than the River Road house and enough to live on.

Smiling, Hope set the receiver back in its cradle. On Tuesday, her mother's boy would deliver the first third of the money to her at the hotel. Lily had promised to keep the contents of the delivery and Hope's identity a secret, even from him. The hotel would be secure, their home and collectibles, her position in society. And Philip would be forever grateful. He would be in her debt.

Hope tipped back her head and laughed. Once again, she had beaten The Darkness.

23

Santos stood just inside the lobby of the St. Charles Hotel. He swept his gaze over the interior, acknowledging awe, acknowledging that this was the most beautiful place he had ever seen. Not in the overblown way of Lily's house on River Road, nor in the crumbling way of the French Quarter. No, the St. Charles possessed an understated beauty, classy and dignified. The wood gleamed, the brass shone and the service people spoke in hushed, almost reverent tones. It all reeked of not only money, but of breeding and heritage, as well.

Things someone like him knew nothing about.

Santos started across the lobby, his gaze drawn to the people who moved around and past him, to the women having high tea on the lobby terrace, to the ones following a bellman, loaded down with shopping bags from Saks Fifth Avenue, Lord & Taylor, and Adler's.

He shook his head. These people sparkled almost as brightly as the hotel's lead-glass windows and doors—the women at their throats, ears and fingers; the men at their wrists and cuffs. And they were all so flawlessly put together, from the tops of their heads to the tips of their fingers and toes, completely coordinated, unrumpled and unfrayed.

This was what it was to have real wealth, he thought. The kind of wealth that wrought power. People like these, he knew, had no use for someone like him. He didn't belong here. Not a young man of such questionable ethnic mix. Not a half-breed, French Quarter–whore's kid whose biggest claim to fame was getting his high school diploma by the skin of his teeth. And from a *public* high school at that. He had heard that fact relayed to him in the doorman's terse, "Can I help you?" He had seen it in the concierge's suspicious gaze, in the way the hotel patrons gave him wide berth—as if he might somehow taint them.

He wondered if they would have a little more respect once he was a cop. Santos shook his head, amused. No, they would probably just fake it.

He shook his head again. They needn't guard their precious world so fearfully—he had no desire to be a part of it, wanted no piece of these pretty, plastic, too-white people with their unholy fears and their unfounded prejudices.

He reached the elevators, pressed the button to summon one, his thoughts turning to Lily. She belonged here no more than he did, though from things that she had said he knew that these privileged people were the ones who had been her patrons.

What business could Lily have with this Mrs. St. Germaine? He drew his eyebrows together and brought a hand to the chest pocket of his chambray shirt and the envelope tucked inside. She had given it to him that morning and instructed him to deliver it here, to a Mrs. Hope St. Germaine. He was to deliver it directly to the woman, putting it in her hands himself.

Could Lily have known the woman from her working days? Maybe she had been one of Lily's girls, though he thought that unlikely. From what Lily had told him, the two groups fraternized for profit and pleasure, but never mixed. In all her years, not one of her girls had been "rescued" from the life by a smitten trick. Some had left the business and made new, respectable lives for themselves elsewhere, but that particular Cinderella story was just that—a story.

So, who was this woman? When he had questioned Lily, she had said the envelope contained personal correspondence; she had said the woman was an old acquaintance. No big deal.

Right. Santos narrowed his eyes in thought. Lily had been as nervous as a cat, as giddy as a schoolgirl. She had been flushed and had kept wringing her hands, as with a combination of excitement and agitation. When he had commented on her behavior, she had assured him he was imagining things—even though he had never seen her act that way before.

Something was definitely up.

An elevator arrived and Santos stepped onto it. He pressed for the third floor, and the doors began to shut.

"Wait! Hold the elevator!"

Santos caught the doors. They creaked back open and a girl darted in. She pushed her dark hair away from her face and laughed up at him. "Thanks. These things are just ancient, I would have been waiting forever for another."

He returned her smile, acknowledging that she was probably the most beautiful girl he had ever seen. And, judging by her girls'-school uniform, too young for him. "No problem. Floor?"

"Six." She tipped her head to the side, unabashedly studying him, not hiding her interest. "I just hate waiting, don't you?"

A smile tugged at his mouth. "That depends."

"On what?"

"On what I'm waiting for."

She flipped her hair over her shoulder. "Oh, you're one of those."

He arched an eyebrow, amused at her obvious flirting but willing to play along. "Those? And who might they be?"

She smoothed a hand over the hip of her tartan-plaid skirt. "One of those who believe that the best things in life are worth waiting for."

"And you're not?"

"Nope." She lifted a shoulder in a breezy shrug. "Who wants to wait? When I see something I want, I go for it."

He laughed. He knew exactly who this girl was—spoiled, cocky, full of herself; he recognized her from all the girls like her he had known at Vacherie High. She intrigued him, anyway. "That seems like a mighty immediate way to live."

She gazed up at him through lowered lashes. "And you think that's bad."

"I didn't say that."

"No, I guess you didn't." Her lips lifted. "What's your name?"

"Santos." He leaned against the elevator's back wall, deliberately not asking hers. But instead of pouting, as he had expected her to do, she narrowed her eyes slightly, as with challenge.

"Santos," she repeated. "That's a different kind of name."

"I'm a different kind of guy."

She opened her mouth as if to say more; the elevator shuddered to a halt, interrupting her. "This is my floor." He pushed away from the wall, crossed to the open doors and stepped into the hallway. "It's been real."

He started off, stopping when she called his name. He looked back at her. She leaned out of the elevator, holding the doors open with her right shoulder. "My name's Glory."

"Glory," he repeated, his lips lifting. "Now, that's a different kind of name."

"Yeah, well, I'm a different kind of girl." She smiled. "See you around, Santos."

Without waiting for a response, she ducked back into the elevator; the doors slid shut. Santos laughed to himself and shook his head. Whoever she was, she was a real firecracker. He would bet she gave her parents fits. Which was probably a big part of her program, anyway.

He should know, he had experience with her type. Lots of it. Girls like Glory always wanted the same thing from him—an adventure, a defiant little walk on the wild side, a way to rebel against their parents.

The whole setup suited him just fine. They used him; he used them back. Everybody was happy. He had no place in his life for silly, spoiled little girls.

Santos took Lily's envelope from his pocket. He checked the number on its front, tucked it back into his pocket and started down the hallway to his right. Several doors down, he found the office and stepped inside. A secretary sat at a big desk that faced the door, her head bent over a typewriter.

He cleared his throat. She lifted her head and moved her gaze over him, her expression suspicious. "Can I help you?" she asked coolly.

"I'm here to see Hope St. Germaine."

"Are you expected?"

"I have a delivery." He took the envelope from his pocket.

She held out her hand. "I'll see that she gets it."

"Sorry. I have to put it directly into her hands. If she's not here, I'll wait."

The woman made a sound of irritation. "Your name?"

"Victor Santos."

"One moment." The woman stood and crossed to one of the two sets of doors that flanked either side of the richly appointed office. She knocked, then slipped inside, careful to shut the door behind her.

A moment later, the secretary reappeared. She motioned Santos into the office. "Mrs. St. Germaine will see you now."

He nodded and followed her direction. The office was large and impressively outfitted. A picture window that looked out over St. Charles Avenue and the streetcar line dominated the far wall. A woman stood before it, her back to him. When the secretary exited the office, closing the doors behind her, the woman turned.

Santos's first reaction to the woman was dislike. He bristled with it, and at the way she looked at him—with blatant distaste, as if he had crawled out from under a rock or someplace equally dark and slimy.

She started toward him, and he cocked his head slightly, studying her. Although she wasn't an unattractive woman, there was something cold about her, cold and unforgiving.

He narrowed his eyes. This woman's nose was so high in the air, it scraped the ceiling.

"Hope St. Germaine?" he asked when she stopped before him.

"Yes." She held out her hand. "You have something for me?"

He handed her the envelope. She took it, then snatched her hand away as if she feared he would contaminate her. He stiffened, offended. "I was told you would have something for me."

Without acknowledging him, she returned to her desk. There, she took a letter opener, sliced open Lily's envelope and checked its contents. As if satisfied with what she found there, she opened a desk drawer and took out another envelope.

She met his gaze and held it out, expecting him to retrieve it, like a dog.

Santos gritted his teeth. He would be damned if he would play step-and-fetch for her or any other diamond-bedecked, society pit bull. He folded his arms across his chest and waited.

Several seconds ticked past. A flush crept over the woman's high, sharp cheekbones, and with a sound of irritation, she came around the desk and strode toward him.

He smiled slightly at having bested her. He couldn't remember ever having disliked anyone as much as he disliked this woman.

She held out the envelope, marked with Lily's name. "Take it and go."

He didn't move. He lifted his gaze from the envelope and met hers, square-on and unflinching. Hers grew hot with anger. This woman thought she could eat him up and spit him out, she thought she was so much better, so much more important than he was. Well, that may be, but he had a clue for her—he wouldn't be treated like a servant, by her or anybody else. Not even for Lily.

"Take it now," she said again, this time with barely veiled contempt. "Or you'll leave without it."

Santos did as she asked, but without hurry. After he had tucked it into his breast pocket, he shot her a cocky grin. "Thanks, babe. I hate to disappoint, but I've got to go."

She made a small sound of shock, of outrage; her face mottled with fury.

Without waiting for another response, he turned and left the office, aware of the secretary's hostile gaze as he passed through the reception area. Once in the hall, he went in search of the stairs, choosing them over the elevator. He jogged down the three flights and made it to the first floor and across the lobby in a matter of minutes, anxious to leave this oh-so-upper-crust, white-bread hell behind.

Santos pushed through the massive lead-glass doors and stepped outside. Sunlight spilled over him, warm for a late-October afternoon. He breathed deeply, letting the beauty of the day cleanse away some of his anger, his distaste and frustration. Although he had left with the upper hand, his meeting with Hope St. Germaine had left a bitter taste in his mouth. She, this place, represented all that was wrong with this city and the entire system of haves and have nots, the worth its and the not-worth-a-shits. It was that system, that fucked-up attitude, that had allowed his mother's murder to go unpunished.

He started across the street, heading toward the streetcar stop. Where had Lily met this cold, arrogant woman? he wondered. And what business did Lily have with her? What kind of "correspondence" that couldn't be handled by phone?

He narrowed his eyes in thought. He had found something familiar about Hope St. Germaine, something that nagged at his memory. He was certain, however, that they had never met. He would have remembered her. Oh, yes, some things were so unpleasant they could never be forgotten.

"Santos!"

He stopped and swung in the direction his name had come. A cherry-red Fiat convertible sat idling at the curb kitty-corner to him, top down, the firecracker from the elevator behind the wheel.

She smiled and waved him over. "Want to go for a ride?"

She was too young and too spoiled for him.

But he was only going for a ride.

Santos sauntered across the street, aware of the doorman's glare. The valet, he noticed, looked none too happy, either.

He stopped beside the car and ran a hand along the front quarter panel. "Nice wheels. Sure you can handle this machine?"

She tipped her face up to his and he saw himself reflected in her sunglasses. "Why don't you find out. Hop in."

"Why not?" Santos went around to the other side of the car, opened the passenger door and slid into the vehicle. He jerked his head in the direction of the valet and doorman. "What's with the bodyguards?"

"They're just overprotective." She waved at the men, then peeled out, burning rubber as she did. "You know how it is."

"Yeah, right," Santos drawled as he fastened his seat belt. "I know just how it is. You want to tell me where we're going?"

"Nope." She laughed. "I think I'd rather surprise you."

She darted into traffic, cutting off a Lincoln. The driver blew his horn. She laughed again, flipping off the other driver. Santos shook his head and settled back in his seat. No doubt about it, he was in for one hell of a wild ride.

They rode in silence for several blocks. She maneuvered the tiny automobile expertly in and out of traffic, then hopped onto the interstate, heading west.

Santos looked her way. "A birthday present?" he asked, shouting to be heard over the roar of the engine and rush of the wind.

"What?"

"The car. Your sixteenth, I'd guess."

She looked over at him and made a face. "You make it sound like a crime."

"Do I?" He started to say that he hadn't meant to, then swallowed the words. They would have been a lie.

"What were you doing at the hotel?" she asked. "I haven't seen you around there before."

"Delivering something for a friend."

"It's mine, you know. Or will be someday."

"The hotel?" he asked, incredulous. She nodded and he shook his head. This girl had just gone from rich to ridiculous. "And they only bought you a Fiat? I'd be pissed. You should have gotten a Porsche."

She tipped her head back and laughed. "We're not *that* rich."

He pushed his hair out of his eyes. "Oh sure. You're just a certified, card-carrying member of the lucky-sperm club."

"Lucky-sperm club?" she repeated, laughing. "You're funny."

"That's me. A laugh riot."

She missed his sarcasm. "But we're really not that rich, you know." She looked at him, her expression earnest. "There're lots of girls at A.I.C. whose families have lots more money."

The car up ahead braked. He motioned toward it. "Maybe you want to keep your eyes on the road."

She hit the accelerator and roared past the slowing car, then glanced at him once more. "Why? I'd rather keep my eyes on you."

He shook his head, a smile tugging at his mouth. She was narrow and naive in her view of the world and, no doubt, deeply prejudiced by her privileged existence. But she was also unabashedly sassy, wild and sexy as hell.

He couldn't help enjoying her and her game, though he knew her flirtation with him went no deeper than rebellion. He liked her forthright approach; she didn't demur about her game playing, she didn't pretend it didn't exist or make any bones about what she was after.

"You're trying too hard, doll. And I'd really like to get wherever we're going alive."

He expected her to pout or feign hurt, instead she laughed again. "Is that so?" She exited the highway, taking the ramp at breakneck speed. "What exactly am I trying too hard to do?"

"Prove to me what a big, bad girl you are. Give me a scare. I don't impress easily. And I don't scare. You can give it a rest anytime."

She shook her head, her dark hair streaming behind her. "Oh, goody. I just love a challenge."

Santos laughed and leaned his head against the seat back. He closed his eyes, enjoying the sting of the wind, the hum of the engine. After a moment, he cracked open his eyes and studied her while she drove. Her cheeks were flushed, her lips tipped up in a hint of a smile, and although hidden by sunglasses, he would bet her glorious blue eyes were sparkling with excitement.

He lowered his gaze, taking in the plaid skirt and white blouse, her school's name embroidered on its front pocket. The blouse pulled slightly across her breasts as if she had recently grown. His body stirred, and he shut his eyes, swearing silently. Jesus, she was only sixteen. San Quentin Quail. An Angola angel. Sassy-mouthed jailbait encased in the body of a twenty-year-old.

He was not about to get burned by this little firecracker. Or any other, for that matter.

She glanced at him. "You were looking at me."

It wasn't a question. And he wasn't embarrassed to admit it. "Yes."

She slowed the car and turned onto Lakeshore Drive. "Why? What were you thinking?"

"I was wondering if your parents are able to sleep nights?"

For a moment she said nothing, and he thought his question had unnerved her. "As far as I know," she said finally, her light tone sounding forced. She angled into a

parking space, cut off the engine, then turned toward him.
"Why shouldn't they?"

"If you were my kid, I wouldn't be able to."

"You make me sound like a baby. I'm not."

"All grown up at sixteen?"

"I think so." Color bloomed in her cheeks, and she
tipped up her chin. "Weren't you? Grown up at sixteen?"

Santos thought of his mother's murder, of the series of
foster homes, of the ride he had hitched in an attempt to
flee the system. He had lived a lifetime by age sixteen; this
pampered princess had probably never even faced one moment of discomfort, let alone horror.

"Apples and oranges, babe."

She searched his expression. "You don't like me very
much, do you?"

"I don't know you, Glory."

"No, you don't."

She looked away, but not before he saw something in her
expression at odds with the girl she purported to be, something soft and scared. Something vulnerable. He thought
that maybe he had been wrong, maybe she had known her
own version of horror.

He didn't like the thought and opened the car door.
"What do you say we take a walk?"

She nodded and they alighted the vehicle. For several
minutes, they strolled silently along the seawall. Sailboats
dotted Lake Pontchartrain's rippled surface; gulls circled
overhead. A car passed, music spilling from its open windows; from the playground across the street came the sound
of children's laughter.

As they walked, their arms or hands brushed every so
often, occasionally she touched his hand or arm to point
something out. With each innocent or accidental touch his
awareness of her grew, until he found himself aroused to
the point of distraction.

Santos reminded himself that he was in control. He could
stop—or start—this anytime he chose. She was a sassy lit-

tle flirt, and nothing more. He would do well to remind himself of that.

"I've always loved it here," Glory murmured, breathing deeply. "It's always seemed more like a world away from uptown than just a drive across the city. I remember the first time my father brought me out here. I thought we were on vacation."

She dragged her hands through her hair, combing it with her fingers. "It was a Sunday, and Mother had one of her headaches. Daddy and I left for mass, but we came here instead. She was furious when she found out."

"Because you cut church?"

"She takes mass very seriously."

He drew his eyebrows together, studying her profile. "You sound like you don't like her too much."

"Mother?" Glory made a face. "I think it's more the other way around. Hope St. Germaine is a hard woman to please."

The ice queen was this girl's mother? In one way he found it hard to believe. But in another it made absolute sense.

They neared what had been the sight of Pontchartrain Beach, an amusement park built on a point of land between Lakeshore Drive and the water's edge. The park had fallen victim to the times, to people's fears and a too rapidly changing world.

"Did you ever go to The Beach?" she asked, referring to the amusement park the way the locals always had.

"Once. My mother brought me out. We rode all the rides and had a picnic. I think I was ten. It was the best time I ever had." The memory made him smile. It made him hurt, too.

He frowned, annoyed with himself for sharing that with her. Annoyed with himself for remembering. "We should start back."

He turned to go; she caught his arm, stopping him. She lifted her face provocatively to his, once more the outrageous, reckless flirt. "Can I ask you a question, Santos?"

He met her eyes, comfortable with this familiar territory. A moment ago had been too personal. He didn't want to know anything but the superficial about her; he wanted her to know only the same about him. Nothing real, nothing close. Just some nice, safe game playing. Just the way he liked it. Nobody got hurt, and everybody was happy.

"It's a free country."

"When you see something you want, what do you do?"

He knew exactly where this was going. He smiled, and slowly, deliberately moved his gaze over her. When he finally met her eyes once more, he arched an eyebrow. "As opposed to just going for it?"

"Uh-huh."

He leaned his head down to hers, not stopping until their faces were so close he could feel her breath against his cheek. He lowered his voice to a whisper. "I weigh the consequences of having it. That's what grown-ups do, Glory."

She laid her hands on his chest. "I'm a grown-up."

"I don't think so."

He made a move to straighten and she curled her fingers into his chambray shirt. "I could prove it."

Arousal kicked him squarely in the gut. He ignored it. "What do you want from me, Glory St. Germaine?"

She batted her eyelashes and leaned toward him. "What do you think?"

He touched her flushed cheek. "I think," he murmured, his voice deliberately husky, "that I'm too old for you. I think you should run home to your mama."

Challenge lit her eyes. "Really? Too old?"

"Uh-huh. Too old. Too experienced. You're way out of your league here, little girl."

"Try me." She splayed her hands on his chest and leaned toward him. "Try me," she said again, lifting her face to his. "I dare you to kiss me."

Santos hesitated, but only a moment. He lowered his head and took her mouth, sweet, hot, already parted. He kissed her as a man kissed, taking, plundering, leaving no doubt what a man wanted from a woman.

She made a small, helpless sound deep in her throat. Her hands flexed against his chest, alternately pushing him away and pulling him closer. He deepened the kiss even more, exploring her mouth with his tongue, leaving no questions or secrets between them.

He slid his hands down her back and cupping her, pulled her more tightly to him. He moved his hips against hers, knowing she could feel his erection, that she would know exactly how aroused he was. And how far she had pushed him.

He drew away. She gazed up at him, her lips still parted, her expression dazed. Stunned. She had never been kissed like that before, he knew. He had given this cocky girl-woman much more than she had bargained for.

Santos laughed softly and dragged his thumb across her bottom lip, moist and swollen from his kiss. "See, little girl. I told you I was too old for you."

He started to turn away from her. She caught his arm, stopping him. He looked at her, surprised.

"No," she said, her voice shaking slightly. "I told you."

She stood on tiptoe and kissed him. As hard, as deeply as he had kissed her a moment before. She threw her whole self into it, probing his mouth with her tongue, pressing herself against him.

Even as he told himself not to, Santos reacted to her kiss, responded to the feel of her exquisite mouth and body against his. Even as he reminded himself to stay in control, it careened out of his reach.

She aroused him to a fever pitch, in a way, and to an extent, no girl had before, not so easily. She set him on fire, made him forget what was right and wrong, smart and not. And all it had taken was her naively hungry kiss and the feel of her lush body straining against his.

She took his breath away.

The truth of that snaked its way through his fog of desire, and he set her roughly away from him. He had set out to prove a point to her; it was he who had been proven to. And though she would never know how much she had shaken him, he didn't like it, not one bit.

"This is over," he said, his voice thick. "It's been fun, babe, but it's time to go home."

She stared blankly at him, then blinked as if suddenly comprehending what he had said. "Will I see you again?"

"No."

He started to turn away once again; she caught his arm, stopping him. He met her eyes. "You're scared," she said, searching his gaze. She shook her head, slightly, as with surprise. "You're running away."

"You *are* young, Glory St. Germaine." He patted her cheek, wanting to be as condescending as possible. "Like I said, it's been fun. But it's time for you to run home to mommy and daddy."

She shook her head again, this time emphatically. "You're running scared."

"Listen, honey," he drawled, wondering how the hell, in a matter of a couple hours, she had begun to see inside his head, "I am definitely not run—"

"You are." She tipped up her chin. "A big man like you shouldn't be scared of being honest with a little bitty girl like me."

He gritted his teeth, furious—at her, for pushing; at himself, for reacting to her. "Look, doll, you're a sixteen-year-old, C-cup, man-eating bundle of trouble. I have no plans to go to Angola for you or any other piece of ass. So if you're looking for an exciting back-seat fuck with an older guy, you're going to have to look elsewhere. Is that honest enough for you?"

Her eyes filled but to her credit, she held her ground. He admitted a kind of grudging respect, then cursed himself for it. She might be made of tougher stuff than the other girls of her type that he had known, but that didn't make her any different. It didn't make her any more honest.

"You prick." She jutted up her chin, though he could see that it trembled slightly. "Feel better now? Feel in control, big man?"

Without giving him a chance to respond, she turned on her heels and marched off, heading toward the car. Santos hesitated a moment, then started after her.

He called her name, but she didn't stop or look back. Finally, he passed her, then swung around, blocking her way.

"Please move," she said evenly, though he could see by her eyes that she had been crying.

Something turned over inside him. Something warm and foreign, something he hadn't felt in a long time. He cursed it even as he held it to him as if it were the most precious gift on earth.

"I'm sorry," he said roughly. "I shouldn't have been—"

"So mean?" she supplied, angry color staining her cheeks. "Such a bastard?"

"Yes, to all of the above." He looked her straight in the eyes. After a moment, she caught her bottom lip between her teeth. But she didn't look away. Again he experienced that small, unwelcome quiver of respect for her.

He pushed it away. Respect ranked right up there with "too close, too real." Those were the last things he wanted with any girl.

But especially this one. This one was trouble.

"You push too much," he said softly. "Too hard. You didn't leave me much choice but to push back. A man like me doesn't play nice, Glory St. Germaine. You should run far and fast."

"I don't want to run. And I'm not going to." She squared her shoulders and met his gaze. "I want to see you again."

"You're determined, I'll give you that." He folded his arms across his chest. "But it takes two, Glory. I'm too old and too experienced for you."

"How old are you?" she asked, eyes wide with exaggerated innocence. "Forty?"

"Very cute. I'm nineteen."

She mock-shuddered. "Ancient."

He laughed and by unspoken agreement, they began walking. "Not ancient. But passed the age of consent. You're not. Besides, it's more than that. There's more than chronological years between us."

She opened her mouth, he knew, to ask him what he meant. He didn't give her the chance. "Let me ask you a question."

"Shoot."

"Why do you want to see me again?"

"Why?" she echoed, obviously surprised by his question. "Because I do."

"The old 'go for it' thing again. Sorry, not good enough."

She frowned, though he wasn't sure whether with annoyance or thought. After a moment, she said, "Well . . . you're really cute and . . . a great kisser."

He laughed, more pleased than he should have been. "Cute and a great kisser. I'm overwhelmed." They reached the end of the seawall, and he touched her elbow, steering her back toward her car.

They walked in silence a moment. He glanced at her from the corners of his eyes. "What school?" he asked, referring to her uniform.

"Academy of the Immaculate Conception."

He stopped. "You've got to be kidding."

"I'm not."

He tipped his head back and roared. "Are all the Immaculate Conception girls as immaculate as you are?"

"No." Her lips lifted. "I pride myself on being the wildest A.I.C. girl, at least in the sophomore class. And I'm quite sure Sister Marguerite would agree with me."

"The school principal?" When Glory nodded he made a sound of sympathy. "She sounds tough."

"She is. And she hates my guts." They reached the car and she held out the keys. "You want to drive?"

"Sure." He took the keys, opened the passenger door for her, then went around to the other side and slid behind the wheel. He started the car and looked at her. "The hotel?"

"If that's good for you."

He nodded and started off; they drove in silence, though Santos was aware of her gaze on him. He glanced at her several times, and regretted it. Her expression—at once resigned and hopeful and hungry—had him almost changing his mind.

The hotel in sight, she broke the silence. "Will I see you again?"

"No."

"I can't change your mind?"

She could. Easily. And that scared him silly. "Sorry."

"I was afraid of that." She sighed and looked away. "Stop right here."

He did as she asked and slipped the stick into neutral. He climbed out and she slid across the seat and behind the wheel. He smiled down at her. "It's been fun, Glory."

She looked so disappointed, he chuckled. "Am I the first fish that got away?"

She laughed up at him. "The first one I really wanted that got way."

He rested his hands on the lowered window and bent his head toward hers. "If it's any consolation, you're a great kisser, too."

"Yeah?"

"Yeah."

She covered one of his hands with one of her own and lifted her face to his. "Then why don't you kiss me again?"

Santos looked across the street, toward the hotel entrance. Both the doorman and valet stood at the curb glaring his way. He indicated them with a jerk of his head. "Here? Where the watchdogs can see?"

"Why not? Let's give them a show."

"You really are a little firecracker," he murmured, even as he lowered his head to hers.

He took her mouth in a quick, hard kiss. She made a sound, deep in her throat. It affected him like a swift punch to his gut.

He drew away, startled. That brief kiss had affected him more than the longer, more passionate one earlier.

She was a firecracker, all right. If he wasn't careful, this whole thing was going to blow up in his face.

He touched the tip of her nose with his index finger. "Thanks for the ride." He straightened, turned and started toward the neutral ground and the streetcar stop.

"Santos!"

He stopped and looked over his shoulder at her. She grinned. "See you around."

For one long moment, he gazed at her. She made a fetching picture, on her knees, elbows resting on her seat back, her dark hair falling across her face. He felt a moment of regret, then lifted his hand in a final wave. "Goodbye, Glory."

He turned and walked away, vowing to never see her again.

24

An entire day passed before Glory realized she knew nothing about Santos but his name. The realization surprised her only mildly: she had been so busy mooning over him, so busy wallowing in the memory of his mind-blowing kisses, that she had been unable to think of anything else.

She still couldn't. She had never met anyone like him; the other boys she had known and kissed seemed like babies to her now, boring, and shallow and immature.

Santos had stolen her heart already. She would die if she didn't see him again. Just die. She had to find a way.

The streetcar approached, the one Liz arrived on every morning, and Glory all but bounced up and down in excitement. She hadn't been able to call her friend the night before. She had arrived home and found her mother and father in an odd, elated mood. Her mother hadn't asked her more than where she had been; her answer of the library with Liz had satisfied her.

That in itself had been odd. Her answers never satisfied her mother; she never *just accepted* them. But she had last night. Thank goodness. If she had looked at or questioned Glory too closely, she would have known her daughter was up to something.

Glory had decided that it must have been fate. She and Santos were meant for each other.

Her mother had insisted they all go to the Renaissance Room for dinner, another odd occurrence. And all through the meal her mother had chattered, sounding more like a teenager than Glory.

Her father's behavior, too, had seemed out of character to Glory. He had drunk less and looked at her mother more—and with affection.

Glory didn't know what was going on between her parents. For a week they had barely spoken to each other. In her sixteen years, Glory had lived through their many fights, their many angry and punishing silences. But even during those times there had always been something between them, something hot and strong. She had always believed, for better or worse—for she did not think her father was happy—that her parents would be together forever.

But this time, this forbidding silence, had been different. It had been more than angry or hurt. It had been ugly and so very cold it had sometimes made her shudder to look at the two of them together. Glory had thought their marriage was over.

After talking to Liz, Glory had hoped it was over. Liz had assured her that, at sixteen, she would be allowed to choose which parent she wanted to live with. Glory had even begun to daydream about what it would be like, living only with her father, going day after day without her mother's constant suspicions and criticism.

Last night's dinner had put an end to those fantasies. Her parents had seemed happier than they had in a long time.

A part of her had been angry at her father; she couldn't understand what he saw in her mother or what her mother's hold on him was. Another part of her had been relieved. By focusing their attention on each other, they had left Glory to wonder about Santos.

The streetcar screeched to a halt; a moment later Liz hopped off. "Hey, Glo. What's up? You didn't call me last night."

Glory grabbed Liz's arm and tugged her away from the group of A.I.C. girls who had alighted the vehicle with Liz. "I have to talk to you. Alone. It's really important."

Liz glanced over her shoulder, then back at Glory. She lowered her voice. "What is it?" she asked. "Your parents?"

Glory shook her head, then leaned toward her friend, feeling about to burst with excitement. "Liz, you're not going to believe this. I met the most wonderful guy. I think I'm in love."

Liz stopped and turned toward her friend, her eyes wide. "In love?" she repeated in a hushed whisper. "Who is he? Where did you meet him?" She caught Glory's hands. "Tell me everything!"

Glory did. She shared every detail of her encounter with Santos, the good and the bad, the way she had pushed, and the way he had pushed back, the things he had said to her in anger. She told her about the elevator, their ride to the lake, their walk. She described Santos—his face and coloring, what he wore, his build, the deep, rich sound of his voice, the way he tilted his head when he laughed and how the husky sound turned her on.

Finally, Glory told Liz about his kisses and about her overwhelming physical reaction to him. "I've kissed bunches of boys, Liz, but this, it was different. It was special."

"But how can you be sure it's love? I mean, you don't really know anything about him."

Traffic cleared and they crossed St. Charles Avenue from the neutral ground to the sidewalk. "I know, but I've never felt this way about anybody, Liz. It's weird, and we barely spent an hour together. There was just something about him...something that..."

Her words trailed off as she searched for a way to explain her feelings so her friend would understand. And she desperately wanted Liz to understand. She wanted her to approve. Liz was her best friend and her opinion meant more to her than anybody else's.

She met Liz's gaze. "When I was with him I forgot everything, where I was, who I was. It was like my entire being was focused only on the touch of his lips on mine, his hands on my body. In a way, it was like I had been waiting my whole life for him, for his kiss. It sounds stupid, like a kid's fairy tale or something, but that's the way I felt."

Glory fell silent a moment, gathering her thoughts, not quite believing what she was about to say. She met her friend's gaze once more, feeling her cheeks heat. "You're going to think I'm crazy, but I had this overwhelming feeling, this certainty that he . . . that he was the one."

Liz swallowed audibly, her eyes wide. "The one?"

"Yeah." Glory hugged her books tighter. "*The One.* The guy . . . the man . . . for me. My destiny or something."

"You mean, like your soul mate?"

They passed under the academy's wrought-iron archway. Glory nodded and drew a deep breath. "At that moment, I would have done anything for him."

"That's so cool. And it sounds so romantic." Liz shivered. "But it scares me, too, Glory."

"It doesn't scare me." She twirled around, laughing. "I feel like I could walk on air!"

"While you're up there," Liz said dryly, "tread lightly. Sister Marguerite has her eyes on you right now."

Sure enough, Sister Marguerite stood just outside the front doors, her eyes on Glory. Glory stopped and turned toward her friend, wanting to talk more without being overheard by the principal. "I have to see him again, Liz. I just have to."

Liz clutched her books closer to her chest. "But how? I mean, how are you going to find him?"

"I figured I'd ask around the hotel, see if anybody knows why he was there. He was delivering something to the third floor and that's where the executive offices are. He might even have delivered something to Daddy. I'll talk to his secretary."

The warning bell rang and several clusters of girls hurried past them, many of whom called out a greeting or waved. Glory started forward, but Liz caught her hand, stopping her.

"Be careful, Glory. Santos doesn't sound like the type of guy your mother would approve of. If she gets wind of this—"

Glory looked into her friend's concerned gaze, and a chill crawled up her spine. "She won't. I'll be really careful."

"Promise? Because I've got a bad feeling about this."

"Yeah, I promise." Glory shook her head against the feeling of dread that settled in the pit of her stomach, and smiled. "You worry too much, Liz. Everything is going to be fine."

After three days of disappointments, Glory began to lose hope of ever seeing Santos again. She had asked everyone who had been on duty at the hotel that day; the few who remembered having seen him had no idea who he was or why he had been in the hotel. When she had questioned her father's secretary, the woman had looked at Glory as if she were crazy.

Glory sagged against the locker next to the one she and Liz shared. She sighed. "I'm out of ideas, Liz. I've talked to everybody."

"Don't be bummed, Glo. You might find him yet." Liz shut the locker door, then snapped the padlock tight. "After all, if he's really your soul mate, you have to see him again."

The final bell had rung several minutes ago, and she and Liz started down the hall, heading toward the main entrance. Glory made a sound of frustration. "Yeah? And why's that?"

"Because, if he's your soul mate, fate wouldn't give you only one chance to be together. That would be too cruel."

"You really think so?" They moved around a cluster of girls blocking the center of the hall.

"Definitely."

Glory laughed, her spirits lifting. "But, what if he's my destiny, but I'm not his?"

Liz laughed, too, shaking her head. "I don't think it works that way."

They stepped through the front doors and out into the bright, cool afternoon. Glory blinked against the sudden, brilliant light.

When her vision cleared, she saw Santos. He stood just beyond the school's gate, his head averted as he watched each girl pass, as if looking for one certain girl. *He had come for her. He felt the same as she did. He must.*

Glory's heart burst into dizzying flight, and for a moment she couldn't find her breath. When she did, she grabbed Liz's arm. "That's him, Liz. It's Santos."

Liz stopped. "Where?"

"There. Standing beyond the gates to the right. In the black T-shirt and sunglasses."

"Are you sure? I can't see his face."

"It's him. I'd know him anywhere. Oh, God, what do I do now?" Still clutching her friend's arm, she dragged her back into the school. "I can't breathe. I feel like I'm going to faint."

"Calm down. You don't want anyone to hear you." Liz glanced quickly around them, then back at Glory. "If you don't feel good about this, don't go out there. If you're scared—"

"It's not that. It's—" Glory sucked in a deep breath, light-headed with happiness. "He's here, so maybe he . . . maybe he feels the same way I do. Just like you said, fate's given me another chance."

"Then get your butt out there."

"Come meet him." Glory laughed again and caught Liz's hands. "I want you to meet him."

"I don't think so." Liz shook her head, and freed her hands from Glory's. "Unlike you, boys really do terrify me. I never know what to say, and I hate feeling so awkward and ugly."

"You're not ugly, you're—"

"Go." Liz nudged her. "You don't want him to get away."

"Thanks, Liz. You're the best." Glory smiled at her friend, then turned and raced outside to meet her destiny.

She was too late.

He was gone.

25

This time, the St. Charles Hotel did not awe Santos. This time, he didn't pause to study the people or surroundings, he didn't wonder at the nature of Lily's relationship with Mrs. St. Germaine or at the contents of the envelope tucked into his pocket.

This time, his head was filled with thoughts of a dark-haired beauty, a firecracker of a girl who had turned him inside out with nothing more than a kiss and a challenge.

Santos muttered an oath. He had tried to put her from his mind. He had told himself all the right and smart things; he had thrown himself into other activities, had even asked out a girl he had met in one of his classes.

But try as he might, he had been unable to stop thinking about Glory, not completely, anyway. And never for long. She had even popped, full-blown, into his thoughts as he had been kissing his date good-night.

He shook his head, disgusted with himself. It had been three weeks now. Three weeks since their stormy, exhilarating, passionate encounter.

Why couldn't he forget her?

The low point of the last weeks had come one afternoon four days after their meeting. He had driven uptown to the Academy of the Immaculate Conception, he had parked his car, climbed out and stood in front of her school waiting for her. Like some silly, love-struck kid. Santos shook his head at the memory. He had felt like a cradle robber, too, as those giggling girls had strolled past, many of them openly staring at him.

He had recovered his sanity in time, before Glory had seen him, before harm had been done.

Before he had actually laid eyes on her and been unable to walk away.

Santos reached the stairs and took them to the third floor. He found Mrs. St. Germaine's office, handed Lily's correspondence to her, took the one she offered in return and left the office. The entire transaction took place without them speaking a single word to each other.

The dislike he had initially felt for Glory's mother had grown in the weeks since he had first met her. And it had festered. He found her to be the coldest, most unpleasant woman he had ever met. He wondered how someone with as much life and fire as Glory could be her daughter.

Once again, Santos took the stairs. He reached the lobby in moments and started for the hotel's front entrance. As he strode toward the doors, he told himself to keep his gaze forward, he told himself it was better off this way, that seeing Glory would be a mistake.

Even so, he looked for her. Against his better judgment, he hoped he would see her. That he couldn't control his own thoughts annoyed the hell out of him.

It was ridiculous. He was obsessed with a spoiled little flirt who had probably not given him a second thought.

Santos made it across the St. Charles lobby and stepped outside. He released a breath he hadn't realized he'd been holding. He had made it. He had run Lily's errand without seeing Glory.

But the hell of it was, he wasn't sure which he felt more keenly—relief or disappointment.

Santos smiled at the doorman, then started for his car, walking briskly. He had parked it several blocks up, on a side street. He turned onto the street, then stopped, surprised.

Glory leaned against the front passenger side of his Camaro, her face lifted to the sun. She wore blue jeans, a white sweater and a short, leather jacket.

She was incredibly beautiful.

His heart hammered against the wall of his chest, and he scowled. Damn, but he felt too stupid for words.

He drew in a deep, determined breath and started toward her. He didn't know how she had found him, but he was going to lose her. And fast.

"Hello, Glory," he said when he reached her.

Without taking her face from the sun, she smiled. "Hello, Santos."

He fished his car keys from his pocket. "This seems an odd place to sunbathe."

This time, she turned her face to his. "Does it?"

"Mmm." He moved his gaze over her face, acknowledging awareness. "Odd time of year, too. Late November."

She turned herself to the sun again. "I was heading for the hotel when I saw you drive by."

"So you followed me."

"Basically." She straightened and met his gaze once more. "I wanted to see you again."

He jiggled his car keys in his right hand, at war with himself. She intrigued him, she turned him on. He would enjoy nothing more right now than taking her up on the challenge in her eyes by dragging her into his arms and kissing her senseless.

He had never been a particularly self-destructive guy, and getting involved with Glory St. Germaine would be just that.

He indicated her clothes. "No school today?"

She shook her head. "It's a feast day. Saint somebody or other."

"Lucky you." Santos jiggled the keys again. "It was nice seeing you, Glory, but I've got to go."

She reached out and caught his arm. "I've been thinking about you. About us."

"Us?" He arched his eyebrows in exaggerated disbelief. "I didn't realize there was an 'us.' I remember a couple kisses and a drive to the lake. That's not an 'us,' babe. Sorry."

"It could be."

She was as persistent as a bulldog, but a hell of a lot prettier. He was flattered and, truthfully, impressed by her nerve. But enough was enough.

He shook off her hand. "I know what you're all about Glory St. Germaine. And I don't want to play."

She drew her eyebrows together. "What do you mean?"

He thought of Hope St. Germaine, of the way she looked at him, as if he were one level below scum, and imagined what her reaction to him and her daughter talking would be.

Oh, no. He understood Glory St. Germaine very well.

"You're rebelling. Against mommy and daddy. Against the limitations of your privileged life. You want to prove something, to them or to yourself. You want to be a little reckless, you want a short walk on the wild side. How better to do all that than by chasing a bad boy like me."

She paled. "That's not true."

"Right. I've been down this road before, babe. I've known girls like you before. Lots of them. And I know there's nothing there."

She shook her head. "There *is* something between us. I feel it, and I think you do, too." He opened his mouth to deny her words, she cut him off. "And I'm not like the other girls you've known. I'm not."

"You are, sweetheart. Sorry."

He made a move to turn away from her, she caught his arm once more. "You're the one playing a game. Not me." She sucked in a quick breath. "Why are you doing this? Why the big act?"

"It's not—"

"I saw you," she interrupted evenly. "At the school. My school." She searched his gaze. "If there's nothing between us, why were you there?"

He narrowed his eyes. Furious at her. And at himself. For getting tangled up in this no-win situation, for wanting her despite all the reasons he shouldn't. "Maybe I was waiting for some other underage firecracker."

For one moment, she looked as if he had slapped her. Then she hiked up her chin. "You weren't. You were waiting for me. And you chickened out."

"'Chickened out?'" he repeated, arching his eyebrows. "Dream on. Being there was a mistake. So I left."

"But it wasn't a mistake." She tightened her fingers on his arm, her expression earnest. "I think we could be good together."

"You do?" He laughed, the sound without humor even to his own ears. "You're too young, and I'm too experienced. Nothing's changed from the other day."

But she didn't seem young, he acknowledged. Not when he looked into her eyes. Then he saw someone wise beyond her years, someone who had seen more than her share of pain. When he looked into her eyes, he saw himself.

He didn't know how that could be, but it was.

Just as he didn't know why standing here with her should feel so right.

He swung away from her, shaken by his own thoughts. Stunned to realize that in a way, he *was* afraid of this girl. Because, despite what he knew to be true, he could find himself involved with her. He could maybe even start to care for her. And if he allowed that, she would hurt him.

He faced her once more. "You want the brutal truth, Glory St. Germaine? I don't think we would be good together. Not at all. And age is only part of it."

He made a sound of frustration and anger, and dragged a hand through his hair. The frustration he understood; the anger came upon him so suddenly it took his breath. He seethed with it.

"It's not just you, doll. It's your type."

"My type," she repeated, her voice small and hurt. "You mean rich and spoiled."

"Yes," he said without hesitation. "Rich and spoiled and pampered. You know nothing of life, of real life. You know nothing of ugliness, nothing of pain. You've been catered to and coddled. You can afford to play these little rebellion games with other people's feelings because you've never had to care about anyone but yourself.''

He had hurt her, he saw. This time, he had penetrated her cocky self-confidence and cut her to the bone. Even though he had meant to, he felt no pleasure in it.

"How do you know?" She asked, her voice thick. "What makes you think you know what I've seen or felt? You don't know anything about me."

"Look at you. What's not to know? You go to that fancy-ass private school. I'll bet your parents had to register you at birth, and that the tuition is more than most people earn in a year. I'll bet, too, that you live in the Garden District. In a mansion that's on the historic New Orleans walking tour. You have servants, two or three, and the only time people like me are let in is through the back entrance, as servants. Daddy may have a Rolls, Mommy has plenty of diamonds and at least two furs."

This time, it was Glory who tried to turn away, Santos who stopped her. He forced her to meet his eyes. "You're so matter-of-fact about what you have. 'I'll own the St. Charles one day,' you told me that first day we met. You have no fucking idea what that means. You are so narrow, you have no conception of the kind of life you live. You and I, princess, have nothing in common."

Her chin trembled; her eyes brimmed with tears. But the tears didn't fall; she didn't allow them to. He wished they would; he wished she was made of softer, shallower stuff. He wished she was one hundred percent the girl he accused her of being. This would be so much easier.

"You're the one who's prejudiced," she said softly. "You're the one who judges people by what they have or don't have. Not me."

"If I do, I've earned it."

She stiffened her spine. "Maybe you have, but that girl, that's not me. I don't care about the things my parents have. They don't mean anything to me." She held out a hand to him. "And they're not who I am."

He caught her hand, angrier than before. Because she reached a place inside him that she had no business touching. A place he didn't want touched, especially not by someone like her. And because he knew he was right; yet, irrationally, he wished he was wrong.

If she understood, she would leave him alone. She would run as far and as fast as she could.

By God, she would understand.

He tightened his fingers over hers and tugged her away from the car. Reaching around her, he unlocked the passenger door. He swung it open. "I want to show you something. Come on."

She rubbed her wrist. "What do you want to show me?"

"That's for me to know and you to find out," he mocked. "Get in."

"Not before you tell me where we're going."

"Not so quick to trust now, are you, Glory St. Germaine? Maybe you want to call it quits? Maybe you should run home to mama?"

She caught her bottom lip between her teeth, obviously frightened.

He smiled. "See, babe? I'm a scary guy. Just ask anybody you know." He slammed the door, so hard the car shook. "Run on home, little girl. Go now, before you do something stupid."

Without waiting for a response, he went around to the driver's side, unlocked and opened the door, then slid behind the wheel. He jammed the key in the ignition, twisted and the engine roared to life.

He threw the car into First. The passenger door flew open, and she tumbled into the seat beside him. He swore silently.

"Okay," she said, her expression defiant. "Show me."

Without a word, he peeled out from the curb. He drove toward the French Quarter, navigating the noontime traffic without speaking, gripping the steering wheel so tightly his fingers went numb.

Finally, as they neared the Quarter, he began to speak. "I spent the first seven years of my life in a broken-down trailer that stank of sweat and booze. My daddy was a piece-of-shit no-good drunk who beat my mama and me. I looked forward to his drunken binges because he usually passed out or puked before he could do much more than bloody my nose or blacken my eye. He was a real man's man, he wasn't averse to breaking a bone or two when the situation called for it.

"I didn't have any friends because I was trash, and half-breed trash, at that. The people around Big Bass, Texas, didn't take too kindly to Indians and Mexicans, especially when mixed together. My daddy was white, and he pretty much felt the same way. I think I heard more racial slurs from him in those seven years than I've heard in all the years since." Santos looked at her. "My own father. Isn't that a hoot?"

She shook her head and huddled deeper into the bucket seat. "No," she whispered, "it's not."

He shrugged and turned back to the road. "Somebody took care of him for me and Mama, though I'm sure when they were slitting his throat, they didn't know how relieved his *loved ones* would be."

Glory cringed and he smiled. "Just wait, babe, it gets even prettier." He crossed Canal Street and drove into the French Quarter. He went several blocks, crisscrossing, getting as close to Bourbon as he could. He saw a parking space and took it.

He swung open his door. "Will everyone please disembark for the next leg of our tour."

She followed him out, though he could tell by her expression that she was uneasy. He followed her gaze. He had chosen one of the rougher, less touristy blocks in the Quarter. Lined by dangerous looking bars and dilapidated buildings, this little slice of New Orleans was about as far from the Garden District as you could get.

"Nice place, huh. Come on." He caught her hand and started down the block, adrenaline pumping through him. He walked so fast she had to run to keep up.

"Our little saga continues," he said, "right here in the world-renowned French Quarter. After my old man's unfortunate run-in with a knife, Mama and I moved here. She had a cousin who lived here, a cousin who said jobs were plentiful and the living was easy. Of course, when we got here, the cousin was gone and jobs for uneducated, untrained women were anything but plentiful."

They reached Bourbon Street and Santos turned onto it. "Here we are," he said. "The street that never sleeps, home to bars and strip clubs and sex shops. Home to Club 69." He saw it just ahead and tugged on her hand. "There it is now."

They stopped before the club. The hawker stood in front of the door, swinging it open, letting it shut, swinging it back open. With each swing of the door, Glory and Santos—and everyone else on the street who cared to stop and gape—got a glimpse of a woman on the stage, mostly undressed, gyrating for the drunken audience.

He hadn't been back—not to Bourbon Street or Club 69. He had avoided both, just as he avoided the memories. When they allowed him to. Most times, they simply swallowed him whole.

"See that, Glory? Take a good look. That's where my mother worked. That's how she supported us."

"Don't do this, Santos." Glory shook her head and made a move to turn away. "Please, it's not necessary. It's—"

"But it is necessary." He caught her shoulders, forcing her to face the door. The hawker leered at her, and Santos felt her shudder.

"Look at that, Glory. Can you imagine? Not even two in the afternoon, and the place is already filled. Of course, my mother worked the late shift, the tips were better."

He rested his chin on top of Glory's dark head. He breathed deeply, catching the ugly scent of the bar but also the sweet smell of Glory's shampoo. Both called sharply to his memory. And the memory cut him to the quick.

"Can you smell that, Glory. Take a good whiff. That's the way she always smelled when she got home from work. She'd reek of booze and cigarettes and dirty old men. I remember how much I'd love Sunday mornings. She'd always smell like flowers."

Glory made a sound. Part revulsion, part pity. He wasn't sure which hurt more. He tightened his fingers on her shoulders, seeing all this through her eyes. Seedy and crass and so very demeaning. He imagined how she would have looked at his mother, what she would have thought of her.

It fueled his anger. "Come on."

He started back to the car, dragging her with him, his hand a vise on her arm.

"Let me go." She tugged against his grasp. "You're hurting me."

He released her, and she stumbled backward. "You want to continue the tour, princess? Or are you ready to go back uptown?"

"You bastard." She caught her bottom lip between her teeth to keep it from trembling. "Why are you doing this?"

"So you'll understand."

Without another word, he turned and continued to the car, though more slowly so she could keep up with him. He unlocked it; they climbed in. He drove to the other side of the Quarter.

Heart in his throat, Santos turned onto Ursuline Street. Another place, another street, he had avoided. He had not been back in the four years since the social worker had taken him away.

He began to sweat—his palms, his armpits and forehead. His hands shook and a feeling of dread settled over him, so heavy and dark that for a moment he couldn't breathe.

"Santos?" Glory reached across the seat, though he was only half-aware of her touch. "Are you all right?"

He didn't reply. He couldn't.

He reached the building. He drew the car to a stop in the middle of the narrow street and climbed out. He stared at the apartment building, seeing it as it had been that last night—the crowd, the squad cars and ambulance, the police lights violating the dark with throbbing red.

Santos closed his eyes and relived the feel of the hot damp air, the smell of sweat and his own fear, relived the panic thrumming through him, and the way they had all combined to create a surreal, dizzying nightmare.

Only it hadn't been a nightmare.

In his head, he heard the low roar of the crowd as the paramedics emerged from the building with the stretcher.

Glory came up beside him. She curled a hand over his forearm, and he glanced at her, though he didn't see her. Not really. He saw two men dressed in white; he saw a stretcher, a still form under the sheet.

"My God." She searched his expression. "What is this place?"

"This is where we lived," he answered, turning back to the building. "Me and my mother."

He started toward the entrance. His chest hurt so badly he could hardly breathe, he heard the thud of his heart, then the rush of blood in his head. "It's where she died. She was...murdered. By a john, they thought. Stabbed sixteen times.

"Here," he said, speaking more to himself than her, stopping at the exact place. "This is where I saw her. This is where I ripped away the sheet and saw her...face."

In his mind's eye, he pictured her just as she had been that night, deathly white and vividly, brutally red. A cry flew to his lips; Santos bit it back. Just as he choked back tears, though they burned his eyes.

"She was so beautiful. And her death was so...ugly. She didn't deserve to die that way. It wasn't fair. It wasn't—"

He swallowed the words and the pain, focusing instead on his anger. He looked at Glory. "I'm going to find the bastard who did it. I'm going to find him, and I'm going to make him pay."

Glory caught his hand and brought it to her mouth. Her tears wet his fingers.

From the street came the blare of a horn and an angry shout. Santos had stopped his car in the middle of the narrow street and jumped out; it was blocking the way. Santos ignored the irate driver and curled his fingers around Glory's. "See how much we have in common, princess? You see who I am?"

Instead of recoiling at all she had learned about him, instead of looking at him in horror or pity, she put her arms around him. She laid her cheek against his chest and held him tightly.

"I'm sorry," she said softly, her voice tear-soaked but strong. She tightened her arms. "I'm so very sorry."

For one moment, Santos held himself stiffly, wanting to deny what she offered, deny what she made him feel. Then he closed his arms around her and buried his face in her sweet smelling hair. "I loved her," he said, his voice low and strangled.

"I know."

To the scream of horns, they held each other.

26

Those moments in the French Quarter changed everything between Glory and Santos. It was as if in the space of a heartbeat, they had gone from two people who hardly knew each other, to two people who had known each other forever—people who were connected by fragile yet powerful threads.

Glory accepted the newfound connection without question, but Santos could not. He fought it. He told himself what he felt for Glory was crazy, irrational and dangerous. He told himself it wasn't real; he told them both that they had nothing in common. Yet it felt real. And right. More right than anything he had ever known.

At first, Glory and Santos were content with seeing each other two or three times a week, often for no more than an hour or two. He would meet her at school, the library, or mall; they would sneak away together. And at first, they were satisfied just kissing and holding each other, they were satisfied just being together.

But the more time they spent together, the more time they wanted. The more they touched, the more their hunger for each other grew. They got greedy. And reckless. Glory began taking chances even she would have thought risky before.

Those chances left her with a knot of fear in the pit of her gut, a knot that grew daily. Before long, her mother would find her out. And when she did, it would be over. Her mother would find a way to tear her and Santos apart.

Even so, Glory could not bring herself to play it safe. The thought of doing without Santos for more than twenty-four hours was inconceivable. It was as if she couldn't breathe without him, as if he were her sun and without him she would shrivel and die.

So she called on Liz to help her, to cover for her while she and Santos spent time together, alone and in each other's arms.

The way she had tonight.

Santos picked Glory up behind the movie theater where she was supposed to be seeing a flick with Liz and drove them to a remote area of Lafreniere Park, parked the car and turned off the headlights. The moment he did, Glory fell against him, laughing and lifting her face to his. He rained kisses over her face, tasting her eyelids, her cheeks, her chin and mouth, as hungry for her as she was for him.

While he kissed her, she stroked him, touching every place she could reach, wanting so badly that touching through clothing was not enough. She tugged his chambray shirt from his jeans and ran her hands up his muscled stomach and chest. Smooth, hot and irresistible; touching his skin was like getting a feel of heaven itself.

"I missed you so much," she whispered between kisses. "I thought today would never end."

"Me, too." Santos caught her mouth in a deep, hungry kiss. Then he broke away. "You taste so good. You feel so—" He groaned and caught her mouth again.

They kissed for a long time, growing drunk on each other, intoxicated with arousal, light-headed with the need for fulfillment. She fumbled with his shirt buttons, he fumbled with hers. She unfastened the last and pushed the shirt off his shoulders; he tugged hers over her head.

"You're so beautiful," he whispered, trailing his fingers across her shoulders, then the curve of her breasts, covered in soft white cotton. Goose bumps chased his fingers, and she shuddered, aching for a closer, more intimate touch.

She flattened her hands on his chest and leaned closer. She rested her forehead against his; his heart thundering beneath her palm. This was the point they had always stopped, the place he had always stopped them. But she didn't want to stop. She told him so.

"You don't know what you're saying."

"Yes, I do." She reached behind her, unclasped her bra, then let it slip down her arms. The cold air stung her breasts; her nipples drew up into tight, aching buds.

For one unending moment, he simply stared at her, his expression almost painfully tight. "Glory," he said finally, bringing his gaze up to hers, his voice thick with arousal, "sweetheart, this is not a good idea."

She caught his hands. "Yes," she whispered, bringing them to her breasts. "Yes, it...please, Santos, touch me."

With a low sound of pleasure, he did. He cupped her breasts, the heat of his hands driving away the cold. But still she shuddered. With arousal, with the need to have an even closer touch. She arched into his hands; then cried out and tangled her fingers in his hair as his mouth found her breast, then nipple.

So this was what real pleasure was, she thought, dazed. She hadn't imagined being touched this way could be so exquisite, so perfect and wonderful. This was the power her mother had over her father, the power Eve had had over Adam. This heady, sense-stealing bliss could free or imprison, she realized. It could be good or evil. With Santos it freed her; she felt as if she were riding on the wings of angels; his touch was so perfect. Being with him was so right.

He was her destiny; if she'd had even a glimmer of a doubt before, she didn't now.

Panting, he tore his mouth away and fell backward, landing lengthwise on the seat, bringing her with him. She sprawled on top of him, her breasts flattened against his chest, her sex molded to his. Hers soft, his hard—terribly, exquisitely hard.

"Santos, don't stop." She pressed her mouth to his chest. Beneath her lips his heart beat wildly. Though the car was cold, their warm breath fogging the windows, he was sweating. She tasted with the tip of her tongue, liking the sting of his salty skin. "I don't want to stop."

He sucked in a sharp breath. "We have to."

"Why? I love you." She moved her hips against his. "After tonight, we won't see each other for three long weeks." She thought of the rounds of Carnival parties and balls and dinners that would keep her away from Santos, and a cry of frustration rushed to her lips. "I want you so much."

"I hate Mardi Gras." He groaned. "I'll go crazy without you."

"Then don't stop now." She rubbed herself against him again. "Please, Santos."

Santos clamped his hands across the small of her back and fanny, holding her still. "You're playing with fire," he warned, his voice thick with desire.

She nipped at his earlobe, then mock-purred in his ear. "And I like it."

"Glory," he warned. "You'd better—"

"What?" She laughed softly and managed to rock her pelvis against his despite his grip on her. "What are you going to—"

He moved so fast, it took her breath. One moment she lay atop him, the next he was sitting up with her straddled across his lap. Her short denim skirt rode up, bunching around her hips, exposing her white panties and the mound of her sex.

"My little firecracker," he murmured, sliding his hands up her thighs. "What am I going to do with you?"

He moved his hands around to her fanny and cupped her, stroking and kneading. The sensation was exquisite. Pure pleasure. She arched her back and purred again, this time without mockery.

He murmured his own approval and moved his hands yet again. He touched her sex, covered with only the thin, soft cotton, and she sucked in a sharp, surprised breath. He drew his hand away.

"No..." She caught his hand and brought it back. Lifting herself slightly to accommodate his hand, she placed it exactly where she wanted it. She shuddered. "Don't stop."

He curved his fingers over her, and again she gasped. He had never touched her there—no one had, though several had tried. Now, she was so glad she had waited, so glad Santos was the first. She arched again and rubbed against him—his hand, his hardness—burning up, needing something she couldn't name but felt keenly.

He slipped his fingers under her panties and found her. She made a sound, one she had never uttered before, one that was deep, guttural, part pain but mostly pleasure.

She curled her fingers into his hair. "Don't...stop. Never...sto—" A moan slipped past her lips; she tilted her head back and closed her eyes.

Santos stroked, softly and lightly at first, then more deeply. She realized with a start that he was inside her, caressing, molding. The sensation defied description—it was hard but giving, invasive but welcomingly so. It was as if he belonged with her, inside her, as if they had been joined this way forever.

Her breathing grew ragged; she felt at once frightened and out of control, yet totally focused and fearless.

She rocked faster; her heart thundered; the breath shuddered past her parted lips. Stars exploded in her head. Glory cried out his name and collapsed against him, catching his mouth with hers, kissing him again and again. She was sweating, her heart pounding as if she had run miles. And her body throbbed, but not as with a wound. She felt deliciously, gloriously alive.

She nestled her face into his neck, murmuring soft sounds of thanks, sounds of complete devotion. Moments became minutes; her world slowly righted itself. She realized he was trembling.

Glory lifted her head and looked into his eyes, understanding suddenly. "Oh, Santos, I'm...sorry."

He ran his fingers tenderly over her damp cheeks, smoothing away the tears she hadn't realized were there.

"For what?" he asked softly, a smile playing at the corners of his mouth. "For making me the happiest guy in the world?"

"But how could I—" She flushed and looked away, then back. "But how could I have made you happy? You didn't..." Embarrassed, she let the words trail off.

He laughed, the sound low and intimate. He cupped her face. "By giving yourself so completely to me. That's how."

A lump formed in her throat. She swallowed past it. "I would give you everything. Now, Santos. Everything."

"No." He shook his head. "It wouldn't be right."

She covered his hands with her own. "Why not?"

"Because of—" He let out a short, frustrated-sounding breath. "Because of this. Where we are. The way we've been sneaking around. It feels wrong. It feels like a...lie."

"It's not." She tightened her fingers on his. "I love you, Santos. How can that be wrong? How can it be a lie?"

"You tell me." He freed his hands from hers, though gently. Even so, she felt the movement like a slap.

She covered his hands again, determined to make him see. "It can't be wrong. I love you more than anything in the world. You believe that don't you?"

For one long moment, he said nothing. Then he shifted his gaze from hers.

She caught her breath, hurt beyond measure. "Santos? Tell me you believe me. Tell me you believe I love you."

"I can't. I'm sorry, but I...can't do that."

She drew away from him. She couldn't have heard him correctly, he couldn't have just said—

But he had. Loud and clear.

He didn't believe she loved him; he didn't believe in her.

She scrambled off his lap. She righted her panties and tugged her skirt over her hips and thighs, feeling suddenly, terribly exposed. And vulnerable. What moments ago had felt more right than anything she had ever known, felt wrong now. Her vision blurred with tears, and she fumbled around for her bra. She found it, turned her back to him and slipped it on.

"I didn't mean to hurt you, Glory," he said quietly, handing her her shirt.

She snatched it from him, then put it on, her fingers shaking so badly it took her three tries to get it buttoned correctly. "You were just telling the truth, right? Just being honest. After everything, you still think—" She bit back the words. "Forget it."

"Maybe I don't want to forget it."

"Tough."

"At least I was honest."

"Meaning?"

"Meaning, you won't even say what you're thinking. Big, bad Glory is really just a chicken-shit."

He'd made her mad now. She hiked up her chin and met his eyes. "You big . . . jerk. You weren't honest, not by a long shot. You still think I'm playing a game with you. You still think I'm a spoiled little princess who cares about nothing but myself."

"Give me a reason not to."

She swung at him. He caught her hand; she swung out with her other. He caught that one, too, and brought them both to his heart. "Grow up. Kids sneak around. I'm not a kid."

"And you don't know everything you think you do."

"Then clue me in."

She wrenched her hands free, hurt beyond measure. "Why should I? You think I'm a spoiled princess? Fine. Great. I'm not going to prove myself to you."

She glared at him, willing him to back down, to apologize, but most of all, willing him to love her the way she loved him. Instead, he glared right back, as angry and determined as she was.

Finally, he swore, looked away then back. "If you loved me the way you say, you would tell your parents about us."

Her heart began to thrum, and she caught his hands, begging him to understand. "That's not true. You know 'why I don't. Why I can't. I told you about my mother. I told you—'' Fear choked her, and she struggled free of it. "Ask anything of me, Santos. Anything. And I'll do it.''

"Anything but this?'' She averted her gaze, and he sucked in a sharp breath. "But this is the only thing I want, Glory. So, what are you going to do?''

"She'll destroy us. She'll find a way.''

He opened his mouth as if to say something, then shook his head. "And this won't destroy us?''

Her tears welled, then spilled over. He drew her into his arms, and she pressed her face to his chest, wishing they could go back ten minutes. If only they could, she would change the future, somehow she would make it better.

When he spoke again, his voice was gentle, but his words firm. "I don't like sneaking around this way, as if we're doing something wrong. I don't like lying. I don't like what it means.''

"It doesn't mean anything, Santos. It doesn't.''

"It means you don't think I'm good enough for you.''

"No!'' She struggled free of his arms. "It's my mother! And my father. They're the ones—''

"Who would think I'm not good enough.''

She heard the anger in his voice. The accusation. Not just toward them, but toward her, too. As if her being a part of them had somehow tainted her. As if being a part of them made their beliefs hers, whether she acknowledged it or not.

Santos made a sound, part angry man, part hurt boy. "If my father had been in Comus, I'd be good enough. If I went to Tulane, if I were in premedicine, if my skin was as lily white as theirs, they'd understand our feelings for each other. Hell, they'd probably applaud them.''

"Daddy's not like that. He's sweet and understanding, but . . . but he sides with her.'' Bitterness and anger rose inside Glory. "He's always sided with her. No matter what she did or said.''

"I'm tired of lying, Glory. We're not wrong, but what we're doing is.'' He dragged his hands through her hair, smoothing it away from her face. "We care about each other. We shouldn't be ashamed of that. We shouldn't try to hide it."

"Don't do this, Santos. Give me some time."

"I want you to meet Lily. Tomorrow."

He had told her about Lily, the woman who had saved him from the streets. Almost defiantly, he had told her about Lily's past, as if he had expected her to cast stones. She hadn't. How could she have? His Lily sounded kind; she sounded as devoted to Santos as he was to her; without her, Santos might have died. But still, Glory was afraid. Irrationally, dizzyingly afraid.

She shook her head, her chest so tight with fear that she could hardly breathe: fear of her mother's power, of the future, fear that she would lose him. "If I meet her, it would be—" Glory squeezed her eyes shut, then opened them again. "I know you won't understand, but I have this feeling, this terrible feeling, that once someone knows about us, it'll be over. They'll find a way to tear us apart, I know they will."

"This is such a bunch of bullshit!" The angry words exploded from him, startling her. He threw down her hands, slid across the seat and out of the car. She followed him, shuddering as the cold, dark night surrounded her.

He stood stiffly, his back to her, hands fisted at his sides. His breath made clouds in the frigid air. "I won't go on this way, Glory," he said quietly, not turning. "If you wanted me, if you weren't ashamed of me, you would tell your parents about us."

"I'm not ashamed of you! You have to believe me." She went to him, tried to put her arms around him, but he shook her off. His rejection cut her to the core.

She clasped her hands in front of her. "I'm anything but ashamed of you. I want to tell everyone about you. I want to show you off. Brag to the world that you're mine."

"Then prove it." He turned and met her eyes. At the expression in his, hopelessness welled up in her. *She was losing him.* And her mother was winning.

She couldn't let it happen. She wouldn't. This time she would not let her mother steal her happiness from her.

Glory stiffened her spine fighting her fear. "I'll talk to my father. I'll get him on our side. But first, I want...I need to tell you something. About my mother. I want you to...understand why I'm so afraid of her. Will you listen?"

Santos nodded, and she began. Choking on the words, she told him about the library and little Danny, about her mother's insane rage when she came upon them, about her brutal, unthinkable punishment.

As she recounted the story, Glory gazed at Santos, but saw her mother's face, twisted into something grotesque and terrifying. She felt the punishing rasp of the nailbrush, the sting of the burning water on her raw skin, heard her mother's ugly, frightening words. She saw the blood leaking from her stripped skin into the water, turning it pink.

"I will cleanse you, daughter. If I have to scrub the flesh from your bones, I will cleanse you."

As Glory spoke, she unlocked the horror of that day; with each remembered word, with each recalled image, hysteria built inside her, like a powerful killer wave that could swallow her whole. Glory felt it happening, but didn't know how to stop or control it, didn't know how to save herself from drowning in it.

She began to shake, so badly she could hardly stand. She realized she was crying, sobbing. She curved her arms around her middle and sank to the ground.

Santos crossed to her. He scooped her into his arms and carried her to the car. He bent and fitted her gently into the back seat, closed the door, then went around. He climbed in beside her, then drew her onto his lap and held her. For a long time, he held her that way, rocking her, making low sounds of comfort and reassurance.

And she cried, until she had no more tears, until the horror of that day more than eight years ago had again receded to a deep, bitter place inside her. A stale, airless place, one without light or warmth.

"I've never told anyone else," she whispered, drained, exhausted. "Not even Liz. I wish I couldn't even remember."

He made a low sound of regret. "I'm sorry, sweetheart. Really sorry you remembered for me."

She glanced up at him; he met her eyes. In that moment, she understood how close to violence he was. She caught her breath. "Don't be. I'm glad I told you. I wanted you to know."

She laid her cheek against his chest, comforted by the steady beat of his heart. "Whatever I love, she takes away from me. Whatever joy I find, she finds a way to kill. It's always been that way." Glory shuddered and nestled closer into his side. "She'll kill us, too. Once she knows."

"I won't let her," he murmured, his voice edged in steel. "I promise you, she will not come between us. No matter what."

But he wouldn't be able to stop her. No one could.

Glory didn't share that thought. The future would come soon enough, she knew. For now, she would cherish this moment and pretend, as best she could, that tomorrow didn't exist.

She brought his mouth to hers.

and the impatient tat-tat-tat being brushed away. Some muffled snatches of words and then, silence.

She called into the phone, her heart... her mind stumbled, unable now to... the right words being. The Darkness had come for her. For now, she could no other short of...

27

The Darkness called her name. Loud, clear, the call echoed in her head, drowning out all but its twisted shouts. Hope dropped the phone back into its cradle and brought her hands to her ears. *She would not heed its call. She would not succumb, not this time.*

The Call became thunder, and she fell to her knees, doubling over, panting like an animal. She pressed her face to her knees. She had made a deal with The Darkness. Now she had to pay. Now, it demanded payment in full.

The Lord's Prayer ran through her head, as did the words of the Rosary and the Twenty-third Psalm. They jumbled together, creating a disjointed mix of promise and plea. Hope clung to the words, using them as a way to push The Darkness back.

"No," she muttered, then repeated it, louder. She squeezed her fingers into fists, so tightly her nails dug into her palms. Through sheer force of will, she fought The Beast's call. Finally, it dimmed. Finally, the thunder became a rumble, the rumble a murmur.

Then it was gone.

For long minutes, Hope remained on her knees, doubled over, exhausted from the battle. Her heart slowed, her breathing became deep and even, her sweat-dampened skin cooled. Triumph spiraled through her. She was safe. She had beaten The Beast again.

Hope straightened, then got unsteadily to her feet. She went to her dressing table and sat down before the mirror. She gazed at her placid reflection, looking for a sign of The Darkness but seeing none. A small smile curved her lips, and she unpinned her hair and began brushing it, two hundred strokes, same as she had since childhood.

She pulled the brush through her hair, her palms stinging, thinking back to the moments before The Darkness had come for her. Her mother had called to whine about having difficulty coming up with the last of the money and to ask if Hope really needed the entire five hundred thousand. Her accountant, she said, had warned her against liquidating all her assets.

Hope narrowed her eyes. She had battled The Darkness all her life. She had paid the price for her mother's sins, again and again. And yet, her mother had the audacity to hesitate to do her this favor. Did her mother think she would have lowered herself the way she had, if she could do without the entire amount? Did her mother really think she could go to Philip now, after he had accepted her story about a loan from an old family friend, and say, "Sorry, but I don't have all the money, after all"?

No, she needed that final payment. She had to have it, and had told her mother so, though in a simpering, pathetically distraught tone. So pathetic it had turned her stomach.

Hope yanked on the brush, wincing as it dug into her scalp, her thoughts turning to Philip. Oh, yes, he had grasped on to that story about an old family friend, grasped on to it like a lifeline. "You remember," she had said to him, "the one who gave us the Baccarat stems for a wedding gift, the horrible ones we exchanged." Conveniently, he had remembered.

Hope made a sound of contempt. He had been so grateful to her for saving him from his own stupidity, that he hadn't asked questions.

Though he'd had them. She had seen them in his eyes.

Hope smiled at her reflection. She had been relieved. And disgusted. Philip was a spineless fool.

In the mirror, she caught the reflection of Glory, trying to tiptoe by her half-open bedroom door. Hope swung toward it. "Glory Alexandra, is that you?"

Hope heard her sigh and smiled. Her daughter was up to something, though she didn't know what. Until she did, she would let her think she was getting away with it. Like her husband, her daughter was easily controlled.

"Yes, Mother."

"Come here, please," she called.

Glory appeared in the doorway, though she did not step into the room. She folded her arms across her chest, her expression defiant. "What?"

"How was *Mask?*" Glory looked confused and Hope narrowed her eyes. "The movie."

"Oh. It was okay." Glory shrugged. "Liz liked it better than I did."

"Did she?" Hope arched an eyebrow. "And why is that?"

Glory hesitated, her cheeks growing pink. Hope pretended not to notice. "She just did." She moved her gaze over the room, then returned it to her mother's face. "Where's Daddy?"

"The hotel." Hope made a dismissive motion with her brush. "One of his little emergencies."

Glory's eyes widened. "Mother! Your wrist, you're bleeding!"

Hope lowered her eyes. A trickle of blood ran from the handle of the brush down her wrist. A red smear marred the cuff of her white terry robe. She stared at it a moment, momentarily off balance.

Glory took a step into the room. "Are you all right?"

Hope swallowed hard, forcing herself to focus. "It's nothing," she murmured, setting down the brush. "Just a little cut."

She grabbed a tissue from the box on the vanity and wiped the blood away, then met her daughter's gaze once more. "You haven't forgotten we have several social engagements next week, beginning with the Krewe banquet?"

"No, Mother, I haven't forgotten."

"Mardi Gras will be in full swing by then. I'm afraid your little friend will have to do without you for the next few weeks."

Glory paled. "My little friend?"

"Why, Liz, of course." Hope searched her daughter's expression. "Who else could I have meant?"

"No one," Glory said quickly, hiking up her chin. "I just...I would never refer to her as my 'little friend.' It makes her sound like a child."

Hope studied her daughter a moment, then picked up the brush. "You know, Glory, if I find you have been lying to me, I will punish you. But if I find that you have been sinning against the Lord—" she met her daughter's gaze in the mirror "—I will make you regret it."

Glory shook her head, her eyes wide. "I'm not doing anything, Mother. Really I'm n—"

"There are places I could send you," Hope continued, enjoying watching Glory squirm, "where you would not be surrounded by constant temptation. Places where they have people who know how to control wayward girls."

Glory took a step backward, her face draining of color. "You would...send me...away?"

"I would hate to, of course. I know how you would miss your friends and your home. But if I have to, I will." Hope smiled at her daughter's fear. "Do you understand?"

Glory nodded. Hope's smile widened. "Good. You look tired, Glory, and mass is early. You should go to bed."

Glory backed into the hall, then stopped. "Tell...Daddy I said good night. And that I...that I need to..." She shook her head, looking almost panicked. "Never mind."

Hope turned back to the mirror. "Close the door behind you, please."

Glory did as she asked. As the latch clicked into place, the brush slipped from Hope's fingers, clattering onto the vanity top, sending several bottles toppling. The scent of *Poison* filled the room. Hope opened her shaking hands and gazed down at her palms, stained with red.

Sacrificial blood. Like that of Christ on the cross.

The Darkness was determined to have its lamb.

Hope brought her hands to her face. They were wet, sticky. A faint, musky scent mingled with that of the spilled perfume. Her stomach heaved, and she leaped to her feet and raced to the bathroom.

28

Liz grew more uneasy by the minute. She checked her watch and frowned. She and Glory had arranged to meet here, in the ladies' room of the Fairmont Hotel, at nine-fifteen sharp. That had been ten minutes ago. Where was Glory?

Liz stood and began to pace, a field of butterflies in her stomach. What was she doing? What had possessed her to agree to this crazy, dangerous scheme? She shook her head, suddenly dizzy with alarm. Switch places with Glory? Pretend to be Glory in front of four hundred or so people? She must have been insane.

Liz crossed to one of the mirrors above the sink and gazed at her pale reflection. She shivered. When Glory had first suggested they switch places at this *bal masqué*, Liz had been skeptical, though intrigued. It hadn't taken Glory long to suck her into the idea, explaining that it wouldn't be as difficult or risky as it sounded. She and Liz were the same size and general build; they even wore the same shoe size. The crowd was always huge, the ballroom dimly lit. Her mother never bothered her; her father stayed busy at the bar. If Liz kept her mask in place and stayed on the fringes of the room, their plan would go off without a hitch.

Liz had not only warmed to the idea, she had become excited. She had always dreamed of going to a real masquerade ball, like the ones she had read about in historical accounts of the Old South and in novels. She was curious, too, to see how the other half—Glory's half—lived. The clincher had been her desire to be Glory, even if only for a night.

Her cheeks heated, and Liz reached out and touched her reflection, more than a little embarrassed by her own thoughts. Who did she think she was? Cinderella? And did she think that just by wearing the glass slipper, she would become the real deal? That she would be the one who got the prince?

Right. Liz made a face and turned away from the mirror. Once an ugly stepsister, always an ugly stepsister.

She went to the bathroom door and peeked out. She could see all the way down the hall that led to the bank of elevators. No Glory. Liz sighed, shut the door and crossed to the powder-room settee. She sank onto it, propping her chin on her fist.

She should have known Glory would be late; she always was these days. Just as she, Liz, was always alone, always covering for Glory so she and Santos could be together. At first, her friend had called on Liz to cover for her every once in a while, and she had been happy to help. But lately, it had been every day. Glory was her best friend, and she would do anything for her, but she was getting tired of this. And resentful.

Liz sighed. She and Glory used to do things together—study or catch a movie, go to the mall or library, sometimes they had gone bike riding in Audubon Park. Now, the time she used to spend with Glory, she spent *pretending* to be with Glory. Liz sighed again. The price for having a best friend who was madly in love, she supposed.

Liz dug the toe of her sneaker into the sumptuous oriental-style carpet. The more infatuated Glory had become, the more Liz had begun to worry that she and Glory would be caught. She had never seen her friend this way, had never imagined she could be so...careless when it came to her mother. It wouldn't be long before Glory's mother noticed the change in her daughter.

If she hadn't already.

Liz shuddered at the thought and rubbed her arms. Hope St. Germaine terrified her, even though the woman had always been cordial toward her, even though she greeted her warmly whenever she saw her.

Liz didn't believe the warmth for a moment, she didn't buy the niceties. She had Glory's mother figured out. Hope St. Germaine had decided that Liz Sweeney was a good influence on her daughter, so she had sanctioned the friendship. For now. That could change, would change, if the woman suddenly decided that Liz was no longer the kind of friend she wanted her daughter to have.

Hope St. Germaine was a powerful woman. And cold. So cold that sometimes when Liz looked into her eyes, she couldn't suppress a shudder. Hope St. Germaine, Liz knew with certainty, would not hesitate to ruthlessly wield that icy power against her.

And if she did, Liz would have no way to protect herself. Liz understood that very well. She was not only distinctly without power, but in a vulnerable position, as well. As a scholarship student, she had to hold herself to the highest standards of propriety and morality. If she slipped up, she was out. The academy had made that abundantly clear.

A mother came into the powder room, two small children in tow, both tired and crabby. She herded them into the bathroom, then into a stall, and Liz gazed blankly at them, her thoughts still on Glory's mother. When she had tried to express her fears to Glory, her friend had insisted Liz was worried over nothing. Her mother did not suspect. And if she did somehow uncover her daughter's romance, it would be Glory who was punished, not Liz.

But Liz couldn't shake a feeling of impending doom, coiled like a snake in the pit of her gut. Glory had told her about her and Santos's fight. Glory had told her she intended to talk to her father soon; when she did, the jig would be up, all of them found out. Glory was scared, Liz knew, but not scared enough. Not enough to be cautious or play it safe, not enough to stop seeing Santos.

Not that she didn't understand Glory's feelings. She did, more than she should. Over the past two months, she had spent a good bit of time with Glory and Santos. Glory had said she wanted Liz to know Santos the way she did, that she wanted her best friend to think he was the greatest, too.

And Liz did think Santos was the greatest. In fact, she thought he was the most wonderful guy she had ever met. He was smart and funny and gorgeous; he made her laugh, he made her think, he even made her feel pretty. Liz drew in a deep breath. And he didn't think her being so smart was nerdy. He admired her intelligence; he had told her so. And they understood each other, in a way he and Glory never would. Because of their similar backgrounds, because they had both, in a way, grown up having to make their own way in the world.

She was more than half in love with Santos herself.

She caught her bottom lip between her teeth. She despised feeling that way. She despised her tiny, niggling, hateful hope that Glory and Santos would break up. It was disloyal and dishonest—even though she would never act on her feelings. Her friendship to Glory came first. She would never betray her. Never.

Not that Santos would ever look twice at her, anyway. Liz trailed a finger along the settee's pretty mauve piping. Even if Glory wasn't in the picture, Santos would be beyond her reach. He was too good-looking, too cool for a little bookworm like her.

Liz sagged against the plump cushions, drawing her eyebrows together, thinking of the future. Her future. Someday she would be rich and respected and successful. She would come up with a cure for cancer or invent something that would change the world. Then it wouldn't matter that she wasn't pretty or curvaceous or bubbly.

She narrowed her eyes in determination. A.I.C. was just the beginning. With top grades from the academy she could win a scholarship to any school she wanted. She would have everything she'd always dreamed of.

The mother and her children emerged from the bathroom; she hustled them through the sitting area and past Liz, sending her a friendly glance as she did. Liz smiled at the woman, reminded of her own mother. As the door began to shut behind them, Liz heard the little girl exclaim, "Look, Mommy, a princess!"

Glory. Liz jumped to her feet. At last.

Glory swept into the powder room; Liz caught her breath. Glory's gown was made of a delicate, shimmery fabric, its color the rich jewel tones of a peacock feather and laced in gold braiding. Glory did look like a princess. Like the princess Liz had always fantasized being.

Liz brought a hand to her chest, almost dizzy with excitement. "You're late," she said breathlessly.

"I wanted to wait for the perfect moment to slip away."

"Your mother?"

"Is playing queen bee, safely surrounded by a group of admiring matrons. She hasn't looked twice at me all night." Glory sucked in a deep breath. "This is going to be fun. An adventure."

"I'm so scared, I'm afraid I'll wet my pants."

Glory laughed, then held a finger to her lips. They tiptoed to the handicapped stall, slipped inside and locked the door. Carefully, quietly, they exchanged clothes. Glory had solved the problem of the obvious differences in their hair with a beaded snood; she helped Liz with it and with the dress's zipper, then carefully fitted on the elaborate feathered mask. Though it only covered half of Liz's face, it concealed her identity.

"You look fantastic," Glory whispered, eyes sparkling.

"Do I?" Liz gazed down at herself, smoothing her hands over her waist and hips, thinking once again of Cinderella. "This is the most beautiful dress I've ever seen. It must have cost a fortune."

"You can have it. Santos is all I want." Glory hugged herself. "Tonight's the night all my dreams come true."

Liz looked sharply at her friend. Her cheeks were flushed, her eyes sparkling. *Something was up. Something more than their switch.* Liz frowned. "Okay, Glo, spill it. What aren't you telling me?"

Glory opened her mouth as if to do just that, then shut it and shook her head. "Come on, you have to look at yourself in the mirror." She unlocked the stall door, peered out to make sure the coast was clear, then grabbed Liz's hand.

They exited the stall and crossed to stand before the mirror. Liz made a sound of disbelief. And wonder. "Is it really me?"

"It is." Glory smiled. "I told you you look fantastic."

Liz cocked her head to the side, studying her image, unconvinced they could pull this off. "Even with the mask, I don't look like you."

"But you look enough like me. Just don't get too close to Mother or Daddy."

Liz shuddered at the thought of Hope St. Germaine discovering their trickery. "Don't worry. I don't plan to get close to anyone. Especially her."

"Here." Glory handed Liz her evening bag, made out of the same fabric as the dress. "My lip gloss is in there. And a hanky. If someone gets too close, have a coughing fit and run to the ladies' room."

Liz took it, her hand shaking. "I can't believe I'm doing this."

Glory pressed a hand to her fluttering stomach. "I have butterflies."

"Me, too." Liz gazed at her reflection, wishing she looked a little more like Glory. "What if—"

"No what ifs. We're going to pull this off."

"Be careful." Liz caught Glory's hands. "Make sure no one sees you."

"No one will." Glory squeezed her friend's fingers. "Stay on the fringes. Let Mother catch sight of you every once in a while. That will satisfy her."

"What about your father?"

"I promise, he'll be at the bar all night. Just don't go near there."

Liz giggled nervously. "I'm so scared. But excited, too."

"I know. I feel the same." Glory hugged her. "I love you, Liz. You're the best friend in the whole world. I'll see you back here, at eleven-thirty."

"On the dot. Don't be late, Glory. Not tonight."

"I won't. I promise."

They crossed to the door. Liz peeked out. There was no one about, and she eased into the hall. Glory caught her hand, pulling her back into the bathroom. Startled, Liz met her eyes. "What?"

"I'm so... Do you—" Glory bit back the words, her eyes growing bright with tears. "Do you think Santos loves me? I just... I just have to know if I'm doing the right thing."

Glory's question, her uncertainty, affected Liz like a stunning punch to her gut. She sucked in a deep, steadying breath. "Oh, Glo... of course I think Santos loves you. I know he does. When he looks at you, I—"

Liz's throat closed over the words. When Santos looked at Glory, she ached. Because she wished someone would look at her that way, wished it with all her heart. And because she feared no one ever would.

She would never really be the princess. And she would never get the prince. He belonged to Glory.

"When Santos looks at you," she finished softly, aching, "I see the way he feels. He's crazy in love with you."

"Then why won't he tell me?" Glory's voice thickened with tears. "If I knew he loved me, I could face anything, Liz. Even my mother."

Liz didn't have an answer for her, and it wasn't until Glory had run to meet Santos and she had made her way up to the ballroom, that Liz wondered what Glory had meant about worrying if she was doing the right thing. What was Glory planning to do?

29

Hope slipped out of the ballroom. Her heart beat rapidly, erratically. Under her elaborate beaded gown she wore an old-fashioned black corset, real hose and nothing else. The corset stays bit punishingly into her flesh, and she was grateful for the pain.

She deserved to be punished. She was weak. And wicked. She deserved to be struck down by the almighty hand of the Lord. She heard the scripture in her head, pleading with her to stop, to go back.

She tried to cling to it, but the voice of The Darkness drove it back, insisting on payment, on satisfaction. The Darkness demanded to be fed.

Hope took the elevator to the fifth floor. She moved down the hall, without worry of discovery. If anyone happened to see her, she would explain that she had taken a room so she could rest during the ball. As she had taken pains for everyone to know, she had been feeling quite under the weather for more than a week now.

She neared the room. Her gown whispered against her legs like an illicit chant. With each step, the corset seemed to grow tighter, the pain becoming insanely erotic. The thunder of blood in her head reached a deafening crescendo.

Number 513. She stopped in front of the door and drew in a deep, trembling breath. Her procurer, a crude but clever little man, would have taken care of everything. He had done this for her before, many times.

A tag hung on the door, asking that the party inside not be disturbed. She knocked, anyway; she was expected.

From inside came a sound, one that was not quite human. Hope grasped the doorknob and twisted. The door swung open; she slipped through. The room was dark but not empty; she heard the man-creature's soft panting.

She fastened the lock and safety chain behind her. She unzipped her dress and removed it, careful to lay it out smoothly, then crossed the floor.

She made out his form as she neared the bed. He was naked and prone, tied to the bed with velvet cords.

With a guttural cry, she fell on him.

30

Santos stood in the doorway of Glory's pool house, gazing out at the swimming pool, finding it incredibly beautiful in the cold, moonlit night. A soft mist swirled up from the heated water, enveloping the area in a filmy cloud, creating a magical, private world.

He had been hesitant to come here, to her parents' home, though Glory had insisted that with her parents at the masquerade ball and the servants gone for the night, they would be alone, they would be safe.

He was glad they had come here. It had been wonderful to be able to lie freely with her, to stretch out and enjoy being together.

He sucked in a deep breath, growing drunk on the night, on Glory's scent, still on his skin, on the realization that she was his now.

He loved her. Santos squeezed his eyes shut. *Dear Jesus, how had he allowed it to happen?*

Santos glanced over his shoulder. The bathroom door was still closed; he heard the faint sound of running water. She had been in there for many minutes, more time, he thought, than she needed to repair her hair and face.

"Dammit," he muttered, knowing he had hurt her. She wanted, longed for, a declaration of love from him. She had for some time; he had seen it in her eyes every time they were together, heard it in her voice each time she had said she loved him.

Now, after this, after their having made love, she longed for it even more.

Their making love. Another thing he shouldn't have allowed to happen.

He stuffed his hands into the front pockets of his blue jeans. But she had offered herself so sweetly. And so passionately. Even as he had told himself to stop, he had been unable to. Even as he had assured himself he could remain in control, it had careened out of his reach.

He breathed deeply through his nose. She had been a virgin. *Had been.* No longer. Now she was his; he would never let her go. Not ever, not without a fight.

She opened the bathroom door, and light spilled through the dark pool house and across his feet. A moment later, the light disappeared.

She came up to stand beside him. "It's pretty tonight."

"Yes, it is." He drew her against his chest and wrapped his arms around her from behind. He rested his chin on the top of her head. "If I lived here, I would spend a lot of time right in this spot. Too much time, probably."

She murmured something he couldn't make out and leaned more fully against him. He realized she was trembling and tightened his arms around her, fitting her body closer to his. "Cold?" he asked, rubbing his cheek against her silky dark hair.

"Not now."

"Good." He trailed his fingers through her hair, a fierce protectiveness moving over him. He would do anything for her. Face any demon; turn his back on all he had known; make concessions he would have sworn an hour ago he would never make.

He loved her so much it terrified him.

If only he could trust her as completely. If only he didn't feel this nagging doubt every time he looked at her. She was too young. Too privileged. They were too different to ever belong together.

If only she had faced down her parents. If she had, he wouldn't be afraid to give her his whole heart, he wouldn't be afraid to trust. He wouldn't doubt.

A part of him understood her fear. But another part didn't. He needed her to claim him, to proudly tell the world, her parents included, that he was the one she wanted.

Until she did that, he couldn't give her what she longed for.

He wanted to. But he couldn't. It was as simple as that.

She sighed. He bent his head close to hers. "You're quiet tonight."

"I guess." She nestled closer.

"Are you sorry?" He held his breath, praying she didn't answer yes. If she did, he didn't know what he would do. He was sorry enough for the both of them.

"No." She tilted her face to his; she searched his gaze. "Are you?"

"How could I be?" he returned softly, evading her. "It's never been so . . . wonderful before."

That much was true. It had been almost painfully wonderful.

She turned in his arms so she faced him. She lifted her gaze to his. "Have there been a . . . a lot of girls?"

"Not a lot." He chose his words carefully. "But some."

She whimpered and curled her fingers into his open shirt. "Did you . . . care for them? Or for one of them . . . especially?"

"No. Not—" His throat closed over the words and he cleared it. "Not in the way I care for you."

She searched his gaze for one moment more, then lifted her chin. "I'm not sorry," she said again, almost fiercely. "I'm not."

He sucked in a deep breath, feeling as if he were drowning in emotion. He had to get a grip on his feelings, he had to keep this relationship in perspective. He acknowledged it was too late for that. Way too late.

"I'm glad," he murmured. "I would hate for you to be sad."

For long moments they simply held each other, not speaking but communicating nonetheless. Santos hadn't thought it could be like this between two people, a man and a woman. Hot and potent, yet sweet and enduring. It certainly hadn't been between his parents, or any other couple he had ever known or observed.

If only she were a woman. If only she were older. They could marry, run away together if need be, and never look back.

"What are you thinking?" she asked, drawing slightly away to look up at him.

He trailed his thumb across her full bottom lip. "Why do you ask?"

"Because you sighed."

"Did I?" He hadn't been aware of making a sound, and he wondered if she had somehow heard his thoughts. "I was thinking about *if onlys*."

"I don't understand."

He smiled. "One of my social workers used to repeat this ditty, 'If if and and buts were candy nuts, we'd all have a merry Christmas. Grow up, Victor.' She wasn't a particularly sympathetic woman."

Glory tightened her arms around his waist. "I think I hate her."

"Don't. I hated her enough for both of us back then. It's okay now."

"So, what..." She hesitated, as if questioning the wisdom of her question, then blurted it out, anyway. "What were your *if onlys* about tonight?"

"I think you know."

She did. He could tell by the way her eyes filled with tears, and she looked away.

"It's all right, Glory."

She returned her gaze to his. "Is it?"

He nodded slowly. "Because it has to be. What time do you have to be back?"

"Eleven-thirty." He heard the regret in her voice. "I promised Liz I'd be back then, on the dot."

"It's almost that."

Glory sighed again. "We'd better go. She'll be fretting."

Neither moved; seconds ticked past. Santos tangled his fingers in her hair and brought his mouth down to hers. He kissed her deeply and possessively, using it to tell her, in no uncertain terms, that she belonged to him. A moment later, he released her. "I wish we didn't have to say good-night."

"If only we—" Their eyes met and they laughed at her choice of words.

"Merry Christmas," he whispered.

"Same to you."

By unspoken agreement, they started for his car. "Are you sure," he said after a moment, "that no one saw you? That your mother didn't suspect or—"

"No one saw me. And no, Mother didn't suspect a thing. She hardly noticed me tonight, thank God."

He stopped and turned to her. "Glory, we need to talk about your parents."

She put her fingers to his lips. "Not tonight. Please, Santos. Tonight is too special. It's our night, and I...I don't want to ruin it."

He nodded, though his chest was so tight he could hardly draw a breath. He wished he could drive his suspicions away, wished he could force them out of his head and trust her completely.

He couldn't. No matter how much he cursed himself and his past, he couldn't let go and trust her. His life lessons had been too hard-learned for that.

"Okay," he murmured finally, taking a step away from her. "We'll talk about it after Mardi Gras."

She nodded. "All right. After Mardi Gras."

They finished making their way to the car. Santos unlocked it and opened the door for her, but caught her hands, stopping her before she climbed in.

She met his gaze, he saw concern in hers. He brought her hands to his mouth. "No one can touch us, Glory. Not if we really believe in each other. If we really believe, we'll be safe. I promise."

31

"Mrs. St. Germaine, there's a girl here to see you. A Bebe Charbonnet. She says she's one of Glory's friends. From the academy."

Hope recognized the name, frowned and glanced at her watch. "At this hour? How odd. Show her in."

Hope tapped her index finger against the gold rim of her china teacup. In the two days since the masquerade ball, Glory had been acting strangely. Excited. Nervous. Guilty but exhilarated. Now this.

Mrs. Hillcrest escorted the teenager in. Hope swept her gaze over the girl. She wore her A.I.C. uniform; she looked like the proverbial cat with a saucer of cream. Hope smiled and stood. "Hello, Bebe, dear. Come right in."

Bebe stopped before her. She clasped her hands together, two spots of color staining her cheeks. "Hello, Mrs. St. Germaine."

"How's your mother?"

"Very well, thank you."

"Do tell her I said hello."

"I will."

Hope took her seat, but didn't offer one to Bebe. She took a sip of her tea, then patted her mouth with a napkin. "What can I do for you this morning?"

"Well, I—" Bebe cleared her throat, obviously intimidated. "I don't know how to tell you this, and I...I want you to know I wouldn't be here if I didn't care so much about Glory. I hate to see her, you know, ruining herself over a...a boy like *that*."

Hope stiffened. So, that was it—a boy. She should have known. Glory was a Pierron, after all. She had The Darkness in her. "Go on."

"I was at the the ball Saturday night, and I saw—" Bebe drew a deep breath "—I saw her leaving the hotel to meet a boy. At about nine. They left in his car."

"Nine o'clock?" Hope searched her memory. "That can't be, Bebe, dear. I saw her at nine-fifteen and...after."

"That wasn't her! It—" She bit the words back, as if remembering suddenly to look sincere. She cleared her throat. "I think that was Liz Sweeney. Because I saw Liz in the hotel, and there was no reason *she* would be there. And I know that was Glory I saw leaving the hotel in blue jeans yet I, too, saw Glory minutes later. Or at least," she added triumphantly, "I saw her gown."

A switch. Glory and her friend had enacted a neat little switch; they'd thought they could fool her. *Devious, treacherous girls.*

Such deception would not go unpunished.

"You noticed quite a lot Saturday night, Bebe dear."

Bebe's cheeks grew pink. "Like I said, I wouldn't even be here, if I didn't care so much for Glory."

"I'm sure," Hope murmured, deciding she did not like this sly, self-important girl. But she could find a way to deal with her later.

Hope stood, shaking with anger. She crossed to the window and looked out at the bright, cold day. "Do you know this boy? Does he go to Jesuit or Christian Brothers?"

Bebe shook her head. "I don't know him and he...he looks older. In fact," Bebe glanced over her shoulder, then returned her gaze to Hope's. "In fact," she continued, her tone hushed, "he doesn't look like the type of boy who would attend either of *those* schools. He's a different type."

"I see." Hope swung to face the girl. "Can you describe him for me?"

"He's tall and dark and very handsome, if you like that type. He looks rough. You know. Kind of wild."

Hope remembered something Philip's secretary had told her, weeks ago now. That Glory had asked about that vile boy Lily had sent, that Vincent or Victor Something. Glory had asked the secretary if she had seen him, if she knew who he was. Of course, the woman had told her daughter no. But still, Glory could have found him, anyway.

Hope narrowed her eyes. Whether that boy was the one, or whether it was another, she had to get control of this situation—and her daughter—immediately. It was obvious to her now, she had been much too lenient with Glory.

"You should get back to school, Bebe dear. Thank you for this information. You've been most helpful."

"I'm glad I could help." The girl couldn't conceal her glee. She all but rubbed her hands together. "I hope Glory and Liz don't get in too much trouble. I mean, I would hate to think I'm responsible—"

"Don't you give it another thought." Hope walked her to the door. "I'm going to take care of everything." She looked directly at Bebe. "And everyone."

32

Two days after the *bal masqué*, during Sister Mary Catherine's lecture on Shakespeare's *Taming of the Shrew*, Liz's worst nightmare became a reality. The principal summoned Liz to the office; when she got there, she saw that Hope St. Germaine waited for her.

She and Glory had been found out.

Liz gazed at the woman in dawning horror, then shifted her gaze to Sister Marguerite. She held out the green call slip, her hand shaking badly. "You...you wanted to see me, Sister?"

The principal stepped forward, her expression forbidding. "Come in, Liz. Close the door behind you."

Liz did as the principal asked, though she could hardly breathe, she was so afraid. She searched for another reason Glory's mother could be here with Sister Marguerite, for another reason she could have been called to the office, another reason they would look so grim.

She came up with none.

Door closed, Liz turned and faced the two women once more, clasping her trembling hands in front of her. She looked from Sister Marguerite to Hope St. Germaine and back. *What were they going to do to her?*

"Take a seat, dear." Sister motioned toward the chair in front of her desk, then went and took her own chair.

Pulse pounding in her head, Liz did, then folded her hands in her lap and met the principal's eyes.

"Do you have any idea why I've called you to my office, Liz?"

Liz shook her head and clasped her hands tighter in her lap. "No, Sister."

"You're here because Mrs. St. Germaine has leveled some very serious charges against you."

"Against me?" Liz whispered, her voice sounding high and scared.

"That's right." Sister looked at Glory's mother, then back at Liz. "Can you imagine what they might be?"

She shook her head, her mouth dry, her palms wet. "No, Sister."

Hope St. Germaine cleared her throat and stepped forward. "May I, Sister?"

The principal hesitated, then nodded. "All right."

Hope faced Liz. "The time has come, young lady, to stop playing games. I know what's been going on. I know you've been helping my daughter to trick me. I know you've been covering for her, lying for her."

It had happened, just as Liz had feared it would. Glory's mother had found them out; now they were both in trouble. *Big trouble.*

Liz looked helplessly at the principal. She saw that there would be no help from the other woman, and her vision blurred with tears. Liz bowed her head.

Why had she agreed to help Glory? Why had she gone against what she knew to be safe and smart and done what Glory wanted her to do?

"You've been helping facilitate a romance between my daughter and a totally unsuitable boy. Haven't you, Liz?" Glory's mother let the words, the accusation hang in the air for a moment, then went in for the kill. "Maybe you even encouraged her. Maybe the lies and tricks were your idea?"

"No!" Liz jerked her head up. "That's not true! It wasn't like that!" Mrs. St. Germaine took a step closer, her icy blue gaze boring into Liz's. Liz shrank against the chair back. "It wasn't," she said again, this time weakly. "I promise."

"Then why don't you tell us what is true, Liz?" Hope smiled, though without warmth. "We wouldn't want to accuse you unfairly."

Liz drew a deep breath, feeling sick to her stomach. She wished she had never agreed to help Glory; she wished Glory hadn't told her what she and Santos had done the night of the ball. And she wished she could lie about her involvement in the whole thing. But she had the feeling Hope St. Germaine knew everything anyway, and if caught in one lie, her position would only be worsened.

"Well?" Hope demanded, impatient. "Did you aid Glory in her deception?"

Liz nodded, but didn't look up or speak.

"Is that a yes?"

"Yes, ma'am," she murmured.

"And on Saturday night, this last Saturday night, did you cover for Glory at the Leukemia Society's *bal masqué,* going so far as to change into her gown and mask so she could slip out of the hotel to be with this boy?"

Liz nodded again. "Yes, ma'am."

Sister Marguerite made a sound of disappointment. "You had such promise, Elizabeth. We believed in you. How could you have let us down this way?"

Liz lifted her gaze to the principal's, her vision swimming with tears. "I'm sorry, Sister. I didn't mean to... to let you down."

"The conditions of your scholarship are quite clear. Moral turpitude will not be allowed."

Liz jumped to her feet, panic taking her breath. "But I didn't know! I didn't do any—"

"Calm down, Liz," Glory's mother interrupted softly. "Perhaps, if you tell us everything you know, perhaps then I'll be able to convince Sister to be lenient with you."

A rush of relief moved over her. It would be okay, all she had to do was tell the truth. That wouldn't be betraying Glory; they knew everything already anyway.

Liz nodded and sat back down. "All right. What do you want to know?"

"Start from the beginning, Elizabeth. Start from when Glory met this boy."

Nodding again, Liz began. She told them everything she could remember, beginning with the morning Glory had met her at the streetcar stop with the news about having met Santos, to the *bal masqué* and what Glory and Santos had done together.

When she had finished, Hope brought a hand to her chest, the color draining from her face. "Are you saying that my daughter... that she and this boy, that they—"

She stumbled over the words, and Sister Marguerite stepped in quickly. "Elizabeth Sweeney, are you saying that Glory and this boy were together in an... an unclean way? A way reserved for married couples only?"

Glory's mother hadn't known. Dear God, what had she done?

"Elizabeth? Is that what you're saying?"

"Yes," she whispered, feeling sick to her stomach.

Sister Marguerite crossed herself; Glory's mother sank onto a chair, her face ashen.

"I didn't know," Liz said, tears slipping down her cheeks. "I only found out what they'd done...after. If she had told me what she...planned, I would have refused to help her." She brushed the tears from her cheeks. "You have to believe me!"

"And why is that?" Hope asked tightly, curving her hands into fists. "You've already proved yourself a liar." She brought a shaking hand to her head. "And now my daughter and this...this scum—"

"Santos isn't scum! He's really not, Mrs. St. Germaine. He's a nice guy. And smart. He goes to the University of New Orleans, and as soon as he's twenty-one, he's going to the police academy."

"That's enough, Elizabeth." Sister Marguerite frowned. "I think we had better—"

"But you have to believe me! He loves Glory." Liz wrung her hands and gazed beseechingly at Glory's mother. "He wanted to tell you and Mr. St. Germaine, he hated sneaking around. He didn't think it was right—"

"He did it anyway."

"Only because Glory begged. They fought about it." Liz swiped at her dripping nose with the back of her hand, and the principal handed her a tissue. "I tried to talk to her, too. I tried to convince her to tell you."

"But she wouldn't listen." Glory's mother stood, and collected her handbag and coat. "How convenient."

"Because she was scared. She said you wouldn't approve, that you would break them up."

"And why shouldn't I have broken them up?" Hope demanded, enraged. "This Victor Santos is worse than a nothing, he's a boy who preys on young and unsuspecting girls. He's despicable."

"But he's...not. He's—" Liz began to cry in earnest, her shoulders shaking with the force of her sobs. "If you would meet him, talk to—"

"I have. I know what kind of boy this Santos is." Hope yanked on her leather gloves. "Did you even once think about coming to me or Sister Marguerite? Did it ever occur to you that maybe Glory was behaving self-destructively? That she needed guidance?"

Liz lifted her tear-soaked gaze. "She's my friend. I couldn't...I had to help her. She loves him so much."

Hope looked at Liz, her icy expression filled with animosity. She bent down so that her face was level with Liz's. "I will not," she said softly but evenly, "have Glory go the wicked way of...so many other girls. Do you understand? Glory is different, she succumbs easily to temptation. I will make sure that doesn't happen. No matter what I have to do."

Liz shuddered and pressed farther back in her seat, feeling as if she had been touched by the icy hand of death. Poor Glory, she thought, her heart going out to her friend. What must it have been like to grow up with Hope St. Germaine for a mother? She couldn't even imagine.

And now she had done this.

As quickly as it had twisted, the woman's expression cleared. She straightened and glanced at Sister. "I can't tell you how distressed I am by this situation. Glory attends A.I.C. to protect her from these kinds of influences. Philip and I donate a great deal of money to this institution to ensure standards are maintained. I expect you to take care of this...situation immediately. Am I making myself clear?"

Sister Marguerite sighed. "We could explore several other options first. I hate to act rashly—"

"Rashly?" Hope repeated, lifting her eyebrows in cool outrage. "I hardly think what we're discussing is rash. Let's hope I don't decide to act 'rashly' at endowment time."

Sister Marguerite inclined her head. "I'll take care of it, Mrs. St. Germaine."

Liz caught her breath, looking from one woman to the other, hysteria building inside her. Glory's mother had said she would try to convince Sister to be lenient. Instead, she was the one insisting that Liz be expelled. Hope St. Germaine had lied, coldly and cleverly. She had just tricked Liz into betraying her best friend.

What was she going to do?

Heart in her throat, Liz leaped to her feet. She turned to Glory's mother. "Please, Mrs. St. Germaine, please don't do this. Glory's my best friend. I was only trying to help." She wrung her hands. "I'd never do anything to hurt her. I promise I wouldn't."

"It's too late for that now, isn't it?" The woman's voice shook with controlled rage. "You've already done plenty to hurt her. She's spoiled now. Ruined."

"I need this scholarship." Liz started to cry, great racking sobs of despair. "Please. I beg you, don't have me expelled."

"You should have thought of that before." Hope St. Germaine made a sound of disgust and turned to the principal. "Sister?"

The nun nodded, and Liz watched Glory's mother leave the room. She turned back to the nun. She saw by the woman's closed expression that she found this entire scene disturbing and distasteful. She saw that all the pleading in the world would be futile. But she couldn't just give up.

"Please, Sister" she begged. "I need this scholarship. I promise I won't get in any more trouble. I'll triple my hours in the office, and the rest of the time I'll devote to my studies—"

"That's enough, Elizabeth. I'm sorry, there's nothing I can do."

"But I didn't do anything, Sister! You're the principal, surely you can see—"

"The conditions of your scholarship are quite clear. You're required to hold yourself to the highest standards, both academic and moral."

"But—"

"You didn't. I'm sorry, but you are no longer welcome at the Academy of the Immaculate Conception. I'll call your parents."

Liz sank to the chair. She covered her face with her hands, crying into them. She had lost everything. Her scholarship. Her chance at the best colleges. Her future. *Everything. She had lost everything.*

Sister handed her a tissue. "I am sorry, Liz. You have an excellent mind, and I know you have a bright future ahead of you despite this setback. I hope you have learned something from all this."

Liz blew her nose. "Wha...what about...Glory?"

"That's none of your concern."

The principal started to turn away. Liz touched her sleeve, stopping her. "But what will happen to her? Has she been expelled, too?"

For a moment, Sister said nothing, then simply, without inflection, murmured, "Her mother, and the Lord, will deal with her transgressions."

Liz stared at Sister, stunned. She couldn't believe what she was hearing. *She* was being expelled for covering for Glory's behavior, but the academy wasn't punishing *Glory* at all. How could Sister do that? It was so unfair. It was so—

Then she understood. If her family donated the kind of money to A.I.C. that the St. Germaines did, nothing would be happening to her, either. The fact was, Hope St. Germaine wanted her gone, removed from Glory's life. And she had the money to see that her wishes became a reality.

Anger at the inequity of it bloomed inside her. And bitterness. So much for a Christian school. So much for the highest standards of moral behavior.

She looked at Sister in accusation, and the nun shifted uncomfortably under her stare. "I'm sorry, Elizabeth. But you have to understand, I have a school to run. I have to do what I feel is best for the entire student body."

"Oh, I understand." Liz stood, trembling. She hiked up her chin. "Money talks and poor folks walk. Is that it?"

"I'll see to it that your permanent record isn't marred. That's the best I can do."

Liz squeezed her fingers into fists, battling hopeless, angry tears. She had just learned a terrible and costly lesson. A lesson that her father—an uneducated laborer—had already known.

Life wasn't played on an even field. Money meant power and everything could be bought for a price.

Even a nun's good intentions.

33

Santos waited for the St. Charles Hotel's ancient elevator. He slapped Lily's envelope against his palm, wanting to open it, wanting to so badly his fingers itched to do just that, only barely fighting off the urge. He drew his eyebrows together. He needed to know what Lily was sending Hope St. Germaine, he needed to know what the two women's relationship was.

Only then would he know how to proceed.

The elevator arrived, and he stepped onto it. He punched the button for the third floor and slipped the envelope into his pocket. That morning, he had begged Lily to give him the answers he sought; she had refused. Again. Instead, she had said that this was the last time he would have to make a delivery to Hope St. Germaine.

He had found that odd, too. Something about this whole thing had his hackles up. Something about it didn't add up. And he was going to find out what. Today.

And today, maybe, he would tell Hope St. Germaine that he was in love with her daughter. Maybe.

Santos drew deeply through his nose, torn by conflicting feelings. He had promised Glory he would not approach her parents, he had promised to give her a little more time, to wait until after Mardi Gras. But in light of what had occurred between them two nights ago, he felt they couldn't wait. For better or worse, they had taken a major step in their relationship, one that demanded honesty. He and Glory had made a commitment to each other, the time had come to stand up and tell the world that they loved each other.

If Glory really did love him.

The elevator shuddered to a halt. He stepped off, angling past a group waiting to get on. He was one selfish son of a bitch. He wanted to press the issue, have it out in the open so he could dispel his doubts once and for all.

His chest tightened; his palms began to sweat, his heart to thrum. Fear. He recognized the symptoms. He didn't fear Hope St. Germaine, but he did fear her power over Glory.

And as much as he longed for the truth, he feared it, too. Because he feared losing Glory. He loved her so much it hurt.

Santos started down the hall, moving in the direction of Hope St. Germaine's office, a feeling of dread settling in the pit of his stomach. He shook it off and squared his shoulders. He had faced much worse than the likes of Hope St. Germaine; and as he had beaten those, he would her.

As always, she was waiting for him. Something about her expression, coldly triumphant, made his skin crawl. He put off the sensation to his complete loathing for her.

She came around the desk. "You have the delivery?"

"Of course." He took the envelope from his pocket. He held it out, narrowing his eyes with distaste as her fingers accidentally brushed his.

As was her custom, she checked the contents of the envelope, then retrieved another for him to take back to Lily. She handed it to him.

Santos looked at it, his mind whirling with indecision. Should he break his promise to Glory? He thought of the things Glory had told him about her mother, thought of the abuse the woman had subjected her daughter to.

Glory had a right to be afraid. He would respect her fear and her wishes—for now.

"Do you have something to say to me?" she asked, a half smile playing at the corners of her mouth. Again he experienced the sensation of his flesh crawling. He met her eyes evenly anyway. "No. I guess I don't."

He took the envelope, turned and crossed to the door

"I know," she said softly.

Hand on the doorknob, he froze.

She laughed. "That's right, Victor Santos. I know. Everything."

He looked over his shoulder at her, not completely certain he had understood her correctly. "Excuse me?"

"I know about my daughter's little defiance with you. I am not amused."

Several different emotions barreled through him: disbelief, surprise, relief. Dread. Heart thundering, Santos dropped his hand and turned back to the woman.

"Don't try to play dumb or deny it, Victor. I have proof."

He squared his shoulders. "I wouldn't do either of those things. I'm glad you know."

"Are you?" She arched her eyebrows. "Why? You want to have it out with me?"

"And what if I do?"

She laughed again. The sound slithered along his nerve endings. "Poor boy. She's really done a number on you, hasn't she? But then, I'm not surprised."

Santos fisted his fingers. He wouldn't ask what that meant, no matter how much he wanted to. If he did, he would be playing right into her hands. "How did you find out?"

"Why, Glory, of course. Eventually, she always tells. She can't seem to help herself. She throws her little tricks and defiances in my face, usually in a fit of pique. Last night was no different."

Santos felt as if the woman had punched him squarely in the gut. He struggled to keep his feelings from showing. "I don't believe you. Glory and I—"

"*Care* about each other," she mocked. "*Love* each other maybe?"

He stiffened. "Yes, as a matter of fact, we do."

She shook her head, her expression pitying. "You mean *nothing* to my daughter. *Nothing!* She's just slumming with you. And deep in your gut, you know it too."

Fury dimmed his fear, making him reckless. In that moment, he realized that without Glory, he had nothing left to lose. Santos took a step toward the woman, the blood thrumming crazily in his head. "That's what you'd like to believe, isn't it? That we don't really love each other. Sorry, Mama, but you lose. And we're going to be together. Forever, whether you're happy about it or not."

Angry color stained the woman's cheeks, and she narrowed her eyes. "You think so? Poor, delusional boy. You are nothing but a defiance to Glory Alexandra. A way to punish me and her father. For what? Giving her too much? For wanting her to grow up right? Poor little rich girl." Hope clucked her tongue. "So what does she do? Goes out and gets involved with a *totally* unsuitable boy. The kind of boy she knows we would never allow her to see. She sneaks around like a thief, she lies, she uses her friends to cover for her.

"It's tragic, really. She's always been this way. Reckless and defiant. And completely selfish. She never thinks about who she might hurt with her little games."

Santos struggled to keep his expression confident. The woman's words cut him to the core—because they were his own, the ones he had said to Glory only months ago, the ones he harbored in his heart.

He pushed the words, and his doubts, away. Glory wasn't like that. He believed in her; he believed in them.

He took a step toward the woman. "You're the one who hurts people. Not Glory. You stand there, thinking you're better than everybody else. Thinking you're so good and righteous." He shuddered with distaste. "Glory told me about you, about what you did to her. A nailbrush? You make me sick."

For several moments, Hope said nothing. She looked surprised, shocked; Santos told himself those reactions were not to what Glory had said, but by the fact that she had told him the truth about her mother.

"What has she told you?" Hope asked, her tone dripping pity. "And told you in an attempt, no doubt, to keep you satisfied with the nature of your little fling. Just another maneuver in her game, I'm afraid. A way to keep you from asking too many questions, a way to keep you from insisting on going to us. I'm sure she cried real tears, I'm sure she convinced you I was some sort of monster."

Santos flinched at her words, though he tried to hide it. He saw by her elated expression that he hadn't been successful.

"She told me the truth," he insisted doggedly, though his tone lacked conviction, even to himself. "I believe in her."

Hope narrowed her eyes and took a step toward him. "Do you really think my daughter could love someone like you? Do you really think she would choose someone like you to be with forever?" Santos felt each of the woman's words like a physical blow. "Do you really think I would let my daughter be with a person like you? Please," she said mockingly. "She's a *St. Germaine*. Who are you? A nobody. Nothing."

Everything she said mirrored his own thoughts and fears. Everything she said mirrored what he knew of the world, of the haves and have nots. Although it took every ounce of his strength of will, he remained outwardly calm and confident.

Inwardly, his belief in Glory and their relationship was crumbling.

He would die before he would let this arrogant and ugly woman know that.

"It's you who are in for a surprise," he said softly, evenly and with a confidence he was far from feeling. "Glory and I love each other. We will be together. Just you wait and see." He turned and started from the room.

"See her again, and I'll have you arrested."

Santos stopped, the coldly spoken threat resounding in the quiet room. He looked back at her, heart thundering.

"Have you ever heard of statutory rape?" She narrowed her eyes on his. "I see by your reaction that you have, though I can't say I'm surprised."

"That charge would be a bit difficult, seeing as we've never—"

"Oh, but I have proof that you have," she interrupted without inflection. "And I'll have your head on a platter."

He met her gaze as evenly as she met his. "I'd like to see you try."

"Do you think the police academy will take you then? Charged and convicted of statutory rape? And you will be convicted, Victor Santos. The St. Germaine family is quite powerful."

He hadn't a doubt about the St. Germaine power. He had seen such power at work before, many times. "Say what you want, Glory would never—"

"Glory will do whatever I say, whatever her father says. Despite her little defiances, she's very much a St. Germaine. It's to us she gives her allegiance. Her family. Don't ever forget that."

"I have nothing more to say to you."

"Not even goodbye? Go to hell, maybe?"

Santos turned and crossed to the door.

"That's right," she called after him, "go back to your dirty whore. Ask *her* about me. Then ask her if you're good enough for Glory."

Santos swung back to the woman. "What did you just say? Repeat it."

"Which part?" She laughed. "The part about Lily being a dirty whore? Or the one about you not being good enough for Glory? And you're not, you know. You're as low, as dirty, as the whore you live with."

He flexed his fingers, furious. He could kill her now, happily, with his bare hands. He had never hated as he did at this moment, never with such depth and fire. He now understood something of the human condition that he hadn't before, something of the extremes one could go in anger.

He strode to where Hope St. Germaine stood, stopping mere inches from her. He met her eyes.

"Say what you want about me," Santos said softly but with an edge of steel, "but never speak ill of Lily again. If you do, you'll regret it. I promise, I'll make you regret it."

34

Glory waited at the locker she and Liz shared. She frowned and checked her watch for the third time. *Twelve-twenty.* Where was Liz? She had waited here for her friend after second period, then again after third. She could explain away those no-shows; the ten-minute break between class didn't leave much time if you had to run an errand for one of the teachers—a frequent occurrence for Liz—or if you had to visit the bathroom. But missing lunch?

Glory glanced up, then down, the hall, her frown deepening. This wasn't like Liz, not at all. Her friend was almost compulsively punctual. Usually, it was Glory who was late, Glory who had to be waited for or hurried.

So, where was she?

A girl Glory recognized as being in Liz's third-period class strolled by, chatting with another girl. Glory hurried after her.

"Pam," she called. "Wait."

The girl stopped and turned. "Hey, Glory. What's up?"

"Have you seen Liz?"

"Liz Sweeney?" When Glory nodded, the girl shook her head. "Haven't seen her. She wasn't in class."

Glory thanked the other girl and returned to the locker. Something wasn't right. Something had happened.

Her mother had found them out.

Even as her heart began to thud uncomfortably against the wall of her chest, she called herself a fool. If her mother had found her and Santos out, Glory would have been the first to hear about it. Not Liz.

No, her friend had probably gone home sick. Or maybe one of her brothers or sisters had taken ill and Liz had been called home to help her mother.

It had happened before. *Sure it had.*

Glory shut the locker and started for the office. She would simply ask, and if Liz had gone home sick, she would give her a call and see how she was doing.

Moments later, she stepped into the office area. The secretary sat at her desk, eating yogurt.

"Hi, Mrs. Anderson."

The woman looked up. A strange expression crossed her face. "Hello, Glory. What can I do for you?"

"I'm looking for Liz Sweeney. Have you seen her?"

The woman's cheeks turned bright red. "Not since this morning."

Glory frowned. "Did she go home sick or something?"

"Well, I—" The woman coughed, took a sip of her Diet Coke, then coughed again. "I don't think—"

Sister Marguerite's door opened. "Joyce, could you get me . . ." The principal's words trailed off as she saw Glory. "Hello, Glory. What can we do for you?"

"Hello, Sister." Glory hugged her books to her chest. "I'm looking for Liz Sweeney. Did she go home sick?"

The principal frowned. "Aren't you supposed to be at lunch now?"

"Yes, Sister, but—"

"I suggest you go. Nothing here concerns you."

Panic took Glory's breath. "What do you mean? Where's Liz? Is she all right? Why wasn't she in class?"

The principal made a sound of annoyance. "I suppose you'll hear soon enough. Elizabeth Sweeney will not be returning to the academy. Now, I suggest you—"

"What do you mean, 'she won't be returning to the academy'?" Glory took an involuntary step backward, feeling as if the rug had been pulled out from under her. "Why not?" Glory heard the note of hysteria in her voice, but couldn't quell it. "I don't understand."

"You don't have to. As I said before, this is no concern of yours. Now, if you don't return to the cafeteria, I'll be forced to put you in detention and call your mother."

Liz had been expelled. Glory brought a shaking hand to her mouth. Why? What had her friend done?

Besides help her?

Heart in her throat, Glory turned and ran from the office. But instead of turning toward the cafeteria, as Sister had instructed her to do, she ran for the main entrance.

Sister Marguerite called out behind her; Glory didn't even hesitate. She had to see Liz. She had to make sure her friend was all right. She had to know what had happened.

Her mother. Dear God, let it not be that.

What else could it be?

She reached her car, unlocked it and slid behind the wheel. Only then did she glance behind her, half expecting to see an army of nuns, habits and rosaries flying behind them as they chased her. The parking lot was deserted. Not even Sister Marguerite or Mrs. Anderson followed.

Glory started the car, roared out of her parking space, then the lot. She darted into traffic, earning the blare of several horns.

Glory knew how much this scholarship had meant to Liz. She would be devastated.

Glory squeezed the steering wheel, fighting hysteria and a feeling of being totally lost. Totally alone. *Her best friend.* What would she do without her?

Glory broke every speed limit in her haste to reach Liz's house, and made it there in record time. She had only been inside the building twice before; usually, she picked Liz up at the curb out front. Liz's father didn't like her and had made no secret of it. Glory didn't care for him, either, so having a reason to stay away had been a relief.

She climbed out of the car, raced across the sidewalk, then into the building and up the sagging central staircase. Liz's family occupied half the top floor of the old four-plex. As she neared their front door, she heard the sound of fighting. Liz's mother and father, she realized, cringing at the sound of the raised, angry voices. She heard her name. And Liz's. Heard weeping. Glory took a deep breath and knocked.

The fighting ceased momentarily; the door creaked open. Through the crack, Glory saw her friend's tear-streaked face. Her heart turned over. "It's me," Glory whispered.

Liz slipped out, shutting the door behind her. They hugged, holding tightly to each other. When they parted, Glory searched her friend's devastated expression. Liz's eyes were red and puffy from crying, a bright red mark marred her left cheek.

Liz's father had hit her.

A lump formed in her throat, and Glory gathered her friend's hands in her own. "When you didn't show for lunch, I went to the office, and Sister Marguerite said you'd been expelled. I couldn't believe it. What happened?"

"It was so awful." Liz started to cry and Glory put her arms around her. "What am I going to do? I've never seen my father so angry. And Mama's hysterical. I don't want to go back to my old school, Glory."

Glory started to cry, too. "How could they expel you? You have the best grades in the whole sophomore class."

Liz drew away, wiping the tears from her cheeks with the heels of her hands. "You don't know?"

"No." Glory searched her friend's gaze, heart thundering. "Sister told me it was none of my concern."

"None of your concern?" Liz made a sound that was part laugh, part sob. "Your mother did it. I was called out of second period, and she was waiting for me."

"My mother?" Glory repeated, feeling the words like a punch to her gut. "My mother was there?"

"It was awful. Just awful." Liz brought her hands to her face. "She knows, Glo. She knows everything."

Glory stared at her friend, a numb sensation moving slowly over her, starting at the top of her head and inching downward.

Her mother knew. Glory took an involuntary step backward. *Dear God, what was she going to do?*

Liz brushed at her tears. "She knows everything. About Santos, the masquerade ball, me covering for you. And not just covering for you that night, but lots of others. That's why I was expelled." Liz drew in a shuddering breath. "Sister wanted to give me another chance, but your mother wouldn't let her."

Her mother knew. Glory began to shake. Her knees gave and she sank to one of the stairs. *Her mother would see to it that she never saw Santos again.*

"Glory, did you hear me?" Liz squatted beside her. "It's your mother's fault. She had me expelled."

"How did she act?" Glory caught her friend's hands once more, her own trembling. "What did she say about Santos?"

"About Santos?" Liz repeated, her voice sounding strange, high and tinny.

"Yes. Did she say anything about him? Did she say what she was going to do about us? How did she know his name?"

Liz shook her head. "I don't know. But I told her that Santos was a good guy. I told her how much you two loved each other, but she wouldn't listen. She called him . . . terrible names. She called me names, too, Glo. She called me a liar and—"

"I'm so scared, Liz." Glory brought a hand to her mouth. "She's going to break me and Santos up. She's going to see to it that we never see each other again. She told me she would send me away if—"

"What are you talking about?" Liz made a choked sound. "You told me she wouldn't take it out on me, Glo. But she did. If she found out, you said she wouldn't hurt me. I tried to tell you, but you wouldn't listen."

Glory blinked, focusing on Liz, on what she was saying, once more. "What?"

"You said she wouldn't blame me, but she did, Glory. She even blamed me for you guys, you know . . . doing it. I told her I didn't know, but she didn't believe me."

"Oh, my God." Glory's world crashed in around her ears. She couldn't breathe; she couldn't think. *Her mother was going to send her away.* She clasped her hands in front of her, squeezing them together so tightly they went numb, and rocked back and forth on the stair. "She knows about that? About what me and Santos did the other night?"

"I thought she knew." Liz shuddered. "By what she was saying, I thought they both knew."

"You told her?" Glory gazed at her friend, horrified. "How could you?"

"How could I?" Liz repeated, bright spots of color blooming in her cheeks. "You weren't in there, you don't know what it was like! You don't know how they—"

"I know *I* wouldn't have told that on you. Not that, not ever."

"Thanks a lot!" Liz jumped to her feet. "What do you know about anything? I was just expelled from school. I just lost my scholarship. And all you care about is your precious boyfriend!"

"That's not true! I do care about you, Liz. You're my best friend." Glory followed her friend to her feet. "It's just that you don't know what my mother's capable of. You don't know what she can do."

"Don't I? She had me expelled today for doing nothing more than being your friend. You're the one who did the deed, and you weren't even called to the office. You were told it was *none of your concern.*" Her voice caught on a sob. "My father was right about all you richies. This is all your fault. I hate you!"

She turned and started for her front door. Glory caught her arm, trying to stop her. "Don't say that, Liz. Please... You've got to understand."

"I do understand." Liz shook off her hand. "I was never your friend. You used me."

"No. That's not true!" Glory shook her head. "Don't you see? It's her. She's doing it again, taking away everything that means anything to me. You, Santos. She does this, it's why I didn't want her to know about Santos. It's why I was afraid—"

"I can't believe this! We're still talking about you!" Liz curled her hands into fists. "You're just like Bebe and Missy and all the rest, aren't you? Selfish. Self-centered. You don't care about anybody but yourself. I was so stupid, I thought you were my friend."

Glory wrapped her arms around her middle, hurting so badly she thought she might be sick. "I am your friend, Liz. You've got to believe me."

"You don't know the meaning of the word. You used me. I was convenient. I was the only one dumb enough to—"

Liz bit back the words, turned and crossed to her door. There, she looked back at Glory. "I lost everything. My chance at a great college, my chance at a way out of living like...this. Do you know what the public schools in this Parish are like? Of course not. How could you, Little-Rich-Girl? A.I.C. was my big chance."

"Please, Liz," Glory whispered, tears welling, then spilling down her cheeks. "Don't do this. You're my best friend."

"And I thought you were mine. Goodbye, Glory."

35

As Hope St. Germaine suggested, Santos went to Lily. He told Lily everything, about meeting Glory, about falling in love with her, about Glory's mother and the vile things she had said. He shared his fury, his fears and finally, he asked Lily the questions Hope St. Germaine had thrown at him.

Go back to your dirty whore. Ask her about me. Ask her if you're good enough for Glory.

Pale, shaken, Lily sank to the couch. She bowed her head.

Santos sat beside her. "Lily," he said softly, taking her hand. "Who is she?"

For long moments, Lily said nothing. Finally, she lifted her gaze to his. The expression in her eyes took his breath. "She's my... Hope is my... daughter."

Santos stared at Lily, stunned, disbelieving. He shook his head. Hope and Lily were... mother and daughter?

He cocked his head and narrowed his eyes, studying Lily, thinking of her daughter. He saw the family resemblance, one of coloring and feature, only now, after knowing the truth. That resemblance was obscured not only by age, but by something that ran much deeper than physical characteristics, by something that printed itself clearly on them.

Kind versus cruel. Light versus dark.

Good versus evil.

A chill ran up his spine. Even as he shuddered with it, he shook the sensation off. He thought of what Lily had told him of her ungrateful daughter and of her heartless desertion. He would expect that of the woman he had come to know as Glory's mother.

He had fallen in love with Lily's granddaughter.

The truth of that hit him like a thunderbolt. No wonder it had felt so right—so fast—between them. Something of Lily lived in Glory, something essential. And he had been drawn to it.

He cleared his throat. "Why didn't you tell me?" he asked. "Didn't you feel you could trust me?"

"That wasn't it," she murmured, her voice choked with tears. "I would trust you with my life, Victor. But I couldn't tell you. I promised. She didn't want anyone to...to know that—"

"That you're her mother." Santos made a sound of disgust, his dislike of Lily's daughter so potent he felt it like a physical thing. "You don't see anything wrong with that, Lily? It doesn't make you angry?"

"You don't understand, you—" She brought a hand to her mouth as if holding back a sound of great pain. After a moment, she continued, "She made a life for herself, a good life. A clean one. She left behind the Pierron legacy of sin. That legacy has been a great darkness hanging over my life. She's free of it."

"Glory knows about you, about my angel of mercy." He smiled, and rubbed her hand between his. "This is your chance to know your granddaughter. You've yearned for her, to be a part of her life, now you can be."

Lily began to tremble, and he tightened his fingers over hers. "She already thinks you're wonderful. Once she gets to know you, she'll love you as much as I do."

"No." Lily freed her hand from his, averting her gaze. "Never. I won't meet her."

"But why? She's not like your daughter. She's warm and loving and...she's like you, Lily."

The blood drained from Lily's face, and she swayed slightly, as if suddenly faint. "Don't say that. Never say that, Santos."

He couldn't believe what he was hearing. Anger took his breath. And frustration. He hadn't realized how deeply ingrained her shame was. And he hadn't realized that, in a way, Hope's hatred of her mother mirrored Lily's hatred of herself.

"This is crazy, Lily. You long to know her, to be with her. This is your chance."

She shook her head, shrinking back as if repelled. "I don't want her to know what her grandmother was. I don't want her to know what she comes from. Not ever."

Santos knew Lily well enough to know that she had made up her mind. He tried one last time, anyway. "That was in the past. That's not who you are. Your good heart is."

He got off the couch and kneeled before her. "Lily, I know good from bad, right from wrong." He caught her her hands again, forcing her to look at him. "You're good, Lily. You took me in, you cared for me and gave me a home. You gave me love. You did that, and I was nobody to you."

He sucked in a quick breath. "What your daughter did, how she treats you, is wrong. Your feelings are wrong. Knowing you would enrich Glory's life. Being with your daughter would enrich hers. They're the ones who are losing out."

Tears welled in Lily's eyes, and her lips quivered with the effort of holding them in check. When she finally spoke, her voice was a thready whisper. "I couldn't bear it if...if she rejected me, too. I couldn't bear it if she looked at me in that...way. I don't want her to know. You must... promise me."

He searched her gaze. "I can't do that, Lily. I won't make a promise I know I can't keep."

A tear slipped past her guard and rolled slowly down her cheek. "Grab your chance at love, Santos. But you must leave me behind. Maybe not today, or tomorrow, but you cannot be a part of Glory's life and of mine. You'll have to choose."

36

For a long time, Glory sat in the stairwell outside Liz's apartment, immobilized by despair and a suffocating feeling of dread. She didn't know what to do; she couldn't think, couldn't focus enough to decide on a course of action.

From outside, she heard the rumble of thunder. From inside Liz's apartment, the sound of silence. Finally.

She dropped her head to her hands. Her mother knew everything. *Everything.* A cry raced to her lips. If only she had listened to Santos. And Liz. But she hadn't, and now she had lost her best friend and faced losing Santos.

How would she go on without him? How could she go back to living the way she had before Santos and Liz? Alone, she had been so alone. And so very lonely.

She couldn't. There had to be a way to make this all right. There had to be someone who could help her. Someone who would understand and side with her and Santos.

Her father. He was the only one.

Glory lifted her head and wiped the tears from her cheeks. If she could get him on her and Santos's side, as she had planned to before, she could enlist his help in facing her mother. All she had to do was convince him that she and Santos loved each other and that they were meant to be together.

Her father would help her.

But she had to reach him before her mother did.

Without pausing for further thought, she jumped up and raced for her car. As she slid behind the wheel, it began to rain. Dark clouds obscured the late-afternoon sky, making it seem much later than it was; gusts of wind bent the branches of the ancient oaks that lined the street and whipped up trash and leaves from the curbs and gutters.

Glory made her way to the hotel, her mind whirling with what she would say to her father, how she would convince him. Once she had talked to him, once she had gotten him on their side, she would call Santos. She wished with all her heart that she had done this sooner, when Santos had urged her to.

But it would be all right. Her father would help them; she and Santos would be together. Somehow, her father would convince her mother to have Liz's scholarship reinstated. She held on to that thought as she fought her way uptown, carefully navigating the slippery streets and rush-hour traffic.

The valets were busy, so Glory parked directly across from the hotel. She hopped out of her car just as the sky unleashed a flood. Oblivious to the cold rain, she darted across St. Charles Avenue and into the hotel, acknowledging neither the doorman nor the concierge's greeting.

She took the stairs to her father's third-floor office, praying he was there. She ran past his secretary and into the office, slamming the door behind her.

Her mother had beaten her here.

Glory stopped in her tracks, out of breath, battling tears and disappointment, disappointment so bitter it burned her tongue. Her mother had wasted no time filling her father in. He looked as if he had aged ten years since she had seen him last, just that morning.

Yet her mother looked almost radiant.

"Glory Alexandra," she said softly but with an edge of steel, "we were just talking about you."

Glory shifted her gaze from her mother to her father, still hopeful. "Daddy, you have to help me."

"Help you what?" her mother demanded. "Lie to us some more? Deceive us? Your father knows about your tricks. He knows how you . . . shamed us."

Glory's eyes welled with tears. She held a trembling hand out to her father. "Please, Daddy, just listen."

Hope shook her head. "We expected better of you. We expected better than the behavior of a . . . a whore."

"That's not true!" Glory spun on her mother. "This is exactly what you expected from me. You're even happy, aren't you?"

"You hear the way she talks to us, Philip? Dear God, what has our daughter become?"

Hope brought a hand to her mouth as if heartsick and horrified; Glory knew better and looked at her father once more. "Don't listen to her, Daddy. She hates me, she always has. She wants to hurt me, to take away everyone I love. Please, Daddy, this time listen to me."

For one moment, she thought he would side with her, that he would stand up for her. Then he spoke and her hope died.

"How could you do this, Glory? How could you lie to us this way? We're your parents, we want the best for you. And you show your respect for us and yourself by . . . by sleeping around?"

Tears choked her. She couldn't have believed her father would ever say such a thing to her, that he would ever look at her the way he was looking at her now. "I haven't slept around! I haven't! There's only been Santos, and I love him. I love him so much—"

Her father made a sound of disgust, cutting her off. "Forget him, Glory. He's trash. He's a bad boy. The kind of boy who uses innocent girls—"

"How can you say that? You've never even met him! You've only listened to what *she* has to say." She heard the note of hysteria in her voice, felt the emotion building to a fever pitch inside her, but she could neither control nor stop it. "He's not trash, he's not bad! He's good to me. He's honest and smart. And I love him."

Hope crossed to stand before her; she looked her square in the eye. "That boy only wanted one thing from you. And he got it."

Glory recoiled from the venom in her mother's voice, the pure hatred in her expression. "That's not true! He... he..." Tears flooded her eyes, and she battled them back. If only Santos had said he loved her. She could hold on to that now; she could throw it up to her parents as proof.

But he hadn't said it.

"I love him," she finished, her tears spilling over. "With all my heart."

Her mother caught her arms and shook her. "Wake up, Glory! This boy is a user. You're only one of many girls for him."

"That's not true!" Sobbing, Glory struggled against her mother's grasp. Her mother tightened her grip, fingers digging painfully into Glory's flesh.

"It is true. He has other girlfriends, lots of them! I checked him out. If only we had known before you... before you threw yourself away on him."

"No! I don't believe you! There were other girls but they didn't mean anything to him. It's me he cares about. It is."

Her father made a heavy sound and crossed to stand beside them. He put his arm around Glory, trying to comfort her. Pitying her. "I'm sure you do believe you're in love with him. He's older, more experienced. A young girl like yourself can be easily convinced."

He drew her into his side. "I'm at fault, I know. I should have told you how boys can be, the things they will say and do to get what they want. Some boys will do anything to... to have their way with a girl. I'm so sorry, poppet. I know how much this must hurt—"

"Don't you call me that!" She jerked free of his arm. "You lost the right to call me that a long time ago. You lost the right when you stopped believing in me!"

He took an involuntary step backward, his expression wounded. "Glory, I—"

"You don't know anything about Santos! He's good and kind, and he loves me. I know he does!" She swiped at her tears. "I'm going to be with him. And I don't care what you two say!"

"I warned him," Hope said evenly, her voice, her words, cutting like a knife, "that if he saw you again, I would have him arrested for statutory rape."

Glory brought a hand to her mouth. *Her mother had seen Santos. She had threatened him.*

"That's right, Glory Alexandra. You're a minor. He's an adult. He took advantage of you. There are laws—"

"Daddy! Please!" She caught her father's hands and looked into his eyes, begging. "Don't you see what she's doing? She hates me. She wants to control my life."

Philip sighed and curled his fingers around her. "Your mother and I have disagreed in the past over discipline, but I'm with her on this one, Glory. She only wants the best for you. And this boy... he's not it."

When Glory tried to pull away, he tightened his fingers. "You won't believe this now, but someday you'll thank us. Someday you'll see that we were right about this boy."

Hysterical, Glory sprang away from him. "I hate you! You always side with her, no matter what she does or says. You never side with me. I hate you!"

Her father blanched at her words, and Glory felt a moment of regret, but she couldn't stop the flood of anger, bitterness and disappointment, from spewing from her. She wanted to hurt him the way he had hurt her, wanted to wound him for all those times he had given his allegiance to his wife, no matter what.

"If you loved me, if you had any guts at all, you'd stand up to her. I pity you as much as I hate you. Do you hear me, I wish you weren't even my father!"

Hope made a grab for Glory, catching her arms, her nails digging, clawlike, into Glory's flesh. "You will not see this boy again," she said, shaking her so hard Glory's teeth rattled. "You will not."

"Hope!" Philip shouted, grabbing Hope's arm to pull her off Glory. "For God's sake! Maybe we should listen to her. She's never lied to us before. Maybe this boy isn't—"

Hope shook off his hand, her face pinched with rage. "You know nothing, Philip! You're blind when it comes to her, you always have been. I'm taking care of this. I'm sending her away, to a school that won't tolerate this kind of behavior."

"No! I won't go. You can't make me!" Glory flailed out with her arms, striking her mother in the shoulder, then neck. Her mother made a sound of pain, released Glory and stumbled backward.

Glory turned and ran.

She cleared the office, and made the stairs. Her father called after her; she didn't stop or even pause. She heard him follow her, heard her mother shout for the secretary to call security.

Glory made it down the stairs and across the lobby. She stumbled and righted herself, then pushed past the shocked doorman and outside. Late afternoon had given way to evening; the storm raged at full peak now, the rain coming down in blinding sheets.

She ran to the edge of the sidewalk. Her hair and clothes were immediately soaked and plastered to her body. She glanced quickly over her shoulder and saw her father. He was right behind her.

"Glory!" he shouted. "Wait! I'll listen. We'll work this out. I promise we will."

She hesitated, then shook her head, tears streaming down her cheeks. Not if her mother had anything to say about it. Her mother would make sure she was locked away; she would make sure she never saw Santos again.

Her father called out to her once more. Glory darted into the street, then raced across it.

As she reached neutral ground, she heard the blare of a horn, the sickening screech of tires. She whirled in time to see the impact of the vehicle throwing her father into the air.

The next moments were a blur. She heard her own scream, the shout of the doorman, the hysterical babbling of the driver who had hit her father. She found her way to her father's side and dropped to her knees beside him.

His head was turned at an odd angle; he was completely motionless. But his eyes were open. "Daddy," she whispered, reaching out to smooth the hair away from his forehead. "Daddy, are you ... okay?"

His head felt warm, sticky. She jerked her hand away. And saw the blood. It was everywhere, mixing with the rain, creating rivers of red. She stared at it in dawning horror. A scream rose in her throat, it came out as a strangled cry of disbelief. Of grief.

She bent down, curved her arms around him and pressed her cheek to his chest, her own hateful words ringing in her head. "I didn't mean it. What I said ... I didn't ... I love you ... Daddy ..."

The wail of sirens cut through the night; she tightened her arms around him, sobbing. "Be okay ... Please, Daddy. I love you ... so much ... Don't ... leave me. Please ... you can't die."

Her mother came up beside her. Glory lifted her watery gaze. Her mother looked down at her, dry-eyed, composed. "Are you happy now, Glory Alexandra? You see what your wanton, reckless behavior has caused? You see what you have done? You did this. This is your fault."

Glory struggled to breathe past her tears, feeling as if she were choking on despair. "No, Mama ..." She shook her head. "No—"

"Yes." Her mother pointed at her. "He was chasing you. It's your fault he ran out into the street. Your fault he didn't see that car."

Sobbing, Glory buried her face in her father's chest, clinging to him. "No ... Mama, please ... It's not—"

"Yes. See what you've done."

Her mother knelt beside her. She pried Glory's arms free and dragged her away from her father. She caught her shoulders, then chin, forcing her to look at his lifeless face, at the rivers of blood. Glory's stomach rose to her throat. She clutched at her middle, doubling over.

"Yes," Hope said again, softly. "You killed your father."

at the door of the room. Glory's shoulders rose to the muscle by the front of her captor, doubt my every...

"...get to the sald eight, soldier." You killed your father.

37

Despite the continuing rain and flooding streets, a crowd had turned out for her father's wake. Friends and family, hotel employees and longtime patrons, all had come to pay their respects. Philip St. Germaine had been loved and respected.

Glory greeted each guest numbly, going through the motions but disconnected from everything but her own pain, her grief. And from the guilt that had a stranglehold on her.

She had loved him so much. He was the only person in her life who had loved her unconditionally. And he had died thinking she hated him. He had died with her hateful and ugly words ringing in his head.

Glory drew in a small, shuddering breath. She wanted her daddy back. She wished with all her heart that she could recall her words and actions; she wished she could turn the clock back to her eighth birthday, the year when everything had begun to change.

But she couldn't. Her father was dead. She had killed him. It was her fault...her fault. The accusation played and replayed in her head, along with regrets, so strong and bitter they burned like acid inside her.

She should have been the one struck by that car, the one who had been killed.

She wished she were dead.

In a way she was.

She drew in another choked breath, her gaze drifting to her father's closed casket. Her mother had been right. She had warned Glory that someday her recklessness would be her undoing. She had told her that someday she would hurt herself or others. Now she had. Her father. Liz.

Santos. Tears welled in her eyes, threatening to spill over. She thought she had cried them all in the last two days, she had thought herself spent. But no, she had more tears. Both tears and pain, it seemed, she had in an unending supply.

Glory squeezed her eyes shut, guilt and longing battling inside her, tearing her apart. If only she had listened to her mother. If only she hadn't been so reckless, so stubborn and selfish. She never should have approached Santos, never should have pursued him.

She couldn't love him. She had been wrong to love him.

From the foyer, she heard the sound of a commotion—raised voices, an oath, the crash of something hitting the floor and shattering.

She turned and her heart leaped to her throat. Just inside the doorway, Santos struggled to free himself from the grasp of two men she didn't recognize.

"Glory!" he shouted.

The blood rushed to her head; she began to shake. She opened her mouth to reply, but no sound came out.

In horror, she watched as Santos swung at one of the men, striking him, then breaking free. A woman screamed, the funeral-home director shouted that he was calling the police; Santos ignored them all and pushed through the crowd, heading toward her.

Soaking-wet, unshaven and wild-eyed, he looked like a crazy man, a savage among the silk dresses and dark suits of the civilized.

Everyone was staring at her. Whispering. Speculating. Glory folded her arms over her chest, shrinking in on herself, wanting to disappear. *They all knew. They all blamed her.*

A cry raced to her lips. She held it back. Barely. She couldn't deal with this. She glanced wildly around her, looking for a place to hide. She saw none and her heart began to pound, so heavily she could hardly breathe.

Her mother appeared at her side. She curved an arm around Glory's shoulders and Glory leaned against her, thankful, so thankful for her support.

Santos stopped before her. Her eyes filled, and she brought a trembling hand to her mouth, torn. A part of her wanted nothing more than to fall into his arms, to have him comfort her, love her. But another part of her recoiled from him. When she looked at Santos, she remembered her father's death. She remembered why he'd died.

Because of her. Because of her reckless, inappropriate love for Santos.

"Did you think I wouldn't come?" he asked softly. "Didn't you know I would fight an army to be by your side, move heaven and earth if I had to?" He reached out and touched her cheek, and her tears spilled over. "I'm so, so sorry, babe. I know how much you loved him."

"You're not wanted here," Hope said shrilly, pulling Glory closer to her side, away from his touch. "Do you understand?" She tightened her arm. "*Glory* does not want you here."

Santos didn't take his gaze from Glory's face. "Baby," he coaxed, "tell her. Tell her how you feel. Tell her how we feel about each other."

"You bastard!" Her mother's voice rose to a hysterical pitch. "This is all your fault! It's your fault Glory behaved as she did. It's your fault her father is . . . dead!"

Glory began to sob. Santos took a step closer to her. "Don't, Glory. You know what your mother's doing. We didn't kill him. It was an accident."

He held out his hand. She stared at it, horrified, feeling as if someone were sucking all the oxygen out of the room.

"Take my hand," he said softly. "Right here, right now. Show them all how we feel. Then I'll go. But we'll know, we'll both know."

Santos stretched his hand farther out to her, she gazed at it, seeing instead the image of her father's face when she had told him she hated him, then minutes later, frozen in death, his blood on her hands.

"If you love me," Santos murmured, "take my hand. Believe in me, Glory. Claim me. All you have to do is take my hand."

Glory whimpered, confused, hurting more than she had ever thought possible. Suddenly, her head filled with the sound of her father's voice, speaking softly and patiently to her, his voice filled with love.

"Family and heritage are everything, Glory. Who you are and who you will be. Promise me, poppet. Promise me you'll never forget that."

She had forgotten. She never would again. Her place was here, with her mother, her family. She owed her allegiance to them, and to the St. Germaine name.

Glory shook her head, her body quaking with the force of her tears. She turned away from Santos and toward her mother, pressing her face into Hope's shoulder.

A moment later, he was gone.

Part 6

Forbidden Fruit

38

New Orleans, Louisiana.
1995

The Snow White Killer had struck again. Santos received notification at 2:57 a.m. Twenty-six minutes later, he wheeled his car to a stop in front of St. Louis Cathedral. The first officers at the scene had already cordoned off the area. The coroner had arrived, as had the crime-scene unit. As he threw his car into Park, the Channel Four news van arrived, and Hoda Kotb and her crew hopped out.

Santos waited until the reporter had moved away before opening his car door and climbing out. He surveyed the scene. The cathedral was lit up like a Christmas tree. A rowdy crowd had gathered, a mix of people—some who worked in the Quarter, some who were residents, but most were late-night partyers, many of them more than five-sheets-to-the-wind drunk. At least a dozen uniforms lined the perimeter of the scene, keeping the area secure and the crowd under control.

Santos drew in a deep breath. In his ten years on the force, he had arrived at hundreds of such scenes. They didn't much affect him anymore. But arriving at this one did. He swore under his breath. This one was his case, his baby; this one was personal.

He wanted to catch this sick bastard, wanted to so badly it burned in the pit of his gut. So far, he had gotten nowhere. This guy was slick. He was smart, he was organized and he was a predator.

Santos flashed his badge and crossed the yellow line. As he did, two tourists nearby snapped his picture, their flashes nearly blinding him. He swung toward the closest uniform. "Take care of that, will you? Jesus, you'd think they'd be happy with a postcard of a riverboat or something."

The uniform shrugged. "What visit to sin city is complete without a photo from a murder scene?"

"Yeah, right." Santos shook his head. "And we think the criminals are twisted."

"Detective Santos?"

Santos turned. A uniformed officer approached him, one he recognized from downtown. "Grady. What've we got?"

"Another dead hooker. No confirmation on that yet, but it seems clear we're dealing with the same guy." He cleared his throat. "That's four in four months."

"I can count," Santos said tightly. "Go on."

"A couple drunk tourists found her. Damn near tripped over the body. The guy lost his cookies. Pathetic."

"Tourists. Fuck." Santos let out a frustrated breath. "The mayor's going to be breathing down all our asses."

"I hear he's on his way."

Santos swore again. "Where are they?" The officer motioned toward a couple huddled under a blanket on a bench in front of the cathedral. "I want to talk to them."

"Got it."

"The body?"

"Our boy laid her out right at the church door. Can you believe that shit? Nobody's got any respect anymore."

Santos nodded, though he only half listened to his fellow officer's editorializing as they made their way across the sidewalk and up the couple steps that led to the cathedral's main entrance.

Just as the uniform had said, there she was, laid out the same as the other three had been, pretty as a picture, this time right at the cathedral's front door. Most killers of this ilk left their victims mutilated or in exaggerated, degrading positions. Not this guy. He arranged his girls with their hands folded on their chests, legs together, eyes closed, freshly washed hair spread out around their heads. Just like Snow White in her glass casket. She could be sleeping. Or praying.

Only she wasn't. She was dead as dead got, brutally murdered.

Santos squatted beside the body. The coroner, a middle-aged woman with sandy hair, freckles and a cherubic face, looked at him. "Hello, Detective. Our friend's keeping busy."

"I see that." Santos slipped on rubber gloves. "What've we got?"

"White female. Dark-haired. Young, I'd guess eighteen to twenty."

"Hooker?"

"That's my guess, if we're dealing with the same perp. You recognize her?"

Santos shook his head. He'd worked French Quarter vice for three years before moving over to homicide, but working girls turned over pretty quickly, especially the young ones. Besides, the Snow White Killer—so dubbed by the press—bathed his victims after killing them, washing and drying their hair, removing their makeup and jewelry, then dressing them in virginal white cotton gowns. The girls were harder to recognize cleaned up.

Santos lifted his gaze to Grady. "There're some working girls out there. See if any of them can make her."

Grady nodded and hurried off.

Santos moved his gaze carefully over the victim, noting every detail. "Cause of death?"

"Suffocation is my guess. I'll know for sure after the autopsy. But the body looks perfect. No bruises, no sign of a struggle."

"She looks pretty fresh."

"She hasn't been dead long." The medical examiner pursed her lips. "Our boy's getting pretty cocky, dumping her here."

"He's taunting us." Santos lifted his gaze, scanned the scene, then met her eyes again. "The apple?"

"Already collected. As before, a bite's missing from both sides. Unlike the others, however, I don't see any residue in her teeth. Look at this."

The medical examiner carefully wedged back the victims folded hands. Rigor mortis had begun to set in, but Santos could clearly see part of the imprint of a cross burned into her palms. Same as the other three. That particular part of the killer's ritual the department had kept from the press.

Santos nodded, and the M.E. eased the hands back into place. "Any chance we're dealing with a different perp?" he asked.

"Not in my book, but the tests will tell the tale."

Santos stood. "I'll call you tomorrow."

"Make that late tomorrow," she murmured, returning to her work. "I've got others ahead of her in line."

Santos didn't reply. He was already thinking ahead to the tourists and the questions he would ask them.

Hours later, Santos stopped in front of a trendy-looking restaurant, shrugged out of his jacket and loosened his tie. The midafternoon sun, warm even for March, beat down on the French Quarter sidewalk. He was hot, tired and frustrated. He'd spent the last four hours working the streets, talking to club owners and bartenders, flashing this latest victim's picture and hoping to find someone who had seen something.

So far, nothing.

And now this. The Garden of Earthly Delights. Damn. His partner had done it again—set out to poison him with health food.

Santos entered the restaurant, a yuppie affair with quirky painted wall murals and an abundance of plants. He glanced around, and spotted his friend and partner—it wasn't difficult, aside from the bartender, he was the only man in the establishment and was nearly six foot four,

completely bald and as black as black got—and picked his
way through the tiny eatery. Santos took a seat across from
the other man, then glanced around the restaurant with
exaggerated suspicion. "I hate this place."

Jackson laughed. "It's new. I hear it's good."

"From Helga the horrible, no doubt."

"Those are fighting words, my friend." His partner
narrowed his eyes, and Santos fought back a grin. "You're
talking about my wife."

"Nice lady. Bad taste in restaurants."

"Fuck you."

Santos laughed and picked up the menu. "I hope they
have something besides rabbit food."

He and his partner—his parents had actually named him
Andrew Jackson—were the antithesis of each other. Jackson, married with kids, was a family man in every sense of
the word. He was practical, his approach to his work cool,
detached. An excellent cop, he believed in leaving his cases
at the precinct when he went home at night.

Santos, on the other hand, was a workaholic and a loner.
Other than Lily, he had no family and no one he cared
about. He approached his work passionately, at times becoming almost obsessed with a case. If his body didn't demand food and rest, he would work around the clock. On
more than one occasion, his passion for his work had gotten his ass in a sling with superiors; those same superiors
had been known to call him dangerous, irresponsible and
a hothead. It really pissed them off that he was also one of
the most decorated officers on the force.

Yet, despite their differences, he and Jackson made a
good team. They had worked together for six years, each
having saved the other's butt more times than either wanted
to count. Next to Lily, Santos counted Jackson as the only
person he trusted enough to call friend.

All that aside, he couldn't abide the healthy crap the man
liked to eat.

Santos scanned the menu, settled on the least unappetizing item, then set the cardboard placard aside. "You're sure it was your turn to choose?"

"Yup." A smile tugged at the corners of his friend's mouth. "Last time, we went to Port of Call. I was sick for a week from all the grease."

"For a tough guy, you sure sound like a mama's boy."

Jackson laughed and rocked back in his chair. He folded his arms across his chest. "I suppose that's so, but this mama's boy's gonna live a long time."

The waitress approached, took their orders, then left. Santos watched her walk away, enjoying the inviting sway of her hips, then turned back to his partner. "Any luck this morning?"

"A couple of hookers IDed the girl. Her name was Kathi. Hasn't been on the street too long. No pimp, no boyfriend, no drugs."

"This guy's really starting to tick me off." Santos frowned, running the details of the case over in his mind, picking them apart, one by one. "We're missing something."

"But what?" Jackson leaned forward and the front legs of his chair hit the wood floor. "We've had four victims now. All working girls. All young, brunette, Caucasians. All from the French Quarter. All killed the same way, no variations. By each is left a red apple, a bite taken from both sides. And in every case, one bite matches the victim's, the other, presumably, the murderer's."

"And the palms of each victim have been branded with the image of the cross," Santos finished, rubbing his index finger along the side of his nose. "I know. But there's got to be... something. Some avenue we've overlooked."

The waitress brought their ice teas, smiling at Santos as she put them down. He smiled back, though his thoughts were, now, miles—and years—away from the pretty blonde. He was remembering another murder, another slaughtered working girl.

And remembering the fifteen-year-old boy who had lost everything with her death, the boy who had wanted to die, too.

"We'll get him, partner," Jackson murmured, as if reading Santos's mind. "One of these days, he'll slip up, he'll get sloppy and leave us a witness or something else to go on, and we'll nail him."

Santos met his friend's eyes. "But how many girls have to die first?"

On the TV above the bar, the talk show in progress was interrupted for a newsbreak. The news anchor announced that the Snow White Killer had struck again, then switched to a clip from the mayor's morning press conference. The mayor, playing the outraged politician, criticized the N.O.P.D.'s handling of the case and vowed to clean up the city.

Santos watched the mayor preach and promise, then made a sound of disgust. "What an asshole."

Jackson shook his head. "More than a murder a day in this town, we're understaffed and underfunded, and he's demanding to know why we haven't caught this guy? Sometimes this job really sucks."

Santos took a long swallow of his tea. "What really sucks is, until now, this case has been a low priority downtown. *Just hookers being killed,*" he mocked. "Now, because a couple tourists stumbled over a victim, everybody's up in arms."

Santos heard the bitterness in his own voice. That's why this case was his baby—he really cared that those girls had been butchered. He felt for them, their families. He knew what it was like to lose someone that way and to have no one give a damn.

Jackson was quiet a moment, then he met Santos's gaze evenly. "These girls aren't your mother, Santos. This guy is not the same guy."

"How do you know he's not the same guy?"

"The M.O. is all wrong." Jackson began ticking off the differences. "He uses suffocation, not a knife. He has sex with them after they're dead, not before. And how long's it been? Twenty years?"

"Sixteen." Santos narrowed his eyes. "It's the apple, man. What about the apple? One was found beside my mother, too."

"A coincidence. The guy was hungry."

"You're probably right, but—" Santos bit back the words as the waitress arrived with their meals. He didn't even glance at it, resuming his thoughts as soon as she'd gotten out of earshot. "I've got this feeling, Jackson. Remember the way I felt during the Ledet case? Remember, right before we busted that scumbag son of a bitch?"

Jackson nodded and dug into his salad. "I remember."

Santos took a halfhearted bite of his vegetarian burger, found that it wasn't bad, then returned to the discussion at hand. "I don't know, it's like . . . I feel the same way, man. And the feeling is strong."

"Wishful thinking, buddy."

"Maybe. You're proba—" He wiped his mouth with his napkin, then tossed it down, frustrated. "No, not maybe," he said. "No, not wishful thinking."

"Santos—"

"Just hear me out. We both know a serial killer's ritual rarely springs forth full-blown. It develops over time, as he learns what most satisfies him. We also know that serial killers sometimes move around the country, killing, then moving on, sometimes operating for years that way."

"Sixteen years?"

"Henry Lee Lucas operated for thirteen years. John Wayne Gacy for over ten. The casebooks are full of them."

"Man, you are dangerously close to losing your objectivity on this one."

Santos narrowed his eyes. "Is that so?"

"It is."

"Well, fuck you."

"Yeah, well, fuck you, too."

They looked each other in the eye, then they both laughed.

During the rest of their meal, they talked about their cases, Jackson's family and Lily's health. Santos didn't bring up the Snow White Killer again or the possibility that he might be the same man who had killed his mother, though it stayed on his mind.

When they'd finished their lunches and paid the bill, they stood and started out of the restaurant. Jackson motioned toward the rest room. "I'm going to hit the john."

"I'll meet you out front." He started for the door, stopping when he heard his name.

He turned. The woman who had come up behind him was attractive in a quiet, wholesome kind of way. She had light brown hair and a slim, willowy build. She worked at the restaurant; he remembered glancing at her when he walked in. But he didn't recognize her.

She smiled. "Santos? Is that you?"

"It is." He returned her smile. "But you have me at a disadvantage here. I'm sorry, do I know you?"

"It's Liz. Liz Sweeney."

It took another moment for realization to dawn. When it did, he shook his head, not quite believing his eyes. "Liz Sweeney?" He laughed. "But you're all grown-up."

"So are you." She echoed his laugh and held out her hand. "It's good to see you again."

He took her hand and smiled, immediately liking the woman she had become. "How are you?"

"Great." She motioned with her free hand. "This is my place."

"Really." Santos whistled softly. "I'm impressed. Good for you."

He realized that he was still holding her hand, and let it go, though regretfully. He had liked holding it. It had felt . . . nice.

Liz cleared her throat. "I was glad to see some men in here. I'm afraid that so far, my clientele has been a bit skewed to the fairer sex." She folded her arms across her chest. "I hope you enjoyed your lunch."

"It was terrific. You—"

"Actually," Jackson said, coming up to stand beside them, "you need to add a little dead cow to the menu for this guy." He held out his hand, and Liz took it. "Andrew Jackson. Victor's only friend."

"Don't mind him," Santos said, rolling his eyes at Liz. "He likes to say that. It makes him feel important. My partner, Detective Andrew Jackson. Jackson, this is Liz Sweeney. An old friend of mine."

"Really? An old friend?" Jackson moved his gaze speculatively between them. "Nice to meet you, Liz."

"Nice to meet you."

"So, how did you two know each other?"

Santos looked at Liz, then away. "I dated a friend of hers." He met her gaze again. "How is Glory?" Even as he asked the question, he cursed himself for it, cursed himself for his weakness.

Her expression cooled. "I don't know. I haven't spoken to her in years."

Ten, he would bet.

Santos gazed at her a moment, seeing the open animosity in her face. An animosity for Glory that mirrored his own. It made him feel strange, it made him remember more than he cared to.

She shifted, as if suddenly at a loss for words. As if she, too, suddenly felt swamped by the past. She cleared her throat. "So, you're partners. That must mean you did it, Santos. You're a cop, just like you always wanted to be. Your dream came true."

Beside him Jackson snorted. "Some dream, buddy. Long hours, low pay, no respect. Get a life."

Santos ignored him. "Yeah, that's me, Detective Santos, supercop, homicide division. At your service."

They talked a moment more, then Jackson interrupted them. "Look, man, we'd better get back." He smiled at Liz. "Nice meeting you, Liz Sweeney. I hope I see you again sometime."

Her gaze slid to Santos, then away. "Same here, Detective."

Santos coughed. "I guess I'd better... It was great seeing you, Liz. I'm glad you're doing so well."

She took a step back. "Great seeing you."

She said another goodbye, then turned and started for the kitchen. He joined Jackson at the door, then stopped and glanced back. At the same moment, she looked back at him.

Their gazes met; he caught his breath.

"Hold on, Jackson," Santos murmured. "I'll be right back."

Santos strode across to where she stood, never taking his gaze from hers. He stopped before her. "Would you like to go to dinner sometime?"

She searched his gaze. "With you?"

"Yeah, with me." He grinned. "Sorry, but Jackson's already taken."

She laughed. "With you, I'd like to go to dinner. Anytime."

He grinned, pleased with her answer, her candor and obvious self-assurance. "How about tonight?"

"Tonight's perfect. It has to be late, though. I don't close the kitchen until nine."

"Great. It's a date, then." His lips lifted. "I'll see you at nine, Liz."

39

Later that night, Santos let himself into his and Lily's apartment. He smiled to himself, thinking about Liz, their date, about their good-night kiss. His smile widened as he remembered the way she had melted against him, the way she had whispered for more. They could have become lovers tonight; if he had made the first move, she would have made the second.

Santos locked the door behind him, and moved through the apartment, turning off lights as he went. He liked Liz. He felt comfortable with her; he had enjoyed their conversation—there had been none of those awkward, first-date silences. And kissing her had been better than nice, it had been new and exciting. He had wanted more, had wanted to make love.

He had decided to wait, anyway.

Because of the past; because of Glory. She had been on his mind too much tonight.

Santos scowled, not liking the truth of that, frustrated by it. Glory had been between him and Liz, a ghost from their shared past, a bad memory. If they had gone to bed together, with her between them, it wouldn't have worked. And he didn't want to screw up with Liz, not so soon, anyway.

They had time. They would become lovers, he was certain of that. But not until the timing was right, not until he had completely expunged Glory from his relationship with Liz.

Lily's bedroom light was on, though Santos doubted he would find her awake at this hour. He moved down the hall, stopping at her door. He peeked in. She had fallen asleep while reading. Santos wasn't surprised; he often found her this way—asleep wherever she was sitting. On occasion, she even nodded off during mass or the afternoon or evening meal.

He gazed at her, a lump forming in his throat, sadness moving over him. The last few years had taken their toll on Lily. Her health had begun to fail, she had little energy, little zest for life.

Her regrets and her shame were eating her alive, he knew. As were her longings. She longed for her daughter, her granddaughter. She scanned the society sections of newspapers until he wanted to shake her. Whenever she found a reference to either of them, she clipped it and put it in a scrapbook. Some days, she would do nothing except go through the scrapbooks, wishing for what she didn't have, hating herself for the loss. He could hardly bear to take her places, because she would gaze at other families with so much longing it made him ache.

Sudden, biting anger swelled inside him. And hatred. He hated Hope for what she had done to Lily. He hated her for her cruelty, her holier-than-thou judgment of others, for her prejudices.

And he hated Glory for what she had done to him. She and her mother weren't fit to lick Lily's shoes; they weren't fit to lick his.

Santos crossed to the bed. He carefully extracted the novel from beneath the old woman's hands, then started to ease the pillow from behind her head. Her eyes snapped open, though he saw that they were fogged with sleep.

"Santos?"

"Yes, Lily. It's me."

She blinked, coming fully awake. "I did it again, didn't I?"

His lips lifted. "At this rate, you'll never finish this book."

"A damnable thing, getting old." She squinted at the clock. "What time is it?"

"After one."

"How was your date?"

"It was good," he said after a moment, softly. "Very good."

She inched toward the center of the bed, then patted the edge. "Tell me about her."

He smiled and sat down, readying himself for the third degree. They had been through this many times before. "She's very nice. Very smart. She owns a little restaurant and bar in the Quarter."

"She's attractive?"

"Very." He rubbed his index finger along the side of his nose, amused. "Actually, she's someone I know from a long time ago."

Lily thought for a moment about that, then nodded, though she didn't ask where he knew Liz from. He was grateful for that.

"That can be a good thing," Lily murmured. "Do you plan to see her again?"

"I think so. Yes, definitely."

"Good." She folded her hands in front of her. "You work too much. You need someone."

"I have you."

"I'm old and sick." She shook her head. "You need a partner."

He grinned. "I have Jackson."

"A life partner. A mate." She bristled at his obvious amusement. "I want you to be happy. I don't want you to be alone." Her eyes flooded with tears, and she looked quickly away. "Being alone isn't the way the Lord intended us to be. That's why He made Eve for Adam."

Santos leaned down and pressed a kiss to her forehead. "Don't you worry about me, Lily. I'm doing good. I'm happy."

When he drew away, she searched his gaze. "Are you, Santos? Are you happy?"

He understood her question. She hadn't forgotten, any more than he had, that once upon a time he had thought he'd found that partner, that love. And, he knew, she blamed herself for his heartache after.

"Yes. I'm very happy." He tucked the blanket more securely around her, then reached across her to snap off her bedside light. "Now get some sleep," he whispered. "Or you won't make it through mass tomorrow."

He crossed to the door, stopping when he reached it. "I'll be here if you need me."

"Santos?"

"Hmm?"

"I heard that man killed another girl. I'm sorry."

"Me, too, Lily. We're going to get him, though. It's just a matter of time."

"I know you will," she murmured, her eyelids drooping. "I have complete confidence...in...you."

She closed her eyes, asleep already. Santos stood at the door, gazing at her, his heart swelling with affection. He had continued living with Lily because she needed him. And because seeing her up and moving around every morning and sleeping peacefully every night reassured him.

But he would lose her anyway, he knew. No matter how often he checked on her, even if he hovered protectively over her around the clock.

One day in the not so distant future, she would be gone.

He sucked in a sharp, painful breath. He had to prepare himself for it, but he didn't know how. How could he prepare himself for something he couldn't even imagine? Life without Lily? His devastation would know no bounds.

He would be alone. Again.

He gazed at her a moment more, a knot of emotion choking him, then dragged his gaze away. He couldn't sleep, he knew. Not now. It would be ridiculous to try. He would make a quick trip to headquarters and see if anything new had come in on the last victim. He had to be missing something. He had to be.

40

The phone awakened Glory from a deep, dreamless sleep. She sat bolt upright in bed, breathing hard. She reached for the phone, pushing her sleep-tangled hair away from her face as she did.

"Yes? Glory St. Germaine."

It was the hotel's assistant manager, a highly excitable man. The way he was babbling, Glory could hardly understand him. "What?" She rubbed a hand across her face. "Slow down, Vincent. I can't make out—" She suddenly realized what he was saying and drew in a deep, stunned breath and sat up straighter.

The Snow White Killer had struck again.

And this time, he had decided to dump the body in the hotel parking lot.

Glory swore and jumped out of bed. "Stay calm, Vincent. And do not, I repeat, do not talk to the press. I'll be right there. I'm calling the PR firm and the hotel lawyer now."

She hung up the phone without waiting for the man's reply and dug in her nightstand drawer for her phone book, already strategizing damage control. The hotel couldn't take another crime-related scandal. Just the week before, two hotel guests, a married couple from Indiana, had been mugged only a dozen feet from the St. Charles's lead-glass front doors. Two months before that, a man had been shot not a half block from the hotel, and although not a guest— thank goodness—he had stumbled into the lobby, bleeding, and collapsed. That incident had prompted a News

Eight special called *Crime Uptown: Are our grand old neighborhoods safe?*

Glory was certain the press was going to have a field day with this one. And this time, considering it involved the Snow White Killer, the St. Charles just might make the national news.

And the hotel's occupancy rate would sink yet again.

Glory found the phone numbers and muttering an oath, dialed her public-relations man first, then her lawyer, dragging them both out of bed and ordering them down to the hotel A.S.A.P. Then she ran for the shower.

Thirty-one minutes later, she pulled up to the hotel, cool, collected and completely put together. She presented the picture of unflappable professional chic, a business barracuda in size seven Manolo Blahnik pumps. Looking at her, no one would guess she had been awakened less than an hour ago, just as no one would guess the turmoil raging behind her calm demeanor.

She intended to keep it that way. She drew a deep breath through her nose, focusing, readying herself for what was sure to be a chaotic scene. It would take every scrap of her savvy and business acumen to carry this off.

Santos. His name and image ran through her head, and a place in the vicinity of her heart tightened. She knew from the *Times Picayune* and the TV news that Santos was the lead detective on this case. In the two months since the last victim had been found at St. Louis Cathedral, he had come under heavy fire from the mayor's office and the media. She had even seen him on TV a couple of times, and she had hated herself for the way she had stared at him, remembering and memorizing.

He had grown into an outrageously attractive man, very masculine, sexy in a rough, macho kind of way. He was the kind of man some women looked at and ached for, the kind of man that made some women want so badly, they forgot what was safe and smart and right.

Glory wasn't that kind of woman. Not anymore. No, she had learned her lesson. She prided herself on keeping her

wits and her emotions in check at all times. And if, when
she saw Santos, she experienced a wisp of longing, a thread
of unwanted arousal, it was only because the past could not
be forgotten or her memories controlled.

The valet ran to her car and opened her door. He was
obviously shaken. "Ms. St. Germaine, did you hear? Pete
found her, and now the police—"

"I heard, Jim." She flashed him a confident, if grim,
smile. "Everything's going to be fine. Just do your job, and
if anyone has questions or concerns, you send them to me.
All right?"

The young man returned her smile, looking almost
comically relieved. "The police have already asked me all
sorts of stuff. The way they questioned me, it was like they
thought I did something."

"Really?" Glory narrowed her eyes slightly. "What did
they ask you?"

"Who was in and out tonight. If I saw anybody or anything unusual. You know, like if one of the guests was acting upset or unusually rushed." He leaned toward her and
for the first time she realized that he was afraid. "Then they
asked me if I could account for all of my time. They asked
me if I had the opportunity, during work, to come and go
as I please, with no one knowing. Why did they ask me
that, Ms. St. Germaine? You don't think I'm . . . I'm a suspect, do you?"

She shook her head and patted his arm comfortingly.
"Those are all routine questions. Don't you worry another
minute, Jim. I'll take care of everything. Where's Pete?"

"With the police." He pointed. "Inside. Man, from what
I heard, they're really giving him the third degree."

"Is that so?" She glanced in the direction he indicated,
then returned her gaze to his. "Have any of the press arrived?"

He shook his head. "Not yet."

"Good. When they do, come and get me. Immediately.
Interrupt whatever I'm doing. I don't want them in the hotel. Is that clear?"

"Yes, ma'am." He straightened. "I'll come get you the minute I see them."

Glory smiled. "Good work, Jim. I really appreciate you keeping your head through all this."

She strode into the St. Charles. As she had expected, pandemonium reigned. She soon learned that Jim and Pete weren't the only ones who had been subjected to the police's interrogations. Several of the housekeeping staff, the girl manning the registration desk, the night bellman. Even two hotel guests, ones who had arrived back at the St. Charles shortly before the body was found, had been roused from their beds and questioned. Glory was seething.

The hotel manager raced over to her, nearly hysterical. "The police want to go door-to-door and question the guests. They're insisting, Ms. St. Germaine, and I don't know what to do."

"Over my dead body," she muttered. "Don't you worry, Vincent, I'm going to take care of this—"

"Ms. St. Germaine!" The valet waved to her from just inside the door. "They're here."

She indicated that she had heard, then turned back to her manager. "I have to take care of this first, Vincent. Do not let them rouse one guest, I'll be right back."

She headed outside. All three network affiliates had arrived, their vans blocking the hotel entrance. The minute the reporters saw her, they began shouting questions. She flashed them all an easy smile and held up her hands. "Please, one question at a time. I'll try to answer each of you in turn. Hoda, how about you first?"

"Is it true the Snow White Killer has struck again and that he has disposed of the body right here at the St. Charles? What are your thoughts on that?"

"My first thought is, I wish he had picked one of the competition, maybe Le Meridian or the Windsor Court." A ripple of laughter moved through the group. "But from what I understand, it is true. However, I haven't talked with the police yet, so I don't know any more than you do. I'm sure they'll be issuing a statement soon.''

"Where was the body found?'' another reporter asked. "Do you think the killer could still be on the premises?''

"Absolutely not,'' Glory said confidently. "The hotel is completely secure. As you all know, this criminal simply chooses a place—any place—to leave his victims. Unfortunately, he chose my parking garage. This murder has *nothing* to do with the hotel. Nothing at all.''

"But, Ms. St. Germaine,'' called a reporter from Channel Eight, a woman she didn't recognize, "do you think your guests can feel safe after this? Knowing that a killer was on the premises?''

Glory shook her head, a smile tugging at the corners of her mouth, making sure she was the picture of confidence. "Let's put it this way, the last victim was found at St. Louis Cathedral. I attended mass there last Sunday and I assure you, I felt perfectly safe. It seems to me, this guy's picking some of New Orleans's best addresses. I have to say, though, the St. Charles has much better security. State-of-the-art.''

She saw that her public-relations man had arrived and was heading her way. She smiled at the reporters. "I'm needed inside the hotel, but Gordon Mackenzie, my public-relations director, will finish telling you about our security team and answer all your other questions.''

After exchanging a quick word with Gordon about what had already transpired, she slipped back inside to save Vincent. And none too soon. He had been cornered by two uniformed officers, no doubt in an effort to get him to agree to a room-to-room search. And he was crumbling fast.

"Perhaps I can help you, Officers?'' She held out her hand. "I'm Glory St. Germaine, the hotel's owner.'' Just as she had suspected, they wanted to search the hotel and wake the guests. She smiled sweetly. "I'm sorry, but that won't be possible. You'll have to do without.''

The men exchanged glances. "We have our orders, ma'am."

"Is that so?" She smiled again, sweet as pie. "Well, I've already spoken with my lawyer and you have no right to search these premises without my permission or a warrant. You have neither. Now," she asked, looking from one officer to the other, "who's in charge of this little circus?"

The younger one cleared his throat. "That would be Detective Santos."

At hearing his name, Glory squeezed her fingers into fists. "And where might I find Detective Santos?"

"He's in the garage. With the coroner. I'm afraid you'll have to wait here."

"Like hell, Officer. It's my hotel, I'll go anywhere I please." Without waiting for an argument, she turned and headed for the elevator. She took it to the third floor and the bridge between the hotel and parking garage.

The area had been cordoned off by a yellow police line. Compared to the chaos in the lobby, however, it was quiet up here. Up ahead she saw a group of people, several of them squatting, studying something on the ground.

Not something. *Someone.* Glory shuddered and crossed herself. That poor girl, she thought.

"Excuse me!" An officer hurried toward her. "You can't be in here."

"I need to speak to Detective Santos."

She started to move by the man, he caught her arm, and none too gently. "I'm sorry, ma'am," he said, his steely voice brooking no argument, "Detective Santos is busy right now. You'll have to wait in the hotel."

Glory jerked her arm from his grasp and squared her shoulders. "My name is Glory St. Germaine. This is *my* hotel, and I demand to see Detective Santos. Now."

For a fraction of a second, the officer looked as if he might try to argue with her. Then he shrugged. "Suit yourself."

He hurried back to the group, and a moment later Glory saw one of the men stand, then start toward her. Not any man, she realized. Santos. *Her Santos.* Her heart began to thunder, the inside of her mouth turned to ash. She called herself a fool and reminded herself of why she was here— she had to protect the hotel, her employees and guests. No matter the cost.

He stopped before her. She looked into his dark eyes, looked into them for the first time in ten years, and all her stern self-reminders flew out of her head. For a fraction of a second, she was sixteen again, sixteen and head-over-heels in love.

"Well, look at the little firecracker," Santos drawled, a snide edge to his voice. "All grown-up and in charge now. Accustomed to giving orders and getting her way. What can I do for you, ma'am? Better make it fast, though. I'm busy."

She stiffened her spine and faced him down, not bothering with preliminaries. "I will not have you harassing my guests or my staff. If you need something, you come through me or the hotel lawyer. We will make ourselves available to you."

"Will you?" He moved his gaze slowly, insolently over her, from head to toe. "Make yourself available to me?"

"Don't push me, Detective. If you so much as say good morning to one of my employees or patrons without consulting me first, I'll have your job. Do you understand?"

"My job? Really?" Santos arched his eyebrows, amusement tugging at the corners of his mouth. "Well, I'll be damned. Who are you going to get it from? The mayor?"

She folded her arms across her chest, feeling the color in her cheeks and hating it. "As a matter of fact, we are acquaintances. And the governor also happens to be a friend of the family."

"Is that so?" He took a step closer, then bent toward her, looking her straight in the eye. "Here's a news flash for you, princess. You can have my job. But until then, I'm going to do it to the best of my ability. To that end, you will provide me with a list of hotel guests and employees. I will question those guests and employees. And by the way, if you don't cooperate with me, in every way, I'll have you charged with obstruction of justice. Do *you* understand?''

"Just try it, Detective."

He narrowed his eyes. "Don't . . . tempt me."

He turned and started to walk away, then as if thinking better of it, stopped and faced her once more. He stared at her a long moment, then smiled. "Why, Glory, you've become the woman your mother always wanted you to be. She must be very proud."

His words affected her like a blow. She caught her breath but held her ground, fighting to keep him from knowing how much that comment hurt. Even as she opened her mouth to deliver a stinging retort, he turned and walked away.

41

By 9:00 a.m., Glory had talked to a reporter from every publication or news department in the South. Or so it seemed. She had also talked to two agitated corporate-meeting planners, managing to convince one not to pull their fall seminar from the St. Charles and persuading the other to at least reconsider their decision to do so. She had been forced to sway them with the offer of additional discount incentives on rooms and banquet facilities. Discounts the hotel could ill afford.

She released a deep breath, exhausted but relieved that the worst was over, though she had no illusions: what she and the PR firm had accomplished was the equivalent of putting a Band Aid on a hemorrhage.

The St. Charles was in trouble.

She sank back in her desk chair, the one that had been her father's, leaned her head against the rest and closed her eyes. Soon, she would have to make some tough decisions concerning the hotel. Decisions she dreaded making, ones her father would not have liked and her mother would fight tooth and nail.

But something had to give. If she didn't get occupancy—and profits—up, hotel services and staff would have to be cut. That would lead to another decline in occupancy, another reduction of room rate. Soon, maintenance of the facility would begin to suffer, then the hotel would slide into disrepair. And on and on in a nightmarish domino effect.

She couldn't let that happen. She wouldn't.

Glory made a sound of frustration and stood. She crossed to the picture window and looked down at St. Charles Avenue. The squad cars were gone, the news vans, the curious. Business as usual. For her. The hotel. For New Orleans.

Business as usual. Glory reached out and touched the glass, its smooth surface cool and unbending beneath her fingers. But today didn't feel like business as usual. This day felt new, different. She felt different.

Santos.

Seeing him had unnerved her badly, more than anything in a long time. She should have been prepared: ten years had passed, she was an adult now, a professional woman with the responsibility of running a one-hundred-and-twenty-five room hotel. Even so, the contempt in his eyes and voice had cut through the years, through the protective wall she had built around herself; it had cut through all her defenses. The contempt in his eyes had hurt.

"Why, Glory, you've become the woman your mother always wanted you to be."

Glory glanced down at her hands and realized they were trembling. She quickly balled them into fists, swearing softly as she did. Had she become the woman her mother had always wanted her to be?

Yes. And no.

Glory tilted up her chin, hating the defensiveness of the movement, but unable to stop herself. He had said it with such scorn. How dare he? What was wrong with the woman she had become? She was a leader in the community, a prominent businesswoman. No, she didn't lead with her heart any longer. Yes, she kept a tight rein on her emotions. So what if when she chose to date, she chose the right kind of man. No more bad boys for her, no more fireworks. No more useless, destructive defiance.

None of her choices were wrong, they weren't to be scoffed at. She was being a grown-up. A responsible adult. Could he claim the same? Running around the streets with a gun, playing cops and robbers, playing the macho supercop. She had heard he was a hothead, had heard that his bad-boy attitude had, on several occasions, gotten him in trouble with his higher-ups.

He had remained true to his dreams, to the person he had always been. Could she claim the same?

Her thoughts grated, and she made a sound of disdain. A case of arrested adolescence, in her opinion. Even if he was one of the most highly decorated officers on the force, she was certainly better off without him.

Sure she was.

Glory turned away from the window and returned to her chair. So what if she had never forgotten him? So what if she had never forgotten the way she had felt in his arms, whole, complete, and completely happy? So what if nothing in her life—before or since—had felt so right?

As an adult, she understood that those feelings had been no more than a childish illusion. She understood that just because something felt right didn't mean it was right.

She had learned that lesson. She had paid a terrible price for it. A lesson she would never forget, a price she would never forgive herself for.

She missed her father still, keenly. It was as if she had a gaping hole inside her, a hole nothing could fill, no amount of food or drink, no amount of tears or laughter or work. She had tried them all.

Glory passed a hand over her face, acknowledging physical and emotional exhaustion. She would feel better after some sleep, she told herself, gazing out at the bright May day. Or a meal. She hadn't eaten, she realized, glancing at her watch. She'd had at least a half-dozen cups of coffee, but no food. No wonder she felt so melancholy and on edge.

"Glory Alexandra, why wasn't I called?"

Her mother's voice affected her like nails on a chalkboard. Glory stiffened, turned and faced Hope. She stood in the doorway, the picture of the fashionable uptown matron. Behind her, Glory's secretary lifted her hands up in apology. No matter how often Glory asked, her mother refused to either knock or be announced.

"Hello, Mother. Come right in."

"I repeat," Hope said, striding across the dove gray carpeting, "why wasn't I called?"

"You're referring to—"

"That unfortunate police matter, of course." The older woman shuddered and sat down. "It's positively ghastly. Dumping that girl *here*. Really."

Her mother's prejudice raised Glory's hackles. She leaned back in the chair, liking the feel of it around her, feeling ridiculously, childishly safe in it. "That poor girl was one of God's children, same as you and I. My heart goes out to her and her family."

For a moment, her mother said nothing, then she made a fluttering motion with her right hand. "Of course. The poor thing certainly didn't deserve to die. But to dump her *here?* Awful, just awful."

Glory gave up. It never did any good to argue with her mother; she would never see the world as Glory did. Instead, she met her mother's gaze evenly and directed the conversation back to the woman's original question. "I saw no reason to call you, Mother. There was nothing you could do and it was the middle of the night."

Her mother leaned forward, eyes narrowed. "Not only am I half owner of the hotel, but need I remind you, it was *my* family money, *my* inheritance, that bailed out Philip and the hotel from certain financial ruin. We could have lost the St. Charles then, but we didn't." She pressed a fist to her chest. "Because of me. I repeat, I should have been called."

When Glory had taken over five years ago, she had discovered a discrepancy in the books—loans that had been paid off, debt that had disappeared as if by magic. Her mother had explained, but ever since, any time they disagreed about the hotel, her mother had thrown the fact in Glory's face. She was tired of it.

Angry, Glory placed her palms on the desk and stood. "And I run the hotel, Mother. If you'd like to take over that job, we'll talk. Until then, I stand by my decision. There was no reason for you to be here, there still isn't. Everything's been handled."

Her secretary buzzed. A reporter from the *Times Pica-yune* was calling for a quote. Glory excused herself and took the call, watching as her mother stood, crossed to the desk and picked up one of the framed photos that decorated its top. She chose one of Glory's father, taken for publicity reasons shortly before his death. A lump formed in Glory's throat as her mother lightly, lovingly touched the glass.

After Philip's death, men, many men, had called on her mother. She had turned them all away. She had told Glory that no one could take the place of her sweet Philip. For a long time, Glory had wished that her mother would relent; her loneliness only accentuated Glory's feelings of guilt.

Finally, Glory had come to accept that her mother would never date, never marry again. But acceptance hadn't eased her burden of guilt, it had only made it a permanent weight around her neck.

Swallowing hard, Glory returned her attention to the reporter. "Yes, that's right. You can quote me on that. If you need any additional information, please don't hesitate to call."

A moment later, she hung up the phone. As she did, her mother carefully set the photograph back in its place, then returned her gaze to Glory's. "I suppose you saw...*him* last night."

Glory's heart began to thud; her mouth went dry. "If you mean Santos, yes, I saw him. He's working this case."

"I'd heard that." Hope smiled thinly. "I'd heard he'd become a...policeman."

She drawled the word as if becoming a cop was the equivalent of falling into a bucket of slop. Glory felt her cheeks heat, and she jumped to his defense. "He's a very good detective, I hear. One of the N.O.P.D.'s best, as a matter of fact. I'm glad he's on our side." She glanced at her watch. "If there's nothing else, Mother, some matters need my attention."

"Of course. You're very busy." Hope crossed to the office door, then turned back. "Oh, there is one other thing. I'm giving a small dinner party Saturday night. The Renaissance Room, eight o'clock. Why don't you bring that nice plastic surgeon you were seeing. What was his name?"

"William," Glory answered, then shook her head. "Mother, how small a dinner?"

"Only twenty." She made a fluttering motion with her right hand. "But don't you worry about a thing, I already made arrangements with both the restaurant manager and the chef. Everything's set. All you have to do is show up."

And pay for it. Glory made a sound of frustration. "We've talked about this. You can't continue entertaining this way. You can't continue to give away rooms and food and services. The hotel can no longer support that kind of life-style."

"I'll do as I please, Glory Alexandra," her mother said softly, her tone measured. "It's my hotel."

"You don't understand, if you continue to—"

"I understand very well. But why have the bother of the hotel, if we can't enjoy its advantages?"

Glory shook her head. "The hotel is our business. It's how we support ourselves. But it's more than that, too. It's—"

"What is it?" Hope mocked. "Your heritage? A part of the family? Please. Without the freebies, it would be nothing more than a boulder around our necks."

"A boulder around our necks?" Glory repeated, stunned. "If you feel that way about the hotel, why did you save it? Why did you use your family money to hold on to it?"

"Because your father was going to sell our personal assets to bail it out. He was going to mortgage our home, sell the summer place, my jewelry, the Rolls. That was unacceptable."

Hope shook her head, her expression disgusted. "People would have talked. They would have laughed at us behind our backs. I couldn't have that."

Glory digested what her mother had just told her. Her father had loved the hotel beyond measure; he had passed that love on to his daughter. But her mother felt none of that affection for the place. She talked as if she hated it.

"What about now, Mother?" Glory asked. "What if there was talk now?"

Hope met her daughter's eyes. They were clear, determined and so very cold that Glory shuddered.

"I would do whatever necessary to stop the talk. Of course."

Without another word, she left the office. Glory watched her go, her last words, the meaning behind them ringing in her ears.

42

Liz lay in the center of her rumpled bed, staring up at the ceiling, her thoughts a disturbing jumble. Santos had left hours ago, before dawn; even so, she hadn't slept a wink since.

Right now he could be talking to Glory, looking into her eyes. Remembering. Beginning to want her all over again.

Her head filled with images, ones from her memory, of Santos and Glory together, of the passionate way they had looked at each other, the hungry way they had touched each other. It filled, too, with images from her taunting, cruel imagination, of Santos and Glory together now, two consenting adults who knew exactly what they wanted and how to please each other.

Liz moaned and pulled the pillow, his pillow, over her face, cursing herself for her insecurities, her traitorous thoughts. He wouldn't want Glory again, she told herself. He wouldn't. He hated Glory as much as she did; he had told her so.

Liz breathed deeply. The pillow smelled of Santos. She buried her face deeper into it, growing drunk on the scent.

She loved him so much.

He didn't love her back.

Moaning again, Liz sat up, bringing the pillow with her. Not yet, anyway. He liked her—a lot, he had told her. He enjoyed her company, their lovemaking. But he had no desire for permanence. No desire for love or the kind of commitment that comes with it.

Liz knew he was being honest with her. She felt the distance he put between them, she felt the walls he erected around himself. There were parts of him he didn't share. That he would not share. His feelings. His hopes and dreams. His heart.

She blamed Glory. For just as Glory had stolen Liz's future, she had stolen Santos's ability to love and trust. She had stolen his heart.

Liz curled her fingers into the feather pillow, hugging it to her. They had been lovers for nearly two months. Since their third date. She had initiated their lovemaking, shamelessly, wantonly. But she had wanted him so badly; she hadn't been able to bear the thought of waiting. It seemed as if she had already waited forever.

Because she had loved him forever.

She drew her knees to her chest. He needed time, she told herself. In time, he would realize how good they were together, how good they were for each other.

If Glory didn't steal him from her first.

Liz pressed her face to her drawn-up knees. She thought back two hours ago, trying to recall Santos's exact reaction to the news that he would be paying a visit to the St. Charles Hotel. She struggled to remember each word they had exchanged, every nuance of his expression. He had gotten a call from headquarters about the murder. The phone hadn't awakened her, but suddenly she had realized he wasn't beside her.

She remembered opening her eyes and seeing him tugging on his jeans. His expression had been tight, angry. She remembered a shiver of apprehension had moved over her. "Santos?" she had asked. "What's happened?"

He'd met her eyes, then looked away. "I've got to go." He sat on the edge of the bed and put on his shoes. "They found another body."

She sat up and pushed the hair out of her eyes. "The Snow White Killer?"

"The very one."

She stroked his thigh. "I'm sorry."

"Me, too." He opened his mouth as if to say more, then closed it. He stood, retrieved his shoulder holster and slipped it on.

"I'll get you some coffee."

"There's no time." He bent and kissed her. "Go back to sleep."

"Are you coming back?" she asked sleepily, lying back down and curling up with his pillow.

He shook his head. "I'll stop at the restaurant later."

She nodded, a lump in her throat. She loved him so much that watching him leave hurt, physically hurt. "Wait!" He stopped in the doorway and looked back at her. "This time, where did he . . . leave the body?"

Santos had hesitated for one long, damning moment, as if he hadn't wanted to tell her, as if he had wanted to hide the truth from her. And in that moment, Liz had known— Santos still had feelings for Glory.

Now, Liz jumped out of bed, too agitated to remain still another moment. If she didn't throw herself into some sort of task or activity, her thoughts would drive her crazy.

Although she had originally planned to let Darryl, her bartender/assistant manager, open up, she would head down to the restaurant. Santos would stop by later, and when she looked into his eyes, she would see that everything was going to be all right.

Sure she would. With that thought fixed firmly in her mind, she went to shower.

It was nearly three o'clock before Santos made it by The Garden of Earthly Delights. By that time, Liz's mood had progressed from agitated to despondent. Her fears, her insecurities, had eaten at her all day. She had been unable to halt her runaway thoughts, to dim the images in her head.

If only Santos loved her. If only she didn't know how much Santos and Glory had once loved each other.

"Hey there." Santos came up behind her and looped his arms around her. "Boy, are you a sight for sore eyes."

Liz ducked out of the circle of his arms. "Am I?"

He frowned. "I wouldn't have said it if it weren't true."

"Of course you wouldn't, not an upstanding guy like you. Not Mr. Honesty." She was so angry she was shaking. Angry at him. At Glory. At herself for not being able to control her feelings.

He placed his hands on his hips. "What's the problem, Liz?"

"No problem." She lifted a shoulder in feigned indifference. "Glad you found the time in your busy day to stop by."

"So that's it." He narrowed his eyes. "I'm on a case, you know what that means."

"But this case is different, isn't it? This particular victim was different." She folded her arms across her chest. Even as she said the words, she wished she could call them back. She sounded jealous, she sounded whiny and clingy. And she wasn't normally that way; she hated it.

And Santos wasn't the kind of man who could take that kind of woman. He needed space, freedom. She could almost see him withdrawing from her.

"Look, Liz—" he dragged a hand through his hair, making a sound of frustration "—I've been up most of the night. I'm tired, I'm hungry and I'm pissed off. So say what you mean, because frankly, I'm not in the mood for childish innuendos."

Liz hiked up her chin. "You saw her, didn't you?"

"If you mean Glory, yes, I saw the high queen of the St. Charles and I didn't particularly enjoy it."

"Are you sure? I mean . . ." Liz blinked against tears, feeling like a total jerk.

"Don't do this, Liz." He took a step toward her and cupped her face in his hands. "Just let us be . . . here and now. The way we are. Let the past go."

"I want to, I do." She drew in a shuddering breath. "But I can't seem to stop myself. I keep remembering how it was . . . between you two. And I know how she is. Selfish. Self-centered. She wouldn't think twice about—" Liz shook her head. "I hate her so much. She stole my future from me, and she didn't even care that she had done it. If not for her, who knows what I would have done or become."

"You own your own business. You've done so well." Santos searched her gaze. "Don't you like what you're doing, Liz?"

She struggled to find the right words. "I do like it. And I feel...good about it. But I had such dreams, Santos. Such big dreams." Tears welled in her eyes, and she fought their spilling over. "I was going to do something important with my life. I was going to be a scientist or a surgeon. Or I was going to invent something that would change people's lives...maybe even the world."

"But you are," he said softly. "With this place, your food. You're making people healthier."

She shook her head, not buying his comment, focusing instead on her anger. "That's not the point. She didn't care what I lost. All she cared about was herself. All she could think about was herself.

"I thought she was my friend," Liz said, hearing the bitterness in her own voice and wishing she didn't. "I would have done...anything for her, Santos. Of course, I believed she felt the same way, I believed she would go to the same lengths for me. She told me she would. She lied."

Liz covered his hands with hers. "You see why I don't trust her?"

Santos bent his head to hers. "Yes, I understand. She hurt me, too. She betrayed me, too. But...it's me you have to trust. I'm not interested in Glory St. Germaine. What I thought we felt for each other all those years ago was a lie. She was not the person I thought she was."

"But your memories—"

"Are all bad." He looked deeply into her eyes. "She's not going to come between us. And she's not going to stop me from loving you."

She searched his gaze, aching. "Only you can stop you from loving me, is that it?"

He hesitated. "I'm sorry, Liz. I didn't mean that the way it sounded."

"Yes, you did." She swung away from him. "I need to get back to work."

He caught her arm. "Let's not fight. Don't let her come between us. We have something good here. Something really good. Let's not . . . blow it."

Something good. But not great. Tears flooded her eyes. "I don't want to blow it. I don't want to lose you."

He bent to kiss her. "I've got to go."

She curled her fingers into his lapels. "Stay and eat." She smiled. "I added cow to the menu, just for you."

He returned her smile. "I want to, but I can't."

"Will I see you later?"

"I'll try."

He was already moving away from her, feeling trapped. She saw it in his eyes, in the slight tightening of his mouth. She cursed her insecurities, cursed Glory St. Germaine and the number she had done on Santos all those years ago. "Call me. Let me know."

"I will." He kissed her again and walked away.

She watched him go, feeling as if she had lost him for good. Vowing to herself that it wasn't true, she went back to work.

43

Santos and Jackson faced each other across the scarred wooden desk, its top littered with stacks of papers, folders and used foam coffee cups. Around them the chaotic sounds of the homicide division ebbed and flowed; they had worked around such sounds so many years that neither noticed them anymore.

Santos cleared a space in the center of the desk and laid out photos of the six Snow White Killer victims. He handed a photo of the last victim to Jackson. "Autopsy's in."

Jackson studied the photograph a moment, then looked up. "So what have we got?"

"First off, she put up a struggle." Santos handed Jackson two more photos, ones that documented the dark purple bruises on her arms, shoulders and back. "She must have realized what was going down before our boy got a chance to do her."

Jackson studied the photos, then tossed them back on the desk. "And the apple?"

"The last two girls didn't voluntarily take a bite. He had to take a bite and stuff it down their throats after they were dead."

"Charming."

Santos pursed his lips. "I bet our boy didn't like having to do that one bit. And I'm damn sure he didn't appreciate this last girl putting up a fight. He wants his girls to be perfect, angelic and unmarred." Santos frowned. "Unmarred," he repeated. "But he picks prostitutes."

"And cleans them up."

"Purifies them."

"Right." Jackson steepled his fingers. "He gets them ready for God."

"But," Santos said, "he has sex with them *after* they're dead. After he's sent them to God. I don't get that. That's the piece of the puzzle that doesn't work for me."

"Maybe he thinks he's God. He marks them with the cross, branding them with his sign. Not *His,* but if our theory holds true, his, the killer's."

Santos met Jackson's eyes, chilled. "And the apple's the forbidden fruit."

"Bingo."

Santos jumped to his feet, frustrated and restless, the need for action damn near making him crazy. "God made the apple off limits. The serpent tempted Eve to taste the fruit. She did, then offered it to Adam."

"Goodbye, paradise, hello, Original Sin."

"So these girls do it," Santos continued, "they taste the apple, they sin. They need to be cleansed, they need their sin taken away. He does that by killing them. He's doing them a big favor, he thinks. The sick bastard."

Santos crossed to the water cooler, then strode back, flexing his fingers. He wanted this guy so badly he could taste it. He stopped in front of Jackson. "So, where's the semen? Where's the biological evidence associated with a sex crime?"

Jackson linked his fingers. "You're thinking foreign object?"

"Yeah. Maybe." Santos narrowed his eyes in thought. "Or... our guy could be a woman."

For a moment the silence deafened. Jackson shook his head. "I don't think so. No way."

"But it's a possibility."

"Yeah. A possibility. But with what we've got, anything is."

Jackson was right. They had nothing. Except bodies. Six of them. *Damn.*

Santos dragged his hands through his hair. "The girls are catching on. They're scared. They know his M.O. And the problem is, if he can't have things his way, he'll move on."

"And we won't get him."

"We've got to get him. He's right under our noses." Santos hesitated, thinking. "He's a Quarter regular, I'm sure of it. He's someone these girls know. They trust him. Otherwise, we would have seen more signs of struggle before now. I have a feeling about this."

Jackson rocked back in his chair, his arms folded across his chest. "Let's look at the crucifix again."

Santos reached around the desk and tugged open the top-right desk drawer. He took out a half a dozen jewelry boxes and tossed them on the desk. They all contained cheap tin crucifixes, all of the type the killer used to imprint the victims' palms, all had been procured in the French Quarter.

In a town as Catholic as New Orleans, one in which salvation was as deeply embedded in the psyche of the people as sin, religion had made its way into every area of life. Even the bacchanal of Mardi Gras had its roots in Catholicism, and religious items like these crucifixes could be found in every tourist shop, sometimes on the same shelf as coffee mugs shaped like tits and G-strings emblazoned with Y'all Come on the crotch.

Santos selected a crucifix and held the pendant up for inspection. "I got this one from a bible thumper on the corner of Royal and St. Peter the other day." He dropped it into its box, then selected another, only subtly different from the first. "I got this one in the Cabildo gift shop—" He picked up another. "And this one in the voodoo store on Bourbon."

Santos ran the last one through his fingers, then dropped it into its box. "No witnesses, no clues. Damn."

"What about that kid from the St. Charles?" Jackson studied the photos. "I'm not sure I buy his alibis."

"They checked out."

"Yeah, but if you ask me, two of 'em stink like last week's shrimp po'boy." Jackson leaned forward, his expression intent. "He had the opportunity. He frequents hookers. He's around the Quarter a lot."

"But the way he came to pieces during questioning? That kid's no killer." Santos returned to his desk, sat down and reached for one of the photos. He studied it a moment, frowning, then tossed it down. "The way he fell apart when we put on the pressure, hell, he would have confessed if he could have. I'm telling you, he's not the one."

"I'm not convinced. I still think we should hav—" Jackson bit back the words. "Don't look now, partner, but trouble's heading our way. And I think it's got your name on it."

Santos swung in the direction of his partner's gaze. Glory strode across the room, her gaze on him, her cheeks bright with angry color. He couldn't help noticing the way she drew the gaze of every male she passed. It was no wonder. She was one gorgeous woman. Even as he reminded himself that her beautiful exterior housed a heart of ice, he moved his own gaze over her appreciatively. She looked like a million bucks, like a diamond among pieces of cut glass, like a sleek, pampered pedigree in a roomful of junkyard dogs.

And she looked as if she wanted someone's head on the chopping block. Santos lifted his lips in an amused smile. And he had a damn good idea whose.

She stopped before his desk, all outraged fury. "How dare you!" she began without preamble. "How dare you...interrogate my employee that way."

"Good morning, Ms. St. Germaine," Santos said, smiling, deliberately taunting. "To what do we owe the pleasure of this visit?"

"Cut the crap." She placed her palms on the desk and leaned toward him, glowering. "I forbade you to question any of my employees without clearing it with me first. Who gave you the authority to defy my instructions?"

"You forbade me?" Santos eased to his feet, his gaze not leaving hers. "Defy your instructions?"

"I think I'll just move my chair back a bit," Jackson murmured, rolling a foot back from the desk. "Wouldn't want to get caught in the cross fire. Shrapnel can be a real bitch."

Santos sent him a furious glance, then turned back to Glory. He mirrored her stance, placing his palms on the desk and leaning toward her, not stopping until they were nose-to-nose. "First off, Ms. St. Germaine, you have no right to give me instructions of any kind. I'll do whatever I damn well need to, to get the bottom of this case. Second off, we talked to Pete on his own time, not yours." He narrowed his eyes. "Back off."

Twin spots of angry color bloomed in her cheeks. "Just because you can't find this guy, Detective, doesn't give you license to single out an innocent boy for harassment. Might I suggest that instead of picking on hardworking kids, you get out in the street and find the maniac who's butchering these girls."

Activity in the room ceased. For one moment, save for the creak of Jackson's chair as he rolled back several more inches, silence reigned. Santos straightened, fury too mild a word to describe what he felt.

He came around the desk to stand before her, stopping so close she had to tip her head back to meet his eyes. She did, meeting his challenge, not backing down a fraction. Oh, yes, he thought, arrogantly sweeping his gaze over her. She had grown into one hard-as-nails, cold-as-ice broad.

He narrowed his gaze. "And how do you know your Pete's not the guy? Hmm, Princess St. Germaine? What if you have a killer working for you?"

She made a sound of disdain. "That's ridiculous. Pete's a nice young man. He's responsible and a model employee."

"And I'll bet the hotel guests like and trust him."

She hiked up her chin. "As a matter of fact, they do. Very much."

"Especially the women. They like…and trust him a lot. Don't they?"

Glory paled. He had struck a nerve, he knew. Because it was true. She shook her head, anyway, making a dismissive motion with her right hand. "You had him in an interrogation room for four hours. No Miranda rights, no lawyer. You all but outright accused him of being the killer."

Santos arched his eyebrows in exaggerated innocence. "Why would we read him his rights? He wasn't charged with anything. We were only questioning him. Right, Jackson?"

"Right."

"See?" Santos ran his index finger along the side of his nose, a smile tugging at the edges of his mouth. "He didn't request a lawyer. He didn't ask to call one. Of course, if he had, we would have made one available to him. That's the law, Ms. St. Germaine."

This time, it was she who narrowed her eyes. "If I were you, I'd wipe that smirk off your face. You know as well as I do that you strongly hinted to him that calling a lawyer would only make things look worse for him. You hinted that consulting a lawyer would make him look guilty, when in fact, we both know you simply wanted him unprotected and vulnerable."

Santos looked at Jackson in feigned shock. "Did we do that, Jackson?"

"Not that I remember, partner. Maybe she's thinking of some other homicide detective. Or maybe some TV show."

"Yeah," Santos said. "Maybe that's it. Too much TV."

"Don't insult my intelligence." She let her breath out in an angry huff. "I've had enough of your intimidation and games. Next time, I'll go right to Chief Pennington."

"No so fast, princess." Santos met her eyes once more. "Is your employee feeling guilty about something? Why's he so nervous?"

"He's not nervous." She jerked her chin up. "He was simply shaken by your accusations."

"Excuse me, ma'am," Jackson said softly but with a steel edge, "but we made no accusations. We questioned the man. That's our job."

"Implied accusations, then." She folded her arms across her chest. "Anyone would be shaken by what you put him through."

Santos tipped his head, studying her. "Sounds like maybe you have a soft spot for this boy, Ms. St. Germaine. Sounds like maybe you're paying him for more than parking cars."

She drew in a sharp breath. "How dare you! How dare you suggest that I—"

Santos cut her off. "And what makes you so sure he's not the guy?" He cocked his head, studying her expression intently. "Maybe you know who is? Maybe you're the Snow White Killer?"

"Oh, please." She made a move to swing away from him, he caught her arm, stopping her. Startled, she met his eyes.

"You have no idea who you're dealing with," Santos said softly. "You think the serial killer can be picked out in a crowd. You think that, somehow, you can look into his eyes and see the monster he is."

He leaned a fraction toward her, smiling grimly. "For he is a monster, Ms. St. Germaine. A monster that walks among us. Cold, brutal and calculating, a killing machine without compassion or regard for human life."

Santos saw fear race into her eyes and felt a grim satisfaction. He meant to scare her. Because her accusations and demands were so arrogantly off base that she deserved it, and because he wanted to punish her. For the present. But for the past, too.

"But," he continued, "we don't know he's a monster, we don't see it. He wears a mask, he fools us. He wants us to believe he's a . . . nice guy. A model employee."

Glory was as white as a sheet. Jackson cleared his throat. "Santos—"

Santos lifted a hand, cutting him off. "Your Pete had the opportunity. He lives in the Quarter. He likes . . . working girls. Just think, Ms. St. Germaine, he's mobile all night long. He parks cars. He could use any one of those cars, at any time. Cars he knows won't be needed for hours."

She darted a glance from Santos to Jackson, then wetted her lips. "What are you saying? Are you saying that Pete . . . that he's—"

"What I'm saying is, don't you ever come in here and tell me how to do my job. I know how to do my job. I take it seriously, and I'm damn good at it. So if there's nothing else, princess, I've got a killer to find."

"Don't call me that." Though shaking, she yanked her arm free of his grasp.

"Why?" He arched his eyebrows. "Do you prefer Your Highness?"

"Go to hell," she said succinctly, then swung away from him. As she did, her gaze lighted on the photographs spread across the center of the desk. She caught her breath, and took an involuntary step back, her hand going to her throat.

"Ms. St. Germaine." Jackson jumped up. He steadied her with a hand to her elbow. "Why don't you sit down a moment?"

She dragged her gaze away, struggling, Santos saw, to compose herself. He could almost see her armor going back up, fitting snugly into place. But for a moment before, when she had been angry, when he had goaded her, she had been alive with fire. In those moments, she had reminded him of the girl he had once known.

"Thank you, Detective," she said stiffly to Jackson, easing her elbow from his grip. "But I'm fine. If you'll excuse me."

She turned and walked away, back straight, head held high, though Santos suspected she would not sleep well tonight. The image of the dead girl would haunt her. In truth, they sometimes still haunted him.

"Ms. St. Germaine," Santos called after her. "About your employee . . ."

She stopped and looked over her shoulder at him. He saw the hesitation in her gaze, the apprehension.

"He's clean. He's got an airtight alibi." Santos smiled, acknowledging that he had won round one, acknowledging that he liked the feeling. A lot. "I just thought you'd like to know."

"You son of a bitch."

He smiled and tipped an imaginary brim. "At your service."

44

Lily awoke to the sound of birds singing. Gently, sweetly, they coaxed her from her heavy sleep and into the new day. She opened her eyes. By the softness of the light, she judged that it was early, just after dawn.

She folded back her blankets and climbed out of bed, though not without difficulty. She crossed to the French doors that led to the small balcony that overlooked the building's central courtyard. Smiling, she opened them and stepped outside to admire God's handiwork.

The dappled light on the courtyard floor reminded her of her youth, though she couldn't pinpoint exactly why. Her mind was flooded with memories of the mornings of her past, and with the sensory reminiscences that came with them: the clean, sweet scent of the air; the feel of morning dew on her toes; the enticing smell of bacon frying; the warmth of the sun on her face as she lifted it to heaven.

Lily tilted her head and listened. The birds continued to sing; they sounded like a choir of angels.

The cold came upon her so suddenly that for a moment she thought it January instead of June, thought the cold that enveloped her came from outside her rather than from within.

But no, she was cold. To the touch cold. She rubbed her arms and found them wet. Slippery wet, as if she had been working in the garden during the day's zenith.

The birds were singing.

And she was dying.

Lily didn't know how she knew, but she did, with a kind of clarity she couldn't dismiss.

She moved her gaze over the courtyard, searching for the birds, finding peace in the fact that she could hear, but not see, them. Perhaps He would take her, after all. Perhaps He had forgiven her sins. Her many, many sins.

Lily turned away from the new day and left her bedroom, though she didn't bother with her slippers or robe. Santos was up. She smelled the coffee, heard the crackle of newspaper pages being turned. Santos never slept deeply or for long. He never had. His demons robbed him of that pleasure, of the sweet perfection of deep, dreamless sleep.

Lily moved slowly to the kitchen, the cold becoming almost unbearable. She wished Santos would find someone to love, a mate, a life partner. She wished he would find someone who loved him so much and so completely that he would never feel alone or unloved again.

She had spent too many years feeling both. Life, she realized now, was too short. Life needed to be grabbed with both hands; it needed to be enjoyed, to be basked in.

Lily found Santos in the kitchen. He sat at the kitchen table, coffee mug and newspaper before him, head bent as he read. He was so strong and handsome, she thought, moving her gaze over him almost greedily. He was so good. Her being filled with such love, such pride that for a moment, the cold receded. He wasn't hers; she wasn't his mother, she hadn't brought him into this world.

But she felt as if she was, as if she had. She couldn't be more proud of him, couldn't love him more if she had given birth to him, if she had held him in her arms and to her breast, if she had nourished him with her own body.

She would look his mother up when she reached her destination. She would tell her about him.

Although, Lily suspected, she probably already knew.

"Santos?"

He lifted his gaze and smiled. "Good morning. You're up early."

"There's something I need you to do for me. Some things I need to tell you."

He frowned and searched her expression as if suddenly realizing that something was wrong. "Lily, are you...all right?"

Her left arm went numb. The sensation unsettled, robbing her of some of her peace. A modicum of her relief. She drew in a deep breath, forcing herself to focus. "I must tell you this now...in case I can't...later."

He stood and rushed over to her, his expression alarmed. He touched her, then snatched his hand away. "I'm calling 911."

"Wait!" She caught his hand, her shoulders growing tight. "Santos...I want you to call Hope. I must see her before...I have to see her before I—"

The pain hit her like a foot to her chest. Lily squeezed Santos's hand, holding on to him, on to his life force. "Promise me you will...promise to...call her."

He promised, then raced for the phone and called 911. A moment later, he swept her into his arms and carried her down the flight of stairs to the building's entrance to await the ambulance.

Lily gazed lovingly at his face, unfooled by his set, emotionless expression. Inside Santos there had always raged an inferno of emotion. And a bottomless well of love.

"Everyone goes sometime," she said softly, her voice small and slurred with pain. "If this is mine, I welcome it."

"You're not going to die." Santos tightened his arms. "I'm not going to let you die, Lily."

"Silly boy," she whispered, wanting to reach up and stroke his cheek but finding she didn't have the strength. "I want you to...know how much I...love you, Santos."

"I know, Lily. I—"

She shook her head, though she couldn't feel her head move. "I think of you like a son. My son. Without you...my life—"

She gasped, struggling past the pain, wanting, needing to share this with him. "I was dead before you came into my life. You took my loneliness away. You gave me something I thought I would never...have. You gave me love, Victor. You're a good boy, and I want you to know everything before I... before I die."

"Lily, stop this." He pressed his face to her hair. "You're scaring me."

"You deserve everything...good. I don't think you know that about yourself. Promise me... be kind to yourself. Don't cheat yourself as I... Victor!" She brought a hand to her chest, her head emptied of everything but the pain. She closed her eyes.

"No, Lily! Wait!" She heard the panic in his voice, felt it in the way he clutched at her. "You gave me those things, too, Lily. A home and a family. You gave me love... Lily, don't do this. Please...don't die. You can't leave me. I need you."

"Hope," Lily said again, her voice small and breathy. She curled her fingers into his T-shirt. "I must see... her. Must... make... peace. My baby, I..."

The pain took her breath, her ability to speak. She heard the wail of the ambulance, heard Santos's frantic, muttered pleas, the cry of the neighbor's baby. And she heard the birds. Singing. Sweetly, sweetly calling.

Then she heard nothing at all.

45

The next two hours passed in a panicked blur for Santos. Lily had suffered a heart attack, though the extent of the damage to her heart was not yet known. The doctor had administered the highest allowable amount of morphine to ease her pain, then later, when he had been sure what they were dealing with, he gave her a miracle drug he described, simply, as a clot buster.

Though Santos had never considered himself a particularly spiritual man, a prayer ran continually through his head, one in which he begged God to keep Lily alive. His prayers had been answered, though the doctor had given him no pretty illusions to hang on to. Lily was old, her health poor and she had suffered what looked to be a major heart attack. The probability that she would have another was great.

But she was alive. Santos gazed at her, so thankful he could weep. She was finally free of pain and was resting. The doctor had said she would sleep for as many as twelve hours and had suggested Santos get some shut-eye, too. The next few days would be long ones.

Santos bent and pressed a kiss to her forehead, whispered that he would be back, then left the room in search of the pay phone. He called the division and Liz, then swallowing both his pride and his hatred, he called Hope.

She answered on the third ring and oddly, she didn't sound surprised when he identified himself.

"What can I do for you, Detective Santos?"

A shudder ran up his spine. He found something almost snakelike about her voice, about the way it moved over him. "I've called with some bad news, I'm afraid."

"Oh, and what could that be? Another murder at the hotel?"

He amused the woman; he heard it in her voice. She thought she was so much better than he, so much above everything, even the law. That was obvious. She made him sick.

"It's about your mother," he said stiffly, controlling his anger and dislike, but not hiding them. "She's had a—"

"I'm sorry, Officer," Hope said, cutting him off, "but you've been misinformed. I have no mother. She died years ago, traveling abroad."

The image of Lily, pale, near death, filled his head. As did her plea that he bring Hope to her side. His anger swelled, taking his breath, stealing his self-control, his ability to think. *For Lily,* he reminded himself, gripping the receiver tightly. He would do this for Lily.

"You can forget your little fairy tale, Mrs. St. Germaine. I know who you are. And personally, I don't think you're good enough to lick Lily's boots, but she asked me to call you. For some reason, she actually thinks you're worth a crap."

Hope laughed, the sound had an almost girlish lilt. "Is that so? Go on, Detective."

"She's had a heart attack. And it doesn't . . . it doesn't look good." Saying the words out loud hurt; they shook him to his core. His throat closed over them, betraying his feelings. *What would he do without Lily?* "There's every chance she might . . . die."

For a moment, Hope was silent, then she made a small sound of impatience. "Is this supposed to concern me in some way, Detective?"

"Did you hear what I said? Your mother is dying."

"Yes, I heard you. But I don't understand why you're calling me."

He could detect no regret in her voice, no remorse, not even a trace of sadness. How could she be so heartless? he wondered. How could she be so cold?

He drew a deep breath, struggling to keep his fury and hatred in check. Hope St. Germaine would love having him lose it, he knew. She would love rubbing his nose in it.

For Lily, he reminded himself again. For Lily he would do anything, even beg. "She wants to see you. She wants to make her peace with you."

"I'm sorry, Detective, but that won't be possible."

"Are you saying—"

"That's exactly what I'm saying."

"She's dying, for Christ's sake!" He struggled to get a grip on his rage. "She wants to see you. It's her dying wish."

"Is that supposed to mean something to me? I can assure you, it doesn't."

"Please." He choked out the word, thinking of Lily, hearing her weak plea, remembering all the years she had longed for her daughter. "Please," he said again. "I'm begging you. Give her this. Let her die happy."

"No, thank you," she said sweetly, as if he were a canvasser who had called for a donation. "Good day."

The phone went dead. Santos stared disbelievingly at the receiver, adrenaline pumping through him, his fury knowing no bounds. *The bitch had hung up on him! She had refused her dying mother's last wish.*

He slammed the receiver of the pay phone back into the cradle, so hard he heard the plastic housing crack. He would show Hope St. Germaine; he would get her where she was most vulnerable. He would not allow her to treat Lily this way.

He pressed the heels of his hands to his eyes. Sweet, generous Lily. Lily who had loved and shared so much and been hurt so often. He would give Lily's her heart's desire, no matter what it cost him.

Or rather, he would give her *one* of them.

After checking with the doctor and on Lily, then leaving his beeper number at the nurses' station, he went to his car. His fury in check, he slid inside, slapped his police light onto the roof and peeled out. He drove as only a seasoned police officer could—like a controlled madman.

And made it to Glory's Garden District cottage in less than fifteen minutes. He wheeled into her driveway, beacon flashing. A neighbor, retrieving her Sunday paper, gaped openly at him, obviously aghast, then hurried inside. No doubt to inform the rest of the family and neighborhood that *that nice Glory St. Germaine was in some sort of trouble.*

His lips lifting in amusement, he slammed out of the car. Glory was about to become the talk of the 'hood.

She answered the door within moments of his knock. She was wearing faded blue jeans and a short, soft knit top. Her feet were bare, her face free of cosmetics. She looked young and vulnerable; she looked like the sixteen-year-old girl he had fallen in love with.

Seeing her that way affected him like a shock to his system. Memories flooded him, hot and sweet, electric and electrifying. In those moments, he remembered things he had managed to put out of his mind for twelve years. Things that made him ache, things that made him wish for the past, wish for a way to turn back the clock.

He scowled at his own thoughts. She was not the girl she had been all those years ago. Hell, that girl had never even existed.

"What?" she asked, searching his expression, hers concerned. Nervously, she brought a hand to her throat. "What's happened?"

"Police business," he said stiffly, struggling for just the right tone of voice. "You'll have to come with me."

"Come with you?" she repeated, alarm racing into her eyes. "What do you mean? Am I under arrest or—"

"Nothing like that," he said quickly. "I need you at headquarters. For questioning."

She frowned. "Has there been another murder? Is the hotel involved or—" She caught her breath. "Is this about Pete?"

"I can't discuss this until we're on our way. I'm sorry." He cleared his throat. "Could you please come with me?"

"All right." She nodded and stepped back from the door so he could enter. "I'll get some shoes and my purse."

While he waited, he looked around her place. The large, open foyer was flanked on the right by a parlor, on the left by a dining room. As were the majority of homes in the Garden District, her raised cottage was old, probably dating from the late 1800s. The windows ran almost from floor to ceiling, the wooden floors and molding looked like cypress and had been buffed to a high shine.

He had expected something grand, more a showplace than a home. He had expected a place that screamed wealth. Instead, her home looked lived-in and comfortable in a warm, unpretentious way.

"You look perplexed," she said, returning to the foyer.

"Do I?"

"Yes." She slipped her purse strap over her shoulder and tipped up her chin. "Maybe you expected different digs for a princess?"

He met her gaze evenly, hating that she had been able to read his mind. "Sorry to disappoint you, Ms. St. Germaine, but I don't have any expectations when it comes to you."

She flushed. "For you to disappoint me, I would have to care what you thought. I don't."

"Good." He motioned the door. "If you're ready."

Together, they walked to his car and without speaking, climbed in. Santos started the car, glancing at her from the corner of his eyes. "Your seat belt, Ms. St. Germaine. It's the law."

She shot him an annoyed glance, but did as he asked. Moments later, they were heading down St. Charles Avenue as if going to Lee Circle; instead, he darted onto the interstate, heading west.

She frowned. "I thought you said we were going to headquarters?"

"I did say that." He eyed the speedometer, seeing that he had reached sixty-five. "But I lied."

It took a full ten seconds for his words to register. When they did, her eyes widened with alarm. "Let me out of this car right now. Do you hear me, Santos? I demand that you stop this car and let me out."

"Sorry, Glory, but I can't do that. Somebody needs you. Somebody I care a lot about. I'm not going to let her down."

"This is ridiculous." She drew in a sharp breath. "If you don't stop this car right now, I'm going to report you for... for kidnapping!"

Santos laughed and shook his head. "You're being melodramatic. I didn't kidnap you. We're just going for a little ride."

"Against my will." She grabbed the door handle. "That's kidnapping."

He pressed down on the accelerator. The speedometer shot up to seventy, then seventy-five. "I wouldn't jump out just now, if I were you. It might hurt."

"You jerk, I'll have your badge for this."

"That's the second time you've said that to me. Sounds to me like you have a pretty serious case of badge envy."

She glared at him. "Go to hell."

"Okay." He took his eyes from the road to meet hers. "But first I have a story to tell you. I didn't think you would listen if given a choice."

"So you're not giving me a choice?"

"Basically. But if, after I tell you this story, you still want to jump out of the car while it's moving, you'll have my blessing."

"What a guy." She folded her arms across her chest. "So, what kind of story is this?"

"One about a mother and a daughter." Santos cut her a quick glance, then returned his gaze to the road. Glory had turned her face to the window, deliberately ignoring him.

"This mother loved her daughter more than anything in the world, and she wanted her to have a good life, a better one than she'd had. You see, the mother was a prostitute, a madam, actually. She ran a house, a brothel, the same one her mother had, the same one her grandmother had."

He had Glory's attention now. He saw her look his way. "Anyway," he continued, "the mother arranged a new identity for the daughter. She arranged for the girl to go away to a school where no one would know who she really was. Or what she had come from.

"But the daughter had her own plans. She had decided to take all her mother had provided for her, and use it as a way to escape forever. The daughter made that fabricated identity her own, lying to everyone, even to the man she eventually married. She broke her mother's heart, refusing to see her again, no matter how her mother cried, no matter how much she begged. This daughter even refused to go to her mother's deathbed, though seeing her one last time was her dying mother's only wish."

For a moment, neither of them spoke. Finally, Glory cleared her throat, obviously more moved by his tale than she wanted to admit. "An intriguing story. But what does it have to do with me?"

"I'm getting to that," Santos continued, ignoring her question. "The daughter went on to marry very well. She had her own daughter. But no one knew the truth. No one questioned the woman's past or the story she told about how her parents died."

"Please, Santos, I have to be at the hotel in a couple hours." She checked her watch and made a sound of frustration. "Make that an hour and a half. Could we quit the cloak-and-dagger? If you have something to tell me, I wish you would just do it."

"All right. The daughter attended a fine, old boarding school in Memphis. She told everyone her parents died while traveling abroad."

Glory turned toward him. "What did you say?"

"I think you heard me."

She shook her head, disbelieving, the full impact of his words hitting her. "You're not actually suggesting—"

"But I am."

"That's ridiculous. That would mean my mother—"

"Is a liar." He tightened his fingers on the steering wheel. "My Lily is the mother of the story." He looked at Glory. "She's your grandmother."

Glory shook her head again, bright spots of color staining her cheeks. "This whole thing is absurd. I don't believe you."

"It's absurd, all right. But it's also true."

Glory brought a hand to her temple. He saw that it trembled. "If, all these years . . . Lily knew how to contact me, why didn't she? If she longed to know me, why didn't she simply make it happen?"

"Because she's ashamed of who she is. She's ashamed of what she spent a good part of her life being. Because she was afraid you would reject her, just as her daughter had. She bought the bullshit line your mother fed her, about how she would ruin your life. How she would *taint* it." He took a deep breath, angry again. More determined than a moment before. "She needs you, Glory. She longs for you. She's dying."

Glory caught her breath. "Dying?"

"Yes." Santos tightened his fingers on the steering wheel, fighting off the hopelessness that washed over him, focusing instead on his anger, his hatred for Hope St. Germaine. "And your mother refused to go see her. It's the only thing Lily wants, her last wish. And your mother said no."

He glanced at her and saw from her expression that, even though she didn't believe him, she was starting to wonder. He saw, too, that his story had touched her heart. "I know this is hard for you to swallow. I know what its being true will mean, to you. But I have no reason to lie about this."

"Why should I believe you, Santos? Just tell me that. Your story is so farfetched it's ludicrous."

"Because it's true. And because, if you'll let me, I can prove it."

She hesitated again, obviously torn. She glanced at her watch, then back at him. "How long will this take?"

"Longer than you've got. To prove my story, we're going to have to take a little drive." She opened her mouth as if to refuse; he cut her off. "Think about this, Glory. What if it's true? How will you feel, knowing you let an old woman die alone?"

For a moment, Glory said nothing. He could almost see her considering her options, weighing her choices, the ramifications of each. Finally, she sighed. "This would mean that everything I know about my mother is a lie."

"I know. But isn't knowing the truth, even if it hurts, better than believing a lie?"

She caught her bottom lip between her teeth, then nodded. "You say you can prove this?"

"Yes."

"All right, Santos. Prove it."

Santos took her to the River Road house. During the drive, she said little, lost, he knew, in her own thoughts. He could only imagine what was running through her head right now; he understood that this was going to hurt her.

But he would do anything for Lily. And Lily needed her granddaughter.

They reached Lily's property; Santos stopped the car, climbed out and unlocked the huge iron gates. "Are you ready for this?"

She met his eyes, her expression tense. "Does it matter if I'm not?"

He smiled grimly. "No."

"Then let's go."

He drove up the oak-lined alley, slowly so Glory could get a good look at the house, and so he could, too. He understood Lily's unhappy feelings for this place, but he loved it. He thought it the most beautiful place in the world.

"It's beautiful," Glory said, as if reading his thoughts, a catch in her voice.

"This was Lily's house. Her home, the brothel. And it was her mother's, and before that, her grandmother's."

"It's the Pierron House," she murmured, realizing suddenly. "I read about it. I remember a classmate pointing it out on a field trip to Oak Alley plantation."

"I imagine most Louisianians have heard of it. The Pierron women, and this place, were quite well known. Especially in its heyday." He stopped the car. "Here we are."

Santos said nothing more until after they were in the house. Their footsteps resounded in the quiet. He and Lily had left most of the furnishings, covered now in white sheets. The apartment hadn't had room, and she hadn't wanted most of these things around her.

"I come as often as I can," he said. "To check up on the place. A building as old as this always needs something. Lily can't afford to hire someone to take care of it, so I do what I'm able myself."

After that, he didn't speak. He trailed behind her as she made her way through the massive rooms, her head swiveling from side to side as she tried to take it all in. Occasionally, she would stop and lift one of the sheets to see a piece of furniture. Her face wore an expression that he had never seen before—one of wonder and fear, doubt and certainty.

Glory stopped and stared up at a portrait above the fireplace. As a young girl, Glory had borne a resemblance to her ancestors. As a woman, she had grown into their image. She could have been gazing at a portrait of herself.

"My God. She looks just like . . ."

"I know." Santos stopped beside Glory. "That's Lily's grandmother, Camellia Pierron. The first Pierron madam. There was Camellia, Rose, then Lily."

"They were all named after flowers."

"Until your mother. Lily wanted to break the chain. She hated being what she was. And she wanted better for her daughter."

"So she named her Hope." Glory made a strangled sound, part amusement, part despair. "I guess I come from a long and illustrious line of career girls."

"You could say that." A smile tugged at his mouth. "They were all smart. They kept this place going long after it was fashionable. And they were all beautiful. Incredibly beautiful."

"And trapped," Glory whispered, almost to herself. She turned to him. "What of their sons?"

"There were none." He shook his head. "Only daughters. One for each Pierron woman."

Just like her mother.

The unspoken thought hung in the air between them. Glory rubbed her arms, visibly shaken. "This could be a coincidence. Many southern Louisianians of French descent have similar coloring and features. I went to school with a girl who was often taken for my sister."

"Come." He led her to photographs that could not lie. She picked up one after another, studying each, growing pale, her hands beginning to tremble.

"You see? You're the image of them. And look, there's one of your mother."

This time she said nothing, but met his eyes, hers bright with tears, then quickly glanced away. "Is there anything else?"

"Yes. This way."

He led her to the attic and a trunk he had discovered years ago, though Lily had never known. It was filled with letters, ones that Lily had sent to Glory's mother, ones that Hope had opened and read, then callously returned to sender. They were letters from a desperate and lonely mother to the daughter she adored. They were pleas for forgiveness, pleas for love. He had cried when he read them, though he had been eighteen years old and had thought himself pretty tough.

Glory sank to the floor. With hands that shook, she selected one, though she didn't open it. She stared at it, and he had a sense that she was afraid to read it—because she feared what she would learn.

He understood. Because he had read the letters himself. And because, although she was selfish and spoiled and self-centered, Glory was not mean the way her mother was. What Hope St. Germaine had done to her mother, Glory could never do.

He cleared his throat. "I'll give you some time alone. If you need me, I'll be downstairs."

"Thank you," she murmured, not looking up.

Forty minutes later, he returned. The pattern of light on the wall and floors had shifted and mellowed, the stack of letters beside Glory had grown. But she sat just as he had left her, head bowed, hands closed over a letter in her lap.

Only now, her shoulders shook. Now her breath came in short, ragged gasps.

She was crying.

He stepped into the attic. "Glory?"

She looked up at him. He caught his breath at her expression, soft and guileless with pain.

"How could she?" Glory whispered brokenly. "How could she have read these and not relented? How could even my mother have been so heartless? So cold and unforgiving?"

"I don't know."

Her tears welled and spilled over again, dropping onto the letter in her hands. She wiped them carefully away. "How long . . . how long have you known?"

"I learned the night your father died. Lily told me then."

She nodded, her lips trembling. "I don't know my mother at all, do I? All these years, I thought . . . all these years, she told me my grandparents were dead. She lied to me." Glory drew in a trembling breath. "All this time . . . I've had a grandmother."

"One who needs you." Santos squatted beside her and cupped her face in his hands. Her tears ran over and between his fingers. "All she longs for, all she's ever longed for, is you and your mother. I called your mother this morning. She refused to see Lily. I begged her, Glory. I swallowed my pride and begged.''

Glory searched his gaze. "Is my . . . is Lily very ill?''

"She's had a heart attack. A bad one. We don't know the extent of the damage yet, but the doctor isn't encouraging.'' Santos tightened his fingers. "She needs you. Will you come with me? Will you give her this?''

Glory covered his hands with her own, and for one long moment, simply gazed at him, her heart in her eyes. Then she nodded. "Take me to my grandmother.''

46

Glory gazed at the elderly woman, pale even against the white hospital sheets. She looked so vulnerable lying there, hooked up to machines and an IV, so fragile that Glory doubted she could fight off even a strong gust of wind.

This woman, this stranger, was her grandmother. Glory drew a careful breath, emotion flooding her. She could have lost her before she'd had a chance to know her.

Glory pulled a chair up to the side of the bed. Hesitantly, she reached a hand out to the older woman's hand and covered it with her own. Lily's skin was papery with age, so translucent Glory could see each vein. But warm, Glory thought, curving her fingers around the other woman's. Still flowing with life. Thank God.

Glory swallowed hard. She felt light-headed, as if she'd had one too many cocktails or had been deprived of oxygen. She couldn't quite grasp what had happened, couldn't quite place all the things Santos had told her.

In the space of minutes, she had learned she had a family and a history she had never even suspected existed. *Prostitutes.* She came from women who had sex with strangers for money. She breathed deeply through her nose, remembering being twelve or thirteen, remembered she and some other girls giggling and whispering about the Pierron House. About the women who lived there and about what they did inside those walls. One of the girls had snickered and called it a cathouse.

Those women had been her women—her people. She was one of them. She was a part of that place.

Trembling, she tightened her fingers around Lily's. In those same minutes, she had learned that her mother was a liar and a fraud. Dear God, which, of all the things her mother had told her of her childhood and youth, had been true? Had any of them?

Tears stung her eyes. The grandparents she had thought she'd known, didn't exist. The stories her mother had told her—of growing up in the big, sunny house on a hill in Meridian, Mississippi, of the times she and her daddy had walked hand in hand to get ice cream on Saturday afternoons, of Christmas Eves spent singing carols around the huge tree they had cut themselves—they were all lies. All of them.

Despair built inside her. Panic with it. Now, here she sat, holding the hand of a stranger she had been told was her grandmother, holding her hand and hoping, praying, she didn't die.

Glory squeezed her eyes shut, fighting back the wave of emotions that threatened to swallow her. How could her mother have done this? How could she have lied this way—for all these years, to the people she loved and was supposed to trust? To her daughter? Her entire family?

Family.

Glory thought of her father, of the things he had taught her. About family. About heritage. What he had told her of knowing who she was by her family name and history. Those things, he had told her, could never be taken away from her, just as they could never be erased.

Though her mother had tried. *Her mother had tried to steal her heritage from her.*

The panic returned, swelling inside her. Half of who she was was a mystery. A lie. Who was Glory St. Germaine? How could she know herself, if a part of her was a blank?

Her head filled with the image of the River Road house, filled with the scent of the air, with the sound of the breeze through the ancient oaks, the creak of the floorboards beneath her feet, and her lips lifted. She had felt an instant affinity for the house, she'd felt comfortable there, as if she belonged. Before Santos had said a word, before she had seen the photos, before she had *known* the truth.

The River Road house had felt like home. More like home than the house she had grown up in. Why? What did it mean that she had felt that way about that place?

Santos stepped into the room. She knew it was him, though her back faced the door, though he didn't speak. She sensed his presence, she felt it as an almost physical thing. The way she always had. A slow shudder of awareness moved over her, unwanted but unstoppable. His effect on her, too, had not changed in the ten years that had passed since they'd been lovers.

Ten years in which he had known who she was and she had been in the dark.

A cry raced to her lips. She bit it back and glanced over her shoulder at him, the questions clawing at her, needing, demanding, answers.

He only had eyes for Lily.

Glory swallowed hard, forgetting the past, forgetting awareness and longings. Forgetting her questions. Her heart broke for him. She saw such grief in his eyes. Such love.

And she saw fear. He had already lost one mother. Now, he stood on the threshold of losing another.

This woman was not his mother, but he loved her as one, Glory realized. She had earned his devotion. That said something. It meant something.

Lily had been a prostitute. But she was a good woman, anyway, Glory acknowledged. A special woman. One who had made her way into Santos's heart, a boy who had been tough and cynical, a boy who had been let down again and again. And she had changed his life by loving him. By believing in him.

Hurting, Glory turned quickly back to Lily. Santos would not want her to feel compassion for him. He wouldn't like it; he would misinterpret it as pity. Or worse.

Santos wanted nothing from her. In terms of basic human decency, he expected even less than that. *He thought she was like her mother.*

Her mother.

Glory's throat closed with emotion. If she had been forced to beg for her life right now, she would have been unable to utter a sound. How could even her own mother have been so unforgiving? So heartless? How could she have read those wrenching letters, then returned them without a response?

The image from before her eighth birthday, of her mother's twisted features, the memory of the nailbrush moving punishingly over her skin, filled her head. With the image, her frightening words. *"I will cleanse you. If I have to, I will scrub the flesh from your bones. You will be clean, Daughter."*

Glory shuddered, bile rising in her throat, nearly choking her. It made a kind of twisted sense now, why her mother had reacted so violently when she had come upon her and Danny in the library, and years later when she had caught her necking in the church parking lot. As did her constant quoting of scripture, her obsession with Glory behaving like a perfect little lady, her obsession with the vile nature of the flesh.

"It's hard to believe they're mother and daughter," Santos murmured, crossing to the side of the bed, stopping beside Glory. "They're nothing alike. I promise you that."

She didn't ask what he meant or for him to clarify, his expression and tone told her everything. He loved Lily completely. "What did the doctor say?" she asked instead.

"Not much. Nothing happened while I was gone. She's resting comfortably. She's stable for now. She could wake up anytime."

"She looks so...fragile."

Santos didn't answer, and Glory knew he didn't trust himself to speak. She swallowed past the lump in her throat. "I wish I could tell you that it was going to be all right," she said after a moment, softly.

He cut her a glance, then looked quickly away. "But you can't. No one can."

She felt his pain, his isolation, and yearned to take it away. She yearned to touch him, to wrap her arms and herself around him and offer him comfort and support with her body.

She caught herself starting to do just that and dropped her hand. He would rebuff her. Or laugh at her. And it would hurt. She had no right to touch him, no right to try to comfort him. They had ended a long time ago.

"No, I can't tell you that," she whispered. "But I am sorry. So terribly . . . sorry."

He met her eyes, and for a moment, she sensed that he was grateful for her support, for her presence beside him. And in that moment, she felt close to him, close in a way she hadn't felt to anyone since Santos. Close in a way she had missed.

She lifted a hand. "Santos, I—"

He stiffened and took a step away from her. "I need to call headquarters. If she wakes up while I'm gone, will you—"

"Of course." She turned back to Lily, not wanting him to see her hurt. "I'll come get you right away."

But Lily didn't wake up. Not then, not in the six hours that followed. Glory didn't leave her side save to call the hotel, go to the bathroom and grab a bag of chips and a Coke from the vending machines down the hall. She couldn't bear the thought of not being by her grandmother's side the moment she woke up. Too, she harbored the horrible fear that she might have only one chance to be with Lily, that she might awaken once, but never again. And she would miss it.

That couldn't happen. She couldn't let it happen.

Santos, too, rarely left Lily's side. So they shared the small space, like adversaries forced to guard the same post, not talking, not swapping reassurances or even reassuring glances.

Finally, Lily moaned, then stirred. Santos jumped to his feet and crossed to her. "Lily... Lily." He took her hand. "It's me, Santos. I'm here."

Her eyelids fluttered up. Her gaze landed on him. She tried to speak, but couldn't.

Glory took a deep, careful breath. Her heart was pounding, her palms sweating. She was afraid, she realized. Of being rejected by this woman she now desperately wanted to know. Of not living up to Lily's expectations, as she had never lived up to her mother's. Of saying the wrong thing, of hurting this woman more than she had already been hurt.

"Lily," Santos said softly, "there's someone here to see you."

Glory stood and went around to the other side of the bed. The woman's gaze moved to her. Even in her grandmother's weakened, drugged state, Glory could see the hope in Lily's eyes. Then the recognition.

"Glo... ry?"

"Yes. It's me." Glory moved even closer to the bed. "Hello, Grandmother."

Lily looked back at Santos, as if for reassurance. He gave it by smiling. She shifted her gaze back to Glory, tears flooding her eyes. "I've... waited... so long."

She took Lily's hand. "Me, too, Grandmother." Lily curled her fingers around hers, the old woman's grip no stronger than a child's. "It's good to be here."

Lily opened her mouth to speak, but nothing came out. Santos held a cup of water to her lips, and she sipped, then tried again. "Your... mother?"

At the desperate hope in the old woman's eyes, Glory glanced at Santos, uncertain what to say, not wanting to hurt Lily by telling her the truth.

He stepped in without pause. "She couldn't come," he said quietly. "She had an... an engagement that she... that couldn't be..."

He let the words trail off. Lily wasn't being fooled. She closed her eyes and turned her head, tears slipping silently down her cheeks.

Glory's heart broke, even as fury at her mother's callousness built inside her. She tightened her fingers on Lily's. "But I'm here, Grandmother. I wanted to come." Lily looked at her, and Glory leaned closer. She smiled softly. "I want us to get to know each other. I want us to make up for some of the time we missed."

Lily clutched Glory's fingers, her expression so grateful it hurt Glory to look at her. Glory brought her grandmother's hand to her cheek. "I love you," she whispered. "And I'm so glad we're finally going to be together."

After that, Glory sat beside the bed, talking softly, mostly about nothing of great importance. Occasionally, Lily would manage a question, always about Glory, and she would hang on the answers as if they were worth more than gold.

While Glory talked, Santos either paced, seeming to almost crackle with barely contained energy, or he stood as still as a predator studying its prey. She was aware of every step he took, his every breath, his every glance her way.

Her awareness of him exhausted her.

It wasn't long before the nurse scurried in and shooed them both off. Lily needed rest, she said. They could return later.

Together Glory and Santos walked to the elevator. Santos punched the call button, then looked at her, the naked animosity in his eyes taking her aback.

"Will you come to see her again?" he asked. "Or have you done your duty?"

She felt his words, his total disdain for her, like a physical blow. She'd thought that she and Santos had begun to bridge the gap between them, to forge a truce, even though a tenuous one. She had been wrong. It took her a moment, but when she met his gaze, she met it evenly, hiding her hurt.

"How can you even ask that question? Do you think this is some sort of game to me? Do you really think I would so cavalierly hurt that sweet woman? That I would tell her I love her, then never come to see her again?"

"It crossed my mind."

She caught her breath, wounded beyond words. "You bastard. I'm not my mother, despite what you think. I'll be back."

"Good." His mouth thinned. "It meant a lot to her for you to be here. I don't want her heart broken again."

Glory folded her arms across her chest and hiked up her chin. "It meant a lot to me, too. In fact, before you started being such a horse's ass, I was going to thank you."

"Really? For what?"

He arched his eyebrows in exaggerated disbelief. She would take great pleasure in slugging him, she decided, shoving her hands deep into her pockets to keep from doing just that.

"For Lily, of course," she said, gritting her teeth. "I feel as if you've given me a gift."

"Knowing Lily *is* a gift." He looked away, then back, his expression fierce. "But be assured, princess, I didn't do it for you."

Without giving her a chance to retort, he turned and walked away.

47

Hope sat in the white wicker empress chair, her favorite bible open on her lap. The sounds of the summer night drifted in through the screens, the sounds of insects and the occasional frog, children playing, a dog barking somewhere on the block. Above her, the whir of the ceiling fan stirred the warm, moist air.

She rested her head against the chair's high back and closed her eyes. As she had grown older, The Darkness had become more determined, more insistent. She was forced to battle it more fiercely, yet fell into its clutches more often. Most days found her battle weary and drained of energy.

Only after she succumbed did The Beast slumber, only then did it give her moments of peace.

It had slept for over a week now. She smiled to herself. At times like these, she thought life good. She thought the struggle she had lived with all her life no more than a vivid, chilling nightmare.

And at times like these, she felt certain she had beaten The Beast once and for all.

Her peace was shattered as Glory slammed onto the porch, crossing to stand directly before her. "You make me sick, Mother! How...could you?"

Hope stared at her daughter, stunned speechless. Glory had never looked at her the way she was now. Her eyes burned with a fevered light Hope recognized from her nightmares. From her nightmares and from her own reflection when The Darkness held her in its grip.

Her heart flew to her throat. *The Darkness had come for another round. This time, somehow, it had found its way through Glory.*

Hope's hands began to tremble; she steadied them by folding them in her lap. "Glory Alexandra," she said crisply, working to mask the edge of panic in her voice, "you know I don't like being disturbed during my nightly reading of scripture. It's always been that way."

Glory made a sound of disbelief. "Reading scripture, Mother? How very good you are. How very Christian. In fact, you're an example to all of us, aren't you? At least that's what you've always wanted me, and everyone else, to believe."

Hope's heart began to thunder. Something had happened, something awful. Something she had feared since her first, heady taste of freedom from the shadow of sin.

She lowered her gaze to the Bible, open to the Twenty-third Psalm.

*Even though I walk through the valley
of the shadow of death,
I fear no evil, for thou art with me.*

Hope drew a deep breath, focusing on the words of the psalm, letting them soothe and protect her. Carefully, she closed the Good Book and set it aside, then folded her hands in her lap once more. She raised her eyebrows coolly. "What's that supposed to mean, Daughter? Are you upset about something?"

"Upset? Yes, I think so." Glory took several more steps into the room. Hope noticed that her daughter's hands were clenched into fists at her sides. "Tell me, Mother, does the scripture say anything about forgiveness? Does it say anything about the sin of judging others?"

Cold started at the top of Hope's head and moved downward until she felt as chilled as death. A small sound of fright slipped past her lips. "Of course it does. As you know very well. I made sure you were well versed in the words of the Lord."

"Oh, yes, you made sure I went to mass. You made sure I knew the Bible, from cover to cover. You made sure that I was a perfect little angel." Her voice cracked. "And if I fell below your demanding standards, you made sure I was punished for my sins."

"I'm your mother. I always did what I thought best for you."

"Or did you always do what you thought best for yourself?" Glory swept her hair away from her face, and sucked in a sharp breath. "I met Lily Pierron today. *My grandmother.* I saw the house you grew up in. I know what you did, Mother. I know."

The breath left Hope's body. She stared at her daughter, her world crashing in around her ears.

Glory knew.

Dear Lord, she knew.

Hope struggled to get a grip on her emotions. She had feared this day would come; she had prayed that it wouldn't. Now that it had she must find the right, the best, words. "I don't know what you're talking about. My mother and I had a wonderful relationship. It broke my heart when the Lord took her from me at such a young age."

"Stop it, Mother! Stop lying to me!" Glory fought back a sob. "Your mother is very much alive. Although she nearly died today. How could you . . . how could you—"

Glory choked on the words, and she swung away from Hope. She brought her hands to her face. "I don't . . . know what to say to you. I don't . . . know who you are." She dropped her hands and looked at Hope. "I don't know who I am. Because of your lies. Because you kept the truth from me."

Hope squeezed her hands into fists. "You are Glory St. Germaine. Of the New Orleans St. Germaines. And I am your mother."

"And she's yours! You abandoned her!"

"You know nothing! You—"

"Santos took me to the River Road house. I saw pictures. I read the letters grandmother sent to you. She begged you for forgiveness. Begged you, Mother. You read those letters and you sent them back."

Hope flew to her feet, shaking with rage. "She's a whore! Don't you understand? A dirty whore who sold her body to the highest bidder!"

"Stop it!" Glory whirled to face Hope. "She's my grandmother! She needs me. I won't abandon her the way you did. I would never do that!"

"It's so easy for you, isn't it?" Hope cried. "You accuse me of judging my mother unfairly, yet here you stand, so quick to judge me. So quick to abandon me. You have no idea what I lived through."

"How could I? All I know about you is your lies." She swung away from Hope and crossed to the edge of the porch, visibly working to control herself.

"All these years you lied to me," she said finally, her voice thick. "To all of us." She shook her head. "Santos called you today. Your mother lay near death, her only wish, her dying wish, to see you. But still you couldn't forgive. You denied her the small gift of a visit, a last visit."

Glory shook her head again, swiping at her cheeks, at the tears that rolled down them. "I don't know who you are. You're a stranger to me, now. When I think of all the times you spoke of your father, the man I imagined to be my grandfather, I almost can't bear it. He didn't exist. You never even knew your father. You were a trick baby, Santos told me. All the Pierron women were. All except me."

Hope's stomach lurched to her throat. She held back the vomit through sheer force of will. "That's right, all except you. Because of me. Because I wouldn't allow myself to be dragged down into the gutter with them!" She threw her head back, proud. "Thanks to me, you're a St. Germaine. The Pierron part of you doesn't exist. It…doesn't…exist."

"But it does! Don't you understand? You can't simply say something doesn't exist and then it doesn't. And I won't cut away that part from me. The Pierron past is my past, too. Whether you like it or not.''

"You *can* cut it away." Hope grabbed Glory's arms, her grip punishing. ''You must! I did.''

"No!'' Glory yanked free of her grasp, and stepped backward, her expression disgusted. ''I won't do that, Mother. It's not who I am, and I think it's wrong.''

The Darkness would not steal her daughter from her. His instrument, that vile boy, would not steal Glory from her. He had tried once, and she had beaten him. She would again.

No matter what she had to do.

Hope brought her hands to her face, struggling to find tears, praying for just the right words, the right pleas. *She had to save her daughter. She had to save herself.*

"You can't imagine," she began softly, lowering her hands as her eyes welled with tears, ''what I lived through. You can't imagine what it was like growing up in a...in that place. The things I heard and saw, the life-style I was forced to endure. I lived with whores, Glory. Prostitutes.''

"I know that, Mother. But—''

"You know nothing! I was spurned by all but those of the house. I was called foul, hateful names. Not because of things I had done, only because of what I had been born into.'' Hope's tears spilled over, no longer fabricated. She remembered with great clarity and bitterness all that she had endured.

"I had no friends. At school, I was alone. At church, on the playground, the school bus. I was never invited to a birthday party or another child's house. The girls taunted me, and the boys chased me.'' Her voice quivered. ''And when they caught me, they held me down and forced me to endure their hands and...their mouths. Because of who I was. Because of who my mother was.''

Hope lowered her head, the memories clawing at her. ''At night, I couldn't sleep for the sounds of the men and the whores. I would hear their panting and grunting...like animals. Human animals without souls.''

Glory brought a hand to her mouth, her expression horrified.

"You see why I ran? You see why I could never go back? If I had stayed there, Glory, I would have died. My soul would have . . . died."

Glory struggled to speak. "But your mother, she . . . loved you. She tried to protect you. She sent you away."

"Yes, she loved me." Hope brought her hands to her face, a great well of hatred roiling inside of her, though she tamped it back. "And I loved her. But I . . . I couldn't separate her from my life, or from my awful despair. All I wanted was to escape. All I wanted was a fresh start." Hope looked pleadingly at her daughter. "When I had the chance to escape, I took it."

Hope drew in a great, shuddering breath. "Please try to understand. Please try to . . . forgive me. If you . . . if I lost you, Glory, I couldn't bear it."

Glory gathered her mother into her arms. "You're not going to lose me. What you went through sounds so horrible. I understand your wanting to escape. I do. But why did you have to lie? To me and Daddy? Why did you need to totally desert her? Why was it necessary to be so cruel?"

Hope clung to Glory, pressing her face to her shoulder. "I was afraid. For myself. And later, for you." She lifted her gaze to Glory's. "Do you think your daddy would have married me if he had known who my people were? Imagine Grandmother St. Germaine's reaction to the news that I was a *Pierron*. They were notorious women. Anyone who grew up in New Orleans had heard of them."

Hope lowered her face and began to sob, though without tears. "I was so afraid. I still am. I don't want anyone to know. If they did . . . I would lose everything, Glory. I know I would."

"It's all right, Mama." Glory stroked her back. "I do understand. If that's what you want, I won't tell anyone."

"Thank you," she whispered, lifting her head and meeting her daughter's eyes.

"I won't tell anyone, Mother. But I won't desert her, either. She needs me. And I...I need her, too. I want to know my grandmother."

Hope stared at her daughter, aghast, her fragile feeling of safety crumbling around her. *The Darkness had come to call. It very nearly had its clutches on her daughter.*

Hope grabbed Glory's hands. "With everything you know about her, about who and what she was, how can you—"

"That was in the past. I understand what you did. And though I don't condone your actions, I forgive them. I can't judge you." She searched her mother's gaze. "And I can't judge her, either. I won't."

Hope tightened her fingers over Glory's. "I know I was hard on you growing up. I know I was stricter than the other mothers." She drew in a shuddering breath. "But after seeing the depths women could sink, I was so afraid for you. I just wanted you to have a good life. One that was clean, one that followed His word.

"Please," Hope begged, "your grandmother is dangerous. I'm afraid you'll...I'm afraid of her influence, I'm afraid she'll hurt you."

"I'm all grown-up now, Mother." Glory smiled and gently drew her hands away. "I'm not going to suddenly become a scarlet woman. Lily is old and she's sick. She's hardly going to tempt me into a life of sin."

But The Beast never aged. It didn't grow sick and it never died. Glory didn't know, she didn't understand, not its ways or that it lay in wait inside her, just biding its time.

And if she told Glory, she wouldn't believe her. She would think her mother was crazy.

So Hope let Glory go. Her heart in her throat, she watched her daughter step unprotected into the night, a demon at her heels.

Hours later, Hope huddled alone in the dark, sweating, heart thundering. The Beast had been awakened. It was on the rampage. And this time it wanted them both—Hope and Glory.

Hope fisted her fingers, so tightly her nails dug into her palms. To win this battle she would need her wits and her stamina. Through Santos, The Darkness had already gotten a hold on Glory. This battle would be a trial by fire; it would prove to be the most difficult she had ever faced.

But she would win, for herself and for Glory. She would not be bested, not now, not after having spent her life protecting and guiding her daughter.

Hope thought of Santos; hatred for him burned inside her. He would pay for this. Someday, she would find a way to make him pay.

The days moved one into the other. With each day, Lily grew stronger, and it seemed to Santos that more than anything the doctors did, Glory was the reason for her improvement. She was always at Lily's side. No matter what time he visited the hospital, day or night, Glory was there, holding Lily's hand, talking softly, listening raptly or simply watching her grandmother sleep.

Most times, Santos simply stood back, watched and listened as Glory shared the details of her life with her grandmother, filling her in on the person Lily had not been allowed to know. And although he would never be able to completely trust Glory, her gentleness with Lily, her unselfish sharing of herself and her time, had subtly changed his opinion of her. Glory was not like her mother; she wasn't so cold or judgmental. She wasn't mean.

And sometimes, when he listened to her, his memory flooded with the girl he had known all those years ago. The girl he had thought he loved.

Those memories unsettled him, they robbed him of his cool-eyed perspective. When that happened, he had to remind himself that he didn't like Glory, that he wasn't intrigued by the woman she had grown into, and that they had nothing in common except Lily and their concern for her.

They had so little in common that during the past days he and Glory had exchanged few words. They asked things like "How is she?" and "Has the doctor been in?" or "Any news?" And even though they had received the grim results of Lily's angiocardiogram together—with this attack, Lily had lost twenty-five percent of her heart, and the chances of her having another attack on the heels of this first one was great—they hadn't talked about it afterward, they hadn't tried to comfort each other.

In fact, they never touched and rarely glanced the other's way. Except every so often, while she and Lily visited and almost as if by accident, Glory would look up at him and smile. And he would stand there feeling as if she had just reached inside him and turned all his vital organs inside out and backward.

Frowning at his own thoughts, Santos swung into the first parking spot he came to, slammed out of his car and headed for the hospital's front entrance, anxious to see Lily. A homicide had kept him away last night and all morning, and as the hours had passed, a vague uneasiness had settled over him. He feared something was wrong, that Lily had taken a turn for the worse. He had tried to call several times: twice Lily had been asleep, and once no one had answered.

Glory was with her, he told himself, picking his way around several slow-moving groups. She would have called if Lily's condition had changed. Sure she would have. He was experiencing a simple, if irrational, reaction to having almost lost Lily.

He sucked in a quick, deep breath, acknowledging gratitude for Glory's attentiveness. He might not like the woman she had become or have any illusions about their shared past, but he was grateful he'd had her to count on during this ordeal. Crime didn't come to a screeching halt simply because he had a family emergency. Knowing Glory was with Lily had allowed him to stay, at least minimally, on the job.

Santos reached the elevator. Jammed, it stopped on every floor between one and six, loading and unloading at each stop. Finally, he reached six, then made it out and to the end of the hall and Lily's room in a matter of moments.

Heart pounding, he pushed through the half-open door, then stopped in the doorway, stunned. He had expected to find the worst: that Lily had suffered another attack, that she was, once more, only a step away from death. Instead, Lily was sitting up in bed, laughing—a kind of breathless-schoolgirl laugh—as Glory recounted one of her high-school exploits.

Santos swallowed hard, almost light-headed with relief. He had never seen Lily quite this happy, he realized. He hadn't heard her laugh this way in a long time. He shook his head. She had just suffered a major heart attack, and she all but glowed.

Lily saw him then and smiled, a brilliant, breath-stealing smile, one filled with happiness and thanks. A wave of emotion rushed over him, and with it a lightness he had never experienced before. Long ago, he had vowed to take care of Lily, to protect her, in a way he hadn't been able to care for and protect his mother. He had made good on that vow, he realized. He had done this for her, given her this time with her granddaughter. He had made her happy.

"Victor," Lily said, holding out her hand. "You've come just in time to hear about Glory's first piano recital."

He crossed the room and took Lily's hand. "I can't wait." Smiling, he bent and kissed her cheek. "You look wonderful."

"I feel wonderful." She curved her fingers around his. "The doctor says I'm almost ready to go home. Maybe tomorrow."

"Tomorrow? Already?" He shifted his gaze to Glory's, and she nodded. He returned his gaze to Lily. "That's great."

"I'm a tough old bird."

"That you are." He laughed. "You never cut me any slack, that's for sure."

"You bandit!" Lily laughed and slapped his hand. "I gave you so much slack, you nearly hung yourself on several occasions." She turned to Glory and began to recount a story about how, when she discovered that Santos had been sneaking out at night to meet a girl, she had locked all the doors and windows, forcing him to have to ring the bell at 3:00 a.m. to get back in.

"He was so surprised," Lily said, laughing. "I listened as he went from window to window, trying each one. When he was finally forced to go to the front door and ring, he was so chagrined."

"I thought I was being so slick," he said, laughing. "I had no idea she was onto me. I kept thinking I must have left a different window open."

That story led to another and another. They all laughed, chiming in comments and cracking jokes. Before long, Lily could hardly keep her eyes open.

"If you need to take off," Santos said to Glory, "I can hang around."

She shook her head. "I'll stay for a while. Nothing's going on at the hotel, and my assistant manager will call me if something comes up."

"I wish I could say the same for the N.O.P.D." He made a sound of frustration. It had been nine weeks since the Snow White Killer had last struck, and Santos feared he had moved on. He wasn't the only one, even the media had begun to speculate the killer's spree was over, at least in New Orleans.

Santos flexed his fingers. He had to catch this guy, he had to stop him.

He had to know if he was the one who had killed his mother.

Glory watched him, a small frown forming between her eyebrows. "What's wrong? Has something happened?"

"Nothing. And that's the problem."

She searched his expression, obviously confused. "If you need to go, I'll tell Lily—"

"No, I've got a little time." He motioned toward the door. "I'm going to give Jackson a quick call and grab a cup of coffee from the machine. Want anything?"

"No. Thanks. I'll get something in a little while."

"Call me if she wakes up while I'm gone."

"I will."

He stepped out into the hallway, smiling to himself, thinking of Lily's story and the way they had all laughed. For a moment, he had forgotten that he didn't trust or like Glory. For a moment, he had forgotten that she was the enemy.

"Santos!"

He looked up. Liz was coming down the hall toward him, carrying a flowering plant. He started toward her, meeting her halfway. "Liz." He bent and kissed her lightly. "What are you doing here?"

"I came to see Lily." She held up the plant. "Is this a bad time?"

"Of course not." He forced a smile. He hadn't told her about Glory and Lily's relationship. He had anticipated her reaction and decided to leave well enough alone. He should have anticipated this, too. "Unfortunately, she's sleeping."

"Oh." She looked disappointed. She glanced over his shoulder, at the door he had come out of, then back at him. "I haven't seen you much."

He shoved his hands into his front trouser pockets. "It's been crazy, what with Lily and all my cases." His excuses sounded lame, even to his own ears. For whatever reason, he hadn't felt a compelling need to see Liz since Lily's heart attack.

"It's okay. I understand. I remember what it was like when my dad was in the hospital." She shifted. "I've missed you, that's all."

He felt like a first-class creep—because, even though he wanted to, he didn't feel the same way about her, because he knew how much she longed for him to love her. He felt, somehow, responsible for her feelings. And he hated that.

"Once Lily's home, things should start returning to normal."

"How is she?"

"Doing great. Surprisingly well, in fact. The doc says she's well enough to go home. Probably tomorrow."

"No kidding? That's wonderful."

"Unbelievable. I'd thought I'd lost her."

"I'm happy for you." Liz smiled, though to Santos the curving of her mouth looked a bit stiff. She handed him the plant. "I'll send some food over. Let me know."

"I will. Thanks."

"If there's anything else I can do, you'll let me know?" He nodded, and she laced her fingers together. "I should get back. Business has picked up a bit."

"Has it?" Santos smiled, genuinely pleased. "How's my traditional hamburger selling?"

She returned his smile. "At a rate that doesn't bear contemplation. I fear for the health of the American male."

He tipped his head back and laughed. It felt good, he realized. Very good. He wondered when he had last laughed like that. "I'm glad you came, Liz. I'll tell Lily you were here."

He bent and kissed her again, this time lingering a moment to savor.

"Santos, she's a . . . wake."

He jerked his head up, then looked over his shoulder. Glory hung out of Lily's room, her face pink.

"I'm sorry," she said. "I didn't know you were involv—I mean . . . I didn't know you weren't . . . alone."

"It's okay," he said stiffly, drawing away from Liz. "She's waking up?"

"Yes. I thought you'd want to know." Her gaze moved past him to Liz, then her eyes widened in surprise. "Liz? Liz Sweeney, my God, is that you?"

He felt Liz stiffen. "Hello, Glory."

Glory shook her head. "I can't believe it's really you. How have you been?"

"Fine." She narrowed her eyes, trembling, Santos saw, with anger. "No thanks to you."

Glory paled. She opened her mouth to say something, then closed it without speaking. In that instant, she looked totally, heartbreakingly vulnerable. Santos's heart went out to her, then he reminded himself that she deserved whatever she got. She had used and hurt Liz; he didn't blame Liz for her anger.

Glory cleared her throat. "I...I'll tell Lily...excuse me."

She ducked back into the room, the door snapping shut behind her. As it did, Liz rounded on him. "How could you, Santos?" she whispered, her voice shaking. "I really thought it was Lily's health that was keeping you away. But it was her, wasn't it?"

"This isn't what it seems, Liz. If you'll just let me explain."

She tipped up her chin. "You told me you weren't interested in her."

"I'm not. She's here to see Lily. Not me."

Liz made a sound of disbelief. "Right. If my memory serves, she never even met Lily."

"She hadn't, until a week ago." He took a deep breath. "Lily is Glory's grandmother."

For a full ten seconds, Liz simply stared at him. Then she shook her head. "You can't be serious."

"But I am. Lily is Glory's maternal grandmother." He lifted his shoulders. "She didn't know. Nobody did. Her mother kept it from her."

"I don't understand. She didn't know?"

He shook his head and explained, telling Liz when and how he had come to learn of the connection between Lily and Glory, about Lily's longing for her daughter and granddaughter and why he had finally told Glory.

"I see." Liz glanced at Lily's closed door, then back at Santos. "So, all this time, since Lily's heart attack, you've been with Glory?"

"With Glory? No. Sharing space with her is a better description. We've hardly spoken to each other."

"But you didn't tell me." She lowered her voice. "Why, Santos?"

"Because of this." He made a sound of frustration. "Because I knew you would react...negatively."

"And by negatively, you mean that I would be upset? That I would be jealous and suspicious, and probably overreact?"

He met her gaze evenly. "Yes."

She hiked up her chin more, angry color staining her cheeks. "Can you blame me? Not telling the whole truth is the same as lying. And lying is just another way of saying you're guilty. But in your line of work, you should know that, Detective."

"It's not like that, Liz." *But it was, dammit.*

She met his eyes. "Tell the truth, Santos. Do I have a reason to be jealous or suspicious?"

"No," he said quickly, too quickly, shaking his head. "You don't."

"Your words tell me one thing, your eyes another." She held up a hand to stave off his denials. "I love you, Santos. You know that. And I don't want to lose you. But I—" She drew in a deep breath, as if fortifying herself for what she was about to say next. "But I don't want to go on this way."

The blood began to thrum in his head. "What are you saying?"

"I want a commitment from you. I want to know you're mine. I want to know we have a future together." She took a step toward him. "I want kids someday. I want a family. And I want it with you."

He swallowed hard. A part of him wanted to take her up on her offer, to promise things he had no business promising her. Because he liked her and enjoyed her company. Because he thought she was smart and nice and pretty.

But what he felt wasn't love. And it wasn't enough.

He didn't want to hurt her.

Santos cleared his throat. "I don't know what I want. And I'm not sure what you're...wanting is it."

Her eyes filled, but to her credit, she didn't allow the tears to fall. "You need to decide. Not right now, I know this is a hard time for you. But I need you to think about this, about us. I think we're good together and good for each other."

She took a step closer, laid her hands on his chest and tipped her face up to his. "I think we could be happy, that we could make a good life for ourselves. Together. And it doesn't have to happen right away, I just have to know that it's out there.

"I love you," she said again, bringing one of her hands to his face and stroking softly. "I know your feelings don't run as deep, but I think they could. If you would let them. Let yourself love me, Santos. I promise I won't hurt you. I'll always be there for you. We could have a good life together. We could be a . . . happy family."

A happy family. What he had always wanted.

So why wasn't he jumping at her offer?

He covered her hand with his own. "I want to tell you everything you want to hear," he murmured, his voice thick with emotion. "But I can't. Not right now."

"I understand. But I can't go on this way. I can't go on not knowing. Hanging on by hoping." Her voiced cracked, and she cleared it. "The ball's in your court, Detective."

He searched her gaze, then nodded. "All right, Liz. I'll think about it."

She stood on tiptoe, pressed her mouth to his, then turned and walked away.

For long moments, Santos stared after her, thinking not about what Liz had said, but about Glory. And about how it had felt to be in love.

Frowning, he returned to Lily's room. Glory stood at the room's one window, gazing out. Though she didn't turn toward him, he saw from her profile that she was pale and shaken. He shifted his gaze to Lily and saw that she was asleep.

"How long was she awake?" he asked.

"Only a few minutes," Glory said softly, not taking her gaze from the window. "She asked for you. I told her you'd be right back."

"Thank you."

"Santos, I—" She glanced at him, then away. "I'm sorry about...just now. I didn't mean to, you know, to intrude."

"I know. Forget about it."

Silence ensued again. She cleared her throat. "So, you and Liz are dating."

He cocked his head, studying her, wondering what she was thinking, wondering if she thought it as odd as he did, the way their triangle had changed in the ten years since they had all been together. "We're seeing each other. Yes."

She caught her bottom lip between her teeth. "She looks good. She's...grown-up now."

He stiffened, suddenly angry. "We all are."

She turned her gaze to his. He saw that her eyes were sparkling with tears. "I didn't mean to hurt her. I didn't mean to hurt...anyone."

He looked at her a moment, torn between his anger and his response to the regret in her eyes. The vulnerability.

An illusion, he reminded himself. There was nothing soft, nothing vulnerable about Glory St. Germaine. "I'm sure you didn't," he said tightly. "But that doesn't change the fact that you did hurt...people."

She inched her chin up a fraction. "Like you?"

"Yeah, like me." He fisted his fingers, his anger taking him like a swift punch to the gut. He crossed to stand directly before her, forcing her to tip her head back to meet his eyes. "Is that what you wanted to hear? That you hurt me? That you broke my heart? Does that make you feel good, Glory? Does it make you feel powerful?"

"No," she managed to say, her voice small and tight. "It makes me feel like shit."

"Good."

He made a move to turn away from her; she caught his arm. He felt her tremble. "I lost things, too. I paid a price you couldn't...imagine."

He shook off her hand. "Still playing the poor little rich girl, I see. My heart bleeds, it really does."

She stared at him, her expression hardening. "You are such a bastard."

"So I've been told." He crossed to the door, pausing when he reached it and looking back at her. "You know, Glory, I'm certain I *could* imagine the price you paid. Because I paid, too."

49

Once again, the birds awakened Lily, their sweet song beckoning her to arise and fly with them. Lily opened her eyes. And smiled. Her beloved Glory had fallen asleep in the chair by her bed; the nightstand lamp cast a soft, warm glow over her lovely face. The last two weeks, getting to know her granddaughter, had been the most perfect of her life. She wished her daughter could have found it in her heart to forgive her, but she understood why she could not.

Lily moved her gaze over Glory, realizing that she didn't fear death. Her life had been more complete than many lives, and because of Santos, and now Glory, she had known love.

She was old enough to understand that nothing else mattered.

This time, the pain was sudden and unbearably sharp. She gasped and clutched at her chest, unable to do more, so great was her pain.

But then, mercifully, it was gone. It exited her as quickly and as unexpectedly as it had come, leaving her feeling weightless and young. So very, very young. Lily laughed, the sound girlish and bright. She recalled feeling and sounding this way before, but such a long time ago she couldn't recall exactly when or where.

The birds would not be ignored. Their song increased in volume until it drowned out all else, even the sound of her own thoughts. Lily realized then what had happened. She was gone now. Her life had ended—and yet it had just begun.

She left her body behind, without regrets. *There were no regrets here,* she realized. *No fear or pain, no sadness. Only love.* She had always wondered what it would be like to soar with the birds, to touch the heavens and kiss the sun. She laughed again, happy. Happier, more at peace, than she had thought it possible to be.

She had to say goodbye.

Lily reached out to Glory, covering Glory's hand with her own, curling her fingers around it, wanting to hold on forever, but understanding that she had to go. Glory stirred and smiled, though she didn't awaken.

I love you. Be happy.

Night ended and day began, light spilled in the windows, filling the room with a glow so bright it hurt to look into it. A glow as bright, as brilliant as the sun.

And the birds called sweetly. Insistently.

Not yet. She had to say goodbye to Santos.

She found him, then held him, though she didn't know how. She'd only had to think of him to be by his side, although she knew that it would not always be so.

In life, she had hated goodbyes. In life, goodbyes had always meant being left behind, being rejected. But this goodbye was sweet—sweeter than anything she had ever experienced, full of promise, full of forever.

Don't cry. Don't be sad.

It's good. It's very good.

Smiling, Lily released Santos and turned to the light. As the birds called her name, she let it take her.

50

The funeral was sparsely attended by only Glory and Santos, Liz, Jackson and a handful of Lily's neighbors. Glory had begged her mother to come, but Hope had refused. Glory had accepted her decision, though it had hurt her. She wished that her mother could find it in her heart to forgive Lily.

That she couldn't, troubled Glory. What could Glory think when she saw something so fundamentally missing in her mother's character?

Glory made it through the service dry-eyed, but only because she had already cried a river of tears. She felt so wrung-out, so wasted, she feared she wouldn't have enough energy to pick up and go on with the next day, let alone the rest of her life.

Wearily, she brought a hand to her forehead. The days and hours since she had awakened to find Lily gone, had passed in a painful blur. She and Santos had both set about making arrangements, Santos more than she because he had been a real part of Lily's life.

He had been given that opportunity. She hadn't.

Tears pricked at the back of Glory's eyes, then formed a lump in her throat, choking her. She fought both back, her control near the snapping point. She missed Lily. In the short time they had been together, her grandmother had become an important part of her life. Her passing had left a huge whole in its place.

Glory dropped her hand to her side, helpless to stop her feelings of loss, helpless to stop the memories that battered her. Memories of her father's death, his funeral, of the way she had felt as she stood beside her mother at the grave side, the priest's words echoing through her. In many ways, she felt the same at Lily's passing as she had at her father's—bereft, abandoned, completely alone.

Perhaps because Lily, like her father, had loved her without conditions.

Glory sighed and glanced at Santos. He, too, had survived the service without an outward sign of grief, though his grim, tight expression told her what he was thinking and feeling. Her heart went out to him; she understood.

They had both loved Lily.

Santos had invited everyone to the apartment after the service; Liz had supplied the food and drink, and Glory knew how grateful Santos had been to have that detail taken care of. During the service, Liz had stayed by Santos's side, possessively clinging to his arm. And although Liz hadn't once met her eyes, Glory sensed that Liz was aware of every move she made; she felt the distrust and dislike that emanated from her in almost palpable waves.

Glory looked at Liz for a moment, regret mixing with her grief, longing with her loneliness. If onlys clawing at her.

One by one, people began to depart. Liz because the restaurant had called with an emergency; Jackson because he was always needed at headquarters; the neighbors, finally, because it was time.

Exhausted and near tears, Glory began picking up plates and cups, began stacking them in the sink, readying them for washing.

"Leave it," Santos said tightly, from behind her. "I'll take care of it all later."

She glanced over her shoulder at him. He stood in the kitchen doorway, his expression thunderous. "I don't mind."

"I do." He folded his arms across his chest and glared at her. "Leave it. I don't need your help."

His words hurt more than they should have. "It's no bother. I want to help."

He strode across the room, stopping before her, pinning her with his furious gaze. "Why, Glory? Why do you want to help?"

"Why?" she repeated helplessly. "Because I loved her."

For a moment, he said nothing. He stood stiffly before her, shifting his eyes to a point somewhere over her shoulder, clenching and unclenching his hands at his sides. Finally, again, he met her eyes. The open animosity in them took her breath.

"And just what the fuck does loving Lily have to do with helping me clean the kitchen? You didn't live here. You hardly knew her."

His words hit home; they cut her wide and left her gasping. She lifted her chin, though it trembled. "I just thought...she became a part of my life, an important part, so quickly. I wanted to do...something. I needed to somehow..."

She let her words, the thought, trail off. He didn't understand. Because he didn't want to, because he didn't care about her feelings. He had contacted her for Lily's benefit, not for hers. She had served her purpose; he wanted her out of his life now.

She fought back a cry of despair. What had she expected? That they would turn to each other in their grief? That he would be there for her, to help shore her up, to understand? That he would want her to be there for him in those same ways?

A hysterical laugh bubbled to her lips. And why? Just because their relationship had become somewhat amiable? Or because they had been civil to each other, and only for Lily's sake, at that?

She was such an idiot. Such a naive fool.

"You didn't answer my question, Glory." He took another step toward her, crowding her—with his body and his strength, with the awesome anger radiating from him. "What does loving Lily have to do with helping me? Did you think doing a few dishes would bring you closer to her? That it would erase some of your guilt?"

"Fine," she said, sounding beaten even to her own ears. "If you want to clean up this mess yourself, have at it."

She turned off the water and dried her hands, then pushed past him to exit the kitchen. He followed her, grabbing her arm when she reached the doorway. "Dammit, Glory. I want an answer."

She met his eyes, feeling nearly light-headed with grief and exhaustion. "No, you don't. You want a fight. And I'm not going to dishonor Lily by doing that. Let me pass."

He tightened his fingers instead. "You can't make up for Lily's pain and suffering, Glory. You can't take back all those lonely years. It's too late. You're too late."

She caught her breath, knowing what he said was true, acknowledging that, in a way, he had read her mind. She wanted desperately to make up for those lost years, to have them back. And she didn't need him to point out to her that she wanted the impossible.

She wrenched her arm free. "I have nothing to feel guilty about. And don't you dare try to make it sound as if I do. That was my mother's sin, not mine. I would never have done to Lily what my—"

"Your mother's sin? Are you so sure?" He narrowed his eyes. "Are you so sure you're not just like her?"

Rage exploded inside her. Her fists flew to his chest. "You bastard! I never knew I had a grandmother! I was lied to. I was cheated out of knowing her. You can't imagine how much that hurts! You can't imagine what I feel now, having lost—"

Glory bit back the words, tears flooding her eyes. She swung away from him, gulping in deep breaths, struggling for control. What she and Santos were doing was wrong; it was dangerous. They had to get control of themselves and their emotions now, before they did something they would regret forever. Something Lily would hate.

"We can't do this, Santos." Glory moved a distance away from him, then faced him again. She wrapped her arms around herself. "I know how much you hurt. I know how much you loved her, how much you'll miss her." Her eyes filled. "I loved her, too. I'll miss her. So much I—"

He cut her off. "You know nothing of how I feel! You keep saying you do, but how could you?" He advanced on her; she saw that he was shaking with rage and pain. "You have a mother. A family. Lily was like my mother, she was my family. I have no one else." He bent his head close to hers. "Go back to your family. Leave me alone."

Santos wanted blood. She saw it in his eyes. He wanted her to crack; to break down or fly into a million pieces. He wanted to punish her.

She wouldn't allow him that pleasure; she would not fall apart or back off. She had become a part of Lily's life, whether he wanted to admit it or not.

Glory met his gaze evenly, though she was trembling badly. "Lily was my grandmother. And she loved me." Glory poked a finger into his chest. "I won't allow you to minimize that. I won't allow you to tell me I don't belong—"

"You don't belong." He grabbed her hand, closing his hand into a fist around it. "This was our life. You can't compare sixteen days to sixteen years."

"You son of a bitch." She brought her other hand to his chest, curling her fingers into his jacket lapel, wanting so badly to slap him that she shook with it. "You won't understand because you don't want to. You can't believe I really loved her because you don't want to share her memory."

"Are you so sure, princess?" He caught her other hand, anchoring her to him. "Maybe it's because I know you. And you're cold. You're a conniving, lying bitch, just like your mother. You're incapable of love."

Her rage swelled. She made a sound, one she had never uttered before, one that seemed to come from the very recesses of her being. One that terrified her.

"Stop it!" She yanked her hands free and backed away from him, breathing hard. "It's not true!"

But he didn't stop. He kept on pushing, the smell of blood in the air. "I think maybe you're just hanging around, hoping for a piece of the pie. Well, I'll save you the time, Your Highness, there ain't much."

With a howl of pain, she lunged at him, taking him by surprise, knocking him off-balance. He stumbled backward, and she kicked and scratched and flailed at him with her fists. "It's not true! I loved her! But you're too angry and self-centered to see that." She caught the side of his chin with her fist. "I loved you, you son of a bitch."

He swore and captured that hand, then her other. "You never loved anyone but yourself."

"I did! I loved you. I was hurt, too!" She tried to wrench herself free of his grasp, but unbalanced him instead. Tangled together, they hit the edge of the couch, then tumbled onto the floor, hitting it hard, knocking the breath from her. He rolled on top of her, pinning her under him, her arms over her head. "Admit it, you never loved me. I was convenient. Just a fun little defiance to you. Poor little rich girl, bored and misunderstood."

"What did you expect of me?" she cried, struggling, freeing a leg and kicking at him, connecting with soft flesh.

He made a sound of pain and released her. She scrambled away; he caught her and dragged her back. "I expected you to believe in me," he said. "I expected you to stand up for me."

The fight gone out of her, she began to cry. "I was sixteen. I lost my father that night. I lost everything. And I was alone. So...alone."

"You had me." He tightened his hands over hers, his grip punishing. "But that wasn't enough, was it? Not for you, not for the girl who had everything."

She shook her head, her tears spilling down her cheeks. "I never had you. You never trusted me. You never loved me. That's all I wanted, for you to love—"

Santos caught her mouth, her words and her tears. She felt his rage, his frustration and grief; she tasted them. He thrust his tongue into her mouth and ground his pelvis into hers, meaning to punish her, wanting her to pay for their past. Pay for how she had hurt him.

He released her hands, shifting his weight so he no longer pinned her to the floor. But instead of using her freedom to escape, to push him away and run, she used it to anchor him to her. She brought her hands to his hair; she hooked her legs around his.

She wanted him, she realized. And what she wanted had nothing to do with making love. Nothing to do with sharing, or completion, or romance. She wanted him to take her, to be inside her. To fuck her.

And, God help her, she wanted to do the same to him.

Muttering an oath, he ended the kiss and broke away from her, breathing hard. "Glory, hell . . . I'm—"

"No." She tightened her fingers in his hair and dragged his mouth back to hers. "No," she said again, catching his mouth, then tongue, desperate and hungry. So hungry she felt as if she hadn't eaten in years. Ten long, barren years.

She clawed at him, at his clothes. As he clawed at hers. It wasn't easy; she was wearing a dress and hose and full undergarments; he was wearing a suit and tie and dress shirt. Buttons flew, seams gave, finally, in frustration, he ripped her panty hose off her.

Naked enough, finally, they came together. As he thrust into her, she cried out. But not with pain. No, far from it.

Their mating was raw, it was rough and ugly. They didn't kiss or stroke; they didn't murmur sounds of affection or even pleasure. Their joining represented the culmination of ten years of hatred and longing, ten years of wanting and despair. Without uttering a word, they told each other everything they had been speaking and feeling.

And some of what they had to say hurt. Hurt almost more than Glory could bear.

Immediately afterward, she rolled onto her side, not wanting to see his expression, the look in his eyes. What had begun in anger, then taken a twisted turn into passion, had ended in regrets. So bitter they burned her tongue.

Glory drew her knees to her chest, ashamed and humiliated. She had behaved like a whore, like an animal in heat. She squeezed her eyes shut, aching in a way she never had before. How would she face him? How would she look into the mirror and face herself?

Santos stirred beside her, then muttered an oath. "I'm sorry."

The regret in his voice was real, the self-recrimination. "Don't," she said, her voice thick. "Don't apologize."

"Why not? I behaved like—" He bit back the words on another curse. "I never acted that way before."

"You tried to stop it. But I...I was the one who—" Her throat closed over the words, and she rolled onto her back and threw an arm across her eyes. "I'm deeply... embarrassed."

He said nothing. One moment became two, became several. Finally, when her chest hurt so badly she could hardly draw a new breath, he cleared his throat. "I'm sorry, Glory," he said again. "Really sorry."

She moved her arm and met his eyes, her cheeks burning. "You already apologized. Accepted, okay? Let's just stop this now."

She made a move to get up, he caught her arm, but gently this time. "You misunderstand. The first time, that was for the...act. This one is for before. For the things I said. I'm sorry. I didn't mean them."

She looked quickly away, her heart in her throat. "Forget it."

"No." She glanced back. He met her gaze but without apology or condemnation or fury. In the way he looked at her, she saw something of the boy she had known.

"Earlier, you said that I wouldn't listen to you. That I wouldn't believe you because I was too angry and hurt." He searched her eyes. "Tell me now." He hesitated, as if carefully choosing his words. "Tell me why you loved Lily. I really want to know."

Emotion choked her. It took her a moment to clear it away and find her voice. "Because she loved me. Because she needed me." She met his eyes. "Can you understand that?"

He nodded and, a lump in her throat, she looked away. "When you gave me Lily, when you gave me that piece of my past, it was like you gave me a missing part of myself. A part I didn't even know was missing. I felt I belonged with her the minute I saw her. From the minute I saw the house, I felt I belonged there. Really belonged."

"Maybe because you wanted to feel that way."

She shook her head. "I don't think so. The feeling was too strong. Too immediate." She shrugged. "Whatever the reason, knowing Lily made me feel whole. I don't know why, but it did."

He touched her, absently, she thought, trailing his fingers back and forth along the outside of her thigh. She suspected he didn't even realize he was doing it. She didn't point it out because she didn't want him to stop.

"Your being there for her at the end, it was good for her." His fingers stilled and Glory held her breath, hoping, praying he hadn't stopped for good.

He hadn't. His fingers began their magic again and a shudder of pleasure, pure and intoxicating, moved over her.

"She died happy," he finished. "Because of you."

His voice was suspiciously thick, and her heart broke for him. "You made her happy, Santos."

She reached up and touched his cheek, cupping it. She moved her index finger along his high, strong cheekbone, realizing with a sort of shock how vivid her memory of him was—his shape, the way he felt under her hands, the way he smelled, the sound of his breathing.

She realized, too, how he had changed. He had toughened, become harder and leaner, a man now. She wished she could explore his body now, wished she had taken the time to explore him before, learning the changes time had wrought, wished she had taken the time to savor.

She dropped her hand, though when she did, it ached for him. "You were right, you know. Sixteen days can't compare to sixteen years. You made her happy for a long time."

His lips lifted. "I was just being a bastard when I said that. I was angry."

She smiled. "I know."

He increased the length of the sweep of his fingers. She grew warm. And wet. She wanted him again, wanted so badly she ached. But this time she didn't want just sex. She wanted warmth. She wanted sharing. She wanted to make love.

Glory made a strangled sound, part disbelief, part arousal. *How could she be such a fool?* She sat up and reached for her dress.

He followed her up. "What?"

"Nothing." Her cheeks heated. "I was just wishing that I... Nothing."

"Yes, something." He caught her chin and turned her face to his. "After what just occurred between us, you can't possibly be worried about what I might think."

The heat in her cheeks became fire. "All right. Can I ask you something?"

"Ask, though I don't promise to answer."

"Can we try this again?" She made a fluttering motion with her right hand. "Do it over, from the start?"

He frowned. "Do what?"

"You know, do—" She took a deep breath, feeling like a complete fool. "Never mind. I was just being... ridiculous." She slipped her dress over her head, shimmied into it, then dragged her hands through her hair. "I guess I'd better get going. The hotel will need—"

He caught her hand and yanked; she tumbled against his chest. She looked up at him, surprised. He laughed. "Oh, you mean do... this."

He kissed her then, taking her mouth deeply, passionately, but without the fury of before. When he lifted his head, she struggled to find her voice. "Yes," she managed to say, her voice thick. "This."

He gazed at her for long seconds, his smile becoming bittersweet. "We can't go back, Glory. I can't, though a part of me wishes I could." He cupped her face in his palms, his expression almost fierce. "And the future, well, I don't see anything there."

"I know," she said softly, though it hurt beyond measure. The past couldn't be found again; and they had too much past to ever have a future. "But I don't want to leave things the way we were today. And I . . . I need to be held now. I need to not be alone. I thought maybe you did, too."

He answered her by taking her into his arms, by holding her, by stroking and kissing and arousing with touches both gentle and stirring. He removed her dress and explored her body, every part, worshiping and encouraging. Thoughts of the past, of this sad day, of future wishes, all flew from her head. For her, nothing existed but him, his body, his touch.

And when the time came, she gave each of his gifts back to him. Stroking. Worshiping. Exciting. Arousal became passion, then passion spun dizzily out of control. Once again they came together in a frenzy of need and heat. But this time, when Glory cried out with completion, he caught her cries with his mouth, giving back to her with cries of his own.

Breathing hard, Glory rolled away from him and onto her back. She gazed up at the ceiling, aware, so aware, of him beside her, doing the same thing. Aware of each breath he took, of the heat of his body, the scent of him, them, their sex.

It had been almost unbearably good, unbearably . . . sweet. It had rivaled the first time.

All that had been missing was love. And all those years ago, it had been the love that had left them fulfilled and clinging to one another, the love that had made the magic that lasted. Not the sex. The aftermath of this act was empty. It was sad. It hurt.

Glory squeezed her eyes shut. Why had she done this? How could she have acted so . . . impetuously? She had thought she'd left this kind of self-destructive behavior behind a long time ago.

Ten years ago. The night her father died.

Tears of remorse stung her eyes. She had let herself down. She had let her father—his memory—down. Not because she had been with Santos, but because she had led with her emotions; because she had acted impulsively, recklessly.

She curled the fingers of her left hand into her dress, lying in a rumpled heap beside her. Dear Jesus, they hadn't even used protection. What was wrong with her?

A lump formed in her throat, as memories, unbidden and unwanted, sprang into her head. Memories of the first time she and Santos had been together, of the sweetness of the act, of her longings, her hopes for the future.

She had loved him so much. The future had been so full of him, of them, she had been unable to see anything but the two of them. She had been so young and headstrong, so without focus or fear.

And she had paid a terrible price for her recklessness.

She sighed. He stirred beside her; she felt his gaze.

"That bad?" he asked.

She didn't look his way. "What do you mean?"

"You sighed."

What could she say? She had sighed, and she did wish she were anyplace but here. "The sex was great, Santos," she said sharply. "Don't worry, your reputation's intact."

"I wasn't worried."

She felt his words like a slap. "Typically not a problem for you, right?"

"Typically."

"I should have known."

He propped himself up on an elbow, forcing her to meet his eyes by leaning over her. "Are you trying to pick a fight with me?" Heat stung her cheeks, and he smiled without humor. "Don't take your regrets out on me, babe. I have my own to deal with."

"I'll just bet you do." She sat up, forcing him to move aside. "I have to go."

"So, go."

She fisted her fingers, his words ricocheting through her.
"I think I hate you."

For a moment, he said nothing. Then he looked at her
"I think I hate you, too."

51

For a long time after Glory left, Santos lay on the floor, staring up at the ceiling, his mind whirling with all the things he should have done. With all the things he should have said. And with the ways he had gone wrong.

Finally, disgusted with himself, he sat up. He dragged his hands through his hair. What was wrong with him? Hadn't once with this woman been enough to teach him a lesson? Hadn't he learned anything ten years ago?

Apparently not. He groaned. Now what? What did he do with the rest of today, with tomorrow and with the next ten years?

Damn. He did think he hated her.

But right now, he hated himself more.

Liz.

He rubbed his hands over his face. What did he say to Liz? *"I hate Glory, but I want to screw her?"* Or how about, *"I like and respect you, but I slept with her? Twice? And I fucking liked it—a lot?"*

Right. He made a sound in self-disgust. Damn, but he was an asshole. He had really messed up this time.

Santos fell back against the carpet, annoyed when he caught a whiff of Glory's perfume, more annoyed when it went straight to his head, affecting him like a fine, potent wine. Scowling, he turned his head and breathed in the flowery, too-expensive scent. The fact of the matter was, like it or not, he and Liz didn't have a future together. Not the kind of future she wanted with him. Not the kind he wished he wanted with her, but didn't.

God help him, he wanted what he'd had with Glory.

Maybe, if he had never known Glory, if he had never known how deep and strong his feelings for a woman could run, maybe he and Liz would have had a chance. If he had never known how explosive—or how moving—sex could be, maybe the "very good" he experienced with Liz would have been enough.

But he had experienced more; he couldn't go back. And he hated that. He hated that he was going to hurt a very nice woman, a woman who cared for him, and he hated himself for not being able to settle for what he knew would be good for him.

Liz deserved better than he could give her. She deserved everything.

And he did, too.

The phone rang, saving him from his own thoughts. Muttering a word of thanks, he stood and crossed to it. It was Jackson. "Get your ass down here, man. We've got another body."

"The Snow White Killer?"

"None other."

"The son of a bitch is still here." Propping the receiver between his shoulder and ear, he retrieved his clothes. "I thought for sure he'd blown town."

"Hold your load, partner, it gets even better. This time we've got a witness."

Santos made it to headquarters in record time. He slammed into homicide division, adrenaline pumping through him, the scent of the hunt filling his head, every nerve ending crackling with awareness, on the alert and ready. *He was going to get this bastard. He had him now.* He could almost taste it.

So could his fellow officers. A low hum of excitement crackled in the air, a subtle but distinct energy he recognized every time there was a break in an important case. Especially a case like this one—one they had all taken heat for, one that had beaten them more times than their egos cared to count.

Several of his colleagues met his eyes. They didn't speak; they didn't have to. He read their thoughts, their expressions. *Don't screw up. Get this guy. It's time to nail him. Do it.* He understood; they were depending on him. He had been on the other side before.

He found Jackson. "Where's the witness?" he asked without preamble.

"Interrogation two." As they started for the interrogation room, Jackson filled him in on the details. "She's a hooker, name's Tia. Came forward at the scene, said she knew the victim and saw her get a date last night, about 2:00 a.m. Got a good look at the guy, too."

"Out-fucking-standing." Santos rubbed his hands together, anxious to get to her. "Anything else?"

"Oh, yeah. It gets even better. This Tia, two, two and a half hours later, she's walking home. She passes the old U.S. mint. That's where we find the body today, right? She sees something that's not quite right. A guy hanging around in back, looks like he's dragging something."

"Or somebody."

"Bingo. And she's got a general description. Medium height, medium weight, a white guy. Definitely white."

"She didn't think to phone this in last night?"

"Get real." Jackson plucked a file folder off his desk as they passed it. "That's why she came around today. She saw the blue and whites, wanted to check it out. Finds out it's her pal—" Jackson opened the folder and glanced inside "—Billie."

"We're sure this is the work of our sick friend?"

"Not a doubt." They stopped outside the interrogation room's closed door, and Jackson handed him the folder. "Right down to the palms."

Santos opened it, scanned the information, noting each detail, looking for anything unexpected, any detail that didn't seem to fit the other killings. He found none.

"There's a hitch."

Santos met his partner's eyes. "Of course there is."

"She got wind this guy's the Snow White, and she clammed up. Big time. Recanted the whole thing. Claims she saw nothing."

"She *got wind* this guy's the Snow White?" Santos swore. "Who was it?"

"Patterson."

"Remind me to kick his ass."

"With pleasure." Jackson held out his hand for the file. "She's a real cop hater, too. We're going to need some of that famous charm of yours with this one."

Santos nodded. "Let's do it."

They entered the room. The woman was standing against the far wall, nervously chewing on her fingernails. She was white, appeared to be about forty, forty-five, but was probably younger. The street aged a girl. Santos had seen sixteen-year-olds who passed for thirty.

She looked scared. Real scared.

She met their eyes, masking her fear with defiance. "You got a cigarette? I need a smoke."

Santos nodded and looked at Jackson. "Get Tia a pack of smokes. While you're at it, bring a couple Cokes, too."

Jackson nodded, turned and left the room. He didn't mind Santos making him the gofer; this was part of their routine. Santos had been known to work wonders with reluctant witnesses, especially working girls. They trusted him because he didn't judge. A lot of his fellow officers had attitudes when it came to prostitutes, they treated them worse than dirt or expected services for free. So the girls hated them. Santos couldn't blame them.

"Hi, Tia." He smiled and motioned toward the chairs. "Have a seat."

He pulled one out, swung it around and straddled it. She didn't move from her position against the wall. "My name's Detective Santos. Detective Jackson's the guy who went for smokes."

She narrowed her eyes. "Detective Santos?"

"That's right." He smiled again. "Victor Santos."

"Go fuck yourself."

He arched his eyebrows, a little surprised by her venom. She wasn't joking around—she wished *him* ill. It was personal. He met her eyes. "Did we start off on the wrong foot here, Tia? Or have I done something to offend you?"

"Something to offend me? You could say that." She shifted her gaze. "I want out of here."

"Sure. I just need to ask you a few questions first."

"I already answered a shitload of questions. I didn't see anything."

"No?" He opened the folder and scanned it. "Says here, you saw plenty. Saw a john pick up your friend Billie around 2:00 a.m. It says you saw some guy around the mint about two hours later."

"I didn't."

Jackson returned with the cigarettes and soft drinks. He set the open pack of cigarettes on the table, in front of the chair directly across from Santos's. She eyed it, then crossed to the table and snatched the pack. Her hands shook so badly it took her three tries to get one lit. She finally did and took a long, greedy drag on it.

Santos watched her a moment, letting her get in a few good drags, waiting for the nicotine to kick in and calm her. "Why would the officer who took your statement lie, Tia?"

"How should I know? I'm just a hooker." She swept her gaze over Santos, her lips curling with distaste. "Besides, all pigs lie."

This girl not only hated all cops; she seemed to have a special dislike for him. Santos slid a glance to Jackson. His partner arched an eyebrow slightly; he saw it, too.

"You do drugs, Tia?" Santos asked.

"Fuck you. I'm clean. You can't keep me." She sucked on the cigarette. "I didn't see anything."

"You're lying, Tia. For whatever reason, probably 'cause you're scared."

"Prove it." She crushed the cigarette in the battered metal ashtray. "Can I go now?"

"We want to help you." Santos met her gaze, not flinching at the horrors he saw there. "A girl's dead. A friend of yours. You can help us nail this guy."

"I told you, I didn't see anything." She folded her arms across her chest. "And I know how it works. You can't hold me."

"Don't you get it?" Santos made a sound of frustration. "You could be next. If this guy hears you saw something, he's after you. You're safer talking to us, helping us get this guy. Come clean and—"

"And you're going to protect me?" She jumped to her feet. "That's a laugh. I'm just a hooker. You're going to get me to talk, then set me loose. You don't give a shit about me."

"That's not true." Santos stood. "I don't want another girl to die. I don't want you to die."

"I'll take my chances."

"Look, Tia," Santos said, slipping his hands into his pockets, feigning nonchalance, "we'll just talk. About anything. Get to know each other. Then, if there's something you want—"

"You don't remember me, do you?" She all but spat the words at him. "You don't even have a clue." Her teeth began to chatter, and she rubbed her arms. "But why should you? You forgot me the minute you left."

"Do we know each other?" Santos shook his head. "I'm sorry, Tia, but I don't remember you. I meet a lot of girls—"

She laughed. The hollow, hopeless sound crawled along his nerve endings. "I wasn't a working girl back then. And you weren't a . . . pig."

He tilted his head studying her, finding nothing familiar in her hard features. "Okay, Tia, why don't you refresh my memory."

"My name's Tina. Got that? Tina." She grabbed her purse, slung it over her shoulder and crossed to the door, stopping when she reached it and meeting his eyes once more. "Figure it out from there, hero."

For a moment, he drew a blank, then his head filled with a memory from the night his mother died, the memory of a girl he had met at the abandoned school on Esplanade.

Tina? Santos made a sound of surprise, of disbelief. *The runaway he had met that night? Could it be?* He remembered that girl, that Tina, sweet and frightened, vulnerable. He remembered her tears, their kiss; he remembered the way she had clung to him, so afraid to be alone on the streets.

And he remembered his promise to her. "I'll come back for you, Tina. Tomorrow. I promise. I'll be back tomorrow."

But tomorrow had never come. Twenty minutes later, his world had come crashing in on him, and he'd been able to think of nothing but what he had lost.

He met Tina's eyes, his heart heavy with the memories, with apologies and with sadness for the way her life had turned out. He had been so much luckier than she.

"That's right," she said, spitting the words at him. "You never came back, you bastard. I waited. I waited so lo—" She bit back the words, yanked open the door and walked out.

Jackson leaped to his feet. "I'll get her."

Santos caught his arm. "Let her go. We know where to find her."

Jackson made a sound of frustration and shook his head. "Nice girl."

"Actually," Santos said, his voice thick, "she was. Once upon a time, she was a very nice girl."

52

The officer working the front desk buzzed Liz into the third-floor offices of the N.O.P.D.'s homicide division. Liz smiled and exchanged a couple pleasantries with the woman, then started for Santos's desk, located at the back of the large room. As she passed various desks and cubicles, some of the detectives recognized her, smiled and nodded. She returned their greetings, fighting her mounting nerves and the terrible feeling that something was wrong.

She hadn't seen Santos since Lily's funeral three days ago. The few times she had talked to him, she had called him. Each time, he had sounded preoccupied, distant. She had sensed a reluctance to speak with her, and each time he had been apologetic about not having the time to see her.

Too apologetic. He had given her up already.

She shook her head. That wasn't it. There had been a break in the Snow White case; he had been working nearly around the clock. He simply hadn't had time to see or call her.

Or so he said.

She frowned at her own thoughts. Santos was going through a difficult period right now. Lily had been his only family; she'd been his anchor. No doubt, he felt lost right now, cast adrift. It was no wonder he had immersed himself in his work. It was no wonder he had pulled away from her.

Sure. It had nothing to do with him and her, nothing to do with their relationship.

Liz readjusted her grip on the picnic basket's handle. He didn't understand that she could fill the void Lily's passing had left in his life. He didn't see that together, the two of them could form a new family, one that would anchor him just as surely as his life with Lily had. He didn't realize that was what he needed. That *she* was what he needed.

Liz rounded a corner between cubicles and caught sight of Santos. He was at his desk, on the phone. Jackson was standing beside him, his expression grim.

Her steps faltered, and she moved her gaze almost greedily over him. Just looking at him stirred her. Just gazing at him caused her heart to burst into flight. She loved him so much.

What would she do if she had lost him?

Jackson saw her first. He smiled in greeting, then nudged Santos. Santos glanced up and for the space of a heartbeat, he looked trapped. Like an animal who had been pinned in the headlights of an approaching vehicle. Her heart crashed to her toes, and she fought off panic and a feeling of absolute despair. Everything would be all right; it had to be.

"Hi." She forced a bright smile, stopped beside the desk and held out the basket. "I thought you guys might be hungry."

Santos stood to greet her but didn't kiss her. Nor did he meet her eyes, not really. Instead, he slid his gaze guiltily away. "That was really thoughtful, Liz. Thanks."

Her heart began to thunder, her palms to sweat. She set the basket on the corner of the desk. *Why wouldn't he meet her eyes?* She turned toward Jackson, almost desperately. She smiled. "I know how you two get when you're in the middle of a case, too busy to stop."

"It's this maniac I work with." Jackson laughed. "He never lets up. The jerk still thinks he's twenty and can live on coffee and that iron will of his."

"Speaking of busy," Santos murmured, ignoring Jackson's joking. "I wished you'd called, Liz. This isn't a very good . . . time."

Santos's words landed heavily, painfully between them; their meaning obvious to all. Jackson looked at Santos in surprise, then cleared his throat. "I've got to make a call. Liz, it was great seeing you, and thanks for the food. I'll talk to you later."

Right. If she ever saw him again.

Liz murmured goodbye to Jackson, then turned back to Santos, meeting his gaze evenly. "What's going on?"

He glanced at her, then away. "We need to talk. I've been meaning to call, but . . . this isn't the time or place."

Liz stared at him, feeling the color draining from her face, the truth hitting her like a punch to the gut. *Glory. This was about Glory.*

"You son of a bitch," she said, her words choked. "You slept with her, didn't you?"

He looked almost comically guilty. She would have laughed if she didn't hurt so bad she felt as if she was going to die.

He took her arm. "Let's go somewhere where we can talk privately."

She jerked free of his grasp, tears flooding her eyes. "You fucked her, didn't you?" Her voice rose. "Tell me you didn't, Santos. Tell me you didn't do that."

"I can't," he said quietly. "I'm sorry. I didn't mean to hurt you."

"Oh, God." Liz hugged herself feeling sick. "After everything . . . after what she did to both of us . . . How could you?"

"I didn't mean to, Liz. I didn't plan it." He lowered his voice. "It just . . . happened."

"Is that supposed to make me feel better?" She searched his gaze, her own swimming with tears. "That you got carried away by passion? You bastard, it doesn't."

Santos tried to take her arm again; she sprang away from his touch. "Liz, I'm sorry."

"Yeah, right," she said, hearing the bitterness in her voice and hating it. Hating the bitterness that welled inside—toward him and Glory, at the cards she had been dealt.

"When were you going to tell me, Santos?" She jerked up her chin. "Or had you planned to keep sleeping with us both?"

Santos glanced around them, obviously uncomfortable. "This isn't the place for this discussion. Please, Liz, let's go somewhere we can really talk."

"Why? So you can try to explain? Try to make me feel better? Forget it."

"I didn't mean to hurt you. God, that's the last thing I ever wanted to do." He looked away, then back. "What I said before, it was true. It just happened."

"I suppose you're going to tell me now that it was a mistake, and you want me to try to forget it. That you want us to go on the way we had been?" Liz couldn't deny the hateful sliver of hope that bloomed inside her—hope that he did want that, that he still wanted her. Despite how much he had hurt her, if he still wanted her, she would forgive him.

But he said nothing. That damning silence told her everything, and her heart broke. She felt like such a stupid fool. For exposing herself with those last words, for her ridiculous hope, for everything.

She swung away from him. "I never should have trusted you. I never should have believed you when you said you didn't care for her—"

"I don't. But I realize now, that you and I...that it's not going to happen. It wouldn't be fair for me to string you along."

Hate for Glory swelled inside her. Glory St. Germaine had stolen her chance at a great education, had stolen her chance for the future she'd always dreamed of. Now she had stolen the man she loved. What was next? Her restaurant? The air she breathed?

As if reading her thoughts, Santos caught her arm and gently turned her to face him. "This isn't about her, Liz.

It's about us, about what is and isn't there. At least for me."

She struggled with her tears, struggled to keep from humiliating herself any more than she already had. The truth was, she loved him so much she would beg if she thought it would bring him back to her. It wouldn't.

She sucked in a sharp breath. "Well, you can't be much plainer than that, can you, Detective?"

"I'm sorry, Liz. I wished there was a way we could still be friend—"

"Don't say it. God, I love you so much I want to be with you forever and you want to be—" She choked back the words, nearly strangling on them. "That hurts almost more than I can stand."

"Liz, I'm so sorry."

He reached out a hand, but she slapped it away. "You've said that already, Santos. But if you were really sorry, you never would have slept with her in the first place. If you had meant all those things you told me, about your feelings, about her, you couldn't have. But it was all lies, wasn't it? Everything you told me."

He shook his head. "I never lied to you, Liz. I never did that."

"No. Instead, you lied to yourself." With the heels of her hands she brushed the tears from her cheeks. "I never want to talk to you again. I don't want to see you. And I'll never forgive . . . either of you for this. Not as long as I live."

53

In the last days of her life, Lily changed her will. In an ironic twist of fate, she had deeded the River Road house to Glory, and had left everything else to Santos. The announcement affected Santos like a blow to his chest—not because he thought he deserved the house, or that he cared what it was worth, or that he thought Glory shouldn't have it. But because he loved it.

Because he thought of it as his home.

Santos stared at the attorney, knowing he had heard correctly, but not quite believing his ears anyway.

The River Road house was Glory's now. Never again could he go there to seek the quiet, the peace, it offered.

The truth of that left him reeling. Until that moment, he hadn't realized what a big part of his life the house had become.

He shifted his gaze to Glory. She, too, appeared stunned at the news. Overwhelmed, even. As if sensing his gaze, she looked his way. She met his eyes, the expression in hers apologetic.

He looked away. The last thing he wanted—or needed—was her sympathy. It was bad enough that she saw how he felt, bad enough that by sleeping with her he had revealed the depth of his desire for her.

And he did desire her, more since their lovemaking. Since then, wanting her had become like an itch he couldn't scratch, a hunger he couldn't satisfy. And the hell of it was, he knew there wasn't a damn thing he could do about it. Glory St. Germaine was off limits.

Twenty minutes later, they exited the attorney's posh downtown office and crossed the hall to the bank of elevators. Santos summoned one, then glanced at her. "Congratulations."

"Thanks, I..." Glory laced her fingers together. "I'm sorry. I had no idea she'd planned to... I never expected this."

"Forget it." The elevator doors slid open and they stepped onto it. Santos punched the lobby button. "I don't know what I would have done with the place if she had left it to me."

"You could have sold it."

"No, I never could have done that." He made a sound of frustration. "And I couldn't have afforded to keep it up. Not on a cop's salary. It's better off with you."

She touched his sleeve lightly, then as if uncomfortable with the gesture, pulled her hand away. "I know how much you love that house. I know you... wanted it."

He met her eyes, instantly on guard. "So, you're a mind reader now?"

"I don't need to be." She looked away, then back. "That day we were there, I saw the expression in your eyes when you looked at it. And today, I saw your expression when you heard the news."

Santos swallowed hard, feeling exposed and too vulnerable. She saw too much. Far too much. She always had.

He shrugged, feigning indifference. "You love it, too. That makes it okay."

The elevator reached the lobby and they stepped off. They crossed the green marble floor toward the building's grand front entrance.

"I've been wondering about something," Glory murmured, almost to herself.

Santos stopped at the door. She looked troubled. "What's that?"

"Twelve years ago, my mother used family money to bail the hotel out of debt. At least that's where she told me the money came from. I only learned about it when I took over running the hotel.

"It was quite a large sum," she continued. "I never questioned Mother's story because I'd grown up believing her family had been very wealthy."

"But Lily was your mother's only family."

"Exactly." She tilted her head to the side, her expression thoughtful. "So, where did Mother get the money?"

Santos frowned. "How much is quite a large sum?"

"I could check the books for an exact figure." She drew her eyebrows together, obviously searching her memory. "But I know it was several hundred thousand dollars. Four. No, more like five."

Five hundred thousand dollars. An old lady could live quite comfortably on the interest from five hundred thousand dollars. Living, suddenly, without it would be tough.

"When was that?" he asked. "Do you remember?"

"Ten, almost eleven years ago now. It was the year we—" She flushed and looked away. "It was the year Daddy died."

1984. The year he and Glory met. The year he learned that Lily was Hope's mother. The year Lily, suddenly, began to worry about money.

His forehead creased. Up until the end, Lily had taken care of her own finances. He hadn't asked questions; that was her business and none of his. And he had never cared what she had or how much.

However, it had been odd that until that time, Lily had seemed more than financially comfortable. She had never worried about money and had treated herself to whatever she wanted, within reason.

That had changed suddenly. He had noticed it for the first time a few months after his break with Glory. Lily had begun to fret over expenses; she had stopped making donations to charities, had stopped treating herself to the small luxuries she enjoyed, ones like eating out, manicures and movies.

It made sense. Lily would have done anything for her daughter, even financially cripple herself. He had made three deliveries to Hope St. Germaine. In the aftermath of Glory's betrayal, he had forgotten about them. Could he have been delivering a loan all those years ago? And if so, what had Hope sent back each time? A thank-you note? Or something more?

"What is it, Santos? You look strange."

He blinked, realizing that he had been staring into space. He jerked his gaze back to Glory's and shook his head. "Do I? Just lost in thought." He forced an absent smile. "It's been a long morning."

He pushed open one of the glass doors, holding it open so she could pass through, then following her out. It had begun to drizzle while they were inside, and Santos hiked his suit-coat collar up around his neck. "Where are you parked?"

"Up the block."

"I'm right here. You want a lift?"

She hesitated, then shook her head. "Thanks, but it's not that far."

"If you're sure, I've got to run."

"I'm sure."

He started off, stopping and looking back at her when she called his name.

She met his gaze, hers thoughtful. "Where do you think my mother got that money?"

He didn't know. But he intended to find out.

He shrugged, not wanting her to know the direction of his thoughts. Not yet, anyway. "I haven't a clue, Glory. Why don't you ask her?"

54

Hope gazed at Victor Santos, distaste crawling up her spine. She swept her gaze coldly over him, then smiled thinly, not bothering to hide her feelings. "What can I do for you, Detective? I understand you're here on police business."

He lifted an eyebrow, a smile tugging at the corners of his mouth. "Did your housekeeper say that? I don't know where she could have gotten that idea. I'm sorry to say, but no, I'm here all on my own."

She stiffened at his air of amused superiority and motioned toward the door. "Then I'll ask you to leave."

"I don't think you'll want to do that." Without invitation, he stepped farther into the foyer and looked around with unabashed curiosity. "Nice little shack you have here."

Again, amusement laced his tone. She squeezed her hands into fists, resenting that she had to put up with him because he was a police officer. If he weren't, she wouldn't even have received him. "I have nothing to say to you."

"That remains to be seen." He met her eyes. "I have something you're going to be quite interested in."

"I rather doubt I would be interested in anything *you* have to say." She folded her arms across her chest, curiosity piqued, despite herself. "But if you insist on this ridiculous little game, I'll give you a minute."

"I do insist." He smiled. "You heard your mother died?"

"Of course," she said, drawling the words in a way that left no doubt how little she cared. They had the desired effect, she saw, by the tightening of his mouth.

"She left Glory the house. Your childhood home. You knew that, too?"

She did know. When Glory had told her, she had wanted to kill Victor Santos. She still did. Impotent rage swelled inside her. She had spent her entire life trying to protect Glory from the Pierron legacy, and now, because of him and his meddling, her daughter was in possession of the very seat of sin.

"She left me everything else."

"I heard that," she snapped. "You've told me nothing new, Detective, so if there's nothing else..." Hope checked her watch impatiently. "Your time's up, I'm happy to say." She started toward the front door, annoyed when she realized he wasn't following. She grasped the knob and swung open the door, then turned to face him.

"Good day, Detective," she snapped, wanting to claw that smug half smile from his face.

"Do you have five hundred thousand dollars handy, Mrs. St. Germaine?"

Hope froze. The devil-boy laughed.

The Darkness took many forms.

"That's right. A ghost from your past has come to haunt you."

She struggled to remain calm. "I don't know what you're talking about," she said coldly.

"No?" He took a step toward her, and she fought the urge to turn and run. He moved like the Serpent, slow but with unerring aim. "How about three notes that promise to repay, on demand, the sum of five hundred thousand dollars? Is your memory sufficiently refreshed yet, Mrs. St. Germaine?"

He took another step toward her; this time she took a step back, heart pounding. Sunlight spilled over her back, hot and too bright. "Lily helped you out of a costly little jam back in 1984, didn't she? The hotel was in deep debt.

It took nearly everything Lily had, but she lent you that money. I made those three deliveries, each time you sent me back to her with one of those promissory notes."

He narrowed his eyes. "You knew she would never try to collect. You knew all she wanted was a little time with you. It makes me sick to think how much she loved you and how badly you treated her."

"That's right." Hope lifted her chin arrogantly. "She didn't try to collect, it's over now. She's dead."

"Sorry, sweetheart, but it doesn't work that way. Promissory notes are like stocks, bonds and other forms of negotiable assets."

Hope began to sweat. The sun on her back became unbearably hot. The blood thrummed in her head, until it drowned out all else but the sound of his hateful voice.

"I fulfilled my debt to her," she said, voice shaking. She worked to steady it. "I gave her the time she wanted."

"You gave her nothing." He fisted his fingers. "She went to her grave longing for her daughter's forgiveness and love, but you couldn't give her even that much. You couldn't pay her even one small visit to the hospital."

"You can't prove it. You can't prove I didn't—"

"But I have the notes. I inherited them from Lily." He leaned toward her, murder in his eyes. "If you had fulfilled your 'debt', you should have collected them."

Hope brought a hand to her throat. "What do you want from me?"

He arched his eyebrows, as if shocked. "Why, Hope, darling, I want my money."

She took another step back, and the sunlight stung her eyes. "You bastard."

He laughed. "I seem to be called that a lot lately. And always by a St. Germaine."

She couldn't bear the sun, the heat, any longer. She pushed past Santos and into the cool, dark foyer. She struggled to catch her breath, realizing only then how panicked she was. She didn't have five hundred thousand dollars. She didn't have it.

Hope rubbed her arms, chilled now. Chilled to the bone. "How do I know the notes are real? How do I know you even have them?"

"They're real, all right." He slipped his hands into his front trouser pockets. "My lawyer has them." At her expression, he smiled grimly. "Oh, yes. I did my homework. Got myself a good lawyer. You've heard of Hawthorne, Hawthorne and Steele, haven't you? Contact Mr. Steele. He's the best estate lawyer in the city, maybe even in the South."

Hope began to shake. She had heard of Kenneth Steele. He was, indeed, the best. "It doesn't matter," she said. "I don't have the money."

"But you can get it. After all, Lily could." He gestured around them. "And she lived a lot less extravagantly."

"Well, I can't."

He clicked his tongue, obviously enjoying himself at her expense. Obviously wallowing in it. If it wouldn't be so far beneath her, she would scratch his eyes out.

"I'm sure this place is worth that much, probably a lot more. I'm sure the St. Charles, your half of it, anyway, is worth more than that." He slipped his hands into his pockets once more, this time grinning like the devil himself. "Imagine me, lowly, low-born Victor Santos, your business partner. Or better yet, living in the St. Germaine mansion."

"Never!" She spat the words at him, shaking with rage. "I would never be partners with a... *creature* like you! I would burn down this house before I allowed you to possess one brick."

He narrowed his eyes. "Didn't anyone ever teach you to be nice to other people? Where were you when the golden rule was the lesson of the day?" He shook his head, his mouth twisting. "But maybe you think, because you're so rich and powerful, that you don't have to worry about such things. Maybe you think you don't need to worry about retribution. Or punishment. Or about paying your debts.

Obviously, you don't think you have to treat others with simple human decency."

He laughed and The Darkness closed in on her. "Well, the time to worry has come, Hope St. Germaine. The time to pay has come. You owe Lily, and you're going to have to pay."

She spun away from him and crossed the foyer. She stopped before a Sheraton convex mirror and gazed at her distorted image, scrambling to think of a way out of this. The hotel was worth a fraction of what it had once been worth. She had some investments, only enough, combined with her part of the hotel profits, to maintain her life-style. Some of her . . . *needs* . . . had proven quite costly over the years.

Like a house of cards, remove any piece and it all tumbled.

What was she going to do?

"There may be another way," Santos said softly.

Light-headed, she met his gaze in the mirror. "Another way?"

"Actually, I don't care about the money. I don't care about your precious house or hotel. Or anything else you have."

Hope turned slowly to face him. She searched his eyes, looking for the joke, the ever-present amusement. Instead, he looked deadly serious. "You don't?"

"No." He crossed to stand directly before her. "I care about Lily."

"But she's dead."

His expression hardened. "But her memory is not. My feelings for her are not. I've decided to give her the thing she wanted most in life, but went to her grave without."

"And that is?"

"Her daughter."

She stared at him, confused. "I don't understand."

"I'm going to give her you, Hope. You will publicly admit Lily was your mother. You will tell everyone who you are and where you come from."

Hope took a step backward, her legs threatening to buckle beneath her. "You can't be ... serious."

"Trust me, I am serious." He swept his gaze over her. "Perhaps you should sit down."

She nodded and crossed to a chair arranged against the wall by the mirror. She sank onto it and folded her trembling hands in her lap. "Go on."

"If you agree to this, you will have to do several, very specific things." She nodded again, and he continued, "The first, you will take out two full-page ads, both declaring your true lineage. The first in the *Times Picayune*, Sunday main news section, the second in *New Orleans* magazine, inside front cover."

He slipped his hands into his pants pockets and rocked back on his heels. "As I said, in those ads you will admit your true lineage, confess to your years of untruths and express your deep and eternal sorrow at having cruelly abandoned your loving mother."

"And next?" she asked tightly, clenching her fingers together.

He smiled. "You throw a huge party, a gala in Lily's honor. You invite all your fancy friends, all the city's bigwigs—mayor, police chief, maybe even Governor Edwards. Of course, once again you will publicly acknowledge Lily."

"And of course," she added bitterly, "you'll be right there to see that I follow your directions to the letter."

"Don't be naive, this is costing me five hundred thousand dollars. Everything will be perfect."

"And if I do all this ... to the letter?"

"The notes are yours, free and clear."

Hope looked at him in astonishment. "That's insane. Why are you really doing this?"

He swept his gaze over her, his lips curling, as with distaste. But she knew they curled with pure evil. "You can't understand it, I know. That I could love Lily that much. That I could believe I owe her everything, even my life. It's beyond you to comprehend that I could want to give her what she wanted most in the world, no matter the cost to me.

"But my reasons aren't totally altruistic. I'm going to enjoy seeing you do the right thing. I'm going to enjoy seeing you forced to act, for once in your life, like a decent human being."

For a moment, she said nothing. The hate inside her grew, twisting and turning inside her. She would kill him if she could, if she had that power.

But there were other ways to make him pay; she would find one. If it was the last thing she did, and she would find one.

She met his eyes evenly, with malice. "You are a very foolish young man."

He cocked an eyebrows. "What? Are you going to 'get me' for this? Are you threatening me?"

Hope simply smiled. *The Darkness came in many forms. But the Lord would not leave the guilty unpunished.*

55

The River Road house beckoned Glory; it called her name, low and softly, the way a lover would. She stood at the end of the long, oak-lined driveway, gazing at it in wonder, thinking it the most beautiful thing she had ever seen. She shook her head, awed. Still, three weeks after the reading of Lily's will, she couldn't believe it was hers.

Over the past weeks, she had driven out here as often as she could. Sometimes, as she had last night, she slept over; sometimes, she simply stole a couple hours from her busy schedule.

Glory bent and plucked a blade of grass and held it to her nose. The house had a powerful hold on her. She was happy here, relaxed and at peace. Here, she felt she belonged.

She started for the house, moving slowly, taking her time. She had nowhere to be today; the hotel, she had decided, could function without her. In the past weeks, she had spent her time here going through boxes of mementos and photographs, through the house's financial records. Her ancestors had run a thriving little business here—shockingly profitable, actually. Considering that, it was odd that Lily had died with so little.

Glory yawned, then combed her fingers through her hair. Last night she had found a small trunk of journals. Ones belonging to her relatives—some going all the way back to the first Madame Pierron, Camellia. Among those, too, had been diaries of some of the girls who had worked in this house, girls whose days had been empty save waiting for the nights.

The accounts of the girls' lives had fascinated and appalled her. She had read deep into the night, until her eyes burned and her head throbbed. Finally, fatigue had forced her to put the journals aside, but she intended to spend her day reading more.

In the broad branches above her, a bird called out. She lifted her face; as she did, it was kissed by a soft river breeze. From behind her came the sound of a car easing down the driveway.

Glory turned. Her heart jumped to her throat.

Santos.

With a feeling of fatalism, she watched as he drove slowly toward her, a subtle cloud of dust billowing up behind him. She had always thought of Santos as her other half, had always used him as the measure by which she judged other men. It felt right that he should be here now, appearing as if by magic. The way he had first appeared in her life.

He pulled the car to a stop beside her. His dark hair was mussed from the breeze through the windows.

She longed to touch it, to smooth it. She shoved her hands into her pockets instead. "Hello, Santos."

"We should talk."

Glory smiled calmly, though her heart had begun to thunder. "All right. Let's sit on the gallery."

He nodded and pulled the car ahead, to the side of the house. She met him there and together they walked around to the stairs that led to the first-floor gallery.

He moved his gaze over the front of the house, his expression wistful. "It's the first time I've been out since she . . . died."

"It brings back memories, doesn't it?"

"Yes." He met her eyes. "Good ones."

She slipped her fingers into the front pockets of her shorts. "For me, too, though it shouldn't. I have no history here."

"You have more history here than I, though of a different kind."

She thought of Lily and of the journals and a lump of emotion formed in her throat. She cleared it away. "Would you like an ice tea, a soft drink or . . . something?"

He shook his head. "Nothing. Thanks."

Nothing. What he wanted from her. She looked away, then back. "How did you know I would be here?"

"A hunch." A smile tugged at the corners of his mouth. "And a tip from your assistant manager. Funny how a police badge opens doors."

"Vincent isn't my most levelheaded employee, but his efficiency makes up for it." They climbed the stairs. "And what was your hunch?"

"The look in your eyes when you learned Lily had left you the house."

Her smile faded. "I'm sorry. I know you wanted—"

"Don't be. I'm not."

"Liar," she said softly but without malice, surprising herself. "I see the truth in *your* eyes."

He inclined his head in acknowledgment of the accuracy of her comment, then crossed to the gallery's edge and gazed down the tree-lined driveway to the levee beyond. "It's not a bad feeling, Glory."

"Just kind of sad."

"Yes. Kind of sad." He glanced over his shoulder at her, his lips curving up. "Now that it's yours, what do you think?"

"That I love it. That I belong here." She crossed to stand beside him, and followed his gaze toward the horizon. "I don't understand the hold this place, this house, has on me. But it does have one. And that . . . confuses me. It scares me."

He met her eyes. One moment became several, still they simply gazed into each other's eyes. Then he looked away. Back toward the river.

She swallowed hard, missing the connection between them, irrationally hurt. Bereft without it. Santos, too, had a hold on her. On her life and her heart. From the first moment she laid eyes on him; still, now, after all these years. She understood his hold on her no more than she did this house's.

She sighed. A long time ago, she told Liz that Santos was her destiny. That seemed so silly now, such a naive statement made by a silly adolescent girl.

But in a way, it was true. She couldn't seem to shake Santos from her system. She couldn't seem to forget him. She couldn't move on without him.

And since they had been together, she'd been tormented by her longings—for him, to be with him again.

He turned suddenly and met her eyes. She knew he could see each of her thoughts, read them in her face and eyes. She didn't try to hide them, didn't try to pretend. She wanted him to know how she ached for him, how she burned.

She felt bold, unafraid and dizzyingly alive. An incredulous laugh bubbled to her lips, though she didn't release it. Perhaps this place was affecting her, perhaps it was having read the journals that influenced her, having read the accounts of women who had been shamelessly wanton, women who had lived by their bodies but without love.

Or perhaps, she had finally come to understand her own needs.

She brought a hand to Santos's face, caressing softly, first his cheek, then his mouth. "I want you."

He caught her fingers with his own. "Glory, I—"

"No." She brought his fingers to her mouth, kissing, tasting with her tongue, finally sucking. She felt honest. The way she hadn't felt in ten years.

The last time she had been honest with a man. The last she had really wanted a man.

And then she hadn't understood. She had been a girl, untried, inexperienced. Now she knew what she needed. Now she knew how to satisfy her lover.

"You want me, too," she murmured. "I know you do."

"Yes." His voice was thick with arousal, his eyes dark. "Yes," he repeated, searching her gaze. "I do want you. But—"

"No." She shook her head. "No buts. Come." She led him into the house, led him upstairs to one of the big, soft beds. The windows were open; the breeze off the Mississippi stirred the lace curtains. Patches of sunlight dappled the floor and walls. The bed.

Together they sank onto it, the light spilling over them. Moments became minutes, time both stopped and slipped away as they explored and pleasured each other.

Glory asked Santos for what she wanted; he gave her all she desired. As he asked; as she gave. Their mating was exquisite and perfect, by turns tender and rough, frenzied and languorous. Glory understood, completely, finally, what it was to be a woman.

Afterward, they lay twined together, damp and out of breath, yet totally relaxed. He didn't draw away from her and she was glad, though she had no illusions about what had occurred between them.

She trailed her fingers across his chest, loving the feel of his firm, muscled flesh. "Are you sorry?" she asked softly.

"No." He bent his head to meet her eyes. "Are you?"

She shook her head. "How could I be? That was so...wonderful."

He smiled, pleased, then he returned his gaze to the ceiling and the elaborately carved medallion at its center.

She followed his gaze. "This place is quite something, isn't it?"

"Mmm." He tightened his arm around her. "Have you decided what you're going to do with it?"

"No. I haven't gotten that far yet." She pressed her cheek to his chest, torn between thoughts of him and this moment and ones of the future. "There's so much history here. This place is a part of Louisiana, a part of her history. It's special. Unique and wonderful. It would be wrong for me to change it."

She drew in a deep breath. "The women who lived here deserve to be remembered. Not to be held up as role models, but to be remembered as a part of history."

"You could live here."

She shook her head. "I'd like to, but it's too far from the hotel. And I'd be lonely, I think."

Unless Santos was here with her.

The thought jumped unbidden into her head, and she quickly pushed it away. It wouldn't do to start thinking about a forever with Santos, it wouldn't do to start thinking about love. It wasn't going to happen, and if she let herself hope, she would end up hurt.

They had too much past to ever have a future together.

"So where does that leave you?" he asked, interrupting her thoughts.

"I have some decisions to make concerning the hotel, too. Some changes I'm going to have to make." She sighed. 'Changes my father wouldn't have approved of."

"Time marches on, Glory."

"I do know that." She pressed her mouth to his shoulder, tears stinging the backs of her eyes. "But I wish I could have run the hotel so expertly that changes in the city and in the world wouldn't have affected the business. I wish I could have kept it running, and performing, the way he did. I know that sounds silly."

"Not silly," Santos murmured, moving his fingers in slow, soft circles against the small of her back. "But self-defeating. Time changes everything. Don't kid yourself, if your father were still alive, he would have had to make adjustments to meet the challenges of 1995, too."

"Thank you," she said, tilting her head to meet his eyes. "That makes me feel . . . better. I loved him so much."

"I know." Santos's fingers stilled. "There's something I have to tell you."

She lifted herself to an elbow and met his eyes, frowning. "That sounds serious."

"How serious depends on your perspective."

"I don't understand."

"I know where your mother got the money to bail out the hotel ten years ago."

"You do?" She drew her eyebrows together. "Where?"

"Lily."

Santos explained how her comment the day the will was read had gotten him thinking—about the correspondence he had delivered to the hotel all those years ago, about what her mother might have sent back to Lily, and about Lily's altered life-style afterward. Finally, he told her how he had searched through Lily's things and found three demand notes promising to repay the sum of five hundred thousand dollars, all signed by her mother.

"I don't—" Glory drew in a deep breath, not quite believing her ears. "Are you saying that my mother owes you...five hundred thousand dollars?"

"Yes. And no." She frowned, and he continued, "I've offered your mother a deal."

"A deal," she repeated. "You mean, you've already spoken to her about this?"

"Yes. After I consulted with a lawyer."

"I see." She sat up and pulled a hand through her hair, not surprised to see that it was trembling. "How long ago did you find these notes?"

"Two weeks."

She looked over her shoulder and into his eyes. "And you're only telling me now. Very nice, Santos. Thanks a lot for the big vote of confidence."

"There wasn't a reason to tell you before this."

That hurt. Because that omission said everything about their relationship. Relationship? she thought, despising herself her foolishness. They had no relationship. They had gone to bed together a couple times.

Sex wasn't love. It wasn't a relationship. And it certainly wasn't what they had shared all those years ago.

She wanted that. She would never have it. She bit down hard on her lip, refusing to cry. Refusing to acknowledge how much that hurt. How much his not trusting her hurt. He didn't think enough of her to tell her that her mother owed him five hundred thousand dollars.

"What about before this?" She gestured toward the rumpled bed. "You don't think you had a moral obligation to tell me before we made...before this?"

He searched her gaze. "Would it have made a difference?"

She lifted her eyes to the ceiling. Maybe it wouldn't have in the before, but in the after, in this moment, it would have made all the difference in the world. If he had told her, she wouldn't be hurting so bad she could hardly bear it.

She curled her fingers into the bedding. "Is that why you came out here today?" she asked, praying it wasn't. Praying he had come because she had been on his mind, because he had wanted to see her, to be with her.

"Yes."

She sucked in a sharp breath and swung her legs over the side of the bed. "Silly me, I thought you'd come out for other reasons."

"Don't be like that."

He sat up and reached for her; she slipped off the bed, bringing the sheet with her. She wrapped it securely around her, then turned to face him. "And what sort of a 'deal' did you offer my mother? Sixty cents on the dollar? Forty?"

He narrowed his eyes. "And why would I do that, Glory? She borrowed that money from Lily, nearly breaking her. She promised to pay it back and didn't. Lily left those notes to me. She wanted me to have them."

Glory stiffened. "Of course," she said coolly, "you're entitled to your inheritance." She reached for her T-shirt, then bent and retrieved her panties from the floor. She met his eyes once more, lifting her chin haughtily. "I have things to do today, maybe you'd better go."

He narrowed his eyes, furious. "What's with the attitude, princess? You think I should forgive your mother's debt because you're such a great lay?"

"Go to hell."

She turned and marched to the bathroom. He followed her, catching the door with the heel of his hand as she tried to slam it in his face.

"Get out." She clutched the sheet to her breasts, although considering that he was stark naked and had, only moments before, both seen and tasted the parts of her body she was trying to hide, it was a little ridiculous to play the outraged virgin.

"Unlike you and your mother, money means nothing to me. I told her I'd forgive the debt if she would publicly acknowledge Lily. That was the deal I offered her."

Glory stared at him, stunned silent. She couldn't believe she had heard him correctly. She shook her head. "You can't mean you're going to forget—"

"That's exactly what I mean." He laughed, the sound as tight and angry as his expression. "I don't give a crap about the money or the hotel or anything else I could get out of this thing. The way your mother treated Lily was wrong. She hurt Lily. And she's going to make it right, even though it's going to cost me a half a million bucks."

He turned and walked away. Glory watched him go, her heart thundering. She reached out a hand. "I'm sorry."

He stopped but didn't turn. "For what?"

"I misjudged you. I was angry and . . . hurt because you didn't confide in me. That you didn't trust me enough to tell me when you found out."

"Should I, Glory?" He looked over his shoulder at her. "Should I trust you?"

She tipped up her chin. "Yes."

"But do you trust me? Do you believe in me?" When she opened her mouth to reply that she did, he shook his head. "I don't think so. When it comes right down to it, I don't think you ever really believed in me. If you had—" He bit back the words. "Forget it."

"How can I prove to you that you're wrong?" She took a step toward him, heart thundering. "I want to prove it to you."

He met her gaze evenly. "I don't know if you can, Glory. It might be too late for that."

A lump formed in her throat, and she fought to speak around it. She was no longer a sixteen-year-old girl; she was a woman. And she knew what she wanted. She wanted Santos. She wanted to be his lover. She wanted them to have a relationship.

She wanted everything. More than she would ever have with him.

"I'd like to see you again. I'd like to…be with you again. This way." She crossed to him and drew in a deep breath, more afraid than she had been in a long time. "Is that going to be possible, Santos?"

"It depends."

"On?"

"On you. On what you're willing to accept from me. On how much is enough." He bent his head to hers and caught her mouth in a brief but shattering kiss. "My feelings aren't going to change. So long, princess."

56

Hope made her way down the dim corridor, the rancid odor of decay turning her stomach. She held her breath, but the stench still choked her, and she realized with a sense of horror that it was her own smell fouling the air.

She squeezed her eyes shut, her head filled with the image of her and the man-creature writhing on the bed, twisting and coiling together like two serpents. She had reveled in the unholy pleasure of his hands and mouth, then she had wielded the whip, punishing him for his sins.

But still The Beast clamored for more. A sound of terror slipped past her lips, and she brought her hands to her mouth to hold back another. These days, It always wanted more, no matter how often she bowed to its power.

Because of *him*. That boy, Santos.

Up ahead, light speared through and around blackened windows and heavy, metal doors, bolted from the inside. Good struggling to invade, then conquer, evil. Hope dragged her light wrap around herself tightly. Good would reign triumphant; she believed that, she had to.

If she didn't, she would be lost.

She drew closer to the light. Only a few more feet and she would be out of this godforsaken place, and maybe then The Beast would quiet. She counted the steps; she reached the door, threw open the bolt and scurried out.

The fresh air cleared her head, though she couldn't stop trembling. Taking a deep breath, she hurried to her car, praying no one spotted her. She hadn't been able to wait for the cover of night; the Beast had refused to be quelled even for another hour.

She reached her car and climbed inside. Only then did she allow herself a moment of stillness. As she had hoped, sunlight had beaten back The Darkness, and the silence in her head was sweet indeed. She curled her fingers around the steering wheel, and leaned her head against the rest. She closed her eyes.

The days and weeks since Victor Santos had arrived on her doorstep, threat in hand, had been a nightmare. After consulting with her lawyer, she had done as the detective demanded, following each of his instructions to the letter, though it had sickened her to do so. For all, she had played the part of the tragic victim, the loving daughter who, to save her own life, had fled the mother she adored.

Surprisingly, her friends and associates, be they business or personal, had stuck by her, though she had no illusions about the talk that had spread like wildfire through New Orleans society. To her face, they applauded her courage. To her face, they understood, they sympathized. They felt for her, they claimed.

But she saw their glances when she wasn't looking, the horror in their eyes, the repugnance. No area of her life had been left untouched—even Father Rapier looked at her differently.

She was flesh of whores, dirty and common. She had been marked by sin.

Hope tightened her fingers on the steering wheel. The Darkness had ravaged her with its laughter, with its constant, steady call. Ripping away her veil of purity had doubled The Beast's strength. It pounded at her without relief or remorse, giving her neither rest nor a moment's peace.

The control she had once prided herself in, that she had relied upon to protect her, failed her more and more often.

She had been marked by Darkness. Now, all could see.

Hope opened her eyes. The sunlight stung them, but she welcomed the pain. She unclenched her right hand and stared at her palm, red and bruised from the whip. She wished it had been Victor Santos's pain she had heard ringing in her ears, wished it had been he who she had punished. Her hatred for him knew no bounds. It defied logic and restraint; it burned so hotly and so brightly inside her, her skin flushed and blistered with it.

He thought he had won. He thought he had beaten her. She could hear his amusement, his ringing laughter in her head. He and Glory were seeing each other; her daughter had shared that news almost defiantly. Glory didn't understand, she didn't see The Beast beneath the beautiful facade. As it had always been, it was up to her to show Glory the truth, to save her.

Hope shivered as a chill crawled up her spine. She would make Victor Santos pay. She had friends, people who, for a price, would help her. People who had always helped her.

Oh, yes. She would make Victor Santos sorry he had ever dared to corner Hope St. Germaine.

Part 7

Paradise

57

New Orleans, Louisiana.
1996

Chop Robichaux was one of those French Quarter landmarks the tourists never saw, a bit of local color even the locals didn't know about. Unless they were part of the city's dark, twisted underbelly. Unless their sexual preferences ran counter to both the laws of God and man. If so, they knew Chop as a businessman of great wiles and flair, a businessman who had the reputation for always landing on his feet and for being able to supply any perversion for a price.

He had information about the Snow White Killer.

Santos set the phone's receiver back into its cradle, pursing his lips in thought. Chop had said that if Santos was interested in catching the Snow White, he should come now, to his club on Bourbon Street.

Santos rubbed the side of his nose with his index finger. He didn't trust Chop Robichaux. He considered him several levels slimier than swamp scum. But if anybody in the Quarter might be privy to information about who was knocking off young hookers, it would be Chop. After all, young hookers were the man's stock and trade.

"Who was that?"

Santos looked over his shoulder at Glory, naked, sprawled across the bed, half covered by the rumpled sheet. She smiled, and his body stirred. She was so beautiful, she took his breath away. And making love with her defied description. Passionate. Mind-blowing. Erotic. All paled to the way being with her made him feel. These last couple of weeks had passed in a kind of hot, sexual blur.

He shook off his growing arousal, forcing himself to focus on the matter at hand—Chop and whatever information he might have on the Snow White Killer. "You want to take a ride?"

"Sure. Where are we going?"

"To the French Quarter. To see an old friend."

She searched his gaze, as if sensing something was not quite right. "An old friend?" she asked softly, sitting up, pushing her tangled hair away from her face. "What kind of friend?"

He leaned down and kissed her, hard and deeply, then reluctantly broke away. "I'll tell you more in the car."

"I know a place on Burgundy that has killer margaritas."

He laughed. "Frozen or rocks?"

"Either. Great chips and salsa, too."

"You got it." He kissed her again. "We have to hurry."

She nodded and they quickly showered and dressed, not wasting time on talking. He liked that about her, the way she accepted the limitations of their time, the way she didn't feel the need to fill every quiet moment with chatter.

Although he liked that quality in her, it unsettled him, too. Because the quiet never seemed empty; it never felt strained. And it should. When they weren't making love, it should feel awkward and strained and empty as a tomb between them.

Within twenty minutes, they were in his car, heading deeper into the Quarter.

"So, who is this old friend we're going to see?"

"A sleezebag from my days on vice." He cut her a quick glance. "His name's Chop Robichaux."

"Chop Robichaux," she repeated. "That name sounds familiar."

Santos laughed without humor. "I'm not surprised, for a while six years ago, it was splattered across every head-

line in the city. Remember the N.O.P.D. scandal the press
dubbed the French Quarter Four?''

She drew her eyebrows together in thought, then inclined her head. ''Yes, but only vaguely.''

''I'll refresh your memory then. Four N.O.P.D. vice officers were accused, then convicted, of taking pay to over-
look the activities in a club at the fringe of the French
Quarter. The place was a sort of sex shop. But not the usual
above-the-law touristy stuff. Hard-core. Some real sick shit.
A lot of the operation involved underage kids, most of
them runaways. The place was called the Chop Shop. After its owner, the man we're going to see.''

''Underage kids?'' Glory made a sound of outrage.
''That's . . . that's disgusting. It's beyond terrible.''

''That's what everybody thought, once the story broke.
Of course, they thought it even worse that some of New
Orleans's finest were taking money to look the other way.
That was my opinion, too. That's why I blew them all in.''

''Blew them in?'' She frowned. ''What do you mean?''

''At the time, I was a ranking vice officer. I became
aware that some of my fellow officers were on the pay. I
went to Chop to talk a deal. Then I went to Internal Affairs.''

''I bet that didn't make you too popular.''

''That's putting it mildly. Luckily, shortly afterward I got
my transfer to homicide.'' Santos turned onto Bourbon.
''Internal Affairs was a lot more interested in the dirty cops
than in Chop. He turned state's evidence in return for immunity from prosecution.''

''He never did time?'' She looked shocked.

''That's the way it works, babe. Standard operating
procedure. They closed him down, of course. He just
opened up on another block. This time, he's supposedly
straight, on the up-and-up. But I say people like Chop
Robichaux don't know how to operate by the books or by
the law. But that's not my department anymore.''

''And that was it? The end of the story?''

"Not quite." He swung into an illegal spot across from Chop's place. "One of The Four claimed I was involved. He claimed I became aware that I.A. was sniffing around, and sacrificed them to save myself. Seems the bit about Internal Affairs sniffing around was true. I.A. investigated me, but they couldn't find anything."

"They took his word against yours?" she asked, sounding stunned.

"I messed up, and it looked bad." He turned off the ignition. "I should have gone to I.A. with my suspicions right away, and let them take it from there. But I wanted proof. And I wanted to know Chop would back me up."

"So because you offered him the deal, he thinks he owes you."

Santos laughed. "Hardly. He hates my guts. I'm the one who busted his operation, after all."

Silence ensued. Santos darted a glance her way. "What?"

She was silent a moment more, then she shook her head. "I don't understand something. If this Chop hates you, why did he call you about this information?"

"Good question. One that's bothering me. But in another way, it makes sense. I'm the lead detective on the case, and he knows me. It could be he's incriminated in some way and wants some sort of deal. Maybe he wants to feel me out, see where he might stand."

"Maybe you should call Jackson. Or get backup."

"Backup?" he repeated, laughing. "You've been watching too many cop shows on TV. There's a big difference between talking to an informant and going into a life-threatening situation."

He saw her nervous glance toward the front of the nightclub. The street was busy; a usual Saturday night in the Quarter. Every so often, someone would enter or emerge from the club, and he and Glory could get a glimpse inside. The place appeared to be packed.

"Look," he said, "I'm in and out of there. You wait here. It won't take ten minutes."

"You're sure?"

"Yeah." He leaned across the seat, kissed her, then opened his car door. "After that, it's Margaritaville for us."

Santos hopped out of the car and started across the street and into the club. The place was, indeed, packed. On the stage, a scantily clad woman undulated to the deafening music. The place reeked of beer, cigarettes and sweaty bodies. It brought back memories, unpleasant ones. From his youth. From his time working vice.

He caught sight of Chop behind the bar, and started to pick his way through the crowd, being bumped and jostled along the way.

A guy wearing a Dixie Beer T-shirt knocked head-on into him, spilling half his beer on Santos in the process.

"Hey, pal." Santos reeled backward, getting bumped from behind, feeling someone's hand at his back. "Watch it."

The guy grinned, exposing a mouthful of rotten teeth. "Pardon me," he said, weaving on his feet, not looking sorry at all. "My mistake."

Santos flashed his shield. "I think you've had enough, buddy. Take a hike."

The guy backed away, grinning again. "Whatever you say, Officer."

The hair on the back of Santos's neck stood up, and he frowned. He swung his gaze to the bar, only to find Chop watching him. The hairs prickled again; Chop motioned him closer.

He reached the bar. Chop had moved to the other end to serve a customer. Santos studied the man, his skin crawling with distaste. He was short and heavy, with thinning hair, dyed an unnatural white-blond. He had perpetually oily skin, and had suffered a severe case of adolescent acne, as evidenced by the scars that pitted his face. But it wasn't Robichaux's physical person, unpleasant though it was that made Santos's flesh crawl. No, it was what showed from inside of the man. Chop Robichaux had the soul of a monster.

As if aware of Santos's thoughts, Chop looked over his shoulder and directly at Santos. He smiled thinly. A moment later, he sauntered over. "Hello, asshole. It's been a long time."

Santos swept his gaze over him, disgusted, unwilling to play the man's game. "You have information for me?"

"What kind of information are you looking for?"

"Don't screw with me, Robichaux." Santos narrowed his eyes. "You have that information or not?"

The man smiled again, that same thin, unpleasant twisting of his lips. "Nah, I just wanted to see your pretty face in my place."

"I ought to bust your ass right now."

"Try it." Chop laughed. "You've no grounds. I'm clean."

"When hell freezes over." Santos swept his gaze over the odious little man. "Maybe I should just manufacture something. Anything I came up with would no doubt be true."

"You don't have the balls." He laughed again, the sound almost girlish in its glee. "You were always such a fucking Boy Scout. But you know what? Even Boy Scouts have their day. Now, get out of my place."

"With pleasure, Robichaux. Your place reeks."

Santos pushed away from the bar, a knot of unease settling in the pit of his gut, his mind clicking over the reasons Chop could have had for claiming he had information about the Snow White, then playing dumb when Santos arrived. He could have gotten last-minute cold feet. Maybe he couldn't talk at that moment because the perp was close by. Or, he could have been, simply, messing with him.

None of those explanations struck Santos as quite right. None of them lessened the knot of unease in his gut. Why would Chop Robichaux call a homicide detective at home, on a Saturday night, to play games with his head?

The situation stank, big time. Chop was up to something, and it involved him.

Santos made his way through the club without incident. He stepped out of the bar, his gaze immediately going to his car. Glory was just where he had left her, looking his way. She smiled and waved.

"Detective Santos?"

Four men—cops, he guessed, judging from their cheap suits and their regulation haircuts—circled him. Santos eyed them warily. "That's me."

One of the men held up his shield. "Lieutenant Brown, Internal Affairs. These are Officers Patrick, Thompson and White."

Santos met each of the officer's openly hostile gazes in turn, a feeling of *ah-ha* sliding up his spine. *So that was it; he'd been set up. But by who? And why?*

"What can I do for you, Lieutenant?"

"I think you know, Detective. Up against the building."

Santos did as the man asked, and one of the officers, Patrick, he thought, frisked him, taking his service revolver and badge.

"What's this?" Patrick pulled an envelope from his jacket pocket and handed it to the lieutenant.

The officer opened it, then met Santos's eyes. "It looks like about twenty-one hundred-dollar bills, Detective. Marked bills, if my guess is right. You want to tell me where this money came from?"

"I'd love to, but I don't know where it came from. I've never seen it before." Heart pounding, Santos searched his memory. Any of a couple dozen people in that bar could have planted that envelope, but he would lay money on the big guy with the bad teeth. "I've been set up."

"Surprise, surprise." Officer Patrick grabbed Santos's right arm, twisted it behind his back and snapped a handcuff around his wrist, then did the same to his left arm. "I've heard that one before."

Santos swore silently. "I don't doubt you have, but this time it's true."

"Tell it to your lawyer," the lieutenant snapped. "Somebody read him his rights."

58

Liz smiled wearily at her bartender. "I'm out of here, Darryl. You're sure you've got everything under control?"

He grinned and his usually nondescript but pleasant, freckled face became absolutely devilish. "Got it, boss."

"You're certain you know the closing procedure? If you have any hesitation, I'll stay the extra hour and—"

"Get lost," he answered, waving her toward the door. "You look beat."

"I am." She hoisted her tote bag to her shoulder. "Nine in the morning to ten at night makes for a long day."

"So take off." He shook his head. "I've got everything covered. Besides, if anything comes up, I know where to find you."

After making one last, visual check of the place and calling goodbye to her two waitresses, Liz left the restaurant and started for her car.

She had parked it in a lot located two blocks up to Bourbon, then one block over. She didn't mind walking, even though she rarely left before ten-thirty. This area of the Quarter was heavily trafficked and she always carried her ever-faithful can of Mace.

Ever-faithful. Unlike Santos had been.

Liz pushed the thought aside and drew in a deep breath, enjoying the crisp, night air. She had to go on; she understood that. She was a survivor. The long days—and nights—at her restaurant were as much of her own choosing as a necessity. The longer and harder she worked, the less time she had to think about Santos; the less time she had to miss him, to hurt.

Even after everything, she still loved him.

She drew in a swift, angry breath. She wouldn't forgive him for the way he had hurt her. The way he had betrayed her with Glory. If she knew of a way to make him pay, she would.

Liz reached Bourbon Street and started across, glancing to her left and right, then stopped, blinking in surprise. Hope St. Germaine was crossing almost right in front of her, from the opposite side of the street.

Liz frowned, stiffening with distaste. French Quarter nightlife hardly seemed like *her* cup of tea. Unless she was down here on some mission of moral mercy. That was it—she had probably come to the Quarter to sanctimoniously ruin someone's life.

But alone? At this time of night?

Without pausing for second thought, Liz turned in the opposite direction of her car, and followed Hope St. Germaine, becoming more curious when, moments later, the woman ducked into Paris Nights, a strip club owned by a sleezeball named Chop Robichaux. Whenever the Association of French Quarter Merchants met, the man always looked her over, as if wondering what she would be worth on the open market.

Liz shuddered. She had heard about his past operations, about his run-ins with the law. And from some of the other business owners, she had heard stories about Robichaux that had given her nightmares.

She shook her head, told herself that Hope's reasons for being in Paris Nights was none of her business, then followed Glory's mother into the club, anyway. She stopped just inside the door, taking a moment to adjust to the dark, smoky interior. When she did, Liz saw that Hope St. Germaine was at the bar, talking to Chop. But instead of turning away, as if she'd gotten directions to a pay phone or a bathroom, Hope waited while the beefy club owner came around the bar, and the two went toward the back of the club together.

Liz narrowed her eyes. *What business could high-and-mighty St. Germaine have with low-down and dirty Robichaux?*

She followed them, though careful to keep her distance. They had slipped into a booth on the other side of the stage. Liz craned her neck to see around the gyrating dancers; she saw Hope slide what appeared to be an envelope across the table.

"Hey, baby." A man reeking of whiskey fell against her and grabbed her arms. "Wanna dance?"

"No, I don't." Disgusted, she reeled back from the man, wrenching her arms free. "Excuse me."

She began to back out of the club, but the drunken man followed her. "Aw, c'mon, darlin'. I bet you can really shake your wild thing." He leered. "Those girls up there have nothing on you."

They had nothing on. Period. Liz glowered at the man, doing her best to look fierce. "I said no."

He made another grab for her, this time for a spot south of her elbow. She slapped his hand, then kicked him in the shin. Surprised, he made a heavy sound of pain and stumbled backward.

Liz turned and ran.

59

Forty-eight hours after being arrested, Glory bailed Santos out. She took him directly to the hotel; there Jackson waited.

Santos didn't waste time on pleasantries. He barreled into the room and across the floor, stopping to stand before his partner. "What the hell's going on, Jackson?"

His partner folded his hands calmly in his lap. "Seems Robichaux went to the district attorney, claiming you were shaking him down. Said you threatened to hurt him and his family if he didn't pay."

"What!" Santos glowered at Jackson. "That's bull-shit!"

"Hold tight, partner, there's more." Jackson drew what sounded like a careful breath. "Chop claims you were a part of the busted operation six years ago. Make that the French Quarter Five."

Santos sank to a chair. The past was coming back to haunt him. He remembered the suspicious glances, the open hostility from his fellow officers. He had felt so betrayed by them, first when he discovered what they had been up to, the way they had bastardized their badges for profit, then worst of all, when one of them had accused him of being a part of their operation.

To have his integrity questioned, his honor under attack, had been the ultimate slap in the face. And now it was happening again.

Unable to sit still, Santos leaped to his feet and began to pace.

"Chop claims you weren't only a part of the operation, but that you were the leader," Jackson continued. "He claims that you got wind I.A. was onto you, so you let your fellow officers take a dive to save your own ass. Chop went along with you, he says, because you threatened his family. Of course, as he freely admits, he had nothing to lose since he was offered immunity from prosecution."

"The slimy little bastard!" Santos stopped and swung to face his partner. He flexed his fingers. "If I could get my hands on him right now, I'd wring his fat neck."

"What I don't understand," Glory said suddenly, speaking for the first time since arriving at the hotel, "is why Internal Affairs is so quick to believe a character like this. The man's a criminal, for heaven's sake."

Jackson smiled grimly at Glory. "It does seem ridiculous, doesn't it? But, politically, this a bad time to look innocent. There have been so many scandals in the department, so many incidents involving dirty cops, the public's perception is that we're all dirty. Hell, "60 Minutes" has done two unflattering exposés on the N.O.P.D., and Chief Pennington came into office looking for corruption, vowing to clean up the department. It's a witchhunt atmosphere right now. Right now, as far as I.A. is concerned, you're guilty until proven innocent. And they keep coming back to that original officer's insistence that you were involved."

"So," Santos said, beginning to pace again, "Robichaux goes to the district attorney with this fairy tale. They go to Internal Affairs with a deal. I.A. sets up a sting. Robichaux tells them I'm coming by for a payment. They give him the marked bills, and he has them planted on me."

Santos stopped pacing and swung to glower at his partner once more. "Of course, everybody buys his story. Not just those pricks from I.A., but all the guys. They all believe a low-down dirty scumbag before me. Just great." He fisted his fingers. "Just fucking great."

"Not everybody," Jackson said quietly. "But to some, it looks bad. Because of your past involvement with Robichaux, because of the way you handled the original case, going to Chop before I.A. And you were there, in his place that night."

"Robichaux called Santos," Glory said quickly. "He said he had information on the Snow White. I was there."

"But you weren't on the phone. So, as far as I.A.'s concerned, you weren't there." Jackson turned back to Santos. "And you had the envelope of money. The marked money."

"Which was planted on me."

Jackson held up a hand. "I know that. And you know that—"

"But we have to get I.A. to know that," Glory murmured. She looked from Santos to Jackson. "But how?"

"To learn that," Jackson said, "we need to know why. Why," he repeated calmly. "Think, Santos. You don't work vice anymore. You're not a threat to Robichaux. There are enough homicides in this city to keep you busy in your own division. Why risk everything to set you up?"

"Money. That's the only thing a person like Robichaux cares about. Somebody's paying him to do it." Santos narrowed his eyes. "But who?"

"That, my friend, is the question of the day."

The hotel manager called, and Glory spoke with him a moment, then excused herself. "Duty calls," she murmured, crossing to the door. "If you need anything, my secretary will have me paged."

Santos crossed to stand beside her. He caught her hand and brought it to his mouth. "Thanks," he said quietly, meeting her eyes, realizing in that moment that he needed her far more than was wise. "For everything."

She smiled and curled her fingers around his. "You're welcome."

Seconds later, the door shut behind her. Jackson whistled under his breath, then looked at Santos. "That's one exceptional woman. She stood by you like you wouldn't believe. Called everybody she knew. You have any idea what you're doing with her?"

Frowning, Santos glanced back at the door through which Glory had just exited. She had stood stalwartly by him, that was true, publicly challenging the charges, doing what she could to help. The night of the arrest, she had called Jackson, then had contacted a top defense lawyer; when bail had finally been set, she had arranged for it and this meeting with his partner.

And yet, through it all, he had wondered why she was doing it. He had wondered when the ax would fall. And right now, he felt like a class-A piece of shit because of it.

"Do I know what I'm doing?" he repeated softly. "When it comes to Glory, hell, no, I never have."

Jackson nodded. "That's what I thought. Figure it out. Or you'll fuck up. Again."

"Meaning?"

"Liz."

Santos looked away, then back at his partner. "I didn't love her, man. It just wasn't there."

"And it's there with Glory?"

Was it? He had thought he loved her once, but that had been a long time ago. Back when he had still believed the world was made up of shades of gray.

Santos made a sound of frustration. "What's the fascination with my love life? We don't have enough to think about?"

Jackson laughed, then sobered. "Our reluctant witness was in."

"Tina?"

"The very one." Jackson steepled his fingers. "She says she's being followed. Stalked by the Snow White Killer."

Santos searched his friend's expression, frowning. "But you don't believe her?"

"She doesn't fit the profile. She's too old. Her hair and eyes are wrong." Jackson shook his head. "She seemed genuinely scared, though. But I also think the woman's got snakes in her head."

"Probably a case of the power of suggestion causing a runaway imagination." Santos rubbed his index finger along the side of his nose. "You checked it out, anyway?"

"Of course. I also attempted to get her to talk, but that was another no-go."

"Big surprise."

"There's another reason I didn't put much stock in her claim of being stalked by the Snow White."

At his partner's tone, Santos braced himself. He had a feeling this was going to be his least favorite news on a day already filled with bad headlines. "Spit it out."

"We found another body. In Baton Rouge."

"Baton Rouge!" Santos jumped to his feet, fury and impotence raging inside him. "He's getting away. The son of a bitch is walking!"

"We don't know that. He could have been—"

"Give me a break, Jackson! You know as well as I do that he's out of here." Santos flexed his fingers. "This guy doesn't stray. He picks a place he likes, a place he feels safe. And he stays until it gets too hot for him. Then he moves on."

His partner didn't argue, because he couldn't. After a moment, Jackson cleared his throat. "I'm heading over there, to see what they've got and to confirm it's the real deal and not a copycat."

"The palms—"

"Marked with the cross."

"Dammit! This is my guy, Jackson. I'm coming with you."

"Right. Then we'd both be off the case." Jackson stood. "I don't think so, buddy. If the captain found out I was even talking to you, my ass would be in a big-time sling."

"This is such a bunch of crap." Santos scowled. "What am I supposed to do? Sit on my hands and wait around while our guy gets away?"

"Basically."

"Screw you."

Jackson laughed and thumped Santos on the shoulder. "We'll get you out of this. Somehow, we'll get the proof we need to get you off."

For a moment, Santos said nothing, then he met his friend's eyes. "But what if we don't? Forget jail for a moment, I could lose my badge, Jackson. What would I do then? I'm a cop, it's who I am."

Jackson squeezed Santos's shoulder and nodded. "I know. But we'll get you off. Somehow, we'll find out who did this to you and we'll fry their ass. All you've got to do is hold tight."

60

Santos was not about to sit on his hands and wait—not for the Snow White Killer to completely slip through his fingers, or for somebody else to save his butt. He would like to find Robichaux and beat the truth out of him, but figured that, despite how satisfying the act would be, it really wouldn't help his cause.

His other option was Tina. What if she really was being stalked by the Snow White? Maybe this guy knew she had seen him. Maybe he wanted to tie up loose ends before blowing town. Tina had been standing near her friend Billie when she had gotten that last date. Tina had seen the guy clearly. It only followed that he had seen her, too. *If* that john was the Snow White, he would consider Tina a threat.

Santos waited until dark to head for the Quarter. He cruised the streets and clubs, checking the places hookers frequented most. All with no sign of Tina. After a couple of hours, he began to wonder if she had been scared enough to skip town, or at the least to lie low for a while.

He rejected the latter. To make any kind of money, working girls needed to be on the street, all the time. Most of them worked sick, they worked if their kids were sick, they worked if it was broiling hot or freezing cold.

No, if Tina was in town, she was on the street. He would keep looking.

After another couple hours, his diligence paid off. He caught sight of her, coming out of, ironically, Club 69. He drew his car to the curb alongside of her and rolled down the window. "Tina."

She turned toward him, her come-hither smile twisting into a scowl when she saw it was him. "Get lost."

She started walking again, and he inched the car forward. "I'm not getting lost, so you might as well talk to me now. It'll save us both a lot of time and hassle."

She swore loudly, stopped and sauntered over. "What's up, honey? You need a date?"

"We need to talk."

"Really?" She rested her forearms on the open window and bent her head toward his. She wetted her lips. "Talk about what? The condition of your dick?"

He smelled booze on her breath, strong and sickly sweet. It wasn't surprising, a lot of the girls had booze and dope habits. In their line of work, numbing their bodies and brains was not a negative.

Unfortunately, it kept a lot of them in the business. It burned them out and used them up and kept them chained to their backs.

He hated seeing her this way. He hated looking at her now but remembering the way she had been. He wasn't to blame for her life or the way it had turned out. He hadn't been able to help her.

But still, he felt, somehow, responsible.

"Don't be cute, Tina. I want to talk to you about the Snow White Killer."

"About police business?" She arched her eyebrows. "But, Sugar, I heard you weren't a cop anymore."

Santos gritted his teeth at her barb, but didn't bite. "Detective Jackson told me you stopped by headquarters."

"So?"

"So, he said you were scared. He said you thought you were being stalked by the Snow White."

She narrowed her heavily outlined eyes. "That's right. And you know what your pig-partners did about it? Nothing." She straightened. "So, like I said before. Get lost."

She turned and walked away. Swearing, Santos threw open his car door, hopped out and went after her. "I want to help you, Tina."

She kept walking, just lifted her right hand into the air and flipped him off.

"I'm sorry I didn't come back for you," he called. "Let me help you now."

She stopped, but didn't look back at him. "You don't want to help me," she murmured, her voice thick. "You only want to help yourself." She cleared her throat. "You only want to get this guy, you don't give a shit about me or any of the other girls who are in danger. We're just hookers."

He took another step forward, hand out. "That's not true, Tina. I swear to you, I do care."

She looked over her shoulder then, meeting his eyes. Hers were soft with hurt, bright with unshed tears. "If you had cared, you would have come back for me."

"I . . . couldn't. But I'm here now. I believe this sick bastard really might be following you. He thinks you're a loose end, Tina. A threat to him. If he does think that, he's going to kill you." The blood drained from her face. Santos closed his hand over her arm. "Unless we can get him first."

She stared at him, fear naked in her eyes. He tightened his fingers. "Help me, Tina. Help yourself."

For one brief moment, he thought she would acquiesce. Then the fear in her eyes became fury. She reeled away from him, wrenching her arm from his grasp.

"Just leave me alone! I don't know anything."

"Tina—" He made another grab for her; she swung at him with her purse, catching him in the shoulder. The purse flew open and its contents spilled across the sidewalk. She made a sound of frustration, bent and began retrieving her things.

He squatted beside her to help. There wasn't much—a pack of cigarettes, a half-dozen books of matches, a wad of crumpled bills, a handful of condoms.

She began scooping up the foil packets. "Go away."

"It's not going to happen, Tina. Until you talk, I'm going to stick to you like white on rice. Why not make it easy on the both of—"

She reached to collect the last packet, and her necklace slipped out from beneath her shirt and fell away from her body.

It was a cross. Small, plain, cheap. It looked like a dozen others he had in his office desk drawer.

He covered her hand. "Where did you get that?"

She yanked her hand away and stuffed the foil packets into her purse. "They're rubbers, Officer. One hundred percent latex. A hooker's best friend, don't you know? Me and the rest of the girls, we buy 'em by the gross at the Corner Drugstore." She pointed. "It's down that way, if you're interested."

"Not that." He reached out and hooked his fingers around the necklace. "This."

"Hey! Hands off!"

She jerked backward, but he closed his fist around the cross and held tight. "Where did you get it, Tina?"

"A graduation gift," she said sarcastically. "From my adoring mother and stepfather. Remember? I told you about them. He was a pig, just like you."

He curled his fingers around the flimsy chain. "Stop the bullshit, Tina! Where did you get it?"

"A friend who wants to save my eternal soul. All right? Now, fuck off!"

Her eternal soul. A chill ran up his spine. Tina knew the killer; he was certain of it. He pulled her a fraction closer. "Who is this friend?"

"You're the detective. Figure it out."

Santos yanked the crucifix off her. She gasped and fell backward, landing on her backside on the sidewalk. "Dammit, Tina. Do you want to die? It could save your li—"

He muttered an oath. "I didn't come back for you because my mother was killed that night. Butchered, like your friend Billie. I didn't come back for you because I didn't have anywhere to go myself. Because my world had just fallen apart. This might be the same guy who killed her. And I've got to know if he is. I've got to catch him, Tina.

"Now—" he leaned toward her, hand out, seeing her surprise "—tell me where you got the goddamned necklace."

61

Tina had gotten the crucifix from a bible thumper in the
Quarter, a guy who owned a small religious-supplies store
on Dauphine. He was a nice guy, she had said. A bit of a
fanatic, but nice. He liked all the working girls, was always preaching to them about good and evil, always quoting the scripture and trying to get them to change their
wicked ways.

No way was he the guy, she had said. No possible way.

Santos thought otherwise. So did Jackson.

Obviously excited, Jackson told him to hang tight, that
he would get back with him as soon as he could.

The waiting was hell. Santos paced, cursing Chop Robichaux and whoever else had set him up. He wanted to be
with Jackson and the others. He wanted to be in that
scumbag's apartment, he wanted to cuff him and bring him
in.

Dammit, he wanted to be doing his job.

And he wanted this guy to be the one who had done his
mother. He wanted to know; and he wanted the son of a
bitch to fry.

Jackson called him the minute he got back to headquarters. It looked as if he was their guy, he said. They found all
sorts of stuff in his store and apartment; more of the
crosses, newspaper articles about the Snow White. He even
had pictures of a couple of the dead girls.

The only thing they didn't have, Jackson said, was the
guy himself. He traveled, his landlady said. He was sometimes gone a week, but never more. She didn't know where
he had gone this time.

''Is he old enough?'' Santos asked tightly, gripping the receiver so hard his fingers went numb. ''Could he be the one who—'' Santos's throat closed over the words and he struggled to clear it, realizing just how much he had hoped and prayed for this moment. And how much he feared it.

He had to know.

''Could he be the one who killed my mother?''

For one, agonizing moment, his partner said nothing. Santos's stomach did a nosedive. ''Jackson?''

''He could be,'' he said finally. ''He's old enough. He's been in and out of the Quarter for years. He frequents . . . hookers.''

Santos let his breath out in a rush, his knees going weak. *It could be the guy. It could be him.*

''Santos, buddy, don't lose it here. Just because maybe it could be the same guy, sure as hell doesn't mean it is. It's probably not.''

''I know. But for now . . . hell, Jackson. For now, *maybe* is enough.''

62

"Hello, Liz."

Liz looked up from her employee time cards, lined up on the bar in front of her. "Jackson," she said, smiling, genuinely pleased to see him. "What brings you in?"

He grinned. "I was craving one of your tofu sesame salads."

"Just what I love to hear from a customer." She slid off the bar stool. "I'll show you to a table. Are you alone today?"

"Yup. Just little old me."

She laughed and shook her head. "Even your pinky is big, Jackson. What were you, thirty-eight inches at birth?"

"Forty-eight."

She laughed again and stopped beside a window table with a good view of the street. "How's this?"

"Perfect." He took one of the chairs and motioned toward another. "Can you join me?"

She glanced back at the bar, and the stack of time cards. She had to finish them tonight for payroll tomorrow. "Just for a minute." She grimaced and took the seat across from him. "The paperwork never ends. It's my least favorite part of the business."

"That's the thing about life," he murmured as the waitress approached with the menu. "You've got to take the good with the bad. I mean, look at me. I love police work. It's the criminals I can't stand."

Liz laughed. "I suppose, compared to criminals, my time cards aren't so bad."

Jackson didn't even glance at the menu. He ordered the salad and a glass of herbal ice tea, then turned back to Liz. "How are things?"

"Great," she said quickly. Too quickly, she realized. And too brightly. Heat stung her cheeks and she cleared her throat, embarrassed. "I hear you got the Snow White Killer."

"We have a suspect."

She drew her eyebrows together. "You don't sound convinced he's the one."

"Don't I?" Jackson shrugged. "I'm not like my hot-headed partner. I always reserve judgment until we've got all the evidence and the guy's under arrest."

At the mention of Santos, a lump formed in her throat. "How is Santos?"

"If you've seen the paper, you know."

She caught her bottom lip between her teeth, fighting back the feeling of guilt that welled up inside her. She reminded herself that she hated him. She reminded herself that he could burn at the stake in Jackson Square, for all she cared. She only wished Glory could burn with him.

"Liz? Is something wrong?"

"Nothing." She shook her head. "No."

Jackson narrowed his eyes, studying her, and heat stung her cheeks again. But this time, guilty heat. She shifted her gaze. "Is it . . . as bad for Santos as I've heard. I mean, is there a chance he'll . . . you know."

"Get off? Be proven innocent, which he is? I sure as hell hope so." Jackson's mouth thinned. "Somebody's setting him up. Somebody besides Chop Robichaux."

"Besides Robichaux?" she repeated, her voice high. "But who?"

"If we knew that, we could do something. As it stands, Santos is screwed." Jackson looked at her sharply. "You don't have any . . . information about this, do you, Liz?"

"Information? Me?" She shook her head, torn, her conscience tugging at her. "Why should I?" She jumped to her feet and forced an easy smile, knowing she was acting guilty as sin. "Here comes your salad, I guess I'd better get back to that nasty paperwork."

She turned and started toward the bar, stopping when Jackson called her name. She glanced over her shoulder, meeting his gaze, though with difficulty.

"He didn't mean to hurt you, Liz. He's a good man. And he's a . . . he's a great cop."

Tears swamped her, and without another word, she turned and walked back to the bar. But once there, she couldn't focus on her calculations. She couldn't stop thinking about having seen Hope St. Germaine in the Quarter the other night, about having seen her talking with Chop Robichaux.

And she couldn't stop thinking about Santos.

As if her thoughts had conjured him, he walked into the restaurant. Her heart pounded and for one breathless moment she thought that maybe, just maybe, he had come for her.

Of course, he hadn't. He had come to see Jackson; and he looked extremely uncomfortable to be here.

He should, she thought, angry. He should feel like a total shit.

She glanced at him again, from the corners of her eyes. She saw him glance her way, grimace, then motion to the door. Jackson shook his head, and motioned to the chair across from his. Looking like a sentenced man, Santos slid into it.

A lump of emotion formed in her throat, almost suffocating her. It hurt to look at him. It hurt to want something so much, and to know she would never have it.

Why couldn't it have worked out between them? Why couldn't he have loved her? It would have made up for the past, for losing her shining future, a hundredfold. It would have made up for Glory.

For several minutes, she fiddled with the time cards, acknowledging that she would have to redo them, unable to focus on anything but Santos. She sneaked another peek at him, studying him for a moment, then averting her eyes.

He looked bad, she realized. Drawn and tired. Something in his expression made him look like a lost little boy. The way he must have looked all those years ago, after his mother's murder, when he'd had no one.

He had recently lost Lily. Now he had lost his job.

Liz swallowed hard, feeling like a heel. In a way, once again, he was that lost and alone little boy. He had no one, nothing, he could call his own.

Santos loved his job, he loved being a cop. And he was a good one. One of the best. She couldn't hurt him this way, no matter how badly he had hurt her. It was wrong. It was hateful.

And, in the long run, it would probably hurt her more than him.

She stood and nervously smoothed her hands over her skirt. Having seen Hope St. Germaine and Chop Robichaux talking together might have been a coincidence and have nothing to do with Santos. It probably was. But at least her conscience would be clear.

Taking a deep breath, she crossed to their table. They both looked up. She clasped her hands in front of her. "Hello, Santos."

He searched her gaze. "Hello, Liz."

He looked as if he was in agony. He hated having hurt her, she realized. He hadn't done it deliberately. The regret in his eyes was real; the sorrow there was true.

"If you want me to leave," he said softly, "I will."

"No, I—" she drew in another deep breath "—I need to speak to you." She shifted her gaze to Jackson. "To both of you. May I sit down?"

They nodded. She took a seat and without preamble, launched into her story. A couple minutes later, Jackson leaned back in his chair and whistled. "Holy bad-apple, Batman."

Santos shook his head, his expression stunned. "I told myself she couldn't be involved. Even though my gut told me otherwise, even though I kept coming back to her, to the venom in her eyes and voice the last time I saw her. But I thought I was crazy. I told myself it...couldn't be.''

"But Chop Robichaux? You can't get much lower than that dude. So how—"

"Did she hook up with him?" Santos leaned forward in his seat, obviously excited. "You can't just open the Yellow Pages and find a listing for Scumbags 'R' Us."

"And Robichaux wouldn't risk everything for just anybody."

"He would for the right amount of money. I know this S.O.B. He'd do anything for money."

"But how much would it take for him to do this?" Jackson steepled his fingers. "What do you think? Where do we go from here?"

"We get proof. We get something that ties the two of them together. We find out what was in that envelope."

Liz watched them, listening, feeling like a third wheel. Like the outsider, the kid who hadn't been picked to play ball. *She was no longer a part of this team. She was no longer needed or wanted here.*

Tears burned the backs of her eyes. She cleared her throat and stood. "I'll leave you two to...talk. I just wanted—" She bit back the words, struggling with the tears, vowing that she would not shame herself by crying.

Santos stood, too, his expression grateful. "Liz, I don't know how to thank you. I don't know what I would have done if—"

"Forget it." She smoothed her hands over her skirt again. "Really."

"But I don't want to forget it. I owe you for this, Liz. Big time."

She folded her arms across her middle and shook her head. "No, Santos. You don't. I didn't do this because I...forgive you. I didn't do it to help you or because I still...love you." Her voice thickened, and she cleared it.

"I did it because it was the right thing to do. Because you're a great cop. And because I couldn't have lived with myself if I hadn't."

Santos caught her hand. He squeezed her fingers. "Whatever your reasons, thank you, Liz. You just saved my life."

63

"Well, Mr. Michaels," Glory said, closing her office door and motioning to the sofa grouping to her right, "what did you think?"

The man smiled, crossed to the sofa and sat down. "Please, call me Jonathan."

She sank onto the chair across from him. "Only if you call me Glory."

"Done." He smiled again. "It's a beautiful property, Glory. You've taken excellent care of it."

"Thank you." She folded her hands in her lap, hating that they shook. "I love the St. Charles. It's been in my family for a long time. In fact, the St. Charles is like a member of the family."

She hesitated, torn by what she was doing. A part of her felt as if even talking to an investor like Jonathan Michaels was letting her father down, another part knew that times had changed and that she—and the St. Charles—had to change with them.

"I'm sure," she continued, meeting his gaze once more, "that sounds rather silly to a no-nonsense businessman such as yourself."

"Actually, it doesn't." He placed his hands on his knees and leaned toward her. "When my agent contacted you, I didn't think we had a chance. After all, we've tried before. Why are you interested in selling this time?"

"I'm not interested in selling," she corrected quickly. "But, as I explained to your associate, I am considering taking on a partner."

He inclined his head, a smile tugging at his mouth. "Poor word choice. You indicated you would part with twenty-percent ownership?"

"And no more. That's nonnegotiable." Glory tightened her fingers in her lap. "I'm also quite interested in your management service. You have an excellent reputation, as I'm sure you know."

He smiled, indicating that he did. "May I ask, why a partner now?"

"Due to forces beyond my control, the hotel is much less profitable than it once was."

"The location."

"Is the biggest reason, yes. The next is the proliferation of new hotels in and around the city." She drew in a deep, careful breath. She knew these words, these reasons, by heart. She had played them all over in her head many times. "If I can't get occupancy up, eventually I will be unable to maintain the hotel, either its standards or the facility."

"You can lower the room rate."

"I have. Considerably, over the years. But occupancy is still down, and I'm getting less for the rooms. Standards will fall. I don't want that to happen."

"I can understand that. In my opinion, it would be a tragedy. There are few enough grand old places like this left." He searched her expression, his gaze, she suspected, missing nothing. "Are those your only reasons, Glory?"

"No." She stood and went to the window that over-looked St. Charles Avenue. As she gazed down, a streetcar rumbled past. "As you know, running a hotel is a full-time responsibility."

"Full-time plus about forty hours."

"You've got that right." She shifted her gaze to his. "And there's another venture I want to get involved in. Another, much smaller property that has a lot of poten-tial."

He arched an eyebrow. "From the look in your eyes, this property is special."

She smiled. "Very. But it will take a tremendous amount of my time. And a great deal of capital to get off the ground."

"Any chance you're looking for a partner in that venture?"

She laughed again, liking this man. "It wouldn't be your cup of tea, believe me. But I'm every bit committed to it as to the St. Charles." At his expression, she added, "It's also a family property. My mother's family."

She crossed to her desk and rested on its edge, facing him. "We've talked about me and my reasons for wanting a partner. What about you, Jonathan? I know you've done your research. You haven't built your business to its present state by being uninformed. Knowing what you do about the St. Charles, why are you interested in part ownership?"

"That's easy." He lifted his hands palms up. "Because the St. Charles is a gem. Because it's a perfect complement to my other hotels. And because I believe this area of New Orleans will turn around. Eventually. I also believe that if given a choice, affluent, cosmopolitan visitors would prefer to stay in a grand old New Orleans hotel than in one of the large, slick chain hotels."

He laced his fingers together. "Advertising this beautiful hotel is key, getting the word out about what a rare and special experience staying at the St. Charles would be. Travel agents need to know about the St. Charles, we need to be hooked in with tour companies, both in the U.S. and abroad. My management company has had incredible success with European wholesalers. You'll see occupancy back at ninety percent within six months."

She worked to conceal her excitement. Except during Mardi Gras, the St. Charles hadn't been at ninety percent since before her father's death. "That's a big claim, Jonathan."

He met her gaze evenly. "I've done it before."

He had. She, too, had done her homework. Jonathan Michaels had a sterling reputation in the industry. He was financially sound, had a history of success and was considered both wily and honest. The year before, he had been named Hotelier of the Year by *Hotel* magazine.

He stood and crossed to the picture window behind her desk, occupying the spot she had occupied only moments before. He, too, gazed down at the avenue. "I'm also looking at buying several commercial properties around the hotel."

Glory arched her eyebrows. "That would be a tremendous investment of capital in an area most consider dead."

"I have the capital. And I love this city. I believe in it." He folded his arms across his chest. "You know I'm a native New Orleanian?"

She nodded. "Your father worked for a time at the St. Charles."

"As a bellman." Jonathan laughed and shook his head. "I remember coming to see him here, with my mother. I was awestruck."

She laughed. "Sometimes I still am."

"I met your father that day. He was very kind to us. Later, I knew him through business."

Glory swept her gaze over him. Jonathan Michaels looked to be in his mid-to-late-forties. Her father would have been sixty-four this year. "Did you?"

"I was just starting out in the business. He was very highly thought of in the industry. He impressed the heck out of me, that's for sure."

Her lips lifted. "He did me, too. Thank you." She checked her watch. "I know you have a plane to catch, I won't keep you any longer."

He nodded and they started for the door. "What do you think?" he asked. "Interested?"

"Very. I have to talk to my business advisors. My lawyer and the hotel accountant. And my mother. As you probably know, she owns fifty percent of the hotel."

"Do you think she'll be receptive to discussion?"

Glory held the door open for him, then they walked toward the elevators. "She's not as attached to the hotel as I am. But she enjoys the perks. And the prestige of owning it."

"Many of those details can be worked out at the table."

They reached the elevator, and Glory summoned one, inclining her head. "I'll call you."

"You do that. An association between our hotels would be profitable for us both. And good for the St. Charles."

"If I didn't believe that, I wouldn't have agreed to meet with you in the first place. I'll call you," she said again. "Either way."

After she had walked him to the elevator, Glory returned to her office. She stood at the door and gazed at her father's desk, the window and view beyond, a feeling of both sadness and hopefulness moving over her.

Her father would not have wanted the hotel to fail. He would not have allowed it to fall into disrepair. And he would have liked Jonathan Michaels—everything about him, from his reputation in the industry to the fact he was a New Orleans native.

But her mother would not like him. She would not think him "good enough" to be in partnership with. She would not want to give up any of her status, nor would she agree to anything she feared would cause talk.

Her mother would not readily—if ever—agree to this deal.

And Glory wasn't quite sure what she was going to do about that.

64

The club was called the Rack. Located on the edge of the French Quarter, away from the hustle and bustle of tourists and legitimate businesses, this club opened at midnight and closed at dawn; it catered to a clientele whose sexual appetites ran counter to normal, ones whose lives revolved around the giving and/or receiving of pain.

And Hope St. Germaine had just gone inside.

Santos whistled, low and sweet. Five days of following her had finally yielded pay dirt. But this? He shook his head. If he hadn't seen it himself, if he hadn't tailed her from her driveway to here, hadn't watched her climb out of her car—dressed totally in black, her face shielded by a scarf—scurry up the sidewalk and slip inside, he never would have believed it.

He had her now. Almost.

Santos tugged his New Orleans Saints' cap lower on his head and climbed out of his car. Jackson had used sources to discover that Queen St. Germaine had recently cashed in a twenty-five-thousand-dollar C.D. He had also learned that she hadn't redeposited the money in any accounts, at least none that Jackson's sources had access to.

Unfortunately, it wasn't a crime to cash in a C.D. And since he and Jackson had learned of it illegally, the information couldn't be used in a court of law or anyplace else. He needed more; he needed proof that she had set him up.

Santos entered the Rack, keeping his head down. He could be recognized here, though it had been years since he had busted the place as a part of a routine, cleanup sting.

If his memory was correct, the place had been closed for less than seventy-two hours after the bust.

Life went on. The department had neither the funding nor staff to act on every infraction of the law, especially when it came to consensual sex between adults—even dangerous, twisted sex.

Everybody had to have a hobby.

Santos scanned the room. It was elegant and lovely, in a classy old-world kind of way, not at all the interior one would expect of a club that catered to the beat-me, whip-me crowd. But the Rack's clientele hailed from the upper crust: they were accustomed to the best and settled for no less, even in their sadomasochistic social clubs. Besides, if a client desired the more traditional, Bela Lugosi chamber-of-horrors stuff, it could be found in the private party rooms upstairs and in back.

Santos moved farther into the club, working his way through a crowd peppered with an unhealthy amount of black leather, spiked body adornments and chains. He paused to let a man leading his "friend" around by collar and leash pass; at the bar, a woman wearing five-inch spike-heel boots, was using her companion's naked back as a footrest. Santos winced as he saw her shift her weight and lean forward, as he saw the spike dig into the man's flesh.

Mixed into the flamboyant expression of personal preferences were people who looked as everyday, as straight-laced and conservative as every other banker, accountant or lawyer Santos saw on a daily basis in the central business district.

No Hope St. Germaine.

She had gone to a private party. Santos swore and glanced around again. Gaining entry to one of the private rooms would require an act of God or the law; unfortunately, he had access to neither at the moment. *Now what?*

"Hello there, stud." A tall, strongly built woman sidled up to him. She slipped a hand through his arm, her long, blood-red fingernails curling suggestively into his forearm. "You delivering tonight?" she asked in a husky falsetto. "You look like just the kind of man who could make me scream."

Santos met her—or depending on perspective, his—heavily made-up eyes. He recognized Sam/Samantha from previous times their paths had crossed. A regular to this kind of scene, Sam was a gump, a male prostitute who dressed like a female.

And there was a good chance she could help him.

Santos smiled. "Hello, Samantha. What's a nice girl like you doing in a place like this?"

Her eyes widened in recognition, and she tried to pull away. He covered her hand with his, and held her where she was. "You're not going to go and make a scene, are you, Samantha? I'd really hate that."

She shook her head. "I'm not doing anything. C'mon, Detective. I was just having a little fun with you, that's all."

"Fun? That's right, that's what you call this." He tightened his grip on her hand. "Come with me, Samantha, we need to have a little chat."

He led her to a secluded corner of the club, positioning himself with his back to the wall, so he would have a clear view of the place. "I need to know what's happening tonight."

Samantha shook her head again, beginning to tremble. "I told you, Detective. Nothing's going on."

"Private parties, Sam. I need to know who's partying tonight."

Samantha smoothed a hand over her black satin gown. Cut into two separate pieces, it was held together at the sides by silver chains. "I don't know anything. Really."

Santos saw that her hand was shaking. "Nervous about something, Sam?"

"Not at all."

"You're shaking like a leaf. Like you're guilty of something." Santos leaned closer. "You know, I could bust you for about half a dozen different things right now. You never have liked jail much, have you, Samantha? The other boys just don't play nice, do they?"

She paled. "You're killing me, Detective Santos. If anyone found out that I'd told you something, I'd be—"

"I'm looking for a middle-aged woman. A real society broad. Lots of money and attitude."

Samantha bit her lip, glancing nervously to her right, then left.

"You know who I'm talking about?" Santos looked into her eyes. "I'll owe you one, Sam. This is important. It's personal."

For a moment, Samantha said nothing, then she nodded and leaned a fraction closer. "I know who you're talking about." She lowered her voice. "She's a real bitch, too. She hurt a friend of mine pretty bad. He was in the hospital a week."

Santos's heart began to thunder. *He had her.* "What else?"

"She likes her guys young and real macho." Sam sniffed, put out. "There's no accounting for some people's taste."

"She's in there now?"

Samantha wetted her lips and nodded. "Came in a little bit ago. Never speaks to anyone, never looks at anybody, like she's too good for the rest of us."

"So, she comes in," Santos urged, impatient. "Then what?"

"The games begin, obviously. She goes straight upstairs. I hear she calls herself Violet."

She had given herself a flower name. Just like all the other Pierron women. "Chop sets her up?"

Samantha's expression cooled. "I wouldn't know about that."

"Bullshit." Santos caught her hand, holding it so tightly she winced. "Chop sets most of these people up. How much? What she likes, how much does it cost?"

Sam lifted her shoulders. "I've never been in the room, you understand. But from what I've heard, a few hundred to a few thousand. Depending on what she's into that night."

Nowhere near twenty-five thousand. Santos nodded, narrowing his eyes. No, that kind of money was needed to set somebody *else* up. That kind of money was needed for something more dangerous, more out of the ordinary, than what went on upstairs.

"Thanks, Samantha," he said, dropping her hand. "I won't forget this. I owe you."

As he turned to go, Samantha caught his arm. She swept her gaze appreciatively over him. "Why not fulfill your debt now? Hang around a while, we could take a walk on the wild side." She moved a fraction closer. "I bet I could teach you a few new tricks."

He removed her hand from his arm, leaving no question what he thought of her offer, though when he spoke, he spoke kindly. "This old dog knows all the tricks he cares to. Be safe, Sam."

Santos walked away, leaving the Rack behind.

65

Seven hours later, Santos and Jackson pulled up in front of Chop Robichaux's club on Bourbon. Not even 10:00 a.m., the street was nearly deserted. They had it on good authority that they would find Chop there, all but alone. Just the way they wanted him. The game they were about to play was far enough outside the law, they didn't want any witnesses.

Jackson turned to Santos. "We're clear on our plan?"

"Yeah. We go in and convince him that Queen St. Germaine turned over on him. We convince him that he's going to fry because of it."

"Piece of cake." Jackson smiled grimly. "We appeal to his immoral, paranoiac, criminal side."

Santos glanced at the club's entrance, unsettled. He and Jackson had performed these dog and pony shows before. Hundreds of times. But he had never had so much resting on the outcome of one. This time, it was his life on the line.

He looked back at his friend. "This might not work. He might catch on. He might not cave."

"It will work." Jackson set his mouth in a tight line. "Trust me, partner, when we corner him, he'll squeal like a New Year's pig. And if he doesn't, I'll beat the truth out of him."

"That's my line," Santos muttered, attempting humor. "Next thing I know, you'll be ordering steak."

"The big cut, bloody rare."

Santos laughed, though the sound rang hollow to him. "We've got the basics. We know about the money. We know she met with him, we know she passed him an enve-

lope. We know about her...extracurricular activities. All
we do is act and fill in the blanks. Fudge a little. We do it
all the time."

"And damn well, I might add."

"I wish we had more," Santos said. "I wish this visit was
one by the books." He narrowed his eyes. "Funny thing,
filling in the blanks isn't nearly so appealing when it's my
ass on the line."

"No joke." Jackson made a sound of frustration.
"These piece-of-shit scumbags are not going to take you
down. We're not going to let it happen."

"Let's do it then."

They climbed out of the car, crossed to the club's entrance and let themselves in. Chop sat at the bar, eating a
plate of something and smoking. Above the bar, the tele-
vision blared cartoons—Wile E. Coyote was in hot pursuit
of the Roadrunner.

"Bar's closed," Chop called, his mouth full, not turning. "Come back at eleven."

"Afraid that won't be possible," Santos said, saunter-
ing across to the bar. "We've got business that needs at-
tending now."

Chop swiveled to look at them, cursed, then returned to
his breakfast. "Pigs. What next?"

"What, indeed?" Jackson went to Chop's left. He eyed
the plate of food. "Nobody's given you the bad news about
animal fat, have they?"

"Fuck off."

Santos laughed and leaned on the bar to Chop's right. He
met Jackson's eyes. "Somebody woke up on the wrong side
of the bed this morning."

Chop narrowed his eyes on Santos, and shoveled in another forkful of food. Some of the gooey yellow egg yolk
dribbled onto his chin. "You can't be here on police business. You're not a cop anymore."

"That so?" Santos took out his shield, or what he hoped
would pass for *his* shield, and flashed it for Chop's inspec-

tion. "Funny how things can change overnight. Information comes to light, and boom, it's a brand-new day."

Chop looked more amused than nervous. "Who's your big friend?"

"Detective Jackson." Jackson flashed his shield, then pocketed it. "We wanted to talk to you about an interesting chat we had with one of your friends."

"A friend of mine?" Chop laughed. "I didn't know I had any."

"Her name's Hope St. Germaine. Sometimes calls herself Violet. Ringing any bells?"

Chop's smile faded, and he pushed his plate away. "Nope. Maybe you should refresh my memory."

"Glad to." Santos picked up Chop's cigarette lighter, weighing it in his palm. "Heavy. Must be gold." He flipped it open, struck the wheel, then snapped the lid shut, extinguishing the flame. "How much does a lighter like this cost, Chop?" Santos arched his eyebrows in question. "Not twenty-five thousand dollars? Surely not that much. What do you think, Jackson?"

He tossed the lighter, Jackson caught it, then weighed it in his hand. "I'll bet twenty-five thousand dollars could buy quite a number of these. A suitcase full, even."

Chop snatched the lighter from Jackson, then dropped it into his shirt pocket. "You have a point here?"

"Yeah, we have a point." Santos leaned toward the man, pinning him with his gaze. "This friend of yours, this Hope St. Germaine, she says you blackmailed her. Says you threatened to expose her...sexual preferences. Claims she overheard you plotting how to set me up. She'll testify, too. She doesn't want her high-society ass going to jail."

Santos smiled thinly and poked his index finger into Chop's fleshy chest. "And we get you, my friend. We get you for conspiracy and blackmail. Tasty, yes?"

Chop yawned and knocked Santos's hand away. "Bullshit. You've got nothing."

"We've got all we need."

"Right." Chop chuckled and pushed away from the bar. "I think I'm going to give my friendly D.A. a call. He's going to find this incident most...interesting."

Jackson caught the man's arm. "I don't think you want to do that. Especially since we've got a witness. A witness who puts you two together. A witness who saw money change hands." He made a clucking sound with his tongue. "Blackmail is such a nasty thing. Especially when you blackmail a woman like this one. She has many highly placed friends."

Chop swallowed hard, audibly. He began to sweat.

"Look—" Santos leaned closer to the man, though the odor of him made him want to gag. "I think she's involved. We don't like each other very much. But I'll be just as happy if you take the fall. You're a pretty slimy piece of work, and I'll be glad to have you off the street. Either way, I've got my badge back."

"Off the street," Jackson repeated. "About time you did some time. How long you think he'll get, Santos?"

Santos made a show of considering it. "Fifteen to thirty. After all, we're talking blackmail and conspiracy." He smiled at his partner, knowing that they were winning, working to control the elation that would give their game away. "You think the boys at Angola will like him? He's kind of pretty, in a fat, nasty sort of way."

"Fuck off," Chop muttered, though this time the oath lacked bravado.

"Even at the minimum," Jackson continued, "by the time he gets out, he'll be too old to get it up anymore. But hey, that's not our problem."

"Why would I blackmail her?" Chop asked, jumping to his feet. He looked at them each in turn, his expression earnest as a Boy Scout's. "And ruin my reputation? Please, I've got clients wealthier, and with much more to lose, than her. Lots of 'em. She's small time."

"Oh, I believe you," Santos said, amused. He looked at Jackson. "Do you believe him?"

"Oh sure, I believe him. But what about all those up-standing ladies and gentlemen of the jury? I've got a big picture of this. By the time the prosecution is done describing the breadth, or should I say the depths, of your operation—" Jackson shook his head. "Frankly, the maximum sentence won't be enough for those folks."

For a full minute, Chop said nothing. He looked from one to the other of them, nervously chewing on his lower lip. Finally, he swore. "I'm not taking a dive for that perverted bitch. I don't care how much she paid me." He looked at Santos. "She came to *me*. She wanted your ass in a sling. She planned the entire thing."

"Right." Santos snorted, hiding his excitement. "We're talking about a woman from one of this city's oldest, best-known families. We're talking a lady who goes to mass every day. A lady who gives about a gazillion dollars to local charities. And she set me up?" Santos motioned to Jackson. "Cuff him."

"It's true!" Chop took a step backward, mouth thinning. "And I can back it up. I can back it all up. Names. Dates. Pictures. Recordings. Nobody, but nobody screws Chop Robichaux."

He could back it up, Jackson and Santos found out shortly after. If nothing else, Chop was one hell of a careful businessman; it seemed he kept files on everything and everyone. He hadn't been boasting when he claimed he had clients with a lot more to lose than Hope St. Germaine. He was already with the D.A., talking plea and deal. He wasn't going to get off scot-free, though. Not this time.

Santos slapped the manila envelope against his hand. Inside were eight-by-ten pictures of Hope St. Germaine. Pictures of her in her other life. The life she had managed to keep secret from everyone for so long. Even her daughter.

Glory. A lump formed in his throat. *Dear Jesus, how was he going to tell Glory?*

"Hey, partner."

Santos turned. "You have the warrant?"

"It's in the works. We'll have it in less than an hour. Forty minutes, if all goes right."

"I want to be there."

"Understandable. I already talked to the captain. He's listened to Chop's taped confession. Considering the circumstances, it's a go."

Santos checked his watch and frowned. "I need the entire hour. I have to—" His throat closed over the words, and he cleared it. He met his partner's eyes. "I have to tell Glory. I can't let her learn from the media. And she'll want to see her mother, I'm sure. You know, before we get there."

"You'll go with Glory? We can't chance mama's taking off."

Santos nodded, heartsick at the prospect of what he had to do. "I'll be there."

"Good. I'll see to it you get the hour." Jackson searched Santos's expression. "You okay with this?"

"Sure, I... Hell, no, I'm not okay with this." He swore, angry and frustrated—by the situation, by what he had to do. "I'm glad to have my badge back. I'm a cop, Jackson. I bust the bad guys, I look for answers. It's what I am. It's what I do. But how do I look Glory in the eyes and tell her what her mother is?"

"You're right, Santos. You are a good cop. And this isn't your fault. You're not the bad guy here. Remember that."

"Yeah, right. Tell it to Glory." Santos took a long, frustrated breath. "What am I going to say to her? How do I tell her without hurting her?"

"I don't know, partner." Jackson laid a hand on Santos's shoulder. "I just don't know."

66

Santos found Glory in her office at the hotel, instructed her secretary to hold all interruptions, sat her down and relayed the tale, calmly and without inflection, starting with what Liz had told him and Jackson.

While Santos spoke, Glory sat unmoving, staring blankly at him, not believing her ears. When he finished, she shook her head. "You can't be serious about this."

"I'm dead serious about it." He cleared his throat. "I'm sorry, Glory."

"But..." She swallowed hard. "It's ridiculous. Insane. You're saying that you...followed my mother? You're saying that you discovered my mother was involved with this sleazy...Chop Robichaux? That she's a client of his?" Her voice rose. "You're saying you think she was—"

"Was the one who set me up. Yes."

She shook her head again, feeling the blood drain from her face. *This couldn't be happening. Not again.* "I don't believe you."

"I'm sorry, Glory. I wish it weren't true."

He looked down at his hands, then back up at her. She caught her breath at the helplessness in his expression. At the regret. Fear stole over her, and she began to shake.

"It's not true!" She jumped to her feet, her hands clenched into fists at her side. "Why are you doing this, Santos? I know you...dislike her. I know you have reason to, but this is...it's—"

She swung away from him, unable to bear the pitying expression in his eyes. She brought her trembling hands to her face, struggling to find the right words, the ones that would make this go away, the ones that would wake her from this nightmare.

She faced him once more. "This is beyond dislike, Santos. It's sick. You need help."

He stood and crossed to her. At his expression, tears stung her eyes. He gathered her hands in his and rubbed them, as if trying to warm them. "I'm not the one who's sick, sweetheart. Believe me, I hate having to hurt you this way."

She jerked her hands from his. "I don't believe you, Santos. This is a lie. A lie! I can't. You're talking about my mother."

"I know it's your mother." He swore. "You can't imagine how much I dreaded coming here and telling you this. You can't imagine—"

"Spare me, Detective Santos. You're enjoying this."

He stiffened. "You're angry at the wrong person. And killing the messenger isn't going to change the facts. I'm not the one who hurt and betrayed you. And we both know it."

She brought a hand to her eyes, covering them, battling tears. *It wasn't true. It couldn't be.*

"I brought...proof. I have pictures. But I don't want you to look at them." He caught her arm, forcing her to face him. "Just believe me, Glory. I wouldn't lie to you. Not about this or anything else."

"Pictures?" she repeated, her vision blurred with tears. "What do you mean?"

He motioned toward the large manila envelope he had brought in with him, propped by the side of his chair. "Robichaux kept files on all his clients. Every transaction, the date of the transaction, the...services provided and their cost. Your mother's file dates back to 1970."

Glory would have been three years old. Her father had still been alive. Very much alive.

Glory's stomach rose to her throat. *It wasn't true. It couldn't be.*

Glory strode across to the envelope, bent and defiantly snatched it up.

"Glory!" Santos took a step toward her, hand out. "Please, sweetheart, just believe me. Once you look at those photographs... you can never go back. Do you understand? Once you see her that way, you'll never—"

"Don't say anything else!" She drew a shuddering breath, realizing for the first time how close to hysteria she was. "Don't you... speak to me. Never speak to me... again."

"I didn't do this, Glory. I only uncovered it." He took another step. "If you look at those photographs, you'll never be able to forget them. Don't do that to yourself, it's not necessary. Just believe me."

She loosened the envelope's metal clasp. She reached inside, closing her fingers over what felt like glossy photos. She eased one out, her gaze not on it, but on Santos.

Her hand began to shake. Her eyes flooded with tears. The envelope slipped from her fingers, and she doubled over, sobbing. Santos crossed to her. He wrapped his arms around her, holding her up. "Glory, sweetheart, it's going to be okay."

"It's... not," she managed to say around tears, pressing her face to his shoulder. "How can it be okay... ever again? My mother is... my mother..."

She cried for a long time, noisily, the pain inside her too much to bear. While she did, Santos held her, murmuring sounds of comfort, stroking her hair.

Finally, exhausted and spent, she lifted her face to his. "What...what am I going to do, Santos? How am I...how do I...go on?"

"You just do," he murmured, brushing the tears from her cheeks with his thumbs. "But first, you need to go to her. You don't have much time."

She wiped her dripping nose with the back of her hand. "What do you mean?"

"A warrant's been issued for her arrest."

"Arrest?" Glory repeated, her knees going weak, then giving. He held her up. "On what charges?"

"Conspiracy. I bought you a little time. I knew you'd want to see her before..."

Before she was arrested. Before the story broke and the media feeding frenzy began.

His unfinished thought hung in the air between them. Her heart stopped, then began beating again with a vengeance. "How long have you known about this? How long have you been...following her?" She could hardly get the words out, they were so bizarre, so unbelievable to her.

"Five days."

"Five...days." She counted back, thinking of the times they had been together. Realizing what his silence meant.

She eased out of his arms, anger coming upon her so swiftly it took her breath. "You knew about this for five days, but you never said a thing to me? For five days you had suspicions and—"

"And until today, that's all they were. What could I have said to you?"

"You could have told me the truth! We're lovers, we were sleeping together. Yet you kept this from me?" She shook her head, her devastation complete. "You don't see anything wrong with that, do you?"

"No. Without proof, what could I have said to you? That I *thought* your mother had set me up? That she was involved with a criminal? Please. She's your mother, Glory."

"Exactly." Glory pushed her hair away from her face, hand shaking. "She's my mother. You should have told me the truth. You should have let me know what was going on. Dammit, Santos, I deserved that."

"If I had done that, I would have jeopardized my investigation."

"I see." She fisted her fingers, so angry she tasted the emotion. "You were afraid I'd tip my mother off, and she'd skip town. You were worried that I'd find a way to stop you. That I'd tip your captain off about what you were doing.''

For a moment, he said nothing, then he let out a frustrated breath. ''I knew you wouldn't believe me. I wanted to be able to prove to you that it was true. What's wrong with that?''

She loved him, she realized. She had never stopped.

He didn't believe in her; he didn't love her. He never would.

That's what was wrong with that.

She crossed to her desk. She retrieved her purse from the bottom drawer, then turned back to him. ''How much time do I have left?''

''Not much.'' He checked his watch. ''Twenty minutes, tops.''

She nodded, outwardly calm. Inside, she was falling apart. ''I guess I'd better go.''

''I'm going with you.''

She narrowed her gaze. ''Like hell. I'm going alone.''

''I gave Jackson my word.''

''Still afraid I'm going to help her skip town?''

At his damning silence, Glory strode to her office door. There, she stopped and turned to him. ''You know, you keep accusing me of not believing in you. Of never believing in you. But I believed enough in you to love you. Not once, but twice now. You're the one who made an issue over our differences, not me. You're the one who judged, the one who decided I was too privileged, too spoiled and self-centered to *really* love you.'' She inched her chin up. ''*You're* the one who decided you weren't good enough for me to love. Not me.''

Glory yanked open her office door. ''It seems to me, that you were the one who never believed, Santos. Not in me, not in us. You never trusted me. You still don't. But right now, I don't have the time to worry about that.''

She drew in a deep, fortifying breath and met his eyes, daring him to try to challenge her. "I'm going to see my mother. And I'm going alone."

67

Glory drove like an insane person, blinded by tears, her head filled with the things Santos had said about her mother, about her twisted passions, her relationship to Chop Robichaux and her attempt to frame Santos.

There had to be an explanation, she told herself. She prayed there would be. She prayed her mother would put her arms around her and tell her it wasn't true. Promise her it wasn't.

Even as the prayer ran crazily through her head, Glory knew in her gut it would not be answered.

By some miracle, she made it to her mother's house without incident. She slammed out of her car and raced up the walk, pounding on the door when she reached it. Mrs. Hillcrest answered, her eyes widening with alarm when she saw Glory.

"Miss Glory, what's wrong? What's happen—"

"Where's Mother?" Glory pushed past her. "I have to see her."

"She's in her room. Resting. She asked not to be disturbed."

Glory ran for the stairs. "Some people are coming for her. Hold them off. As long as you can."

"People?" Mrs. Hillcrest followed her to the bottom of the stairs, obviously confused. "Coming for your mother? I don't understand."

Glory stopped and looked back at the woman. "Just do it, Greta! Please." Feeling as if the devil himself were snapping at her heels, she ran up the remaining steps and down the hall to her mother's bedroom. She burst through the door and inside. "Mother!"

Her mother had been sleeping. She sprang bolt upright in bed, her eyes wide and disoriented. "Glory Alexandra?" she said, blinking, her hand going to her throat. "What are you doing here?"

"Mama, I...we have to talk." Glory crossed to the bed, shaking so badly she wondered if she would make it. She sank gratefully to its edge. "Mama, they're—"

Tears choked her, and she fought to clear them. She didn't have much time. She had to talk to her mother; she had to hear the truth from her, whatever it was. "They're coming for you. We have to talk. I have to know—"

"Coming for me?" Hope interrupted, pushing the hair out of her eyes, her hand shaking. She reached for her robe and slipped it on. "Who? What do you mean?"

"Santos and...others." She met her mother's eyes, heart breaking. "They have a warrant."

"A warrant?" Hope repeated. "For whom?"

"You, Mama. They say—"

"For me?" Hope reeled back, an expression of horror crossing her face. "But whatever for? I can't imagine what—"

"They say you were involved with that Chop Robichaux. They say you conspired to set Santos up."

Her mother didn't deny it; she didn't make a sound of outrage or disbelief. She simply stared at Glory, her mouth working, the expression in her eyes trapped, panicked.

Her mother was guilty of everything Santos had accused her. Dear Lord, it was true.

Glory's tears welled up, then spilled down her cheeks. Impatiently, she wiped them away. "They know everything, Mama. About Santos and your relationship to Chop Robichaux. About what he...about what he provided for you." Her voice rose. "Is it true, Mother? Did you do those things? And while Daddy was alive, too? I can't bear to think it."

"No!" her mother cried, the sound deep and desperate, as if it had emerged from the very depths of her soul. "No!"

Glory grabbed her mother's hands, clutching at them. They felt as cold and damp as death. "They have proof. Dates and pictures. A whole file on you." She rubbed her mother's hands, trying to warm them. She shook her head. "Tell me it isn't true, Mama. And I'll believe you. Tell me how they got pictures like those, and I'll—"

Hope yanked her hands from Glory's and scrambled off the bed. She raced across the room, slammed her bedroom door and locked it.

"Mother?"

Hope wheeled around, panting, frantic. "The Darkness has come. We must try to hide. We must plan."

Glory's heart began to thunder, and she struggled to stay calm. "You're hysterical," she said as quietly and as evenly as she could. "Let's calm down, and together we'll find a solution to this problem. I promise you, we'll find a—"

"No. . . no, it's coming. The Darkness is coming."

Glory crossed to her mother, catching her hands again, holding them tightly. "What are you talking about, Mama? You need to tell me, so I can help you."

"Yes." Her mother nodded. "I need to tell. Now, I must tell." She met her daughter's eyes; the expression in them took Glory's breath. "The Darkness, The Beast. It comes for us."

Hope swung away from Glory and began to pace, her long silk gown and robe billowing around her ankles. "I tried to protect you. Always tried, I never gave up. You see, I knew. I saw it in you and it was strong."

Glory wetted her lips. "You saw what, Mother?"

"The Beast."

Glory took a step backward, her mother's words hitting her like a blow to her chest. Her mind reeled back to her childhood, to all those times she had awakened to find her mother staring down at her as if she were the devil himself.

Glory made a sound of pain. All she had ever wanted was for her mother to love her.

Her mother looked at her and saw a monster.

"It's the curse," Hope continued. "The Pierron legacy of evil. Passed mother to daughter . . . we all have it. We're sinners, we succumb. I fought as fiercely as I could—" She brought her trembling hands to her face. "It was too strong."

Glory swallowed hard, thinking of what Santos had told her of her mother's perversions. "So you . . . succumbed."

"Yes." Hope lifted her tear-streaked face. "I wanted better for you. I vowed to drive The Beast out of you. I promised you would not fall prey to its litany of sin. Didn't I try to cleanse you of it? Didn't I try to scrub you clean?"

The library. Little Danny. Glory's stomach rose to her throat.

Hope grabbed Glory's hands. "You still have time. Do you understand?"

Glory shook her head, staring at her mother in dawning horror. Her mother was insane. Completely crazy. "You need help, Mama. We can get you help."

"There is no help. No help." Hope backed away slowly, then whirled and raced for the balcony doors. She wrenched them open and ran outside to the railing. She grasped it and leaned over, almost toppling, drawing in gulps of air.

"Mama!" Glory ran after her, catching her from behind, wrapping her arms around her. "You'll fall. Come away from there."

Her mother struggled. They fell against the railing; the wood groaned, then bowed. Frightened, Glory dragged her mother away. She lost her balance, stumbling backward. She hit the door casing, pain shot through her shoulder and her mother broke free.

Hope backed away from Glory, not stopping until she reached the railing. "It waits inside you, waits to feed on your immortal soul. I tried to purge you of it. I tried to purge you of your need for sins of the flesh."

Glory held out a hand. "Santos will help us. If I ask him, he will."

Hope shook her head, her expression suddenly eerily calm. "He has The Darkness, Glory. The Beast has them all. It uses them to get to us."

From downstairs Glory heard the sound of voices. Santos's voice. He would help her; despite everything, he would help her mother. "They're here, Mother. Let me talk to them. I'll buy us some time. We'll figure something out. Together."

"All right, Glory." Her mother nodded and walked back into the bedroom, her calm more frightening than her frenzy. "I'll do my Rosary now."

Glory followed her in, closing the balcony doors behind them. "That's a . . . Good. I'll be right back."

Her mother seemed not to even notice her leave. As soon as Glory cleared the room, she ran for the stairs, hysteria building inside her. Santos and Jackson stood in the foyer with Mrs. Hillcrest, along with two other officers she didn't recognize.

"Santos!"

He looked up. Tears of relief flooded her eyes, and she started down the stairs. He met her halfway, catching her hands. "Are you all right?"

"Yes, but Mother—" She clutched at his hands, struggling to keep from falling apart. "She's hysterical. She's...out of her mind. I'm afraid, Santos. I'm afraid for her. I don't know what she's going to do when you come for her."

Santos looked at Jackson. "Call headquarters. Get someone from psychiatric down here. A.S.A.P." Jackson went to do it, and Santos turned back to Glory. "Where is she?"

Glory told him and together they ran up the stairs. They reached the bedroom; Glory tapped on the closed door, then cracked it open. "Mother," she said softly, afraid of startling her, "it's Glory. Santos is with me. He's going to help us. It's going to be all right."

She cracked the door wider, peeking inside. She didn't see her mother and pushed the door the rest of the way open with dread. "Mother, where are you?"

And then she saw. Her mother stood on the balcony railing, balancing precariously, her rosary beads clutched in her hands. The breeze caught her robe, lifting the gossamer fabric, swirling it around her, creating billowing wings. Her mother looked like a dark angel, an angel preparing for flight.

"Mother!" Glory took a step into the room, hand out. "Don't move!"

Her mother met her eyes. The expression in them was clear and strangely calm. "The Beast has come."

"Mrs. St. Germaine, please. Don't move." Santos moved carefully into the room, his voice low, deep and soothing. "Everything is going to be fine. You just hold tight and—"

The beads slipped from Hope's fingers and clattered to the floor. Glory's heart leaped to her throat; Hope smiled. "Remember, daughter, The Darkness takes many forms."

And then she flew.

68

Santos checked his watch for what seemed like the hundredth time in less than an hour. It had been a slow day in homicide, though every day had seemed slow after the media frenzy surrounding Hope St. Germaine's suicide, Chop Robichaux's arrest and the story that had led to both; then on the heels of that, the arrest of the Snow White Killer.

Tina's bible thumper had finally returned to New Orleans. By the time he had, Santos and Jackson had already nailed down witnesses who placed him with two of the victims, one of them on the night of her death. Santos shook his head. Of course the guy, this Buster Flowers, denied he was the Snow White; he denied having ever killed anybody.

But if being a cop for ten years had taught Santos anything, it was that criminals rarely stood up and shouted their guilt. No, this was the guy. The Snow White Killer and the one who had killed his mother. He was certain of it.

Santos checked his watch again, then muttered an oath. He didn't know why he was so anxious to get out of here; he had nowhere to go and nobody who was waiting for him. Certainly not Glory.

He hadn't seen her since her mother's funeral. Even then, they had hardly spoken to each other. She had been withdrawn and in pain; he had tried to reach her, had tried to comfort her, but had been unable to. There had been a wall between them. Brick-solid and impenetrable. It was as if, with the shocking revelations and suicide of her mother, they had lost the ability—or wherewithal—to reach beyond it.

He missed her. He longed to scale that wall and claim her as his. But he didn't know how.

And even if he did, a relationship between them wouldn't last. Too much stood between them, too much past, too much pain. They came from two different worlds. She wouldn't be happy with a cop, not for long. It was better this way.

His phone rang; he reached for it like a drowning man would grab for a lifeline. "Detective Santos."

"Help me," a woman on the other end whispered. "Please, help me."

He straightened. "Who is this?"

"Santos, please. You have to help me, I have nowhere else to turn."

"Tina? Is that you?"

"He's following me. I know it's him." She began to sob. "He's going to kill me."

A chill ran up his spine. "Tina, we've got him. Buster Flowers, the guy who gave you the cross."

"It's not him! Santos, I don't want to die!"

Her cry shook him clear to his soul. She was scared witless. "Tina, where are you?"

She drew a shuddering breath. "At a pay phone on the corner of Toulouse and Burgundy. Right by the Corner Drugstore and a church."

"Okay." He checked his watch, calculating the time it would take him to reach her at this time of day. "Stay put. Do you hear me, Tina? I'm coming now. It'll take me no more than ten minutes."

"Hurry, Santos. Please."

He hung up the phone and jumped to his feet, grabbing his suit jacket as he did.

Patterson, the detective with the desk across from his, looked his way. "What's up?"

"The hooker who made our guy. She says he's still stalking her." He shrugged into the jacket. "If Jackson gets back before I do, fill him in. She called from the pay phone at the corner of Toulouse and Burgundy."

Patterson's lips curled with distaste. He had taken some heat for his sloppy handling of Tina when she was first in and was still stinging from the captain's dressing-down. "The bitch is nuts. We've got our guy. Let it go."

Something about Patterson's statement, his arrogance, had the hairs on the back of Santos's neck standing up. What if they did have the wrong guy? He didn't think they did, but . . . what if? Everything they had on Buster Flowers was circumstantial. Everything pointed toward him, none of it proved, beyond a shadow of a doubt, that he was their guy.

What if Buster Flowers wasn't the Snow White Killer?

That would mean he was still on the street. Tina could be in real danger.

Patterson snorted. "Did you hear what I said? The bitch is nuts. Certifiable. Do yourself a favor, it's almost quitting time, let it go."

"Yeah, I heard you." Santos swept his gaze over the other officer. "But what if she's not nuts? What if a killer *is* stalking her? You may be willing to take that chance, but I'm not."

The trip from headquarters to the French Quarter took just over the ten minutes he had promised. Santos found the pay phone. He found the drugstore and church. He wheeled his car to the curb and jumped out.

No Tina.

Santos glanced around, checking to be certain he had the right corner. *Toulouse and Burgundy. The Corner Drugstore. Not a church, he realized. A convent. Mary Queen of Peace.* This was it.

So, where the hell was she? He scanned the area, looking for a place she might have ducked into or behind to hide, looking for a place she might feel safe. The store's glass front door caught his eye. The Closed sign swung slightly, as if it had just been tipped over.

Santos checked his watch. Five-twenty. Early for a store like this one to be closing, especially in the Quarter. He stared at the sign, remembering something Tina had said, the hairs on the back of his neck prickling with the memory.

"They're rubbers, Detective. A hooker's best friend. Me and the other girls buy them by the gross at the Corner Drugstore."

The Corner Drugstore.

Santos crossed the street. He went to the door and peered in. A guy stood at the register, counting the cash. Otherwise, the store appeared empty.

Santos tapped on the glass. The young man at the register looked. Santos held up his shield. "Police."

The guy paled, shut the cash drawer and came over. He peered through the glass at Santos's badge, studying it for long moments before unlocking and cracking open the door.

"What can I do for you, Officer?"

"There've been some burglaries in the area," Santos said. "Mind if I come in and take a look around."

"Burglaries?" the guy repeated. "In the area?"

"That's right."

"Okay, then." The kid—Santos judged him to be in his early twenties—stepped away from the door and let him in.

The shop's interior was cool, too cool, and dimly lit. It was the kind of store found on many corners in New Orleans: dirty and cluttered, with an eclectic assortment of goods for sale—pain relievers and snacks, sundry items and cold drinks, magazines and newspapers, all jammed into the bottom floor of a building dating from the thirties or forties.

Santos's gaze landed on a basket of apples on the counter. His pulse began to thrum. He turned back to the other man. His name tag said John. He was of medium height and build and had an average, almost nondescript face. His eyes and hair were light-colored, his eyebrows so pale they were almost nonexistent.

And he was nervous. Fidgety.

"You own this place, John?"

He shook his head. "My uncle."

"A family business," Santos murmured. "That's nice. Where is your uncle tonight?"

"Prayer group."

"No kidding?" Santos started moving slowly up and down the aisles. "He goes every night?"

"Pretty much." John followed him. "My uncle says that if you know the Lord, you'll never know darkness or pain." John rubbed his hands on his blue jeans, as if to dry them. "Are you looking for something in particular, Officer . . . ?"

"Detective Santos." Santos smiled, ignoring his question. "Early to be closing for the night. Seems to me you'd get a lot of business if you stayed open. Quarter's busy after dark."

The kid shrugged. "The crime's gotten too bad. We were getting held up almost nightly."

"What about the working girls? You must get a lot of them in at night." Santos looked him straight in the eye; the kid held his gaze a moment, then slid his away.

"They don't come in. My uncle doesn't like hookers. He doesn't like them in the store."

He was lying. The store was chill as a tomb, but John was sweating. As he turned his head, Santos saw the fine sheen of the stuff above his top lip.

"Actually, I'm looking for a hooker named Tina. You know her?"

"No. I told you, hookers don't come in here."

"But maybe you saw who I'm looking for. She was using the pay phone across the street. Just a little bit ago."

He shrugged again. "I see lots of people at that phone. What did . . . does she look like?"

Santos described Tina, carefully watching John. The kid's face remained completely impassive.

"Come to think of it," he said finally, nodding, "I did see a woman who looked like her. She took off."

"She did?"

"Yeah, she was on her way toward St. Peter."

There was something sly in the kid's voice, or rather, slyly amused. Santos indicated a door at the back of the store. "What's back there?"

"Stockroom."

"Mind if I have a look?"

John hesitated, then lifted a shoulder. "I don't mind."

"After you." Santos followed the guy, his neck hairs prickling again. This might be nothing. But it didn't feel like nothing. It felt like something, something dirty. But what?

Which brought him back to Tina. Where was she?

"Here it is." The guy opened the stockroom door. Empty save for stocked storage shelves and shipping boxes, Santos made his way through the room, nudging boxes, checking for doors.

He found one. The exit-sign light above the door was burned out and there were boxes stacked in front of it. "Where does that go?"

"The alley. We don't use it." John indicated a key pad on the wall. A green light flashed. "It's electronically armed and barred from the outside, too. Criminals were breaking in through the back to rob us. It's bad enough when they come through the front. But that's why you're here, right, Detective Santos?" John folded his arms across his chest. "Because of burglaries in the area?"

"That's right." Santos turned to the kid and smiled. "I guess that'll be it. You've been very helpful. I appreciate it."

John walked him to the front door and unlocked it. "You know," Santos said, "blocking that exit is a fire hazard. If the fire marshal came in here, he'd close you down for that."

"I'll talk to my uncle."

"You do that, John."

"I hope you get those guys."

"We will." Santos met his gaze. "We always do."

Santos stepped out onto the street; John locked the door behind him. Santos turned and watched as the kid returned to his counting.

He narrowed his eyes. Something wasn't right with that kid. He felt it in his gut. But whatever he was up to, it might not a have a thing to do with Tina. And she was his first priority.

But what if it did have to do with her? The kid had lied about hookers coming into the store. He was certain of it. And that bothered him. It bothered him big time.

Santos swore, aware of each second ticking past. Tina could have taken off. It wouldn't surprise him if she had; she wasn't the most stable person. Santos shook his head. But she had been scared, really scared. And she had known he was coming for her. So, why take off?

He walked to the corner and gazed in the direction of St. Peter Street. The kid said she had been heading toward St. Peter Street. Santos started in that direction, stopping midblock as the realization hit him like a thunderbolt. The kid had said she'd been *"on her way toward St. Peter."*

St. Peter. The saint who guarded the gates of heaven. The saint who checked the books and decided if your soul was clean enough to pass through those gates.

The kid was sending Tina to see St. Peter.

Santos doubled back at a dead run, ducking down when he reached the Corner Drugstore, not wanting the kid to see him, wishing he could call for backup but afraid to chance it. Every second counted for Tina—if he wasn't already too late.

Dear God, let it not be too late.

As he reached the corner, a late-model Buick eased out of the alley behind the store and turned his way. The driver's eyes met his. It was the kid from the drugstore.

Santos drew his gun, leaped into the street and shouted, "Freeze!" At the same moment, the kid hit the gas, barreling straight for him.

Santos dived out of the way, rolled, took aim and fired. Once, then twice. The car skidded out of control, slammed through the convent's wrought-iron fence and into a statue of Jesus blessing the masses. The statue rocked, then toppled forward, smashing into the driver's-side windshield, crushing it.

Someone screamed. Clusters of people appeared in shop doorways, some spilled out onto the sidewalk, eager to get a look.

Santos ran for the vehicle. "Police!" he shouted, holding up his badge. "Call 911! Somebody get an ambulance!"

He reached the car. At impact, its trunk had popped open. Stuffed inside, tied up like a sacrificial lamb, was Tina.

Santos knees went weak with relief. She was alive.

69

The popularity of the Garden of Earthly Delights had mushroomed almost overnight. The rave review in the *Times Picayune* by food critic Gregory Roberts hadn't hurt, nor had the notoriety Liz had gained when the scandal involving Santos and Hope St. Germaine had hit the media. Liz and her restaurant had been named, again and again, on TV and in print.

The restaurant had become so popular, in fact, that she rarely got a chance to sit down. This was one of those rare occasions—the 3:00 p.m. lull between the lunch and dinner crowd—and she was enjoying it. She sank onto one of the bar stools and sighed.

Her bartender came over with a cup of herbal tea. "Success is tiring."

"But nice, Darryl." She smiled and curved her hands around the warm mug. "Very nice."

"Hey, I'm not complaining. The tips have been great." The man grinned. "Believe it or not, we made the paper again."

"Not again?" She slipped off a shoe and rubbed her aching arch on one of the stool's rungs. "It's been a month."

Darryl handed her the *Times Picayune,* main news section, open to page four, tapping the article in question. "And this time, they call you 'the proprietor of the trendy and popular restaurant, the Garden of Earthly Delights.' That's a quote, by the way." He flashed her another of his devilish grins, then went down the bar to fill one of the waitress's orders.

Liz sipped her tea, scanned the article and smiled. She found it ironic that her act of conscience had paid off like this. She hadn't expected anything in return for her honesty but the ability to sleep nights, but to get this professional recognition and monetary success, well, it boggled the mind.

She hadn't expected it, but she was enjoying it. Sometimes she wanted to clap her hands and giggle with delight over her newfound success. She had done this, created this place, on her own. Just as Santos had said, she *was* making a difference in the world, she *was* helping people.

Her life had turned out pretty damn good, after all. If only she had Santos, it would be perfect.

"Hello, Liz."

Glory. Liz stiffened, then took a deep, fortifying breath and swiveled to face her former friend. Glory stood several feet behind her, looking hesitant and uncomfortable, but determined. Liz swept her gaze over her. The last weeks had taken their toll on Glory, her face was drawn and tired-looking, the expression in her eyes sad, almost haunted.

What must it be like to learn that your mother was a sort of monster?

Liz tipped up her chin, fighting against her thoughts and the sympathy they brought. "What are you doing here?"

"Can we talk?" Glory laced her fingers together. "Please."

Liz swept her gaze coldly over her once more. "I can't imagine what we would have to talk to each other about."

"About the past," she said softly, her words thick with emotion. "About . . . us."

Sudden, unexpected tears stung Liz's eyes, and horrified, she blinked them back. "There is no us."

"There was. A long time ago." Glory drew a deep breath. "Please, Liz."

Liz hesitated, then nodded and slid off the stool. "All right." She slipped back into her shoe and motioned to her bartender. "Darryl, I'll be in my office if you need me."

He gave her a thumbs-up, and Liz led Glory to her office. Once inside, she closed the door behind them, then faced Glory, not offering her a seat.

"Your restaurant is lovely, Liz. And I hear the food is wonderful. Congratulations."

"Thank you." She folded her arms across her chest, despising herself for being so pleased at Glory's approval. She didn't want, or need, it. "You have something on your mind?"

"Yes, I..." Glory drew a deep breath, then released it in a rush. "There's so much I want to say to you, I don't know where to begin. I guess, first, I want to say I'm sorry. For all those years ago. I never thought my mother would hurt you. Never. I don't know why. I should have thought, I should have suspected..."

Glory made a helpless gesture with her right hand. "I didn't know her very well, obviously. I guess no one did. But I'm sure you've watched the news."

"Yes."

"I'm...sorry, too, that..." Glory's words faltered as she struggled, Liz saw, not to cry. "I'm sorry that I didn't stand by you. That I didn't show you how much you meant to me. How much I...loved you. You *were* my best friend."

She lowered her gaze to the floor, then looked back up at Liz, her eyes brimming. "I was so afraid of my mother, of what she might do to me, that I forgot to be afraid for you. And that day, I...I fell apart."

A lump formed in Liz's throat. She understood. And she wished she didn't. That day, she had fallen apart, too.

Liz swung away from Glory and crossed to her desk. She stared down at its littered top, calling herself a fool for letting Glory get to her, even a little.

She squeezed her eyes shut. If only she could shake the things she had learned about Glory's mother in the past weeks, about the kind of person she had been revealed to be. If only she could stop wondering what it had been like growing up as Hope St. Germaine's daughter.

She couldn't.

All those years ago, Glory had been right to be afraid.

"I came today, too, to thank you for what you did for Santos."

At the mention of Santos, Liz stiffened, anger and hurt sweeping over her, stealing empathy and understanding. She swung to face Glory once more, defiantly. "I didn't do it for him," she said sharply. "And I certainly didn't do it so the two of you could live happily ever after."

Glory drew a deep breath and met Liz's gaze evenly. "I never stopped loving him, Liz. Never."

Something in Glory's eyes took Liz by surprise. Something fierce and sad and hot. Something that spoke to Liz of the depth of Glory's feelings for Santos—feelings too strong, too substantive to be the whim of a spoiled, selfish girl in search of a trophy or an adventure. Something that her own feelings paled in comparison to.

And something that began to heal an old wound.

Liz's mind went spinning back to two young girls, standing by their high school locker, giggling together. Two girls who had had their whole lives before them. One of them had just met a boy. A boy she had loved on first sight. A boy she had claimed was her destiny.

Maybe he was.

Tears welled up in her eyes, and Liz quickly averted her gaze, checking her watch. "If that's all," she said crisply, feigning indifference, "I really need to get back to work."

"Of course." Looking as if Liz had slapped her, Glory took a step backward, toward the door. "Thank you for your time, Liz. Thanks for listening. I know you're very...busy. I'll see myself out."

Liz watched as Glory turned and walked to the door, watched as she opened it and stepped through. *And out of her life forever.*

She couldn't let her go this way, not without the whole truth.

Liz caught her breath. "Glory!"

Glory stopped and looked over her shoulder at Liz.

"That day at A.I.C....that day your mother had me expelled, I fell apart, too." Liz looked down at her hands, then back up at Glory. "You mother told me she would intercede with Sister Marguerite for me. If I would tell her everything I knew about you and Santos."

She drew in a shuddering breath. "I told myself she already knew about you and Santos being lovers, but I knew in my heart she didn't. I was afraid, too, Glory. Of your mother. Of losing my scholarship. Of facing my father."

"You were sixteen," Glory said softly. "Sixteen-year-olds get scared sometimes."

"So do twenty-eight-year-olds." Liz met Glory's eyes and smiled, feeling good, really good. "But you know what, Glo? It's over now. It's in the past. And I think I'm going to let it stay there."

70

The kid from the drugstore, John Francis Bourgeois, was arrested, and in a matter of days, charged with the killing of eight young women. The physical evidence against him was overwhelming and indisputable: matching bite marks from the apples, DNA tests results on blood and body fluids found on the victims and at the scene set the likelihood that anyone else was the killer to be one in six billion; hair and fiber evidence, fingerprints—the list went on and on.

And then there was Tina and her testimony. John Bourgeois wasn't the man who had picked up her friend Billie on the last night of her life. But he had been there. Moments before, Tina had seen him and said hello.

She hadn't thought anything of it. But John had been afraid she would. He had feared, once the police started grilling her, she would remember. And the police, he had been certain, would have thought something of it. Tina had been a loose end.

So he had begun to follow her, watching, waiting for the right time. She had given John what he'd thought was the right time and the perfect opportunity. He had seen her at the phone and had invited her to come inside and wait. Where she would be safe, he had told her.

And then he'd had her.

Santos sat on his living room couch, the silence of his empty apartment deafening. Santos had been right about everything: the working girls had all known and liked him; John had been trying to "save" them. After all, as John's uncle always said, "He who knows the Lord, knows no darkness or pain.'' Santos had been right, too, about the fact that John had been preparing to move on.

But he hadn't been right about one thing. The most important one. Santos tipped his head toward the ceiling. John Thomas Bourgeois was twenty-two years old. He had been five years old when Santos's mother had been murdered.

He wasn't the guy.

Santos drew in a deep, aching breath. He hadn't found his mother's killer; he hadn't avenged her murder.

He never would.

Santos stood and crossed to the window and gazed out at the quiet street. Just after dawn, the rest of the world slept. He longed for sleep, too, but it eluded him. It always had.

He touched the window with his fingertips, finding the glass already warm with the day. He thought back to that evening a week ago, when he had untied Tina and lifted her out of the trunk. She had clung to him, sobbing, grateful, so very grateful, to be alive.

Santos squeezed his eyes shut, emotion choking him. Though he hadn't been there for his mother, he had been for Tina. He had saved her life. By catching the Snow White, he had saved countless other girls.

That felt good. Really good.

It would have to be good enough.

In a fairy-tale kind of ending, Tina had vowed she was getting out of the life. She was going to move somewhere no one knew her, to a small town, get a job doing anything but hooking and start making a real life for herself. The time had come, she had told him, to let go and move on.

He hoped she made it. He had given her some money, as much as he could spare. She had promised to pay it back, though he didn't care. If it helped her begin her new life, it would be the best money he had ever spent. Finally, he would have done for her what he promised all those years ago—he had come back for her; he had helped her.

Santos turned away from the window and gazed at his living room, thinking of his mother. Of her life and death. Of the way she had loved him and despite everything, loved life. The time had come to let go, he realized. Just as Tina had said. Of his past. Of his anger and guilt. Of his pain. Those were destructive, as was hatred, as was affixing blame instead of facing life and accepting responsibility.

The time had come to move on.

The truth of that moved over him and he smiled, then laughed out loud. He felt good, really good, for the first time in forever. He, too, was grateful for life. Grateful to be here, to be in this moment, grateful for all the love he had known and been blessed by.

Glory.

She had been right about him, about his judging her, about him being unwilling to believe in her, unwilling to believe in her love for him. He had wanted her to prove her feelings were true. Because he didn't see his own worth. Even when he went to her father's wake, it wasn't to claim her—but for her to claim *him*. For her to prove she really loved him.

He laughed again. Hope's hatred of Lily had mirrored Lily's own hatred of herself. In Lily, he had never understood it. He had never understood why Lily hadn't been able to see herself as she really was. Good. Loving. Worth being loved.

And yet, he had done the same thing. He had refused to see himself as the man he was, refused to see that he was worth being loved, that he was worth Glory's love.

He saw now.

The past fell away from him, and in that moment he felt light and free and able to soar with the eagles. He loved

Glory. He deserved her love; he could make her happy. He would make her happy.

He went to claim her. No proof required.

71

In the days and weeks following her mother's suicide and the resulting scandal, Glory had fitted together the pieces of her mother's other life. Though at times it had been almost too painful to bear, she had wanted to know and to try to understand. For she had realized that only by doing both would she be able to move on.

To that end, Glory had seen a psychiatrist, and he had helped her to fully understand her mother's state of mind. Her mother had been very ill. The doctor had used the term schizophrenia. He believed that had she lived, she wouldn't have stood trial, but instead of being sent to jail, she would have been institutionalized.

Glory wished with all her heart that her mother could have gotten help, but she also knew that to her mother the scandal would have been a punishment worse than death. Her mother had made her choice.

Glory's own feelings had been more difficult to deal with—ones of loss and betrayal, of anger and helplessness, of confusion. She had felt as if she had been cut loose and cast adrift. In the space of twenty-four hours, her life had been changed forever, and once again all that she had known, about her mother and herself, had been proven a lie.

And again, she had been forced to ask herself, *"Who am I?"*

So she had come here, to the River Road house, to be soothed, to feel the loving arms of a family around her, though a family she had hardly known. She had come here to put the pieces of her identity back together.

And as the weeks had passed, she had done just that. Finally, she felt whole, again—or maybe, whole for the first time in her life.

Glory dug her trowel into the damp, black earth. The June sun beat down on her back, and sweat beaded her upper lip and between her breasts. She enjoyed it all—the heat of the sun, the moist earth, her sweat.

Soon she would have to go back to the city, to her air-conditioned office at the St. Charles. She smiled and fitted the plant into the hole she'd dug, then refilled the hole with earth. She had spoken with Jonathan Michaels several times since their first meeting; their lawyers were working on the details of their agreement now.

She felt good about her decision. Restoring the Pierron House to it original overblown grandeur would take a considerable amount of money. Converting three of the upstairs bedrooms into luxurious guest accommodations and two of the others into an owner's apartment, would also be expensive. She would have to hire a live-in housekeeper/manager, daytime tour guides, and a part-time grounds keeper.

She had no illusions that opening the Pierron House for tours, private parties and overnight stays was going to make her money. If she broke even, she would be doing well. But she wasn't doing it for money; she was doing it out of love. The Pierron House was a part of Louisiana history, and a part of her history. She didn't want it to be forgotten or to fall into disrepair and crumble away, as so many other pieces of Southern history had.

Smiling, Glory stood, and dusting the dirt off her hands, admired her work. She had spent the last week planting summer annuals in the front flower beds. Now, the entire gallery was edged with a triple row of bright red begonias.

Fitting, she thought, for the women who had lived and worked in this house. Women whose lives fascinated her.

She had been engrossed by the accounts of their days and nights; drawn into their hopes and dreams and disappointments. It seemed that those women and girls had had many of all of those, and little of anything else. Certainly not what Glory would call a real life.

Her fascination had led to understanding; understanding to love. They hadn't been bad people. Or evil, as her mother's twisted mind had believed. They had been lost. And trapped—in a world that had created them, yet had no room in their hearts to accept or love them.

A breeze stirred off the Mississippi, and Glory lifted her face to it, smiling at its sweetness, at the way it cooled her damp skin. In understanding the women of this house, she had come to understand herself. She, too, had been trapped. By her mother's inability to love her, her inability to accept the person she was. And by her own enslaving need for that acceptance and love.

A need so powerful, so all-consuming that she had tried to change herself, had tried to mold herself into the person her mother wanted her to be, the person her mother would love.

Glory shook her head, remembering. All her life, her mother had looked at Glory as if she were lacking, as if there was something *wrong* with her. Something bad about her.

All along, the wrong, the bad, had been inside her mother.

Glory laughed. Finally, she was free. To be herself. To love who she was, this moment and the next, on to forever. She would never again try to be a person who she was not; she would never stop believing in herself only because someone else didn't believe. She would never again have to ask herself, *"Who is Glory St. Germaine?"*

Now she knew.

From behind her she heard the sound of a car coming up the driveway. She turned, holding a hand to her eyes to shield them from the sun.

Santos.

He had come at last.

Heart pounding, Glory let him find her, let him make his way from the driveway to the house. She had missed him, longed for him. But she'd had demons to wrestle with; ones she'd had to face alone.

In facing them, she had realized something else: she had come too far to settle for less than everything from Santos. Although, she admitted, watching him walk toward her, her pulse and heart stirring, an offer of anything at all from him would be damn tempting.

He stopped before her and unsmiling, met her eyes. "Hello, Glory."

"Santos." Her lips lifted even as she drank in the sight of him, growing almost intoxicated with longing. "I was wondering when you'd come. If you'd come."

"And I was wondering if you'd want me to."

"I did. I do." She laid her hand on his chest, over his heart. Beneath her palm it thundered, strong and sure. "I'm glad you're here."

He reached out and cupped her cheek in his palm. "Are you all right? I've been worried about you."

She smiled and covered his hand with her own, tipping her face into his caress. "I'm good. Really good, Santos."

"I've missed you."

Her heart began to thud; her palms grew damp. Hope bloomed inside her, as brightly as the rows of begonias at their feet. "And I you. So much."

He lowered his mouth to hers, though he only brushed his against hers, then straightened. "I brought you something."

"You did?" she said, searching his gaze, pleased.

He drew a small, white cardboard box out of his jacket pocket. At least it had once been white. Now, it was battered and smudged, half-crushed. It looked as if it had spent a lifetime clutched in someone's fist.

Santos caught her hand, turned it palm up and set the battered box in its center. "For you."

She looked up at him, heart in her throat. She saw something in his eyes she had never seen before, something deep and hot and strong. Her hand began to shake. She carefully, reverently, opened the box. Inside, wrapped in tissue, was a pair of earrings. She lifted one out, and held it to the sun. Made of colored, cut-glass beads, it sparkled in the sunlight, glittering like rainbow fire.

"They were my mother's," he said softly, taking the earring from her, clipping it on her ear, then doing the same with the second. "They're the only thing of hers I have. She loved them."

Tears swamped her. She met his gaze once more. "I will, too, Santos. Forever."

She took his hand and led him inside and upstairs. There, on a bed drenched in sunlight, they made love. Real love, for the first time since they had been teenagers, back when they had been too young to know that together they had paradise in their hands.

They weren't too young now. They knew.